The

Appearance of

Truth

Rosemary J. Kind

Printed in the United Kingdom

First Printing, 2013 Alfie Dog Limited

The author can be found at: www.rjkind.co.uk

Cover image: Katie Stewart, Magic Owl Design

http://www.magicowldesign.com/

ISBN 978-0-9569659-2-9

Published by
Alfie Dog Limited
Schilde Lodge, Tholthorpe,
North Yorkshire, YO61 1SN
Tel: 0207 193 33 90

DEDICATION

To Megan, the child I couldn't have and the dog that is her substitute.

Other books by Rosemary J. Kind

Alfie's Diary

Alfie's Woods

From Story Idea to Reader

Lovers Take up Less Space

Pet Dogs Democratic Party Manifesto

Poems for Life

The Lifetracer

ACKNOWLEDGMENTS

I would like to thank my dear friend Andy Laker, my mother and my wonderful husband, Chris Platt, for all their constructive criticism in reading the early drafts of The Appearance of Truth.

I would also like to thank those friends, particularly those belonging to Talkback, who gave me insight into some of the harrowing events explored in this novel.

INTRODUCTION

"Write 300 words on verisimilitude," that was the challenge set by Vanessa Harvey a writing friend of mine. I scurried away to look it up in the dictionary. 'Having the appearance of truth', I pondered what that might mean.

At around the same time, I was researching my family tree. I had ordered copies of birth certificates and one was sitting on my desk waiting for me to follow it up. It had been easy to obtain the copies. What if a birth certificate was passed off as belonging to someone it didn't belong to? What if someone was researching their family tree and the first thing they found out was that their birth certificate didn't belong to them? And so Lisa Forster was born in a literary sense and the story developed into a search for identity and what could possibly have happened to lead her parents to pass her off as someone else.

What started as 300 words ended up as 100,000 words and is brought to you as 'The appearance of truth' one woman's search for identity. The places are all fictitious, as are the characters and storyline. If you spot anything that reminds you of real life, that is purely accidental. I hope the book gives you cause to think as well as providing you with entertainment.

Rosemary J. Kind

CHAPTER 1

Billingbrook, Lancashire. 24th March 2007

Of course, there was no such thing as 'Groundhog Day', not in the sense of reliving the same day over and over again. In terms of the groundhog being used to predict the start of spring that was a different matter. Certainly, the shadow of winter had lingered over the whole of the last twelve months. Now it was the first anniversary of that day and the pilgrimage to Billingbrook Cemetery that Lisa had been dreading. It wasn't her first visit, it wasn't her tenth for that matter, but today felt different. Today marked a period of transition.

Her mum's final words had been "I'm sorry." She never said what for. She never said anything else, just "I'm sorry" and then her breathing became shallower and, a few minutes later, there was no more breathing. Lisa shuddered as she remembered. She wondered if her Mum was sorry for dying before her time, sorry for leaving Lisa on her own, sorry for not paying the milkman; she had no idea. She had spent most of the last year worrying about those words. Perhaps it was scary because it threw into sharp relief how little she had moved on in that year. The milkman had been paid and the day to day inconsequential acts of 'being' had continued, but otherwise life hadn't progressed. It was time for the groundhog to find a new home.

1

Lisa looked up and saw the sign ahead, Billingbrook Cemetery. The iron railings, surrounding the cemetery, stood like a barrier between the living and the dead. *Were they there to keep the dead in, or the living out?* She felt the overwhelming sense of trespassing. This was somewhere she shouldn't be, or maybe it was the intense urge of wanting not to be there, wanting it to be some other way. Why had her parents died so young? It seemed strange that both of them had died. A pang of guilt swept over her that she hadn't brought flowers for Dad too. It had been four years since he died; maybe he would understand, today was her mum's day. Mother's Day for the living had been last week. This was Mother's Day for her mum. She plucked a single freesia from the bouquet as she walked along the line of graves. She placed the flower on the grassy mound with the headstone that read 'Hugh Forster 1941-2003'. Her mum had wanted her own plot. Even in anticipation of her own death, she hadn't been able to contemplate being placed with someone who was 'just bones'. There was no logic to it, but it was her choice. It wasn't that her parents hadn't loved each other, they had. They were always so close, happy with just each other's company. She walked two rows along and five graves further up the path.

"Hello, Mum," she laid the bouquet on the grave. "They're your favourites." She felt her vision start to cloud with tears and dabbed her eyes with a tissue. "How've you been? Silly question, I suppose, it's just I don't know what to say. I can't believe it's been a year. I miss you. There are so many things I wish I'd asked you, so many things I should have said. Your house sold in January, there's new people in it now. I wonder if they'll be as happy as we were." She looked down at her watch, ten past eleven; she watched the hands turning and felt a wave of gulping sobs rising up from the pit of her stomach. She closed her eyes and bit her lip, fighting to hold them down. Her hands were shaking as she opened her mouth and drew in a huge gasp of air. She let it out slowly. "I can't say it's the first Christmas since you died anymore, or the first birthday, or the first Mother's Day." The hands ticked to eleven-fifteen. She felt as empty as she had ever felt. "I guess I'll be off then. I'll see you soon."

She stumbled away, head down, lost in a flood of grief. At another time, when her thoughts were less distant, she would have registered the creak of the rusty iron moving on its tired hinges. Instead, she jolted to a stop as she walked straight into the man who had just come through the gate.

"Sorry. I'm sorry," she sobbed and went to move round him. She blew her nose on another scrappy old tissue from her coat pocket and tried to regain some composure. It was a gusty day and she felt the wind driving a tear across her cheek. She'd given up wearing make up on the days she visited the cemetery. It would have needed industrial strength materials to stop it from running into tear-stained clumps.

"Hey, wait. Are you O.K.?"

Lisa felt her neck and back stiffen. She'd struggled through her grief very much on her own. She hated to be seen this way.

"Come and sit down," said the voice, as the man led her towards a bench.

She flinched. He could be anyone. However, there was no real fight left in her and she followed his command.

"I'm Pete," said the stranger. "I hate coming to this place, but it's the only way to talk to Mum these days."

3

She looked up, shocked by the openness of someone she'd only just met. Pete's approach had seemed confident, not the type of person she imagined talking to a grave, but then she was there, so she supposed that it proved nothing.

"I was visiting my parents too," her voice faltered. "It's a year since Mum died. I've been dreading today." Her hands were trembling as she clutched the shreds of tissue. "I needed to be here at the same time she died. I don't know why."

"I didn't mean to intrude," said Pete. "Are you going to be all right? I was going to the pub when I've finished here, if you need someone to talk to who understands."

"I'm not much company at the moment," she said, wondering if it was a way of finding an excuse. "But thanks, anyway."

"Me neither. At least it would be someone to mope with. I'll be in the Red Lion if you change your mind. "

She studied the even features of Pete's face, with his gentle blue eyes and rugged chin, as he broke into a smile and Lisa began to feel better than she had done all morning.

"I'll be there about midday. It usually takes me twenty minutes to have a chat with Mum. Maybe I'll see you there." Pete smiled again, before setting off at a brisk walk into the heart of the cemetery. She watched him go. It felt quite a surreal situation; she almost wondered whether the conversation had taken place at all.

She stayed on the bench for another five minutes, regaining her composure and then started to walk home. She could see the Red Lion from the gate of the cemetery. She walked at least two hundred metres past the door of the pub when a little voice inside said, "What harm could it do?"

Lisa turned and walked back past the pub in the other direction before pulling herself together and approaching the door. The Red Lion was set back from the road behind a gravelled forecourt, with a jaded sign swinging soundlessly back and forth. It had a squat, white stucco exterior, which belied its cavernous, rambling interior. The pub was quiet for a Sunday lunchtime, but she presumed it would get busier over the next hour. She was grateful there were so few people to stare at the 'single female stranger' as she went up to the bar.

She chose a table in a quiet corner of the lounge and was reflecting on her happy childhood and how close she had been to both her parents.

Pete came in on the dot of twelve. She looked at him biting his lip, seeming anxious to see if she were there. He was medium build and height, maybe a couple of inches taller than she was, with dark wavy hair, cut short, but not too short, just enough to prevent a stray curl forming here and there. She struggled to place his age, older than she was, but she couldn't gauge by how much.

"Can I get you a drink?" Pete asked, smiling.

"No, thanks, I'm fine with this." She glanced down at the still full glass of wine. "I probably shouldn't be drinking. I didn't have much breakfast."

"Here, have a look at this." Pete passed the Sunday lunch menu to her when he returned with his pint.

She had thought earlier that a pub lunch would be nice. It was either that or a walk out on the hills. When she was young they would take a picnic up to the lower slopes and eat before heading off for a couple of miles with her dog, Spotty, darting behind every rock in a vain search for rabbits. It had been a while since she'd been up to Low Hill; it never felt the same walking without a dog for company, so she was more than happy to settle for the pub, particularly with someone to share it with.

"I didn't know whether I'd find you here or not."

"You nearly didn't," she looked up from the menu. "I don't go in for meeting strange men. Are you eating?"

"I prefer not to think of myself as strange. I'll have the roast beef if you're having something."

"I didn't mean…" she looked back at the menu, feeling the colour rise in her face. "I'll have the lasagne," she said without looking up.

She opened her bag and took out her purse. Pete put his hand onto hers. "Please, let me. I know today will be tough. Let this be my treat."

For a moment she stared at him. Her instinct was to argue for equality, but there was something in the gentle firmness of Pete's words that allowed her to accept. "Thank you, that's very kind."

As Pete sat down after placing the order, Lisa leaned her head to one side and asked, "Are both your parents in the cemetery?"

"No. Dad was cremated. He was killed in an accident. There was no time to talk about what he wanted. Cremation seemed like the right thing to do. Mum had time to think before she died. I was glad when she chose burial. It doesn't feel as easy to talk to Dad at the crematorium. It doesn't feel as though he's there in the same way that it does with Mum in the cemetery. I've been there a couple of times, in the early days, on the anniversary of his death, but it's been a while now."

"I'm sorry. Was today a special occasion with your Mum?" Lisa knew she used questions as a way of preventing people getting too close to her; it was a habit, a security mechanism. If she was asking, then people couldn't ask her.

Pete was quiet for a moment, "Yes."

She realised she'd touched a nerve. "I didn't mean to pry."

They sat for a while, contemplating their own thoughts. "What do you do?" she said, breaking the silence.

Pete looked relieved to be given an escape route. "I'm an electrical engineer and before you ask, that doesn't mean I run on batteries."

He smiled as she laughed. She was glad the tension had been broken. She found herself starting to tell this stranger about herself. "There was this one time I'd fallen off the climbing frame in the playground and cut my arm open. Mum came rushing over, all efficient practicality as she tied a handkerchief over the wound and bundled me off to hospital. You can still see the scar where the five stitches held it together." She glanced down at the left sleeve of her jacket, where the scar lay cosseted by the layers. "Dad was usually the calm, quiet one, but in a crisis Mum was never flustered. She only really flapped over the things that didn't matter, like the time I spilt my drink all down my dress when we were on the way to someone's wedding. I don't remember whose it was. Neither of my parents seemed to have many friends. I think it must have been one of Mum's work colleagues from the college. She was a teacher."

"And you?"

She looked up, almost surprised to find Pete there. "I'm a librarian. Can't you tell by the clothes?" She laughed. "Mum used to say I could have looked quite something, if I made the most of my appearance." She ran her hands through her light brown, shoulder length hair. "I wondered about having highlights, but it's not really me and besides, I'd stand out too much in the library if I started looking stylish."

"You look all right to me." Pete grinned and then looked into his pint and took a deep swig.

Lisa felt herself blush and added, "I always loved reading as a kid. I wasn't allowed out on my own very often, so I built a fantasy world at home. I just wanted to be surrounded by books. Now I suppose I've got my wish. When you're an only child, there's no one else to play with and torment, you have to find your own amusement. Mine was books."

"I know what you mean. I used to make things. More to the point I used to take them apart. I couldn't always put them back together in the same way they were before; Mum got through three kettles before I got that right and the train set was never the same again. It would have been nice to have had a brother or sister, but I was quite happy in my own little world creating things. I suppose as kids go, I was rather dull."

"And you think sticking your head in books makes you exciting?" They both laughed. It was easy laughter, miles from the tension of their meeting. "I seem to be in another world now, than the girl who spent hours sitting in the crook of the apple tree branches, reading about my latest heroine. I used to love "White Boots" by Noel Streatfield. I don't suppose that was a boy's book."

"I tend to read non-fiction. I've often thought about researching my family tree. There must be books in the library for that."

She smiled. "Yes, I'd wondered about that too. I might be descended from someone rich and famous. I never thought about it when Mum was alive. I know virtually nothing of my family history at all. Maybe if I did, it would help to fill the gap."

"Me neither. We could be related. Maybe you're my long lost sister?"

"I think I'd have known if I had a brother, besides I don't think we were from here way back then."

"Are you saying I'm old?"

"No, I... er, it's just, well you look older than I am."

Pete laughed at her embarrassment, but put her at her ease saying "You do look younger than me, by a few days at least."

It was Lisa's turn to laugh. She hadn't felt like this for ages. The companionship felt very welcome. She had never stopped being the bookish loner of her childhood. She hoped that Pete would keep his word of dropping into the library to look for some books on genealogy. It would be good to see him again.

As she walked home later that afternoon, she reflected on the lightness of spirit she felt, on what could have been a very dark day. Lunchtime had provided such an enjoyable interlude, new shoots in an otherwise barren landscape.

CHAPTER 2

Billingbrook. Friday 14 September 2007

The ten-pin bowling alley was always busy on a Friday night. Lisa and Pete had been waiting for an hour before being called to their lane.

"Wouldn't this be a great place for someone famous to come incognito? You'd never know with the subdued lighting. It's amazing anyone gets a strike." Lisa was trying to find a bowling ball light enough to bowl with without straining her wrist.

"What is it with you and the 'rich and famous' thing?" Pete said as he stepped up to bowl his first ball.

"Well, I don't know who my ancestors are. I prefer to think I'm a somebody, rather than a nobody. Don't you ever think things like that? You've got no immediate family alive either."

"No, I just think I've been unlucky to lose them all so young. I try not to think 'what if?' My guess is that my ancestors did as many exciting things in their lives as I do. They probably lived in Billingbrook for centuries and couldn't write their names. Laundon is hard enough for most people to spell now." He aimed his second ball at the remaining seven pins and missed.

Lisa was shouting to be heard over the music. "I could be an heiress awaiting my inheritance. It's bad enough that Dad had a heart attack at 62 and Mum died of cancer at 64..." The music came to an abrupt halt, leaving Lisa still shouting, "... without having to think that I'm ordinary into the bargain!"

Pete laughed out loud. "You're not ordinary, that I can tell you for certain. As for the rich and famous bit, you may just have read one too many books."

She loved Pete's sense of humour; he sometimes used it to cover difficult moments, but on the whole he made her laugh. Although she had no idea why, she'd always imagined engineers to be dull until she met Pete, but over the last six months they had become close friends and spent a lot of time in each other's company.

"I maintain I could be rich and famous. One day you're going to be asking for my autograph." She selected a bowling ball of the right weight and went up to the lane. Looking to ensure she was central to the pins, she bowled, knocking down six pins. "Yes!"

"Prove it." Pete said, carrying on the conversation.

"What?" A feeling of shock ran through her. The idea of having famous ancestors was something she hid behind, to cover the reality of loneliness and nonentity, she didn't intend to prove it.

"Prove that you're rich and famous." They continued to take their turns bowling as they talked.

"And how am I going to do that?"

"Research your family tree. Let's both do it. Come on we've talked about it enough. We could both find our family history."

"You've had too much to drink." Lisa swirled her wine round in the bottom of the glass. "We don't know where to start."

"That's an excuse."

"I don't know the names of any of my ancestors to

provide a starting point." She sipped some more of the wine, before taking her next turn.

"Another excuse. You know your parents' names."

"You're drunk."

"I might be, I can't tell. I can still bowl straighter than you. Here's the deal. I bet I can find more of my family tree in the next week than you can."

"What are the stakes?"

"I buy the drinks if you win; you buy the drinks if I win."

She laughed. "Situation normal then. We always take it in turns to buy the drinks. What counts as more? Is it more people or more generations?" She knocked all the pins down for the first time with her next ball and did a little celebratory dance.

"Oh, I don't know. We both only know the names of our parents, so I suppose more people in our family tree would be as good as anything."

She looked at his eyes, visible over the rim of his pint glass. A challenge of any type wasn't to be turned down. This one, however, held special interest. Where did Lisa Forster fit into the world? It was a question she had tried hiding from for a long time, maybe it was time to break through the myths and learn how long other members of her family had lived. She'd been developing something of a phobia that because her parents had died young, she would face the same fate. Maybe if she found her grandparents had lived longer, she could stop taking life so seriously. There was no proof that their problems had been hereditary. If they were, she didn't want to know.

There was only so long she could run away from herself. It wasn't a new thought. Tracing her family tree might give her more of a sense of place and purpose than she seemed to have at present. She was almost thirty, single, childless and alone, barring a few close friends. She knew little detail about her parents' families. She knew they weren't close and with the move to Billingbrook, the physical distance meant the links hadn't been maintained. As a child, she asked why they couldn't see her grandparents for Christmas, but the distance from Lancashire to Sussex had meant it never happened. She didn't know what other family members there were. Her grandparents were no longer alive, but she thought her mum had at least one sister. As a result of the mystery, the question 'Where do I fit in the greater scheme of life?' was one that she had shied away from. Instead she hid behind the notion that somewhere along the line her family were rich and famous and despite a longing to know where she fitted in, she'd made no effort to find out.

It hadn't been so bad when her parents were alive. It was easier to feel she belonged with them around. Now things were different. Perhaps she just needed a bit of a kick-start. Pete's friendship over the last six months had already given her the courage to confront many of her fears. Feeling ordinary was no longer an issue.

"Deal," she said, thrusting her hand towards Pete to shake on it.

***

Billingbrook. Saturday 15th September 2007

On Saturday, once the hangover had worn off and she could face the day, Lisa made a start on the bet. It was too late for a cosy chat with a parent about what they could remember of their childhood and what their own immediate family was like. These were the types of conversations she thought she could always have tomorrow, until there were no tomorrows to have them. It meant that she would have to discover who her ancestors were through research. As she got dressed, she tried to remember what she did know about her family. Her mum had a sister, or was it a brother? If she could remember the name it would give her a good clue. Her mother's mother had been the last of her grandparents alive and even she died when Lisa was only four. They hadn't smoked or been heavy drinkers, but neither did they exercise regularly. They were just an ordinary, middle class, suburban family. She didn't remember her parents being unfit, but it hadn't made any difference to their lifespan, so much for 'three score years and ten', or was it supposed to be even more than that now?

She'd bought her house from new, about five years ago. It was on a modern estate with roads that wound round in dizzying crescents, like elongated centipedes, with cul-de-sac legs on either side. She moved in when her dad was ill; staying close to her parents was important. It was her choice. They encouraged her to follow her dreams, but she wanted to be there for them. As it turned out, with having to spend so much time with her mum it had been a Godsend. She had no regrets about her decision.

She had turned the dining room into an office. That was the thing about living on her own, she could use rooms in any way she wanted. She switched on the computer and whilst it ran through its infernal start up routines, she went to make some coffee. She thought she was slow getting going in a morning, but the computer was ridiculous. She needed to buy a more up to date model.

She put her cappuccino down on the desk, waited for the computer to finish and then typed 'family tree' into the internet search box.

She and her friends often used the chat programmes to talk to each other whilst they worked on their computers. It meant she could see which of her friends were on-line when she was. It meant she could have virtual company, which for the most part suited her rather well. A message popped up in the corner of the screen. 'How's it going?' Pete.

She typed back, 'Just starting. You are so going to be buying the drinks.' Then she scanned down the list of search results.

The message notice flashed again. 'What date was my Dad's birthday? Pete.'

She laughed out loud as she typed back, 'How should I know? You are so going to lose this bet.'

There was a link through 'Friends Reunited', a web site she already used to look for school friends. It took her to another site she hadn't noticed before, 'Genes Reunited'. This one allowed her, with free registration, to build her family tree on line. The site also provided the facility to search for missing information. She went through the registration process and logged in. Finding the 'Family Tree Builder' section, she thought it best to start by capturing the information she did know, before thinking about the next stage of the jigsaw. She began by putting in her own details and those of her parents. Her birth certificate was in front of her. She had removed it from her alphabetically sorted and labelled filing system when she came home from ten-pin bowling the previous evening. Her real first name, according to the certificate, was Patricia, but she'd been known by her middle name 'Lisa', since she was tiny. She entered Patricia Forster and her place and year of birth as her first record and hit 'enter' to load it to the tree.

'I've found my dad's birth,' Pete's message interrupted her again. She could sense his excitement.

'It's a bit late to remember his birthday now,' she joked. 'What site are you on?'

'I'll send you the link.'

She went back to Genes Reunited and was stunned to see that it was flashing with a little tree in the corner of her record, indicating that the name and year of birth gave a match with another person's family tree. The same thing happened as she entered the details of her parents. She looked to see who her matches were with. She started by following her own name and found the tree match was with someone called Julie. The date and place of birth given for Patricia Lisa were similar. When she looked up the information for each of her parents, they were matches. She felt a sudden tension. This was real; someone out there already knew something about her family. This Julie would know about other family members too. She must do, there must at least be the part of the family that made it fit with her own tree.

Lisa sat at the desk wondering what to do next. Whilst it was obvious that she needed to email Julie, it felt like quite a big step. This was the time to get to the truth and begin to build a solid knowledge of her origins. She started tidying the desk around her in an attempt to delay writing the email. She never did seem to stick to her annual New Year's Resolution to be tidier at home. When she did file things she was meticulous, the librarian in her coming to the fore, but she never wanted to do those things, she left them until they became essential. She smiled as she put the pens and pencils back in the little stand and then began to tidy up the stray paperclips. She looked at the piles of papers waiting to be filed and decided it was easier to give in and send the email than to start on all of those. She took a deep breath and went back to the keyboard.

To contact Julie, she needed to become a paid up member of the website. She rummaged through her bag for her credit card. Then she sent a brief email to Julie.

'Dear Julie, I'm new to researching my family tree, but I seem to have matches between my family and yours. The matches are Patricia Forster, Hugh Forster and Maureen Forster nee Richardson. I wonder if you could provide me with any other information. Thank you, Lisa.'

Being aware of all the stories of identity theft, she decided to provide no other personal information. She pressed 'send' and wondered what to do next. There was no indication on the site as to where Julie lived, but even if it were in Billingbrook itself she may not be online. It might take a while to receive a reply to the email. She decided to leave her research while she did the grocery shopping instead. She sent Pete a message, 'Just off to Tesco's. I'll be back online later. Do you need anything?'

'Can't stand the pace and you've only just started! You could do my whole week's shopping! (Just joking – about the shopping anyway.) Bye. Pete.'

She wandered through the shops for a couple of hours before going to Tesco's and as she drove home it was already five o' clock. She was due to meet Pete to compare progress at seven-thirty, even though they'd given themselves a whole week for the challenge. She wondered whether she'd received a reply to her email yet. Maybe she wouldn't get a reply at all. Then what would she do? She'd 'bookmarked' sites that allowed her to hunt for birth, marriage and death records, but she hadn't looked at what information they would give her. Julie could be anywhere, even if she lived in England, she might be off trekking in Timbuktu, which made it difficult to gauge when she might reply. Lisa turned the computer on the minute she got in and by the time she'd put the shopping away it had finished going through its start-up ritual. She went straight to her email and logged in. Her heart missed a beat as she found a Genes Reunited email saying she had received a reply. She clicked the link and held her breath as the message loaded.

'Dear Lisa, Maureen Richardson was my great aunt. She was my grandmother's younger sister by some ten years. She married Hugh Forster in 1972 and they eventually had a daughter Patricia in 1977. Patricia was my mother's first cousin, but sadly she died aged about three months and they were not able to have any more children of their own. I think they may have gone on to adopt a child fairly soon after Patricia died, but I don't have any of the details. My parents moved to Sydney, Australia when I was four, in 1975, so we didn't see Aunty Maureen after that. I have opened up my tree so that you can look at it. Can you let me know what relation you are to Aunty Maureen please? Best wishes, Julie.'

Lisa clutched her birth certificate in her hands, Patricia Lisa Forster born 12th December 1977, Triford, Sussex. That was what the paper said. Perhaps Julie had made a mistake, maybe she was thinking of someone else. She reread the email. After all, by the time Patricia Lisa was born, Julie was living the other side of the world in Australia.

Lisa's hands were shaking. She breathed deeply and tried to picture a calming image of a green field with a stream flowing through it. She drew another full breath.

There was a mistake, of course there was. It was even possible there were two families in the same area that just happened to have the same names. She reasoned that there must be a sensible explanation. She sent a quick message to Pete, trying to remain light hearted, 'I've found me, but I'm dead.'

'That's just the hangover,' Pete replied. 'See you soon. p.s. You're not really dead are you?'

She opened a new web page and went to one of the websites she had bookmarked. The site gave details of all births, marriages and deaths. She input Patricia Forster, selected the options of 'all types of record from 1977 to 1978' and chose 'Triford' as the search area. With trepidation, she hit the 'search' button. Two records came up on screen. They were listed by the appropriate quarter of the year. 'Patricia Forster, born Dec quarter 1977' and 'Patricia Forster, died June quarter 1978, aged 4 months'. There was one Patricia Forster in Triford, and it wasn't her. She stared at the screen in disbelief.

Her stomach was beginning to rebel and her throat felt like a windswept dustbowl. Had she understood this right? Did it say she was dead? Swallowing was almost impossible. She thought about the implications. Had her death been faked for some reason, or was this someone else's birth certificate? And if this wasn't hers then...

Nausea swept over her and she knew she was going to be sick. She rushed upstairs to the bathroom and was just in time to raise the toilet seat before throwing up. She sat on the floor of the bathroom feeling drained and stunned. She stared at the little butterfly pattern on the wallpaper, fixing on it for so long that it began to fly around her. She had no idea how long she sat there before the world started to flutter back into place. She wiped her mouth with toilet paper. The computer did suggest she was dead. If Patricia was dead, then who was she? How could she research her family tree when she no longer knew who she was? She felt dazed. The answer was to get in touch with Julie's mum and find out whether she knew any more. How on earth would she begin that email?

After getting a drink of water, she went back to the computer. She sent a message to Pete. 'I think we'd better say you've won, but I'm going to need you to buy me a drink anyway.' Then trying to console herself she typed, 'As it turns out, I may well be descended from someone rich and famous after all.'

CHAPTER 3

Billingbrook. Saturday evening 15th September 2007

Lisa was sitting with Pete in the Red Lion later that evening.

"Now let me get this straight," said Pete. "Whilst I've found the names and dates of birth of my grandparents, you've found out that you aren't Lisa Forster."

"That's the long and the short of it, yes." She felt much smaller than her 5'8", slumped on her stool, fiddling with a spare beer mat. "I suppose I am still Lisa Forster at least that's what I'm known as, but I have no idea who I started life as." The beer mat spiralled onto the floor and she didn't even have the enthusiasm to pick it up.

They were sitting in the lounge near the fireplace. It was too early in the year for a fire, but the grate was cascading with unburnt logs, challenging the weather to give the first hint of cold. They were regulars now, on first name terms with the bar staff, but the bar was busy with occasional traffic and despite the hubbub, it was easy to find some privacy and anonymity amongst the crowd. Pete was waiting for his steak and chips to arrive, whilst she clung to her white wine, her eyes cast down. After being so sick earlier, she wasn't able to face eating. The wine wasn't going to do her any good, but she needed it.

"This is the last time I'm entering into a bet with you," said Pete, looking stunned by her revelations. "Was it only last night that we started this?" He shook his head. "What was I thinking? It isn't as though we don't take it in turns to buy the drinks anyway."

"Don't blame yourself. It isn't your fault things have turned out like this. You knew I wanted to trace my family tree. You just gave me a little push. Besides it could still turn out O.K." She tried to force a smile.

"What are you going to do now?" Pete asked, as he moved his glass out of the way for the barmaid to place the large oval plate, piled high with steak and the usual accompaniments of chips, onion rings and mushrooms, in front of him.

"I wondered if you'd help me to find out who I am?" She bit her lip. She couldn't face doing this alone, but if Pete would give up on his family tree, to work with her, she thought she might have the strength to follow it through. They could always work on his family tree later.

Considering it was twenty-four hours since the challenge had begun, it seemed incredible how much her world had changed. She was tempted to start questioning everything around her. If her identity wasn't real, then perhaps everything else was an illusion. Had her childhood been as happy as she remembered? For thirty years, she had thought the birth certificate was hers. How funny, the significance that could attach to a single piece of paper. No one had ever mentioned that she was adopted and, if it hadn't been for the challenge, the secret might have successfully gone to the grave with both her parents. If it hadn't been for the bet she still wouldn't know. She would still think herself the product of a conventional middle class suburban family.

Friends and neighbours had always said she looked like her mum but she'd got her dad's nose. There were so many ways in which they all seemed similar. She laughed like her mum, but had her dad's contemplative nature. On balance that was the better combination than the opposite. Perhaps none of it was real and she had imagined it all. All the habits they had in common could as easily have been things she'd picked up by copying her parents as things that were genetically programmed responses. Did she see similarities because she wanted to, rather than because those similarities were there?

Either she needed the strength to forget the whole thing or she would have to follow it through to discover where it would lead. The latter was a daunting course of action, but she knew now she'd started, she had little choice. The whole situation was going to eat away at her until she did. She would have needed a great deal of self-confidence for a revelation such as this not to change her whole world forever. Whatever self-confidence she might have had until yesterday, had been knocked away in one glancing blow. How could she change that fast? She needed the courage to reply to the email from Julie. That was going to be a difficult one. As yet, Julie had no idea that Lisa was the adopted child.

"Hello. Anyone in there?"

She became aware Pete was talking to her. "Sorry? What?"

"I didn't think you were listening," he said finishing another mouthful of steak. "Of course I'll help you. You don't think I'd let you go through this on your own do you?"

She shrugged. "I don't know, I guess it's not your problem."

He laid his knife down and put his hand on hers. The gentleness of his touch was comforting, like the inherent security of a child being taken care of by a parent and yet the electricity it gave her, made it feel so much more. Did he feel it, or was this all in her imagination too?

"Look," he said. "I can't begin to imagine how you must be feeling right now. What I do know is that if it were the other way round, you'd help me. It's what being friends means."

She looked at him and smiled in relief. She realised how fond of him she'd become in the last six months. Did he feel the same? "Where do you think we should start?"

Her workmates often teased her for her unwavering organisational skills and it wasn't that uncommon for her to be called a control-freak. They didn't see the vulnerable core that it masked. This childlike admission of a need for help felt alien to her. Pete had seen the person underneath that first day at the cemetery when she walked into him. Their friendship was based on who she was, rather than the façade she showed the world.

"Well, presuming this isn't like the film *The Truman Show*, where I would be part of the plot, and even this pub is just a prop. I don't know," said Pete. She felt a wave of shock. "I'm kidding, about the pub anyway. No seriously," Pete took both of her hands in his. "I'm not part of any plot. You have to be able to trust in some things and trusting me would be a good start. I'm guessing we could use the internet again. Is it possible that Julie's mum will have more information?"

"I'm almost afraid to ask," she said. "After the last bombshell."

"It has to be your decision," Pete said. "I'll work with you on it, but if you're not ready then we should leave it for a while."

"I've got to do it. Stepping back isn't an option. I'm

terrified, but I have to do this. I have to find out who I am. Yesterday I thought I knew, today I have no idea. It's dawned on me that I don't know my own date of birth, or how old I am. Pete, I don't know when my birthday is. I thought I was going to be thirty in three months' time, but it could be today for all I know. Do you realise how scary that feels?"

She could tell from Pete's face, he could see this was a startling thought.

"Happy Birthday," he ventured, "just in case."

She managed to raise a weak smile.

Pete became serious again, "Look Lisa, whatever happens, you mustn't lose sight of the fact your adoptive parents loved you and you loved them, they were still your parents wherever this leads. You've said yourself, you had a happy childhood. How can any of this take that away?"

She shrugged. "Memories are all about perception, what you know now affects how you see things from the past. I think it was a happy childhood, but then I thought they were my parents. I remember when we first got Spotty. I sat in the back of the car with him on my lap. It was amazing, this tiny bundle of fur, cuddling up to me, nibbling my finger. I didn't need an imaginary friend with Spotty around. He'd be there if I needed a companion for a pretend tea-party and I used to read to him for hours. . . Why didn't they tell me?" There were tears in her eyes. She needed answers that Pete couldn't give.

"I don't know. Maybe they were scared things would change. Maybe they were frightened you wouldn't love them anymore. Maybe there was a good reason not to tell you. What if your real parents were killed in a tragic accident and the adopters were trying to shield you from the pain?" Pete began to warm to his subject. "Perhaps you're a foreign princess, smuggled out of the country when your parents were killed in a military coup."

This at least, made her smile. "You don't believe that do you?"

"Well, no, I'm just saying there might have been good reasons not to tell you. I can't believe it isn't something they thought about."

Lisa nodded. "When will we start?" She used Pete's napkin to wipe away her tears.

"We could write an email to Julie tonight," he said. "Why don't you come back to my place and we could do it there."

"Yes, all right, I'm not sure I want to go back to my house at the moment anyway," she replied.

Once Pete had finished his steak, they started the walk back. The stars did their best to glimmer between the breaks in the cloud which were moving with the mild autumnal breeze. The intensity of the starlight was masked by the light pollution from the town. For a moment, the lights of an aeroplane through a break in the cloud looked like a planet's constant light, but by the next break it had moved on, leaving Lisa wondering where it was going and whether running away would be an option. Who was she kidding? She would still be there when the plane landed in some distant place, as confused as she was now. She could never run away from herself. Whether she knew who she was, she had as much chance of coming to terms with her life here as she had anywhere and at least here she might find answers to the basic questions.

Pete slipped his arm around her shoulders. It was something he'd never done before, but she didn't protest.

They walked in silence for a while. Where would all this lead?

"What do I do if I find my real parents and they don't want to see me?"

"We're a long way from that right now," Pete said. "There are lots of hurdles to clear before we can get that far and besides, why would anyone not want to meet you?" He brushed her cheek with his finger and a not unwelcome little shiver ran through her.

"Pete," she said. "You don't have to do this."

"I'm not doing it because I have to," he said. "I want to." Then once again they fell into a comfortable silence as they walked.

Pete's house was at the end of a row backing onto another matching row of terraced properties. They were all built of dark, weather worn brick, in a regular pattern of houses and passages between. The one thing to differentiate the mirror images was the little name plaque at intervals along the rows, 'Porchester Villas 1898', 'Rose Villas 1901', 'Ivy Villas 1897'. The terraces had all been built at the turn of the twentieth century when the railway had first come to Billingbrook. Now the railway was long gone, but the terraces remained as a legacy of an era of steam trains and quarry workers. She tried to imagine what it must have been like when they were new. How long had it taken for the sooty deposits from the neighbouring railway to darken the outside of the bricks? Perhaps the members of the family who didn't work on the railway, had operated cottage industries from home. The children had worse lives than hers, starting work at a young age with little chance of an education. Maybe they had no idea who their parents were either.

The road was still and silent at this time of night, the

houses slumbering with their night lights glowing behind curtained windows. It felt as though nothing had changed in that hundred years until a voice broke through the stillness as they walked past 'Holly Villas 1899'.

"Ryan, will you turn that telly off and get into bed."

"Go away. You can't tell me what to do."

"Don't you talk to me like that you little…"

The sound drifted away as they walked further along the road.

"They're not a bad family," said Pete laughing as they reached his own house. The front doors of the houses opened almost onto the pavement, but Pete went through the passageway to the back, where the row of terraces behind looked down indulgently on the comings and goings of their neighbours.

Pete let her in through the back door in the little yard. It was tidy for the house of a single man. As they went through the kitchen, the washing up was arranged to drain and the tea towel was hanging on the hook. She smiled. How domesticated Pete was compared to the mess in her own kitchen. She tended to go in phases with these things. The clutter built up and then she sorted it all out. She claimed it was a backlash to being so organised at work, but she knew she might be kidding herself. Maybe it was a reaction to how she was brought up. The house was always spotless, although she and her parents were the only ones who used to see it. They never had visitors. She went through to the lounge and sat down whilst Pete made coffee.

It was a large lounge, covering most of the ground floor of the house, with the kitchen as a long thin room on the back, almost an afterthought. She presumed that at one time, there had been a separate hallway but this had been opened up so that the staircase to upstairs now went up in one corner of the room. The traditional straight staircase had been replaced by an attractive but impractical spiral.

"There's some paper on the side, if you want to start thinking about what we need to say." Pete called through from the kitchen. "The pen's by the phone."

"Do you mind if I wait for you?" she asked. She looked round and saw the phone was on a table near the front window, next to a large leather armchair that she presumed was where Pete sat when he was on his own. The settee was free from clutter. It would be a beautiful room, if Pete weren't colour blind. The bright red curtains clashed with the terracotta carpet and the blue rug. As she waited she heard the sound of the cat flap thud shut and a cat strutted into the lounge, her tail held high. She stopped half way across the floor and began to wash, her green eyes fixed on Lisa the whole time. Her black and white coat looked immaculate with further washing appearing unnecessary.

Pete stood at the kitchen door, whilst he waited for the filter to finish. "I see Toffee's found you then. She'll make friends once she's sized you up. Of course, I don't mind you waiting for me," he smiled at her.

There it was again, the warmth flooding through her, because of his smile. How could she not have noticed it before? Toffee moved to rub herself around Lisa's legs, but moved away when Lisa went to stroke her.

Pete came back in, carrying two steaming mugs of coffee. "Sorry," he said. "My machine doesn't do cappuccino."

"I'd rather have it black now anyway," she said. "I'd forgotten you had a cat. She must be good company."

"Not bad, but she's a bit too independent. Fudge was better when he was alive. Fudge would be on your lap in a shot." Pete picked up the pen and paper and after turning on the computer, sat next to her on the settee. The suppleness of the leather told its own story of well cared antiquity. "Now what are we going to say?"

Lisa looked up at him, wanting him to take over; not knowing where her determination of earlier had gone. "Dear Julie?" she proffered more as a question than a statement.

"I'm not sure that will be enough," he laughed and she found herself laughing for the first time that evening.

"No," she said, "I suppose not."

Pete started to jot some ideas down on the pad. Then he handed them to her to see what she thought.

Without a word, she went to the computer and after logging into the Genes Reunited website, she typed the email as Pete had written and sent it to Julie. "I couldn't have put it better myself," she said. "Now all we have to do is wait."

CHAPTER 4

Triford. 1977

"I am not spending Midsummer's Day naked at Cerne Abbas and that's final."

"I know, Hugh. I can't say I fancy it either, but nothing else has worked. You have to ask yourself whether there might be something in these old wives tales."

"Maureen, are you listening to yourself? When did you start believing any of that old clap-trap?"

"Hugh, I'm desperate for a family. What else can we do?"

He drew me into his arms. "Maureen, last summer might have been the hottest in living memory, but did it send you stark raving mad? We've got the details of the Adoption Agency. Be honest, wouldn't it be easier to make an appointment to see them then to lose our dignity at Cerne Abbas?"

I nodded meekly. He was right as usual. I didn't fancy sex on a public monument, but I was thirty-four. We'd been trying for a family for four years. You know what it's like when you talk to people about things like that. They all have their theories of what you should do. It's funny how it's always the ones with children who are convinced they know where you're going wrong. I just wanted to scream.

"It's hard to let go of the thought that it will be our

own baby."

"I know," he said, "but we can at least think about it."

We got in touch with the agency just before Christmas and once we'd started the process, I stopped thinking so much about becoming pregnant. Having children still meant everything to me, but becoming pregnant stopped being the focus.

"Surprise," said Hugh, handing me an envelope.

"What is it?" I asked.

"It's your birthday present. Open it."

"Oh, Hugh, a weekend away on the Isle of Wight. How lovely."

"I thought we could do with the break."

He was right again. It was unspoilt. We stayed in a little guest house in Shanklin. It was good for both of us, relaxing. We were like a pair of teenagers, in love with each other.

We'd been back a couple of weeks when I realised my period was late. I didn't say a word to Hugh, I didn't want to raise his hopes, but as I made an appointment to see the doctor my pulse was pounding so hard that I was surprised the receptionist didn't ask if I had a heart problem.

Waiting for the result of that pregnancy test seemed like a lifetime and when I was given the news it was positive I kept opening and closing my mouth, unable to find a single word. I couldn't settle to anything when I got home, impatient for Hugh to arrive. I'd sit down for two minutes then be up and pacing the kitchen, putting on a kettle and forgetting to make any tea. Normally, by the time he came home I had dinner ready. That day, I hadn't even started. He looked at me as he came in and it must have been written all over my face.

"You look different, Maureen, what is it?"

"Oh, Hugh" was all I could manage to say.

"Have you had your hair done?"

I threw my arms round him, "No, silly, nothing like that. We're going to have a baby. I'm pregnant."

"Oh, Maureen, say that again." There were already tears forming in the corners of his eyes before I got another word out.

"We're going to have a baby of our very own."

We held each other and cried such tears of joy. I needed to get my handkerchief out to wipe my eyes, but Hugh had still got hold of my hands.

"Have you told your mum?"

"No, not yet. I wanted to tell you first."

"Come on, let's see her now."

Mum needed the good news. She hadn't been so good since Dad died the previous year. She was old for her sixty-seven years, but was still looking after herself. When we got there, Elizabeth, my sister was there too, so we told them both together. We all cried. Elizabeth's daughter, Sylvia, had moved to Australia with her husband a couple of years earlier, we all needed a bit of life introducing to the family. Hugh and I never did have dinner that evening. By the time we got back from Mum's, we just had a bit of cheese on toast and went to bed.

"Will you finish work at the end of the summer term?" Hugh asked as we sat down together one quiet evening.

"I'd rather work up to the October half-term. It will give them longer to replace me. Besides, what would I do sat around here all day?"

"Well there's the spare room to turn into a nursery, but I'd rather thought I might do that," said Hugh, grinning. "My contribution."

"I think we've already had your contribution," I said laughing until my eyes watered.

The early stages were easy. I did have morning sickness, but not too much. The funniest thing was wanting to eat Marmite and bacon sandwiches. I'd never even liked Marmite before that. I was six months gone when I finished work. I was getting larger and it was a relief to have a bit of a rest.

"What are we going to call the baby?" I asked, looking through a book of names.

"It depends if it's a boy or a girl," said Hugh. "I'd rather like to call a boy Robert, after my father."

"I quite like the name Patrick. He could be Robert Patrick Forster."

"What about a girl? Why don't you choose a name for a girl?"

"I still like Patrick, what about Patricia? Patricia Lisa."

"That's lovely." Hugh put a hand on my growing tummy. "Hello, Robert Patrick or Patricia Lisa." I felt the baby wriggle in response.

I was doing O.K. until the end of November and then I felt tired. Not the normal tired you feel when you've done too much. It was a 'being sucked into oblivion' sort of tired, with no energy for anything. Hugh laughed and said I had to remember I was carrying another person and I presumed he was right. Then the headaches started. I didn't usually get headaches, so I thought it was a bit strange and to begin with we put this down to the size I was and the difficulty of being pregnant. Then I got the pain in my abdomen.

"You've got to see the doctor, love."

"I know, Hugh. I'm scared."

"Come on, I'll take you down now."

The doctor took my blood pressure and gave me a general examination. He sat down with us and explained that he thought I needed to go to the hospital for further tests and that they would keep me in.

"But we're not ready. Hugh, I was going to prepare some meals for you for while I was in hospital. I was going to have a bag ready. We haven't finished buying everything. What about Christmas?"

"Maureen," he said taking my hand. "We'll get through this. It's more important that you do what the doctor says."

I nodded, my shoulders slumped. "Can we just go home to pick up a few bits first?"

"O.K., we can do that."

We got to the hospital at midday. My head and abdomen were hurting and I'd been sick while we were at home. The nurses were very good and it wasn't long before I was admitted.

"Mrs Forster," I was dozing when the doctor spoke to me.

"Where am I?"

"It's O.K., love, you're in hospital. I brought you in earlier." Hugh had been sitting in the chair by my side, reading his paper.

"Mrs Forster," the doctor said again, "We're going to keep you under observation over the next few hours. Mr Forster can stay with you until the end of visiting time."

"Then what?" Hugh asked, standing up.

"You'll need to leave like all the other visitors. We'll look after your wife."

"Sorry, love," said Hugh shrugging. "I don't suppose there's any point in me arguing."

I was already tearful. I think that was my hormones,

but I just couldn't stop crying. "I don't want to be on my own, Hugh. I'm frightened."

"You won't be on your own, Mrs Forster. We'll be here to look after you," said the nurse. "And Mr Forster can stay for another ten minutes."

The nurse came and took my blood pressure again. Then the doctor was back and looking at the results. "We're a little concerned about your raised blood pressure. It is possible we may need to induce the baby."

"But I've still got another five weeks. The baby might die."

"Mrs Forster, it's starting to look as though both yours and the baby's health may be at risk. We'll continue to monitor you and hope that you stabilise. We'll ring Mr Forster if the situation deteriorates."

Hugh was just getting ready to go. He'd already stayed beyond the visiting time and the nurse was trying to usher him out of the way.

"I'll be back as soon as I can, love." He didn't let go of my hand until our arms wouldn't stretch any further.

They monitored my progress for the next few days. I stabilised as far as the blood pressure went, but the pain in my abdomen was excruciating. It was too bad for me to think about how Hugh was coping at home. He came to see me at visiting times and then went back to sit at home and worry.

There were four weeks to my due date and the doctor said, "You do realise Mrs Forster if we leave it any longer we are risking both yours and the baby's life?"

"Will the baby survive if I have it now?"

"There is a good possibility."

I wished Hugh was there. There wasn't a decision to make, but I would have been happier if he had been part of it. "Will you ring my husband?" The nurse nodded.

They started preparing me to go down to the delivery suite. It would be a while before the drugs they gave me took effect, but they needed me under a different type of observation. I remember thinking that it would be Christmas Day in two weeks and praying that we'd have a healthy baby and we would all be at home together.

That was when things started to go wrong. They checked my pulse and blood pressure again as they had been doing at regular intervals and through the haze of pain in my head and abdomen I was aware of activity.

"We're going to have to do a caesarean. Is the patient's husband here?"

Everything was a bit of a blur. There was a nurse holding my hand and telling me everything was going to be fine. It was late at night and I wasn't expecting them to do anything until the following day, but the next thing I knew Hugh was there and he looked very white.

"You'll be fine, love. I'm sure of it. Be my brave girl."

They wheeled me away and gave me a general anaesthetic. I don't know how long these things last, but I remember starting to regain consciousness and there was Hugh's face coming in and out of focus.

"It's a girl. We've got a little girl." He was crying and it took me a moment to work out what he was talking about.

I wasn't completely awake yet, but I remember drifting back off to sleep thinking "Patricia, we've got a daughter called Patricia," and feeling so much better than I had been feeling, despite the surgery I'd just been through. The pain had gone and in its place I'd got Patricia.

It was some time before they sat me and Hugh down and explained how serious it had all been and told me that they recommended that I didn't have any more children. I asked what the risks were if I did and all they would say was that in their experience, women who had had these symptoms were prone to have them again and my life as well as the baby's life would be in danger.

Despite having been born prematurely, Patricia was growing well and although we would have liked more children, one would be just fine to be going on with.

CHAPTER 5

Billingbrook. Saturday night 15th September

"Pete, would it be all right if I stayed here tonight? I don't think I can face being at home on my own." In the six months they'd known each other, she'd never stayed at Pete's house. The issue hadn't arisen. It struck her that there was no evidence of anyone but Pete around the house. He'd never talked about his previous relationships. She wondered how long it had been since any of his female friends had stayed. "I don't mind sleeping on the settee," she ran her hand over the luxuriant hide. "Although to be quite honest I don't think I'll do much sleeping." Tired as she was, her mind was churning through all the possibilities.

"Of course you can stay." He sat next to her and stroked her hair. She was surprised by the gesture, but more surprised by the disappointment she felt as he took his hand away. Pete cleared his throat sounding uncomfortable. "You're quite welcome to have my bed. Otherwise you'll have to fight over the settee with Toffee, although she goes out for some of the night. Maybe I could stay up with you a while? I don't feel that tired either. I'll put some more coffee on."

"I'll be fine on the settee, thanks." She picked up her bag and after delving into several corners and pockets found a clean tissue. She blew her nose and returned the tissue to her bag. She must sort the bag out. Ruefully, she looked at the mess. She checked the corners of the bag until she felt her contact lens holder and nodded reassured.

Why was everything such a mess, her bag, her house and now her life?

"What am I going to do if Julie doesn't reply to my email? I need answers. I've been struggling to tell myself I'm still the person I was yesterday, but it doesn't feel as simple as that. For years, I've been expecting to turn into my mum, Maureen, as I've got older. I listen for the inflection in my voice, I watch for the inches round the hips, but I've been looking for the wrong things. I don't know what to expect anymore. Maybe I should have been noticing the differences rather than the similarities. I can't even remember many details. I know my fingers were a different length to either of my parents. I remember holding the palm of my hand against theirs and measuring. Dad's fingers were quite short and stubby, Mum's were, well, just normal." She held out her long slender hands and looked at them.

"I don't know," Pete said. "I suppose it's too easy for me to say that you could see it as an opportunity to think about who you are, for your own sake. Maybe that's all a little way down the road. Why don't we make a list of the things we do know and the things we need to find out and then take it from there? There must be organisations that can help you find out things like this, who your parents are anyway. It would take a lifetime with a psychologist to unravel the rest of who we both are. Just let me do the coffee first. Then we'll try to come up with a plan."

The clock on the mantelpiece had stopped at 4.25 on a nameless day. It was a beautiful Ormolu clock that she presumed was an heirloom, as it seemed out of keeping with the rest of Pete's taste. She wondered whether it worked at all or whether it was one you needed to wind on a daily basis, making it difficult to keep going. She looked at her watch; it was 9.40 They had sent the email about half an hour ago, but she presumed it was too soon for Julie to have seen it. In any case, Julie would be in bed, it was ridiculous to hope for a reply so soon.

"What's the time difference to Australia?" She called through to the kitchen.

"It depends where they are. I think it's eight or nine hours."

She counted forward eight hours using her fingers. "Funny how you never get the hang of what time it is when you add a number of hours," she said laughing. "Perhaps I should have worked harder on the twenty-four hour clock when I was at school. I make that about six in the morning, give or take. I wonder when Julie gets up or looks at the computer? It's funny waiting for something so important from someone you don't know. Her grandmother was Mum's, well Maureen's sister, but I still don't know her name. She was older. I don't know if she's still alive. Can you still hear me in there or am I rambling to myself?"

"Pardon?" Pete grinned as he came back with the coffee. "Yes, I heard you, but you're right, you are rambling! To keep things simple, why don't you still refer to Maureen as Mum for the time being, at least I know who you mean then. This is confusing enough for me; goodness knows what you're feeling. I don't think we should check for the email again until at least eleven Australian time. Otherwise we're going to be looking every five minutes. Right," he said in a commanding voice, "what do we want to know?"

"I want to know who I am." Then the floodgates opened. "I want to know who my real parents are. I want to know if they're still alive. I want to know why they gave me away. I want to know why my adoptive parents didn't tell me. I want to know if I have any brothers and sisters. I want to know if they want to meet me after all these years and why they never got in touch. I want to know if I'm going to die young of some hereditary disease. I want to know when my birthday is."

"Streuth, I hadn't even thought of some of those. So in summary," he said, "we need to trace your birth parents."

"Yes. I think that sums it up."

"So what do we already know?"

"That's the hard part. I think I was born in 1977, but I can't be certain. I must have lived with my adoptive parents since I was a baby, because there are photographs and because otherwise someone would have known I was adopted. Beyond that, I'm not sure we know very much. I suppose we know where my parents worked and what town they came from. We know where I went to school, but the adoption must predate that. We know what I look like and that I'm short-sighted, but I don't suppose that helps without knowing some other stuff. I know my blood group," she added her face lighting up.

"When you cleared out your parents' things after your mum died," said Pete, "what paperwork did you find?"

"Nothing that's relevant to all this. It was just routine stuff. You know…"

"Did you help your Mum sort through things when you're Dad died?"

"No," she said. "No, Mum was quite insistent that she did it on her own. She was a very capable lady. I accepted that."

"I'm sorry if some of these questions are difficult, but we've got to start somewhere."

"That's O.K., go on. You're doing well. It's a good job one of us is thinking straight. I keep thinking things like, if my real parents were criminals, would it make any difference to who I am? I need to take this one step at a time. My imagination is doing overtime."

"What do we know about your parents? What friends did they have? Did they have a lawyer? I mean your adoptive ones, not the criminals," he said smiling.

She ignored the joke. "They never seemed to have many friends. Just work colleagues. They always seemed happy with their own company. As for lawyers, yes, at least their will was with a lawyer. I don't think they'd used him for other things, but I suppose it's worth asking."

"How long had they lived in Billingbrook?"

"All my life, as far as I know. Maybe that's something Julie knows."

"Did they keep all their papers at home or did they have a safety deposit box? Who did they bank with?" Pete continued, making notes of her answers.

"They banked with Natwest in Billingbrook for some things, but they had accounts here and in Triford. Good heavens. I didn't think about a safety deposit box at the time. Do you think the bank would have told me if they had? I didn't ask the question. I didn't come across any papers of interest, perhaps they did keep them elsewhere."

"I think they tell you if the box is at the same bank as other things, but people often seem to use a different bank for things like that. Or is that just in the movies?"

"I've still got some of the files of paperwork at home," she said. "I've just finished sorting it all out from Mum's death last year. We could go through it again tomorrow to look for clues." The prospect of raking through papers left from an event that itself still felt so raw was unappealing. She was grateful for the comfort that at least this time she wouldn't be alone.

"I know it's your life we're talking about," said Pete putting the pad of paper down and grinning at her, "but it does feel a bit as though we're solving a mystery doesn't it?"

She yawned. "Yes, it does. It's just a shame I'm at the centre of it." The constant gymnastics of her thinking was getting too much. She'd had enough for one day. She curled up on the settee and put her head on Pete's lap. It felt a very natural thing to do. Pete didn't flinch; perhaps it felt the same to him. She was glad he hadn't tried to insist that she had the bed, but then he knew her well enough to know she wouldn't let him.

"I'll get you a pillow and duvet." He lifted her head from his knee and put a cushion underneath it whilst he got up.

"Pete," she said as he came back with the bedding, which to her pleasant surprise had a Snoopy pattern on it, she imagined he'd have something more boring, well more masculine anyway, she approved of this part of his taste, even if his colour choices were odd. "Can I stay with you tonight?"

"But you're already here," he said, missing the point of what she was saying and then blushing as he understood. He sat down next to her and stroked her hair again. "Lisa, there's nothing I'd like more than that, but you're in a very vulnerable state. I'd hate you to wake up tomorrow and regret it. I couldn't bear to lose your friendship. I'll sit with you here until you go to sleep. Besides, Toffee would think I was being unfaithful."

He kissed her cheek very softly, and the feint smell of cologne drifted into her sleepy world. He wrapped the duvet round her, tucking it under her feet.

"Sleep well, my beautiful friend," he said smiling.

She snuggled into the warmth of the duvet. She knew he was right and yet his chivalry made him seem all the more attractive to her. How had she never seen all this in him before?

CHAPTER 6

Noosa, Australia. Saturday 15th September 2007

It was Saturday evening on what had been a very warm day for mid-September; the first indication that spring was taking hold in Noosa. There had been little breeze off the sea, which was unusual at this time of year. Julie was exhausted from her day in the gift shop. It had been a slow day with few people for company. She couldn't afford to pay for additional help out of season, other than the few hours a week she needed to keep her sane. Julie had worked in the shop for ages but only bought it when the previous owner retired, four years earlier. It wasn't a bad life. She made enough to get by. Now she was sitting down, recovering from the day with a glass of chilled white wine, from one of the finest vineyards in New South Wales. She flicked on the television using the remote control and then turned on the computer.

She'd lived up here on the east coast of Queensland since she married fifteen years ago. Now the marriage was long gone. Dave claimed that 'business reasons' had intervened. But Julie knew that the 'business reasons' had long slender legs, piercing blue eyes and a date of birth nearer to their daughter's than to her own. Dave had left for the bright lights of the city, but Julie had stayed here, rather than move back to where her mum lived near

Sydney. Growing up near a city was fine, but here there were unspoilt beaches, blue seas and out of the tourist season, peace and quiet. She depended on the tourists for trade but she was always happier when they'd gone. Happier when the detritus of their self-indulgent lives had been swept away by the local garbage department and when the lifeguards could concentrate on real rescues, rather than ill-prepared holiday makers.

Tired as Julie was, there was no going to bed until Susie was delivered home safely from her friend's house in another half an hour. She might be very mature for fourteen, but Julie wasn't ready to leave Susie to let herself into a sleeping household just yet. She had time to get a bite to eat and check her emails before Susie's return.

The house was like so many in this area; cut into the hillside with a view of the sea, if you stood on tiptoe. Before the houses were built, the plots of land had fixed wooden step-ladders you could climb, to see what the view would be. The ladders were about the height of the stilts the houses were built on. The stilts helped to keep the houses cool, but in the hot summer months, you could be forgiven for thinking they failed. The step-ladders had been a way you could choose your view and then decide which house you wanted to build. Julie had been lucky, hers was one of the earlier houses to be built; at least the view wasn't a complete figment of her imagination. The houses on the coast were too expensive, but it wasn't a long trip down to the sea. It took no more than five minutes in their sports utility vehicle. SUV's were almost standard issue in a community that spent its life surfing and lounging on the beach. The four-wheel drive capability meant you could drive right onto the beach without fear of getting stuck, unlike some of the holiday makers with their two-wheel drive hire cars. It was so much better to be able to throw all the wet gear onto the flatbed at the back and not have to worry about the state of the boot or the car seats.

Julie loved her home. She preferred the brick to the wooden construction of so many. She enjoyed the open plan layout that was so typical of Australian homes. The kitchen flowed into the living areas, with nothing but a work surface separating the cook from the guests. It made for a sociable life, but could be a bugbear if things went wrong in the kitchen. These days it was not something she had to worry about often. Most of the entertaining was done by Susie, with Julie called upon to provide the cooking expertise. Salads and bar-b-qs were her specialities; they took little work and suited the climate.

Julie chopped some peppers and put them together with the cucumber, tomatoes and lettuce in a salad bowl. She put some onto her plate and the rest back in the fridge for later. She took her plate through to the lounge area and sat by the computer. She had an email from the Genes Reunited website. It was a while since she put the family tree together. It was a popular pursuit amongst her acquaintances. It was as though the newer generations of arrivals had a pressing need to establish their link back to their homelands. With nothing better to do, Julie clicked to go through to the page to see what the email said. "Dear Julie..." she scanned through the rest of the email researching her Gran's sister's family and sent a quick reply, outlining the person's relationship to her and asking where the sender, Lisa, fitted in. Julie wondered what relation this person was. She turned the computer off and slumped in front of the television, until she heard Susie.

"That you, love? Had a good time?"

"Hi, Mum," Susie came and dropped onto the settee next to her. "I'm whacked. You're not working again tomorrow are you?"

"Afraid so darling, it's my weekend on. I'll be free next weekend though. Was there something you wanted to do?"

"Not really. I'm just fed up with getting my own lunch." Susie grinned at her Mum.

"You lazy little..." said Julie laughing. "Perhaps it's about time you got a weekend job of your own."

"O.K., enough already. I'm going to bed. Night, Mum."

"Night, Susie, I'm coming too in a minute."

Julie finished off her wine and took the glass through to the kitchen. Then before going to bed, she made a note on the pad by the phone, "Ring Mum and tell her about Aunty Maureen." Then she turned out the lights and went through to her bedroom.

***

Noosa. Sunday 16th September 2007

It was just after six when Julie woke; the sun streamed through a gap in the curtains and was already promising a warm day ahead. This was the best time of day to get housework done, before it got too warm, with the incentive of a refreshing shower at the end of it. Julie forced herself out of bed and put on an old tracksuit. She put a pot of coffee on to brew, but made a start on the chores rather than wait for it to finish. It was eight before she sat down for a coffee and turned the computer on to warm up. She showered and changed before returning to look at her emails.

"What you doing, Mum?" Susie yawned as she came

into the lounge where her mother was sitting at the computer.

"Just looking at email, I had one from England yesterday, from someone tracing her family tree. I wanted to see if she'd sent any more information on how she's related."

"You and that family tree," said Susie. "Sometimes, I think you'd rather be English."

Julie laughed. "No, I don't think so. I feel every inch an Aussie, but something deep down makes me want to search for distant roots. Maybe it's an age thing. You might feel the same when you're older."

"Yeah right!"

Julie cleared out all the email that had come in as spam overnight and then went back to her inbox. There was one marked Genes Reunited that read 'You have received a reply from Lisa Forster' click here to read the reply'. "I didn't spot that yesterday, her surname's Forster too; she must be directly connected to the family." She followed the link to the reply. As she read it, she gasped.

"What is it, Mum?" Susie's interest was sparked and she came over to the chair and read over her Mum's shoulder.

"Dear Julie,

Thank you for your email reply earlier. You asked me what relation I was to your Aunty Maureen, until your email, I thought I was her daughter. Now I realise I must have been adopted, following the death of Patricia. I had always been led to believe that I was Patricia Lisa Forster, known as Lisa. I was never told of my adoption, or indeed of Patricia's death. As you might imagine, this has all come as a considerable shock and I would appreciate any help that either you or your mother could give me in working out who I am. When my parents died, I found no details of my adoption and wonder if your mum might be aware of any information that might help me in tracing those details.

Please reply as soon as possible.

Best wishes

Lisa."

"Oh no, Mum, what have you done?"

"I don't know. I had no idea. Oh, what can that poor girl be going through? I feel dreadful about it. Somehow I've got to help. If it hadn't been for me she would still think she was Aunty Maureen's daughter."

"Mum, it's not your fault, you can't blame yourself. She'd have found out somehow."

"I'd better ring your Gran." Julie walked across the lounge, picked up the cordless phone and came back to the computer whilst typing in the number for her mother.

It was several rings before her mother answered in a bright cheerful voice.

"Morning, Mum, you sound in a good mood."

"Oh hi, Jules, I'm just feeling full of the joys of spring. What's the weather like up there?"

"Great as always. Look, Mum, I've got a bit of a problem that you might be able to help with."

"Uh oh. There goes my good mood," her mum laughed. "What have you done 'this time'?"

"What do you mean this time? Anyone would think I was always getting into scrapes."

"Well," said her mother, "what about that date three weeks ago, when...?"

"O.K. point taken, but you might be able to help with this one." Julie began the story at the beginning and read the series of emails to her mother. Julie's Mum was quiet for a minute. "Are you still there, Mum?"

"Yes, darling, I was just thinking. I've still got most of my old diaries, but I know some of them got lost when a box went missing in the last house move after your Dad and I split up. I can't remember which years got lost without checking. I wasn't planning anything for today. I'll see what I can find. To be honest, I don't remember ever knowing very much about it. Your Gran would have known more if she were still around. I've still got her old letters somewhere though. There may be an answer amongst those. I don't know if I can find them, but that poor girl must be in a dreadful state. I'll do what I can."

"Thanks, Mum. I'll send Lisa an email telling her we'll do our best. I'll call you later when I get back from work. It won't be until about seven this evening, maybe a bit later."

"I won't have gone anywhere," said her Mum, still showing signs of her good mood.

Julie said her goodbyes to her Mum and looked back at the computer screen. She typed a reply to Lisa, expressing how dreadful she felt about being the one to reveal the truth. "You know," she said to Susie, "I wanted an excuse to visit England, maybe this is it."

"Get real, Mum, who's going to look after me?" said Susie in a horrified voice. "Getting my lunch on a weekend is bad enough. I don't think I want to look after myself just yet."

"You could always come with me, or stay with your Gran. I suppose it's the start of term so I couldn't do anything before your holidays."

Susie sat up, "You serious? Take me to England? I'm in."

"Let's just wait to see what happens first. I'll think

about it. Now I must get ready for work. I'll take pity on you and make a sandwich before I go, on condition you clean your room while I'm out. Oh and get your homework finished."

"Deal," said Susie, grinning.

It was 7.30 before Julie came back that evening. She lit the gas bar-b-q on the veranda and put some chicken on to cook. It was dark, but the warmth of the day lingered as the crickets chirruped from their grassy hiding places. The fragrant scent of early blossom mixed with eucalyptus teased the senses, mingling with the mouth-watering aroma drifting up from the food cooking on the wood-effect fire.

She prepared some salad to go with the meat.

"Susie, dinner," she called through to Susie's bedroom. There was no reply. Julie went through to her daughter's room, turning the computer on as she passed. She opened the door. Susie was lying on her bed doing her homework, with headphones in both ears. Julie turned the music off to get her attention. "I don't suppose you'll know if Gran rang back then."

"No, sorry, Mum," she said getting up off the bed.

"Why do you do your homework on your bed like that, when you've got a perfectly good desk in your room? I can't say much about the music, I used to do mine with music blaring. I should at least be grateful that you've got headphones; I just let everyone suffer the noise. Anyway, you can switch it off for now, dinner's out. I'll ring Gran after we've eaten." As she said it, the phone rang. She answered after finding the handset from under some papers on the table. "Mum, yes, do I need a notepad?"

"There isn't a lot to tell so far, Jules. I found my diary

for 1977, listen to this from January 25th, it was a Tuesday. 'Took Julie for her first day at school. I was trembling and didn't want to leave her. Julie was fine and after a brief introduction by her teacher to one or two of the other children, she went off to play and forgot I existed. Went home crying. Why is it so hard to let go as they get older.'"

"Oh, Mum," said Julie, "that's sad. I'm sorry. It was much the same with Susie. Perhaps that's nature's revenge. I suffered through the next generation."

"Don't be silly, darling," said her Mum with a slight quaver in her voice. "It's funny what you come across when you're looking for something else. I read right through all of 1976, 1977 and 1978, in the hope there would be something there."

"And?"

"Nothing. Nothing useful anyway. I found a line about Aunty Maureen being pregnant and one about the baby being born. Most of the time, in those days, your Gran communicated with her sister by letter. It took a while for news to be exchanged. I think it was her own mother rather than her sister she spoke to on the phone, but your Gran wasn't a great letter writer, high days and holidays. With me having moved out here, we got the news last of all. Mum did write and tell me about the baby dying, but everyone back in England was very upset by it all and didn't want to talk about it. I knew there was an adoption, but I don't know how I knew. I don't know who told me. I brought your Gran's letters back to Australia with me after she died, I've still got those to go through and there's one other possibility, but I might need your help."

"Go on," said Julie, sounding disappointed that there wasn't any more helpful news.

"Every so often we used to exchange a tape of Christmas greetings, birthdays etc. The whole family used to sit round the microphone and we would all get to take part."

"I remember," said Julie, "I used to recite little rhymes and things for Grandma. Read her bits I'd written at school."

"Yes, that's it, we used to send the same tapes backwards and forwards to England, rather than keep buying new ones. There were four different tapes altogether. I kept all four of them when Mum died. I don't know whether there's anything on them that might help. We always did a bit that was just the adults. That might have included something."

"I don't understand where I come in to all this?" Julie said.

"Don't you remember?" said her Mum. "You borrowed my old reel to reel tape recorder as part of one of your college projects. I've got one of the tapes, but you've still got the machine and the other tapes."

"Oh yes," said Julie in a distant voice. "So I did. I must still have them somewhere. I presume they're in the loft. I haven't been up there since Dave left. Gosh, it's been years. I can't think of anywhere else they would be. I don't think I've even got a ladder to get up there."

"Well," said her mum, "You've got until five-thirty tomorrow afternoon to get a ladder and find the tapes and the tape recorder, before picking me up from the coach station. If I get a flight to Brisbane in the morning, I can get the coach to Noosa from there. There have to be some benefits to taking early retirement."

"What if it doesn't work, Mum? You'll have come all this way for no reason."

"I'll see my daughter and granddaughter, that's reason enough for me. I'd better pack."

"Have a safe journey, Mum. I'll pick you up tomorrow. Bye." Julie turned to Susie who was still munching away at her dinner. "You heard most of that I presume?"

"Yeah, Gran's coming to stay. Does that mean I need to be on my best behaviour?"

"Second best will do, pretty much as usual. Did you tidy your room? If you didn't, now would be a good time to think about doing it. I'll make up the spare bed after dinner. I should send Lisa an email too. I'm just not sure what to say to her."

"I could write it for you," said Susie. "Dear Lisa, Yeah you're adopted, get over it."

"Susie! Don't be so heartless."

"I was joking, Mum."

"Well, teenage humour isn't what I need right now."

"Whatever," said Susie and drifted back to her bedroom.

Julie shook her head in despair and as she ate her cold chicken, she made a quick list of the things she needed to get done.

- Borrow stepladder
- Find tape recorder
- Make up spare bed
- Shopping
- Pick up Mum 5.30pm
- Email Lisa

She moved the computer mouse to bring the screen back to life and went to the Genes Reunited site. She clicked on Lisa's email again and then clicked on 'reply'. She began to type.

"Dear Lisa,

It might be best if we exchanged email addresses rather than keep going through the Genes site, mine is…"

CHAPTER 7

Billingbrook. Sunday 16th September 2007

It was eight before Lisa woke up. Her joints ached from sleeping on the settee and for a minute she couldn't think where she was. She yawned, stretched and looked around the room. The clashing colour scheme gave her an instant reminder.

"Morning, sleepyhead," Pete sat straddling the chair by the computer. He was watching her. "I was starting to think I was going to have to open this email without you."

She shot off the settee and over to the computer, tripping on the edge of the duvet as she went. There was a howl as Toffee, who had finished the night curled up on Lisa's feet, was hurled from the settee.

"What does it say?"

"Hey, steady." Pete reached up and caught her flailing arm. Toffee had already picked herself up and stalked out to the kitchen. Once she regained her balance, Pete said, "I don't know." He moved to sit on the chair properly. "I haven't opened it yet." He clicked on the message button and they waited anxiously for it to appear. Lisa was biting the edge of her finger.

"I haven't got my lenses in. Can you read it to me?"

"Dear Lisa,

What can I say? I can't begin to think what you must be going through right now and I feel as though it's all my fault. I am very sorry. I'm afraid that I was too young to know any of the details of the adoption at the time. I'm not much use to you. I've rung Mum. She used to keep a diary. She's going through all the entries for the months around 1977, to see if she can find out any more. She'll do that today. I should be able to send you another email this evening if I find out anything.

Best wishes

Julie."

There was a long silence before Pete said, "Some good news there."

"Not a lot," Lisa replied. "It's odd to think I might just have been a replacement for the baby they wanted. Not wanted for myself at all."

"Don't talk like that." Pete sounded hurt by what she'd said. "Of course, you were wanted because you were you."

"I guess so," she said.

"You still are," he said.

"I still am what?"

"Wanted because you're you." He slipped his arm around her. "I was thinking about last night and wondered if you still wished you'd spent it with me. If you don't then I'll never say another word about it, but if you did, well, I just wanted you to know that I feel the same way. And I'm sure in time Toffee would forgive you too."

She stared at him, feelings of confusion flooding over her. "I did mean it. I do mean it. It's just that..." She paused, it was just what? What was it that was holding her back? She knew how she was feeling about Pete. Her fear had always been that if you let yourself feel like this, the person you relied upon, might not be there when you needed them. She remembered the pain of losing the people she loved. "It isn't that... Oh, I don't know." She thought how much simpler it was not to rely on other people and how good it felt not to answer to anyone else for the everyday decisions. "Can I think about it?" She looked into his clear blue eyes. Her pulse quickened.

Pete smiled and kissed her on the cheek again. "Take as long as you need. I'm not going anywhere." He reached up and ran his fingers through her hair, lingering when he reached its ends. "I'll make some breakfast."

Lisa went for a shower. The upstairs of Pete's house was as tidy as downstairs, but she was reassured to see that the colour schemes were just as bad. She poked her head through one of the doors that appeared to be the spare bedroom. It had a set of drums where the bed should be and a guitar leaning against the wall. It was tempting to try the drums, but maybe Sunday morning wasn't the time. She thought how much Pete's neighbours must appreciate the noise through the wall of a terraced house. The second door she opened was the bathroom.

The smell of bacon frying wafted through the lounge as she came back downstairs. "Something smells good," said Lisa as she came into the kitchen and tentatively put her arms around Pete.

"Yes, doesn't it?" said Pete, as she stood clad in his dressing gown with a towel wrapped round her still wet hair.

She twisted the end of the towel in her hands, "I've always found the shower a great place to do my thinking and well, I was thinking about what you said before I went upstairs and I do feel the same." Before she had chance to change her mind, or for him to speak, Lisa kissed Pete on the lips, lingering long enough for the smell of burning toast to make them separate.

"I think these are for the bin," said Pete laughing as he blew out the little flames. "I'll put some more on. You go and sit down and I'll bring it through, or we could skip breakfast?"

"Not yet," she said running her finger across his lips and turning away from the kitchen. She could see Pete trying to hide his disappointment, but the time didn't feel right to her. There were too many thoughts churning around her mind and whilst in her experience, this wasn't always an obstacle to men, she wanted their first time to be special and not distracted by the chaos she was feeling.

Pete had set the dining table, in the corner of the lounge, for two. He had already put the coffee pot, cereal and marmalade on the table. "Are you trying to spoil me?" she called through to the kitchen.

"No. I'm just making sure you have enough strength for the day ahead. Besides which, you didn't eat anything last night." He came through carrying the toast. "The bacon will keep warm in the oven while you have some cereal." He sat opposite to her. "When we've finished breakfast are you up to going through the files of papers from your mum and dad's estates?"

"I think so. At least, I will be if you're there to help." She realised relying on someone felt quite good. At heart, she was frightened of not being in control of her own life. Now her life had gone completely out of her control and she needed Pete's help to try to get it back.

Try as she might, she couldn't eat much breakfast. She felt guilty not doing justice to Pete's hard work.

"Don't worry," he said. "There'll be other breakfasts and Toffee is rather partial to bacon."

It was already 10.00 by the time they headed to Lisa's

house. She lived about the same distance the other side of the pub as Pete did this side. It was far enough to make it worth Pete getting his Mini out of the garage and driving rather than walking. The garages were in a separate block along the street.

"The distance makes me think twice about using them," he said as they walked along. He ducked to avoid a mis-kicked football that some kids were playing with in the road. "That," he said laughing, "reminds me why I keep my pride and joy in the garage in the first place. I don't want to leave it parked on the road, at the mercy of every local urchin."

"Are these the same urchins we heard shouting last night?"

"Yes, that one's Ryan," Pete pointed to a lanky boy of about ten, with his hair shaved to within a fraction of existence. "His brother's the one with the torn t-shirt. Apparently that's 'fashion'." He picked up the football that had once again come towards him and tried to aim it at the mismatched clothing goalposts. The ball went in the general direction of the children. "I need more practice," he said laughing again. She loved his childlike enjoyment of life. Then changing the subject he said, "I had thought of using the money from Mum and Dad to move somewhere a bit bigger. I'd like a house with my own driveway. I want to give the Mini pride of place. My dad bought it new and cherished the old thing, even after he bought a bigger car. The car gives me a very special link to Dad. I've thought about it, but I'm settled here in Garden Street. There was an optimistic name if ever there was one."

It was Lisa's turn to laugh, as she looked round at the matching rows of gardenless houses spilling life out onto the street. What was missing was the lines of washing hanging between the houses and the image would be complete. The terraces seemed less sombre by day with the contrast of the light grey stone steps and lintels against the darkness of the brick and their paint-card range of front door colours.

The garage had everything sorted and stored in labelled containers on neatly arranged racks. The order it represented appealed to her; amidst the chaos she was feeling, order was good.

As they drove along, she started to worry about the state of her own house. "I'll just need a minute to do a bit of tidying up before we start," she said. Pete grinned but said nothing.

"When did you move to Billingbrook?" he asked as they drove past a school.

"I don't know. I've lived here all my life as far as I remember, but I always knew that my birth certificate said Triford, so presumed it was when I was very small. Maybe I was born here. I don't know."

"We do have a lot of gaps to fill in, don't we?"

"That was where Mum taught." They were passing Billingbrook Community College. "She taught History."

"Right," said Pete. "I don't suppose you can give me directions from here can you? I know the general area you live but not which road to turn down. Do any of your Mum's colleagues still work there?"

"Second left after the crossing. No, well I don't know. Mum retired when she was fifty-five I don't think she stayed in touch with the college after that."

Lisa's house wasn't as bad as she feared; at least she'd put the rack of washing away the day before. She wasn't ready for Pete to see her unfashionable old undies just yet.

"I'll bring the boxes down here," she said. "There's more room to spread out."

"D'you need a hand?"

"No," she said. "It's just that I think upstairs might be a bit more of a mess." Lisa screwed her face up as she spoke, which served to emphasise the extent of the mess. She hoped he wouldn't think badly of her for it after the neatness of his own house.

Lisa left Pete looking out at the garden as she went upstairs. She wondered what he would make of the sound of her throwing things in cupboards and closing the doors. She'd worry about sorting them out later, besides they were in good company with the piles of things already thrown in.

She carried a box of papers downstairs and went back to get three box files. As she put them down on the table in the lounge she said, "I think that's everything. To be honest I didn't keep all the papers, just the ones I needed for probate and tax. I hope I didn't throw away anything that mattered."

"I think we should go through everything systematically," Pete said. "Do you want to go through separate boxes or shall we do it together?"

"I know it would be quicker if we each did some, but would you mind doing it together? Going through all these the first time was harrowing, delving into the lives of the dead. Somehow it felt like unpicking the people they were and pieces of people aren't as attractive as the whole thing. I had to tell myself it was just another person I was dealing with; rather than my own parents. Then every so often I would come to something that brought back memories and I couldn't carry on."

"We don't have to do this." He took her hand.

"I can do it," she said forcing a smile.

"Why don't you write down anything we find out whilst I go through the papers?"

"O.K.," she said handing him the first box file. "We might as well start here, although this is the most recent stuff so it's less likely."

It took six hours to go through all of it. They had a break at lunchtime for long enough to eat a sandwich and to go into the dining room to log on to the computer, in case they'd received a reply. As there was nothing there, they continued until they were tired and dusty from the paperwork. The smell of old papers hung on the air. Lisa opened the French window to let the breeze through.

"So what have we got?" said Pete smiling.

She handed him the piece of paper. 'Column 1 Relevant Information' remained blank. 'Column 2 People to contact' had a long list of company and individuals' names, but they had no idea whether any of them would prove promising.

"Remind me again who Dorothy Farmer is?"

"She worked with Mum. It looks as though they stayed in touch. I think Dorothy retired just before Mum. She was an English teacher."

"It's a shame she moved to Spain. We could have visited her first. She's the one name we've come across that wasn't a company."

"I do remember going to her house when I was young. It was before I went to the college, because I can remember being relieved when I found I wasn't in her English class. She was nice enough, but no one wants to be taught by a friend of their parents. Right then, what do we do now?"

"We need to start by ringing each of them, but with the

companies we may have to go in person and take some ID before we can get anyone to talk to us. The ones that aren't local we might have to write to," Pete said.

"This could take ages. I can do some research whilst I'm at work, for the phone number or addresses, but I can't make calls from the library."

"We could do some of the research tonight, if you aren't too tired," he said. "Are you owed any holiday? I've got six days that I'm supposed to use before the end of this month."

She didn't know what to say, so she kissed him. "Thank you. I am owed some time."

"Shall we check for email again?" he said.

She went through to the other room, with Pete following. "I suppose if they haven't replied by now then we won't get anything today. Why don't you do it? I don't think I can look."

CHAPTER 8

Billingbrook. Sunday night 16th September 2007

Pete opened the email and began to read aloud. "Dear Lisa, it might be best if we exchanged email addresses rather than keep going through the Genes site ..."

"It's O.K.," Lisa said, "I'm reading too. Nothing interesting to report, they haven't found out anything that can help me. I've been sat here all day thinking about what they were doing and maybe they haven't even looked. They've had a fun Sunday doing other things, going out enjoying themselves and then remembered to email as an after-thought. It's not their problem anyway. Why should they care?"

"Lisa, don't be like that. You don't know they haven't done anything, for all we know they might have tried. Don't take it out on them."

"Oh that's it, you stick up for somebody else. I thought you were supposed to be on my side," she kicked the waste paper bin as she made her way across the dining room and out to the hall, slamming the door as she went. The bin made a satisfying thwack as it hit the desk leg and spewed its fragments of torn up papers onto the floor.

"I know you're hurting, Lisa, but you can't spend the evening feeling sorry for yourself and I don't think the bin can take it," Pete said. She could hear him scrabbling around on the floor putting everything back in the bin.

"Don't tell me what I can and can't do." She sat in a huddled mass on the stairs and began to sob. The stairs had always been a place she'd gone for comfort. Ever since being a small child, it had been the ideal place to huddle in the semi-darkness, separated from the world, but in reality just a door away. On the rare occasions that her mum and dad had argued, she sat in the dark trying to understand what it was about. She would catch part sentences from the conversation and try to fill in the gaps. It was never about anything very much and Dad had never been one to raise his voice. Every so often she would hear her mum stamp her foot and the words "Why won't you argue with me?" would come drifting out to the stairs. It was another house and another set of stairs, but for a moment Lisa could have been back there, a child again, safe in the comfort of the world around her. She could remember her mum getting cross because she'd lost her keys and wanting her dad to take part in the frantic search. Her dad had sat there asking questions about when she'd last used them and as a result, directed her to them without so much as getting up. She wondered now if the arguments had ever been about her, but they had never sounded like that at the time.

Pete came through to the hallway and squeezed onto the step next to her. "Do you want to shout at me some more?"

"Not really."

He tentatively put his arm around her, then drew her to him; she relaxed at his touch and sobbed on his shoulder until she could sob no more. Pete held her in his arms, "Look," he said, "to be honest I don't know what to say. I would love to be able to take the pain away right now. I'm not good in these situations; I didn't mean it to sound as though I was on their side. Maybe you're right, maybe they haven't tried, maybe we will just have to do this without them."

"I used to make an advent ring, out of wire coat hangers, like the one on *Blue Peter* and hang it above the stairs," she pointed to the ceiling above them. "How the candles didn't set fire to the tinsel I'll never know. I used to sit in the candlelight in my own little world, dreaming of the characters in the books I was reading. Imagining that their life was my life and I was facing their trials and tribulations. I never saw myself as the heroine. I don't know why? I always saw myself as one of the supporting cast. Sometimes my role was key to bringing the hero and heroine together; sometimes I was just a nobody on the edge of the action. I don't think I've ever worked out who I am." She turned to Pete and looked at him through blurry, tear-ridden eyes; he looked fuzzy round the edges. She blew her nose to stop the drip that was forming. "I know you weren't sticking up for them, it's just that I was sort of relying on them coming up with something."

"She did include the immediate family tree, that's something."

"Yes, but it's not my family tree," Lisa sniffed.

"No, I suppose not, but it's still interesting to see how it fits together."

"I suppose so, I didn't look at it," she got up and went back through to the computer to have a proper look. "It's a shame none of the other members of the family are alive except Julie and her mum - Sylvia, I think her name was. It would have been Sylvia's mum or her grandmother that would have been most likely to know anything."

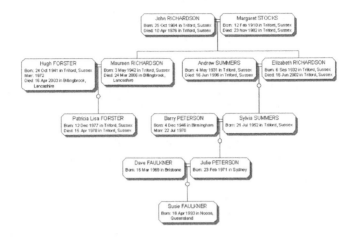

"Have you seen this? Sylvia was eighteen when Julie was born. I wouldn't have been ready to be a mother when I was eighteen. I sometimes wonder if I ever will be. Mum was thirty-five when I..., when Patricia was born. I wonder why Mum didn't see more of her family, I suppose the age difference to her sister meant they didn't have so much in common, but you'd think she would have wanted to see her niece when she was small."

Pete looked over her shoulder. "You're right that none of them lived to be all that old. Perhaps it's a good job you're not related to them. I don't suppose there's very much we can learn by looking at this. Let's get on with our list of jobs."

Lisa liked her lounge. It had the look of lived in chic. Everything was coordinated in shades of brown and beige, but there was none of the clinical minimalism that so often beset the homes of the young free and childless. There were half-read books on the coffee tables, together with magazines in unstraightened piles. Pictures hung in an irregular pattern that defied the precision of a tape measure and an abandoned green sweatshirt was draped at an angle over the back of a chair. Pete picked up the photograph of Lisa's graduation, "Is this your mum and dad?"

"Yes. Oh dear, I still wore glasses then. Don't I look dreadful?"

"No. I don't think you do. Where did you study?"

"I wasn't that adventurous. I went to Lancaster, not a million miles from home. I liked the fact it was easy to come home for weekends, besides Mum did a better job of the washing than I did in the launderette. It's hard to believe it's already been nine years since I graduated. It seems as though a lot's happened in that time. Although in reality apart from working, there's been Mum and Dad dying. Well, there's no good my starting to feel sorry for myself. Where were we?"

Pete picked up the list of people to contact. "So apart from our elusive Spanish retiree, we've got several banks, a lawyer, your mum's pension fund, the Council, Social Services or whatever they're called, the people who issued your national insurance number, the people who paid child benefit, the tax office. What about neighbours?"

"I didn't know Mum's neighbours very well, not the recent ones anyway. They were very sweet when Dad died and when Mum was ill, but I wouldn't say we knew them. I think one side had lived there for about four years and the other side for a little longer. There've been a couple of changes over the years; Mum and Dad were unusual living in the same house for so long. I think they bought it when they first moved here and liked it so much they never wanted to move. It had got a nice little garden for me to play in and it was quite private, they liked that. The neighbours that were there when I was younger moved a long time ago. I used to visit them when I was small. Mum would send me with some apples from one of our trees. I think Mrs Gardiner stayed in Billingbrook, but I'm sure she died a few years ago. Mr and Mrs Jones moved to Stockport when I was still at school. I've no idea where they are now. They had grown up children in the Stockport area. I think they moved to be near them."

"I'm surprised you didn't think of it. I would have thought that by the age of six it occurred to every child, 'I must remember to make a note of where the neighbours move to. They may be the ones who can tell me who I am when I get older.' I'm sure I must have made notes somewhere."

"Pete, are you taking this seriously?"

"Sorry, I just don't know what to say. We keep drawing a blank before we even get started. It isn't as though the name 'Jones' would be easy to trace either. Still, at least it wasn't Smith!"

"I've had enough for one day. I suppose we might need to start finding out about adoption agencies too. I can't quite believe that any of this is happening to me. Can we leave it for now? I'll start trying to get the addresses tomorrow."

"Oh, right, do you want me to go?" Pete got up and picked up his keys from the table.

"No. Oh dear, I didn't mean I wanted you to go, I just wanted to do something different. I feel so confused by all this; I just need some time to digest what we're doing. Let's get a takeaway and watch a film."

A look of relief swept over Pete's face, "I thought perhaps my bad jokes had upset you. Sorry."

"The bad jokes are fine, although I prefer the good ones. It's just that my head's spinning and I keep thinking of questions that just don't make sense. How can I have a National Insurance number if I don't exist? Whose number is it? How did Mum and Dad pass me off for so long as their dead baby? You'd think that someone would notice. Why did they have so few friends?"

Pete gripped Lisa in his arms. "We don't know most of that for certain yet. This could all still be a mix up. We haven't had any proof that you aren't Patricia Forster. You said yourself there could be two of them. Couldn't the records on the internet be wrong? Isn't the first step to ring the Record Office in Triford tomorrow to see if they can confirm whether or not the death you found matches the birth certificate you've got?"

"I suppose so, but what…"

Pete placed a finger on her lips, "No buts. Let's start to deal with some facts instead. I know that's my science background, but it is the way to get through this. Now the first fact is that we need a takeaway menu and a phone number."

The strength of Pete's voice pulled Lisa together. She kissed him, "Thanks," she went to the window ledge by the phone. "Do you fancy pizza?"

"Fine by me. I guess you're going to want a trashy film to go with it?"

"It depends what you call trashy. I need something that'll make me laugh."

"Not *Silence of the Lambs* then?"

"No, Pete, not *Silence of the Lambs*. Have a look on the shelf and see what you can find. They're over there," Lisa pointed to the bookcase.

She dialled the pizza company and ordered an extra-large deep pan meatfeast with a side order of cheesy garlic bread. "That ought to keep us going," she grinned as she came off the phone. "They said it'll be about forty minutes. What film have you found?"

"I can't find anything that won't make you cry. How about an old series of *Friends*?"

"Perfect, although having your humour is bad enough without having your jokes matched by Chandler's." Lisa ducked as Pete hit her with a cushion from the settee. "Hey, mind my cushions!"

"Oh sorry," said Pete, turning serious.

Lisa hit him with a cushion, "I was joking, they're old anyway." She hit him again, the tensions of the weekend giving way to a release of energy.

They landed in a heap on the settee, laughing and giggling. "It's just a thought," said Lisa regaining her composure, "but maybe we could skip the film."

"And the pizza?"

"You could always answer the door in my pink frilly dressing gown."

"That's a funny place to have a door." Pete laughed, as he launched the cushion in Lisa's direction and as she ducked to miss it, caught her in his arms and pulled her towards him.

CHAPTER 9

Triford. Early April 1978

I was quite depressed after Patricia was born. The hospital said that often went with the illness and that I'd soon get over it. It wasn't post-natal depression with me wanting nothing to do with my baby, just a general depression from the illness. 'Snap out of it, you'll be fine.' What did they know? They weren't the ones having to look after a new baby every day without the least idea of what they were doing. It doesn't matter how many pre-natal and post-natal classes you have, nothing prepares you for the real thing.

With being born prematurely, Patricia was very small, but she was soon making progress and on my good days, I enjoyed having her. She was beautiful. On my sleep deprived, depressed days, I couldn't cope with anything. I would sit in tears, with no idea what to do with myself. I had even less idea of what to do with Patricia.

By the end of March, I was beginning to stabilise. Life was getting into a pattern of feeding, sleeping, nappy changing and cuddles. I was starting to feel that this tiny precious bundle was the blue sky of a bright spring day. I loved being with her. I loved holding her. I'd sit with her on my knee, rocking her very gently and singing to her.

Her little outfits were winsome and those tiny shoes, they were so... oh, I can't think of the word, but they were perfect. Knowing they were wrapping up those tiny pink toes was a beautiful thought.

Hugh and I had no time for ourselves once Patricia was born. To be honest, it was a long time before I was back on my feet. I didn't realise how long it took to get over a caesarean until then.

Then last week, Hugh came home and said, "How about we go out for an evening, just the two of us?"

"But who's going to look after Patricia? We can't just go out."

"I do know that. It's all sorted. Your mum says Patricia can stay there overnight, if we'd like her to. Otherwise, she'll look after her here for a couple of hours while we go out."

"Oh, I don't know about a couple of hours, but maybe just for a little while. I'll talk to Mum."

Hugh laughed. "She said you wouldn't want to be out long the first time. How about I book us a table at the *Bernie*?"

"That would be super. I can give the number to Mum in case she needs me."

"Maureen, everything will be fine. You'll see."

We booked to go out the following Saturday. I wasn't at all sure about leaving Patricia, but Mum pointed out she'd brought up two daughters of her own, so she had some idea of what she was doing. I shrugged, but then agreed. It doesn't matter how logical it is, in your heart you believe no one knows how to look after your child right, except you. Mum came round at six, so that there was time for me to settle to the idea before we went out at seven.

I won't say part of me wasn't excited about going out, as things have turned out, that's part of the problem. I was excited. I wish it hadn't been that way.

"Come on, Maureen, you must be ready by now?"

"Just a minute, Hugh. I just want to look in on Patricia one last time before we go."

He poked his head round the door of our room, where Patricia's cot was in the corner. "See she's fine isn't she?"

I nodded hating to admit he was right.

"Your mum's got the monitor plugged in. She'll hear any noise if she wakes up. I promise we won't be out long. If all goes to plan you'll be home before Patricia so much as stirs."

"I know. Just look at her, Hugh. She's so beautiful. Our little girl."

"She gets her looks from her mum. Come on, let's go and enjoy ourselves." Then he kissed me so tenderly and slipped his hand into mine.

"O.K., Mum, I've left the bottle on the side in the kitchen and ..."

"You've already told me all that. Now go along, or you'll miss your reservation."

"Bye, Mum. I've put the number on the ..."

"Go on, Maureen," and she ushered us out through the back door.

It was a beautiful evening, cloudless, which meant there was a bit of a chill in the air, but the stars were almost clear and I smiled, a satisfied smile.

"We've got a table for two in the name of Forster."

"Come this way, Sir, Madam."

The waitress led us to a dimly lit alcove, away from other diners. It felt so romantic to be out just the two of us, although I couldn't stop wondering how Mum was doing with Patricia.

"Do you think I should find a phone and ring to see

how they're doing?"

"Maureen, we've just left. I think you should limit yourself to one phone call per course."

"I can do that. O.K."

I had the breaded mushrooms and Hugh had the garlic ones. We both opted for just a glass of wine. We've never been big drinkers.

"Can I ring now?"

Hugh smiled at me, "Go on then. Tell her, Daddy misses her too."

Mum answered the phone on the first ring.

"Not a murmur. Now stop worrying and enjoy yourself. Yes, I'll look in on her in a while."

I felt more relaxed as we tucked into our steaks. As usual, Hugh had my onion rings and I had his tomato. It was good to feel so in love.

"I'm not sure that I want to stay for dessert. We should be getting back."

"Maureen, it's eight o' clock. We've been gone just over an hour. Why don't you ring your mum again and then see how you feel?"

"O.K."

"Mum, how's it going?"

"Maureen, will you stop worrying."

"Have you been in to check on her?"

"No, but she hasn't made any sound at all. She'll be fine."

"Can you check on her while I'm on the phone?"

"Maureen!"

"Please, Mum?"

"All right. Just wait there."

I was standing in an alcove near the door of the restaurant. There were blasts of cold air every time someone came in, or out of the door. It seemed like forever waiting for Mum to come back to the phone. Then I could hear her in the background. It was faint, but I could make out the words.

"Oh my God! Patricia! Patricia!"

"Mum? Mum!" My heart raced. I didn't know whether to hang up and head home or wait for her to answer. "Mum!"

There was no reply. I hung up and ran through the restaurant to get Hugh.

"Hugh. Hugh. We've got to go now. Quickly!"

"What's wrong?"

"I don't know, just hurry up."

"Maureen, I'm sure everything's fine."

"Hugh! Now! We've got to go!"

He took some money from his wallet, threw it on the table then followed me out to the car park.

"Drive faster."

"What exactly did she say?"

"I sent her to check on Patricia." The tears began to stream down my face. "I could hear her shouting, 'Patricia! Patricia!', in the background. She didn't come back to the phone."

"It may just be something silly. Maybe she'd worked her way out of her nappy."

"No, Hugh," I sniffed. "Mum sounded as though she was panicking."

As we turned the corner into our road, I saw the blue flashing lights of the ambulance before I made out its shape. "Stop the car. Let me out." I ran the last few yards, kicking off my shoes as I went. "Patricia. Patricia."

The ambulance man stopped me. "Are you the child's mother?"

"What's happened?"

"Oh, Maureen." It was Mum, she was shaking and crying.

I took her by the shoulders. "Mum what happened? Will someone tell me what's happening? I want to see my baby."

Hugh had parked the car and caught up now. He was out of breath.

"The ambulance driver says one of us can go in the ambulance with her to the hospital. You go. I'll follow in the car."

"I'll get my bag," said my mother.

"You stay where you are," I said. "I don't want you anywhere near her. In fact, go home. I don't want to see you."

"But she'll be fine. Don't be stupid, Maureen."

"Just keep away."

"Mrs Forster, we need you to calm down if you're coming in the ambulance with Patricia. We're putting her on breathing apparatus and will be doing what we can during the journey."

I turned and saw Patricia for the first time. She was lying there, her skin had a blue pallor. She was motionless. "Patricia. You can't leave me. Be strong. We've come this far. We can do it." There was no time for the medics to comfort me as well as look after Patricia. I wanted someone to hold my hand. I wanted someone to tell me it was going to be all right; that everything was going to be all right. I hated myself for having gone out and left her with Mum. I wanted to turn the clock back. I wanted to have the evening again.

The journey to the hospital took forever. When we got there, they rushed Patricia through Accident and

Emergency direct to the special rooms they have for the serious cases; the ones with all the equipment in them. A nurse took me by the arm and tried to guide me to a waiting room.

"Where are you taking her? I want to be with my baby." I was convulsed by sobbing as I spoke.

"Mrs Forster, we need you to wait in here. Patricia will be in the best hands. She'll get all the treatment she needs."

"I want to be with my baby!" I howled. I could feel others in the waiting room pulling away from me. "I want my baby!"

"I'm here now, Maureen," said Hugh taking my hand. He turned to the nurse. "Is there any news?"

"No, I'm sorry, Mr Forster. It's too soon for any news yet. I'll find out what's happening and come back to you as soon as I can."

"Thank you." He wrapped his arms round me. "Maureen. Oh, Maureen." I felt his tears on my shoulder. We sat and clung to each other.

Time stood still. Despite the bustle of any casualty department on a Saturday night, the drunk and boisterous clientele barely pricked my awareness. I was dazed. They'd taken my Patricia. What were they doing to her?

I have no idea how long we waited before the nurse came back. "Mr Forster, Mrs Forster, can you come this way please?"

"Can I see her? How is she?" We almost tripped over each other in our haste to follow her.

"Where are we….? No! Oh, God, no!" As the nurse led us into a side room I felt my legs give way. Hugh caught my weight as I fell and he hoisted me into a chair.

"Can we see her?" It was Hugh asking, not me.

"My baby." I wailed.

A young doctor in a white coat sat down opposite us.

"No, please no."

"I'm very sorry…,"

"Noooooooooooo!"

***

Triford. 22nd April 1978

"Your sister's on the phone."

"Tell her I'm out."

"Maureen, darling, she knows you're not out. You haven't left the house all week."

"Then tell her the truth. Tell her I never want to see or talk to any of them ever again."

"They want to come to Patricia's funeral on Monday."

"Well, I don't want them there. If it weren't for them there wouldn't be a funeral."

"You know that's not the case. The hospital said it was nobody's fault. It was just one of those things. It happens."

"Will you stop being so damned reasonable?"

"It's how I deal with it. If we both gave up, if we both blamed the world, if we both stopped eating, then what?" He went back out of the bedroom and closed the door.

I reached the cushion from the bed and held it to me. I longed for it to be Patricia. I longed to hold her and rock her. I longed to smell her hair. Instead, all I had to remind me were breasts that hurt from the pain of the milk that wouldn't dry up for weeks, a nursery that we'd finished decorating ready for her cot to move into in a month or two – and those shoes.

My eyes were sore from crying as I sobbed into the cushion. It felt as though they had cut a Patricia sized hole out of my inside and left me empty. I was dead inside.

Everything I wanted was gone. How could my child be a 'cot death'? I hadn't done anything wrong. Why me? There were times when I thought there must be a mistake and that I would look over at her crib and see her asleep, her tiny pink fingers wrapped around the trunk of her cuddly elephant. Instead, all there was tucked up in the crib was the elephant, his trunk sticking out over the blanket. I went over and picked it up. I held it to me, desperate for it to have the warmth of life, desperate for it to breathe. Then I threw it across the room, knocking our wedding photo off the dressing table. The photograph clattered to the floor, where it lay in a heap with the elephant.

Hugh came into the bedroom to see what the noise was. He picked the photo up and sat down on the corner of the bed. "Why us, Maureen? Why us?"

I sat next to him.

"How can the world carry on as though nothing has happened? Why can't anyone understand that our world will never be normal again? What are we going to do?" Then we clung to each other as we had so many times that week and we cried.

"Was it something we did wrong, Hugh? Aren't I fit to be a mother?"

"Don't talk like that, Maureen." He held me by the shoulders and looked me full in the face. "Don't talk like that. It was nothing you did. It was nothing we did."

"Perhaps there's something wrong with me. I mean medically, that I passed on. Perhaps it is my fault; they just didn't find the cause."

"Maureen, listen to me. It was not your fault."

"I just want to hold her. I want to feed her. I want to change her nappy. I even miss changing her nappy. I want to see her smile. I want to feel her soft warm skin close to mine. I want to dress her in all the little outfits in the cupboard. Hugh, she needed me and I wasn't there. I was out enjoying myself." Then I broke down again. "I don't know whether I believed in God before, but if there is a God, right now I hate him. How could He do this to me? How could He take away my child? How can He be so cruel?"

CHAPTER 10

Billingbrook. Monday 17th September

Lisa was already half-awake when the chirpy radio voice told her it was 'Seven o'clock and time for the news read by…' She turned it off before hearing who it was, as she did every morning. It was pointless having it tuned to a news channel, given that she wasn't ready to hear the worst the world had to offer at this hour.

She was coming to, in the slow 'animal out of hibernation' way that she did every morning, taking those first few minutes to remember what day it was and what getting up involved. She always started with a few stretches to loosen up her arms and legs before… As her foot touched Pete's she came too with the sudden realisation that she was not alone. She felt a thrill and awkwardness wrapped into one as Pete rolled over and propped himself up on his elbow, facing her, his upper body exposed above the duvet.

"Morning," he said, running his finger down her nose and following the contours of her face. "Sleep well? I slept like a log, in fact if it hadn't been for the radio I could have slept all morning."

She moved herself over towards him and nestled into his arm. It was surprising how comfortable she felt. "Morning. It's been a long time since I haven't woken up on my own."

"Yes," said Pete, confirming her thoughts without saying too much. "It's a shame we've got to get up for work. I need to get a move on. I'll need to go home to get some clean clothes first. I'll get a lecture from Toffee about staying out all night, though I do deserve it. I say the same to her when she comes strolling through the cat flap at eight o'clock, without so much as a word as to where she's been all night. Will I see you later?"

Lisa curled round him, all awkwardness gone, she nodded. "That would be nice. Shall I come to your house after work?"

"I'll cook dinner," said Pete, kissing her as he moved away and got out of bed. Lisa hugged the quilt as she sat up watching Pete get dressed. She smiled, enjoying the sight of his naked body stretching and straightening as he pulled on his clothes.

"What time do you have to go?" He asked.

She came out of her coddled warmth into the reality of the day. "Oh no, I'm supposed to be in early today. We've got a staff meeting at eight thirty. I'd better hurry. I'll see you later."

She shot out of bed gave Pete a quick peck and disappeared into the shower. She heard the door slam shut downstairs as she started shampooing her hair and despite her lateness found herself starting to sing. "I'm a pink toothbrush, you're a blue toothbrush, have we met somewhere before…"

Her voice trailed off as she remembered singing along to the record as a child. It reminded her that today wasn't just about Pete. It was about starting the search for information to clear up the mystery surrounding her birth certificate. Her mind turned to where she would start. It had to be the call to the Record Office first, the one in

Triford. They must be able to tell her whether there was another person of the same name or whether the two records tied together.

Dressed in plain trousers, shirt and long cardigan, she went down to the kitchen. A pot of coffee was already brewed and next to it stood a little note, which read 'See you later, Love Pete'. She slipped the note into her pocket to remind herself in her moments of doubt that this was real, then she poured a coffee. Despite the weight of the day's thoughts, she couldn't help smiling.

It was eight twenty-seven as Lisa rushed up the fan of semi-circular steps to the building.

The library had been an important part of her life right from being a small child. The building had seemed imposing in those days. It was an old stone building along from the town's museum. The double-wooden front doors, with their heavy iron hinges had always made it feel an important place. It was this as much as the books that had made her want to work here. The doors opened into a hallway with stone steps leading away in curves on either side, meeting again on the open landing. It might all look impressive, but Lisa was out of breath by the time she ran up the stairs and to the right. Here there were a suite of offices along the front corridor of the building. She made it into the staff room with just enough time to take a coffee from the machine before everyone settled down for the meeting.

"This won't take long." Derek had been the Head Librarian at Billingbrook for what seemed like forever. Lisa could remember him being there when she used to visit the library with school, although she had no idea what his role was then. "Joan has been taken into hospital and will be off for at least the next six weeks. It's going to be tight covering everything, but at least we're out of the main holiday season, so we will have a full complement of staff."

She whispered to Trudy who was next to her, "Do you know what's wrong with her?"

"The usual."

"Oh, not another. What is it with this place?" Hysterectomies were the curse of middle aged women. "Anyone would think it was catching!"

Derek looked over at her, "Was there something you wanted to say Miss Forster?" She shrivelled under his glare. After all these years he was still so formal in how he addressed them, even though he always stressed that they should call him by his Christian name. Lisa wondered whether it was just that he had difficulty getting close to women. There was no Mrs Derek that she knew about. Despite his efforts to the contrary he did rather make her feel like a school child. She had to concede that the library ran like the mechanism of a Swiss clock under his leadership, but he had never been the easiest man to work for. She had no idea if the men felt the same.

Lisa wondered about how to ask for some time off after this little 'pep talk'. If everyone was being asked to pull together to cover, did it look as though she was being disloyal asking for time off so soon? She didn't feel ready to share the reasons with any of her colleagues at the library. This was work and that was her private life and as far as possible the two would not be allowed to overlap. Whilst Lisa had been busy with her own thoughts, Derek had finished talking to everyone and her colleagues were starting to drift off to their positions for the day. She checked the chart on the wall of the staff room and confirmed she was on 'lending', then made her way towards the stairs, dropping the holiday request form, which she had completed before the meeting, into Derek's pigeon hole as she passed. She didn't fancy asking in person today.

"Lisa," she turned to see Trudy catching up. "Are you all right? You don't seem quite yourself."

"I'm fine, thanks." Her tone didn't match the words, but she spoke with a finality that would have left even the most thick-skinned person knowing not to pry further. "I need to have lunch at twelve today, can we swap?"

"Yes, sure, are you going out somewhere?" It was an obvious question but Lisa wasn't prepared for it.

"No, I ... No there's just something I need to do. Thanks, Trudy." Lisa marched down the stairs before there was time for further questions.

She couldn't help thinking that the building and Derek were a reflection of each other. His formality in dealing with them, contrasting with the informality of how he wanted to be addressed, whilst for the building the splendour was brought back to earth by the laminated card signs; with arrows pointing 'up' for the reference library and through the doors to either side of the back of the hall for the lending library. In the middle of the hall stood a beautiful large circular oak table with leaflets advertising local attractions and events, many of which were now memories. People were as different as buildings. She wondered what made a person the way they were and how the different types of people left their own stamps on the world. Some people left beautiful marks in stone and carved wood, but others left tatty laminated cards. She wondered which she was and whether even now she might have a choice in the matter.

The library was quiet first thing, just the stalwarts

coming in to read the magazines and newspapers in the reference library and the committed researchers with their notebooks and pencils at the reading tables and the computers. Lisa set about clearing away the pile of waiting book returns to their proper shelves and moving errant books to their rightful place within the Dewey decimal system. The shelving was as old-fashioned as the rest of the library, light oak, solid without being either attractive or cumbersome, fanning out in a semi-circular pattern away from the counter. For efficiency of reach, though not of the usage of space, the book cases were no more than four shelves high, their wood marred by the plastic numbers placed on top of each of them. Lisa knew every nuance of this library, but it was today that she appreciated the contrasts.

She stood thinking about all the things that had appealed to her as a child and the things that she had not considered back then. The ceiling was high, with tall windows letting in light, but designed to obscure the view. The whole building spoke of faded philanthropy, functional, effective but in need of investment and modernisation. Even a lick of paint wouldn't improve the austerity of the metal-cased windows, the fluorescent lights, with their plastic covers or the pragmatic and 'cost effective' carpet tiles with their occasional gaps and regular wear. The smell of musty books in their pungent plastic straightjackets hung in the air. The smell lingered on her clothes by the end of the day. It was something you had to get used to if you wanted to work in a library. None of that had mattered to the child she had been. How could she so easily shift her perspective on a building, but find it so difficult to comprehend a change in perspective of her life? She'd been happy hadn't she? None of that had changed. It was just the way she was viewing it that had altered.

As Lisa placed the last of the returns back on the shelves, she looked across at the large clock with its clear black numbers above the desk. She smiled at the way it matched the uncluttered efficiency of the library. There were minutes before the first school party would mar the order. She didn't mind. It was great to see children developing a love of books. It was how she started, with her scrappy ticket allowing her to borrow no more than three books at a time. How times had changed. Now you could borrow up to twenty items at once. She went over to the counter, at least it wasn't her turn to read the stories this morning, but she would need to be available to help with all the queries the young readers may have. They weren't so different to the queries she and her friends had when they were young.

"Excuse me, Miss, I want to be a fireman when I'm older. Have you got any books on fire engines?"

"My dog's going to have puppies. Mummy said you might have a book that would help me to understand all about it."

"Have you got a book about insects and spiders? I want to frighten my sister with it."

"Where can I find the *Harry Potter* books?"

Even some of the books they read were the same as the ones she read, although this seemed less true of the older children. How had things become so much less innocent? Had there been an equivalent of Jacqueline Wilson in her days? Lisa tried to remember the books she read as a teenager, but could get no further than remembering studying *Great Expectations* for her exams.

"Miss Forster." Lisa didn't stir. Derek shouted, "Miss

Forster."

She gave a start and straightened herself up. "I'm sorry, I was miles away. I was thinking about when I used to come in from school years ago."

"Well, I'm sure that's very nice for you, but I wanted to talk to you about your holiday request. Were you not listening to what I said this morning?"

Lisa's heart sank. "Yes, yes I was listening. It's just, well…" She didn't want to have to explain why taking the time off was so important to her. This was private. "I could manage with less than a week. When I filled the form in I didn't know about Joan, maybe if I could have just a couple of days and it doesn't have to be this week. Would next week be better?"

Derek smiled. "Thank you, Miss Forster, I'm glad you weren't totally ignoring what I was saying. I think we could stretch to three days, perhaps Wednesday to Friday?"

Lisa nodded. "Yes, thank you. That would be fine."

She was saved from any further conversation by the sight of thirty children aged around seven or eight filing through the 'In' door. There was the usual 'sssh chorus' as they all made more noise reminding each other to be quiet. At least this age group didn't come with the challenge of unsilenced mobile phones.

It wasn't long before the hum of voices and giggles spread out through the library and it became a place of excited discovery rather than sombre reflection. She rather enjoyed the school times. She knew inside out the books held by the library and could almost always put her hand on a book that would appease even the most outrageous request.

Eventually, the children were trooping out, clutching

their newly stamped borrowings and the library returned to the grip of its more seasoned visitors. There were a few comfortable chairs stationed at the end of rows of shelving, where the public sat in their untidy piles, clutching coats, books, bags and writing materials for want of anywhere to put them. Lisa smiled as she viewed the odd bunch of people filling the spaces around the library, the long-scarved students and the long-haired artists, the shopping-trolleyed elderly and the bespectacled readers. They were a medley of the bookish and the bookworms in their flat shoes and practical rainwear, with not a scrap of fashion sense between them. Lisa thought how much more at home she had always felt with books than people. Her current problems showed just what happened when people got involved. Books never let you down. You might not like the ending, but you could always rewrite it in your head. The hero always saved the day, the heroine was always successful and if you wanted them to, everyone could live happily ever after. Why didn't real life work like that?

An elderly gentleman came over to her. "I'm sorry, but I can't find computer number seven. I've booked it for the next two hours, but I don't know where it is."

Lisa looked at her watch. "I'm going that way myself. I'll show you."

She walked across the library and round the corner by the DVDs to a line of computers tucked out of sight from the books. Perhaps they were here to prevent them causing any offence to their paper rivals, the modern age tucked away from the sensitivities of the books. She pointed to the little numbers on their laminated cards, directing him to the seat for number seven, then sat herself at computer number four. She had meant to look up the number for the Triford Record Office at home, but the day had taken an unexpected turn. She smiled thinking of Pete. She'd tried to put him out of her mind during the morning, but it had been impossible. It would be good to see him at the end of the day. She jotted the telephone number down on her pad and made her way back across the library. If the staff room was empty she would make her call from there, otherwise she would have no choice but to go outside. At least with mobile phones, she didn't have the problem of asking for permission to make a private call.

As Lisa passed through the hall to go up to the staff room, she noticed that it was raining outside. Perhaps she could still make the call even if there were others in the staff room. She was relieved when she opened the door to find the room deserted.

She stood over by the window, her paper ledged on the windowsill and dialled the number. Her heart beat faster as she waited to hear a voice. It was answered on the third ring.

"Triford Record Office."

"Oh, hello, I wonder if you can help me. I don't know who I need to speak to. My name is Lisa Forster, but I was christened Patricia. I'm trying to find out whether there could be two people of that name who were registered with you at around the same time."

"It's not the Records Office you need, I'm afraid. You need to ring the Registrar's Office. Just hold the line and I'll find the number for you."

Lisa felt deflated as she scribbled the number on the pad. "Thank you." she said and hung up.

"Problems?" said Celia who had come into the staff room whilst Lisa was on the phone.

"No, everything's fine."

"Oh, don't mind me, carry on, I was just picking my sandwiches up from the fridge."

As Celia left the staff room, Lisa dialled the Registrar's Office. She ran through the same explanation for a second time, but they needed a written request in order to respond.

"Yes, thanks," said Lisa. "But can't you give me any more than that? You see, I've just found out that I may not be the person I thought I was. I need to be sure whether there was more than one Patricia Forster born in Triford."

The voice at the other end carried the tone of professional concern and warmth. Perhaps dealing with bereaved relatives registering a death wasn't so very different to a bereaved woman mourning the loss of her identity. "I'm very sorry that I can't help you further. I'm afraid the Birth and Death Registration Act of 1953 doesn't permit me to give out such information, whatever the circumstances. If you would like to come in to our offices, then I'm sure we will do everything we can to help. You will need to bring in sufficient information to identify the record. This can either be the reference of the registration you're looking for, or it can be the name of the person and of their parents, we can then reprint a copy of the appropriate certificates for you."

"Are the death records linked to the original birth records?"

"No, I'm sorry. What age was the person when they died?"

"Four months."

"Well, for a child the death certificate will give the names of the parents if that helps you."

Lisa brightened, "Yes I guess that would be what I

need."

Lisa noted everything down on her piece of paper and rang off. She checked her watch, just time for one more call. She dialled Pete's number.

"Hello, this is Pete Laundon, I'm sorry I'm not available to take your call, please leave your message after the tone."

She left him a quick message about the holiday she had booked and hung up. Then she hurried back downstairs and out of the front doors in search of a sandwich.

Afternoons were often busier than the mornings and Trudy came to join her on the lending counter. Lisa was quiet. She was thinking about the phone call.

"Lisa, what is wrong with you today?"

"There's nothing wrong," she snapped at Trudy.

"You're stamping the books to be returned by 6th October 2009. That's two years away."

"Oh, Trudy look what I've done," Lisa gasped. "Instead of moving the day wheel on the stamp forward by two days from Saturday to Monday, I've moved the year wheel two years forward. It must have been like that all day. "Please don't tell Derek."

"Don't you think you'd better tell me what's going on? I did rather think we were friends."

"But I always keep my private life and my work separate."

"Hey, Lisa, I've got news for you, you're a woman, you can't do that. None of us can. Men might be able to leave all the personal stuff outside, although I don't believe that either, but I do know that women can't. Is it a man?"

Lisa's mind raced. Which was worse, to tell Trudy about Pete, or to tell her about the birth certificate? She chose the birth certificate as she couldn't bear women using their love lives as an excuse for behaving out of character. Even then she thought she could get away with telling Trudy part of the story. "I've started to trace my family tree and it turns out things weren't quite as I thought."

"Weren't your parents married? You know that's O.K. now, don't you?" said Trudy, laughing.

"Oh, they were married, they just weren't my parents."

It was Trudy's turn to gasp. "You mean you were adopted?"

"I suppose so. I haven't got that far yet."

"How did you find out?"

"Because the birth certificate I have seems to be for a dead person. Now can you see why I might have stamped the books with the wrong date?"

"Oh, Lisa, I am so sorry. Can I help at all? Is there anything you need someone to do?"

"I don't know yet. I only found out at the weekend. Thanks for the offer. I'll think about it. Please would you do me a favour? Don't tell any of the others. I can't bear being the centre of gossip."

"My lips are sealed. Do you want to go for a meal this evening and talk about it?"

"No, thank you. I've, er, well, I think I want some time on my own." Perhaps she should have told Trudy about Pete. Well, maybe she would tomorrow.

CHAPTER 11

Billingbrook. Monday evening 17th September

Lisa parked round the corner from Garden Street. There was still a chance that Ryan and his brother were miss-kicking their football into the sides of unsuspecting cars. She had finished work an hour earlier, but decided to go back to her own house first, to pick up a change of clothes and her wash bag, just in case. There hadn't been time to think of things like that this morning, or for that matter agree a time with Pete. He'd said 'after work' and he knew this wasn't her week to be on the late shift, but this didn't stop the butterflies trying to break out of the chrysalis of her stomach. She couldn't decide whether to leave her bag in the boot and collect it later or take it in with her. She wondered whether taking it in would look too presumptuous. On balance they knew each other too well and there were more important things to be thinking about than being precious over a sports bag. She lifted it over from the back seat, got out and locked the car. She opened the passenger door and picked up the mobile phone she'd left on the seat, slipped it into the pocket of her jeans and relocked the car.

Walking up to Pete's house, she had no idea whether to go to the front door and ring the bell or use the back. Before she had time to worry further, the front door opened and Pete, who she realised must have been watching for her, came out. He took her bag without a word and carried it into the lounge.

"I've cooked *duck a l'orange* for dinner. You do eat duck, don't you?"

"Do you mean was I a fan of Jemima Puddleduck as a child and has it scarred me for life?" They both laughed and Lisa felt an easy comfort re-established between them. "Yes, I like duck, thanks. It smells good."

"It'll be ready in twenty minutes. I thought cooking for about seven should be safe."

"Sorry, I should have let you know what time I'd be here. Did you get my message about the holiday?"

"Yes, I picked it up at lunch. I've booked the same days off." He moved through to the kitchen. "Do you want a drink? I've already opened a bottle of wine, it's on the table."

She poured some into a glass and went over to the settee where Toffee was sitting, using her front paws to balance, with her back leg in the air, washing the back of her knee. She repositioned herself as Lisa sat down and went back to the business of washing.

If Lisa had children now what would she tell them about their grandparents? It seemed wrong to say that Hugh and Maureen were their grandparents, but it would be even harder to tell them the truth, that she didn't know. Would it matter to them whether their grandparents were dead or just unknown? She doubted it. Children had a way of dealing with things, but to her, at the moment, it was everything.

She got up and moved to stand in the doorway to the kitchen, leaning against the doorframe and swirling the amber wine in the glass.

"I've been thinking about the circumstances that might

lead me to offer a child for adoption. It isn't easy to do when you aren't in that situation. I'd love to have children of my own. I can't imagine ever choosing to give them away. It must be heartbreaking if you feel like that about a child, but have no choice. I wonder how many teenage girls are faced with that situation. Having their parents think it's best for them, while all the time wanting to keep their baby." She went quiet. She wandered through to the lounge and ran her finger along a bookshelf one book at a time, looking at the titles of the books, until she came to an A-Z map of Billingbrook. She stretched out her index finger and pulled the book towards her.

She came back to the kitchen doorway. "I guess there are children who are adopted because their parents die and there's no family around to take care of them, but what makes someone decide they don't want their child?"

Pete opened the oven to check on the duck and then looked at the timer on the front of the steamer. "Four minutes," he said as much to himself as anything, then turned to look at her. "I don't know. I really don't know. I suppose there are people who feel they aren't ready to be parents. There are those who just can't cope, financially or mentally." Pete hesitated. "I'm not sure whether to say this, I don't want you to start assuming anything bad of your birth parents, but there are some children who are taken away for their own safety, ones who are abused."

She started to fidget with the map. "I know. You hear all these stories about people remembering violence and sexual abuse from their childhood and much as I've tried to remember back to infancy, there's nothing bad there at all. I think for me now, the worst thing is not knowing. Not knowing why, not knowing who they are, not even knowing when or how it happened. I wonder if you grow up knowing you're adopted you find yourself so desperate for answers to all those questions or whether it's because it's all come on me suddenly."

Pete started putting the food on the plates. "Can you bring my glass of wine through, please?"

She followed him through to the lounge carrying the wine glasses. "I keep coming back to the same question. Would you have been the same person if you'd had different parents?"

He put the plates down on the mats. "That's a good point. I've been thinking about that too. I don't know the answer. I don't think it's quite as simple as that."

"Simple!" Lisa laughed. "None of this is simple. But what do you think?"

"Oh, dear, I'm not sure I can put this into words. Let me think for a minute." Pete started tucking into a roast potato coated in some orange sauce. "Well," he took a deep breath. "I think some of who I am is genetic. I do think I get some of my mannerisms direct from my parents. My sense of humour is a carbon copy of my Dad's, or should that be scan in this day and age? That's not to say it isn't because we were exposed to the same things, but it seems to run deeper than that." He chewed some duck before continuing. "But my character and how I behave has been influenced by so many things. I suppose where I grew up and the school I went to made a difference, but so did the friends I had and the situations I found myself in. Even as an adult there are things that have happened to me that have changed the way I look at life. That's got nothing to do with who my parents were. I suppose how much money we had when I was growing up might have made a difference. It changed the things we did and what pressures there were. There are a hundred and one factors to take into account."

"Yes."

"Is that all you're going to say? Just, yes."

"No."

Pete took a mouthful of wine. "Have I said the wrong thing?"

"No. You're saying some of the things that have been going through my mind. I'm torn between wondering who I would have been if things were different and reminding myself that it's as much about the choices I've made as it is about my parents. I didn't have to become a librarian. It wasn't something my parents wanted, it was my choice. I didn't have to study at Lancaster. Oh, I don't know. You can trace your choices back across the years. It makes you wonder what influences the choices right at the start." She opened the map on the table and pointed to a road near the middle of Billingbrook. "I went to a playgroup there. How times change! I suppose it would be called a nursery now. It was a couple of mornings a week. I think the building was part of a church. It was built from red brick, it's still there. We were in a big room that took up the whole of the upstairs. I hated it. Mum never knew that, not at the time anyway. It was when she told me that I didn't have to go there anymore that I said anything. But why did I hate it?"

While she carried on eating Pete looked at the page of the map. "There's a police station along there isn't there?"

"Next door."

"Well, that could have been handy if you misbehaved. They could have threatened you with the cells."

"Pete, I was three!"

"Some people start young!"

She wasn't in the mood for jokes. He seemed to realise

and stopped grinning.

"This is where I went to infant school," she pointed to a small road in another part of Billingbrook. "I remember there were two buildings at either end of the playground. Then there were the toilets between the two. Why are school toilets so disgusting? I don't know if it's the smell the kids leave behind or the bleach that's used to cover it up." She wrinkled her nose as she remembered. "I always loved it when we had story time. I used to sit with my hands folded across my knees in rapt attention." She smiled at the recollection. Changing tack she said, "Why did I sit by Fiona in primary school? I'd never met her before but something made me think she looked nice. What is it that attracts you to some people and not others?"

"I don't think I should be the one to answer that for you in case it breaks the spell." Pete said, "I would hate you to realise what I was like."

Lisa wasn't listening. She was lost in a world of childhood. "What made me want a bright yellow teddy bear? No one went into the shop and said 'Look, Lisa, why don't you have the yellow one?' I just saw it in the window and wanted it. I wanted it for weeks and weeks before I was bought it for my birthday." She went quiet and started to tuck into the duck, the sauce had congealed as it had cooled, but despite her soul searching, she was hungry. "I was a fussy eater as a child. Now I'll eat most things. Do we get our taste from our parents?"

As she chewed the meat, Pete put his hand over hers. "I think we inherit our taste buds, but then children have the chance to try more foods than their parents. This isn't going to be easy. I suspect we're going to learn a great deal about each other and about ourselves over the next few days. I'm willing to listen or talk whichever you need."

She ate in the quiet of her own thoughts, studying the map. Despite the time it had had to cool, the tang of the orange offset the duck and there was little left by the end of the meal.

"There was some waste ground," she said pointing to the map. "Fiona and I had a den there when we were a bit older. It was near where she lived." She turned the page to the end of Billingbrook where Pete had grown up. "I didn't come to this end of town very often."

"Wrong side of the tracks." Pete laughed.

"The other thing I've been thinking about is what makes someone adopt a child? O.K. so I now know that their child died, but is that enough to make you adopt? Wouldn't you try for another of your own first?"

"But if they knew they couldn't have any more." Pete looked anxious. After a pause he said, "Perhaps they'd always wanted to adopt in addition to their own children - some people do. Given the number of children in children's homes, it's a good job they do. I was reading the other day, there are thousands of children brought up in care homes. Where are they? I can't remember any in our school that were in care. Do they have separate schools? You sometimes hear their life stories as having achieved great success despite their start in life, but where is that start? ... Sorry I think I've gone a bit off topic."

"I can't ask Mum and Dad all the questions I want answered. It's too late. Was I just to fill a gap, or were they these incredibly good people with so much to give? Perhaps it was both. I wish they'd told me."

"Which would you like them to be?"

"I didn't expect you to say that, but you're right. I

don't know if I can cope with thinking about them being that good. If they were, why did they leave me with all these questions?" She looked back at the map. "I don't suppose you fancy going for a walk do you?"

"Where do you mean? Do we need the car?"

"No," she hesitated. "I don't want this to sound corny, but I'd like to walk round Billingbrook to all the places that have been important through my life. It feels a bit like reconstructing a crime scene, but on a bigger scale."

"O.K., I can do that. Am I playing a leading part or am I just an extra? A passer-by on the street of life."

"Pete!"

"O.K., O.K., I can be serious. Where shall we start?"

"Well, I'd like to do it in chronological order, but that isn't going to be possible unless we walk all the way to the other side of town to start."

"Come on, let's start with the car. Shall I get mine from the garage?"

"No, mine's in the next street. Besides, I think I'd like to be in control of this journey, if you don't mind."

"Always willing for the girl to be in control." He reached across and kissed her.

"In which case it should be me reaching across to kiss you."

"Oh, yes, good point. I just couldn't resist. Shall I sit down and we'll try that bit again?"

CHAPTER 12

Billingbrook. Monday night 17th September

"This is where Fiona lived." They stood outside a small modern end of terrace. "The waste ground was round the back, just past the driveway for the garages. "I need to find out where she lives now. It's been a while since I saw her." They'd walked from her house out of the estate and along towards the railway. "It's amazing that we grew up in the same town but never met before," she said as they walked away from Fiona's old house.

"That's the funny thing though. We don't know our paths never crossed. We just know we're not conscious of having met. I suppose we didn't go to the same doctor's surgery, or the same youth club, or even the same school, but we don't know we didn't push past each other on the way out of Woolworths or NatWest," said Pete. "I've pushed past an awful lot of people over the years."

"I suppose not. I suppose we mixed in different circles at different times."

"I guess with us both being loners, it made meeting unlikely. We might have met in the library. I used to borrow books on electronics. You could have a look in the records to see if our books were stamped on the same day."

"The records don't go back that far," she said. "And if they did, it might have been a different time of day or my mum getting something for me."

"My mum didn't know about electronics. I had to get my own. I suppose we'll never know whether we met or not."

Lisa stopped outside a small modern church. "I joined the Girl Guides here. I didn't stay long. It wasn't my thing. A bit too sociable, I suppose. I'd rather read a book about camping than go and put a tent up. I did play on the swings at the park though." She pointed to the rusty green railings further along the road. "There was a bowling green on the park. I used to watch the old people playing and wonder if that would be me one day. Mum and Dad never used to do anything like that. I suppose they never had time to grow old and do the things old people do." She turned to Pete and nestled into his shoulder. Her eyes were damp with tears. "I wish they were here now, so that I could ask them about all this. I'm sure it must be a simple misunderstanding, at least that's what I'm hoping is going to be the case."

Pete wrapped his arms round her and held her. "Somehow, we'll find out."

"I think I've had enough for now. Let's go home."

They walked back past the row of shops selling everything from hardware to tattoos, bread to bicycles. "I worked in that cake shop when I was fourteen," she pointed to a mid-terrace property with the bay window replaced by a shop front. "Until they decided they didn't need me. They could have told me before I bought the blasted apron they insisted on. It was a dreadful nylon thing. I hated it. You'd think they'd provide the basic uniform. Dad went and told them what he thought of them. They said they'd taken on too many of us. I suppose they expected some not to turn up, either that or they hadn't the courage to say I was no good! It was a good thing for Dad to do, but at the time I was so embarrassed. You don't always understand about sticking up for yourself against the 'big people' when you're younger. It just feels like unnecessary confrontation. Whether they were my birth parents or not, I could never doubt that they loved me and would have done anything for me. We were so close, it doesn't make sense that they didn't feel they could tell me."

"We've still not made much progress with finding the addresses and phone numbers of people we have to contact. It's going to be too late tonight." Pete looked at his watch, "I can always get a cab home rather than you drive me."

"Or..." Lisa's voice trailed off.

"Or what?"

"Oh, dear, this sounds a bit brazen. It's just that I brought my bag of stuff to your house tonight. I could drive you back and stay over."

Pete's face lit up, "I'd like that." He stopped walking and kissed her. They were standing outside the bicycle shop, Lisa felt lost in the moment. It took her back to memories of her first boyfriend. She stopped. "Steve Henson! I'd forgotten him."

"What? Where?"

"No, sorry. I was just remembering my childhood. Oh dear, I'm sorry, the timing of that was all wrong. Can we do that bit again?" She smiled at Pete and then before he had time to argue she kissed him, another long lingering kiss that said everything that was needed.

***

Billingbrook. Tuesday 18th September 2007

"Trudy!" Lisa called, out of breath as she rushed

towards the library steps, not wanting to miss the chance to catch her friend.

"Good morning, you look pleased with yourself. Have you found out about the adoption?" Trudy waited for her to catch up.

"What? Oh, no!" Lisa was so focused on how she felt about Pete that for a moment she'd almost forgotten there was anything else going on in her life. "It's just that there's something else that I've got to tell you about. I told you half the story yesterday." They were walking up to the staff room to get a coffee before making a start on the day. "I've got a man."

"What?" Trudy almost shouted.

"Shhh!" Replied Lisa.

"Ooops, it's just that you've not been out with anyone for ages. I was starting to think you weren't interested in men. Sorry, I'm joking, I know what a tough time you've had over the last few years. Oh come on, who is he?"

"Are you free at lunchtime? If we can both get the same time I'll tell you everything then."

"Spoilsport. You can't just give me a snippet and then not tell me any more until later."

"Watch me," said Lisa laughing again as she moved towards the staff room door to head into the library. "I'll see you in the foyer at twelve-thirty," and with that she went through the door with the grin re-established on her face. In her pocket she had a piece of paper listing the organisations for which she needed addresses. Sometimes in the morning when the library was quiet, Derek didn't mind them spending time doing 'appropriate research'. Many of the staff wrote in their spare time and were always looking into one subject or another for an article or a book. There was no need for Lisa to explain why she needed access to electoral rolls and out-of-area phone directories. Most of it was on computer these days, but she still preferred the feel of paper.

In the odd quiet moments of the morning, Lisa was able to find the details for most of the official bodies that she needed to contact. She was still struggling to trace the previous neighbour and her mother's friend who had moved to Spain. At lunchtime, she was ready and waiting for Trudy.

"Sorry, I'm late," said Trudy, "I seem to have had my share of hopeless cases this morning. Now I want to forget all about them for a while and hear the whole story."

"Pizza Hut?" said Lisa as they headed through the front door.

"That'll do just fine. Now who is he? You can tell me about the whole adoption thing afterwards."

"Well, you know how there are those times that you can't see for looking? When what you want is right there and you just hadn't noticed it before." Lisa took a deep breath. "Well, it's Pete."

Trudy stopped in her tracks and the people behind her on the pavement walked straight into her. "Sorry," she said turning round to them as they grumbled obscenities at her. She carried on walking, "Pete, as in 'cemetery Pete'?"

"I might have met him at the cemetery, but please don't call him 'cemetery Pete'!" Lisa frowned. "It makes him sound so, so... well so dead!"

"It's my day to upset everyone! Sorry," said Trudy holding her hands up in a mock gesture. "When did it happen?"

By now they had entered Pizza Hut and were waiting to be noticed and shown to some seats. As the waitress directed them to a table in the window and was about to fetch menus for them, they said in unison "Pizza buffet and a Coke please." The girl went off to fetch them their drinks and they made their way straight over to the buffet.

"To cut a long story short, Pete bet that he could find out more of his family tree in a week than I could. Then I found out that my birth certificate belonged to a dead baby and then I fell in love with him."

"Wow, steady on there with the 'dead baby' stuff, it makes it feel so clinical."

"Sorry. I guess I've got so wrapped up in the trauma I've almost forgotten there must be another human story underneath it all."

"Now can I have the long version? Excuse me" Trudy was addressing one of the waitresses. "Is there any more pizza coming out? There's not much here." She groaned as the waitress told her it would be five minutes and headed back to their table.

For the next forty minutes Lisa told Trudy all her news, then she told her about trying to trace both her parents' old neighbours and her Mum's friend.

"Do you mean the Miss Farmer who taught English at school?" asked Trudy.

"Yes, she was friendly with Mum, but retired ages ago."

"Yes, I know," said Trudy, "I know you and I didn't know each other then, but I've got a feeling that my Mum knew Miss Farmer through the Billingbrook Historical Association. I don't think she kept in touch with her, but I'm sure she must know people who have. Hang on." Trudy pulled her mobile phone out of her bag and rang her Mum's number.

"Hi, Mum, it's me. Yes I'm fine … Yes, Mum sorry this is a quick call, I'll ring you later for a chat. I'm with Lisa from work. She needs to get in touch with Miss Farmer who used to teach English at school and I wondered if you knew anyone who's in touch with her? … Yes… Ok, I'll tell her. Thanks, Mum. I'll ring you tonight."

"Oh, Trudy, you're wonderful." Lisa reached across and hugged her friend. "It's just our old neighbours still to find, the almost anonymous Mr and Mrs Jones of Stockport."

Trudy laughed, picked up the bill and made her way towards the cash desk. "This one's on me. I think you need it."

"Thanks, Trudy. I'll pay next time."

As they walked back to the library, Lisa longed to ring Pete and tell him everything she'd found out so far. She looked at her watch, another five hours until she would see him.

It was half-way through the afternoon and Lisa was standing by the lending counter when the phone rang on an internal call. She picked up the receiver, "Hello, Lending, Lisa Forster."

"Lisa, it's me Trudy. I've just had a thought. You could always put an ad in the Stockport paper asking for the Jones's who moved from Billingbrook to get in touch with you."

"What a great idea! Why didn't I think of an advert? No, don't answer that. Thanks, Trudy. I'll try to sort something out. See you later."

"So what's the name of the Stockport paper?" Lisa said aloud as she put the phone down.

"Stockport Express," said the man at the counter.

"Pardon," said Lisa, coming out of her reverie.

"You asked what the name of the Stockport newspaper is. It's the Stockport Express, it's my home town."

Lisa looked at him, "Thank you. Thank you very much."

"It's part of Manchester Evening Newspapers, if it helps."

"Thanks. It does." She stamped the book he had placed on the counter and was left with that awkward feeling you have when saying goodbye to someone you don't know, but feel you need to say something more. "See you again soon." She curled up with embarrassment inside as she realised how trite she'd sounded.

She wouldn't see him again and yet that was the sort of thing you said to people, meaningless comments to cover for difficult situations, pleasantries you don't mean, smiles you don't feel. In fact there were lots of behaviours she had been taught and never questioned. If she wasn't Lisa Forster, if she wasn't Hugh and Maureen's daughter, perhaps it was time to start thinking about whether she believed in all the things they had passed down to her. She came back to the present as a lady was coughing to attract her attention.

"Excuse me, dear, if it isn't too much trouble, please could I renew this one?" The lady pushed the book over the counter.

"Sorry. Yes, of course." She stamped the book and entered the updated details on the computer. She concentrated on the lady and for the first time meant what she said when she smiled and said "Thank you for using Billingbrook Library. Have a pleasant day."

Tesco wasn't busy when she got there after work. On the way in the car, she had decided to go for the simple option and cook spaghetti carbonara. It wouldn't take long to put together and they could spend their time writing letters to all the companies and official bodies that she'd found the addresses for. She wondered if there'd still be time to ring the Stockport Express, but thought maybe that could wait for now. Her phone rang as she got to the checkout.

"It's me, Trudy. Mum has managed to get the phone number for Dorothy Farmer in Spain."

Lisa gasped.

"Do you have a pen?"

"I'm at the checkout in Tesco's, I don't have... hang on, Excuse me," she interrupted Trudy to speak to the checkout girl at the neighbouring till, who was just gazing into space whilst she waited for her customer to get her purse out. "Can I borrow your pen please?"

Lisa grabbed an old receipt that had been left behind by a previous customer "O.K. Trudy, I'm ready."

She wrote the number down as Trudy read it out and then had to finish the call as her shopping moved off down the conveyor leaving her behind. "I'll let you know how I get on. Thank your mum for me. Bye." She felt excited. At last she felt she had a real lead.

As she drove up to her house, she saw Pete's Mini parked outside. In her haste to get out to see him, she made a complete mess of parking the car, almost hitting the gatepost as she pulled in.

"Hi, have you been waiting long?" She kissed him as he got out of the car.

"No, I've been here about five minutes. Is the car all right there?"

"Yes, it's fine, they don't play football on this stretch of road, thankfully."

Lisa filled Pete in on the information she'd found and

ended by telling him about Trudy finding the phone number.

"How about I start drafting some letters while you get tea?"

"Great idea. When do you think we should ring Spain? They're an hour ahead."

"When do you want to do it?"

"First, I think. I can't stop thinking 'what if she knows the whole story?'."

"O.K., but do you know what you're going to say?"

"No. I think I'm just going to see what happens."

"Right. Do you want me to go out of the way?"

"No, you're fine there." Lisa took the scrappy receipt out of her pocket and dialled the number. She heard the longer, deeper, international ring tone and her breath caught as it was answered. She took a deep breath to say hello when she realised it was an answer machine. Breathing out she mouthed 'answerphone' to Pete and frantically thought about what message to leave. "Hello, this is Lisa Forster, Maureen Forster's daughter in England. You used to work with my mother at Billingbrook College. I'm not sure if you knew that my mum died last year, but if it's possible I'd like to talk to you. I'll try again later or you could call me on..." she gave both her house and mobile numbers and then replaced the handset. "Well, that's a start, not a very good one but a start none-the-less. I don't know what to do with myself now. I'll get on with tea." She was disappointed. She wasn't sure what she'd expected, but it hadn't occurred to her that she wouldn't get to speak to Dorothy in person.

Pete came over and hugged her. "We'll get there in the end."

It was harder drafting the letters than she expected. "O.K. I'm on the one for the National Insurance number," said Pete. "What we want to know is what checks they do on the information they're provided with, in order to issue a number, but I suppose I need to give them the background story first. Even then it's a long shot. They'll have rules about that sort of thing."

"I thought something like a straightforward explanation that I am trying to trace my birth parents and wondered what information they hold on file. It sounds a bit odd to start to explain the birth certificate thing. I don't want them to think it's a hoax."

"Good point. Although I don't think even I could have thought of this situation as a prank just to wind people up." Pete started scribbling down some notes.

"I think we'd be better to make appointments with the banks. We could go next week. Perhaps we can just write to say we would like to talk to them about my parents who used to bank with them before they died. Some of the details will still be on file from when I dealt with Mum's estate last year."

"Right." Pete was writing again.

"How do you know what you believe in? I mean what you Pete Laundon believe in, rather than what you've grown up taking for granted," Lisa asked, while they were eating.

Pete thought for a moment, "Well, for example my parents believed in Santa Claus, so I've grown up knowing with absolute certainty that Santa Claus is real and his elves of course... No, seriously, it's real in the sense that I believe in the spirit of Christmas, and regardless of what I think about the birth of Jesus, I know that every human being has the same value."

"It's hard. It's all part of the same question of 'who am I?' It feels as though I have to rethink everything. Test it out to see if it's real."

"Hmm. I know what you mean. I went on a course once where we had to think about what our core values are. You know, a bit like a stick of rock, if they cut you through the middle what words would they find written round the inside."

"And what words did you find?"

"Bognor," he said with a straight face. "Sorry. No, I don't think I should say until you've had chance to think about what yours would be. I don't want to colour your thinking. I'd never stopped to think about mine before. I just accepted so much of what was around me without questioning it. It was just after Dad died; it helped me to see what was important for me. I'd lived in his shadow so much up until then. It helped me to get some perspective."

"That's what I need." She sat up straight feeling an intensity of concentration. That was it. She needed to know her core values. She had to decide what Lisa Forster believed in. "It isn't easy is it?"

"No," Pete smiled. "Why don't I go onto the internet to find out what we need to do to order birth and death certificates while you're thinking?"

"Thanks, yes please." She sat twiddling a pencil in her fingers as she thought. It felt strange to realise she had reached the grand old age of thirty and never asked herself before what she believed. There were the big questions that everyone paid some heed to at some point in their lives, such as whether they believed in God and which party to vote for in the elections, but had she ever thought about what any of them meant to her? She hadn't.

Maybe whether she believed in God wasn't the place to start right now, that one was too big a starting point. She did think that equality was important, at least equality of opportunity. Justice, that was another thing or perhaps it came back to the same point - equality of opportunity before the law. Her thinking was going in circles when Pete's voice broke in.

"I've found the site that we can order certificates from, do you want me to go ahead or do you want to do it?"

"Sorry? What? I was miles away. I've got as far as equality of opportunity."

Pete smiled, she was tempted to ask if he came up with something similar, but she wanted more thinking time first.

"I asked if you'd like me to order the certificates."

"Yes, please." She got up and went through to the dining room where Pete had been working on the computer. "I don't suppose we've heard any more from Australia have we?"

"I haven't looked. I didn't think I should open your email."

"Are you worried I might have some dark secrets?"

"No," he said grinning, "but I do think privacy is important."

She laughed. "That wasn't one of your core values by any chance was it?"

He nodded agreement.

"Do you think they're doing anything to help in Australia? It's easy to say you'll do something but so many people don't do the things they've said they will."

"You've hit another of my beliefs."

"What? Do what you say or be honest about what you will do."

"No, always think the best of people. Of course, it means that every so often they let you down, but you have to start by having faith in people. Or at least you do in my book."

"Oh, dear, perhaps I'm too intolerant. Maybe I've got to work out what matters in life. O.K. perhaps I'll say instead that I hope they are having some success in what they're doing in Australia."

Pete kissed her. "You know, I think I'm falling in love with you. I didn't think I'd hear myself say that to someone again."

"Again? That sounds very pointed." She looked at the pain that spread across his face. "I'm sorry I shouldn't have said that. I should have said something like how glad I am that you are." She leant towards him and kissed him. She continued to wonder what he meant but said instead, "I think I'm falling in love with you too." She snuggled up to Pete's chest and sighed. She was still there when the phone rang.

"Do you think that'll be Miss Farmer?"

"Answer it, that's the way you'll find out."

She picked up the receiver; she could feel her hand trembling. "Hello."

CHAPTER 13

Noosa. Monday Afternoon 17th September

"Mum," Julie called across the road as she hurried in the direction of the bus. Sylvia was just collecting her suitcase from the pavement and starting to wheel it in the direction of the shelter. She turned as she heard Julie shouting for the second time. Sylvia was still young for her fifty-five years and with her slim, elegant build and neat dyed brown hair could have passed as Julie's sister.

"Hello, darling, I was all set to find a coffee while I waited for you. Your timekeeping's improving then." Sylvia hugged her daughter.

Julie laughed. "I've passed it on to Susie. We can't both be hopeless at punctuality, nothing would ever happen. How was the journey?"

"As bad as ever," said Sylvia in a resigned tone. "Flying has become one of those necessary evils. I remember the days when it was an adventure, something to look forward to. Now it's only worth looking forward to if you like being frisked by strangers and questioned as though you're a criminal. But I'm here now."

Julie took the handle of the suitcase and wheeled it towards the SUV. "I managed to borrow a step ladder from my neighbour just before I came out, but I haven't had chance to go into the loft yet. To be honest, I was rather hoping he'd offer to help, but the reason I needed it didn't come up and I didn't like to ask."

"Oh, for heaven's sake, Julie. What are you expecting to find up there? A dead body."

"I just don't… well. I know it's stupid it's just I've not been up there before. I can't help but wonder if there might be something I didn't know about."

"You've been watching too many horror films."

"You're probably right." Julie smiled. "Susie is going through all the usual teenage angst. She thinks I know absolutely nothing. I was never that bad, was I?"

"Oh, I think you can assume that whatever Susie is dishing out is just desserts for the teenager I brought up. It's part of being a teenager. At fifteen, you think you know everything. At eighteen, you know you know everything and at twenty one, you begin to realise that you have a whole world ahead of you and you know nothing."

"Were you as bad as that, Mum?"

"I got married the day after my eighteenth birthday already pregnant with you. What do you think?" They both laughed.

"Do you suppose Lisa is the result of someone's teenage fling? You don't think it was one of Maureen's students do you? One of the teenagers at the school she taught at. She was a teacher wasn't she?"

"Yes I think she was. It's a thought. Do you think we should mention it?"

"I don't know. Susie's gone round to a friend's house. She'll be back in time for dinner later. I thought we could all go out for something to eat. There's a new restaurant on the seafront I thought we could try."

"Sounds good. I could do with a shower first. When are you thinking of looking in the loft?"

"I'll have to do it as soon as we get in. I'm working tomorrow, sorry. You can have the car if you drop me off and pick me up."

"No worries. I don't suppose I'll want to go anywhere that I can't walk."

Julie pulled into the drive and stopped at the side of the house. "I hope we find something. I owe it to Lisa."

"I know," her mother said. "I've been looking for an excuse for a trip to England for a long time. I went back last time because Mum died. I'd like to go and have a good look round. I don't know what good it can do, but we're just so far away here. I've been thinking what it would be like if it were me, and I can't even begin to imagine how confusing it must feel."

They unloaded the case and went into the house. "I'll put the kettle on," said Julie. "Unless you fancy something stronger?"

"No, you don't," Sylvia put her hand on Julie's arm. "I'll do the drinks you need to look in the loft."

Julie sighed, "I know." She brought the step ladder in from the veranda and positioned it under the hatch. "Here goes." She picked up the torch that she had already placed on the side and climbed the steps. She lifted the hatch gingerly. "Why can't we live somewhere that doesn't have deadly spiders? If I meet a funnelweb peering back at me, I'm out of here." She shone the torch through the hatch and flashed it around the inside. She let out the breath she had been holding. "It doesn't look too bad up here. It smells a bit musty, but apart from the dust you could almost hold a party up here. It would be a bit on the cosy side, but who's complaining? At least there are boards down and... Hey there's a light. I didn't know we'd got a light up here." She flicked the switch and a bare light bulb illuminated the whole area. Julie looked around her. "Now I can see a bit better, scratch the party there wouldn't be room. There's a pile of old suitcases from the days before cases had rollers." The cases were battered and beaten from their travels. "Why on earth are we keeping these? We'll never use that type of suitcase again."

"They might be collector's items," Sylvia shouted up to her.

"I doubt it." She went over and shot back the locks of the top case. They creaked open. "I don't think I'll be needing this one anytime soon. It's got Dave's old school reports in it. Here you go. 'Could do better if he put some effort in.' You can say that one again."

"Just remember what you've gone up there for. You can sort everything else out another day."

"Sorry, Mum, I got side-tracked." She looked past a pile of empty boxes that came with many of the household items. The items had since been thrown out and replaced by new ones. The boxes for the new ones had also been kept and now filled the shelves of the garage. "Hey, I've just found Bruno." She picked up a large clear plastic bag containing a faded brown teddy bear. "There's no way he can breathe in this thing."

"Julie, he's a stuffed toy."

"Don't say that about Bruno. Do you remember when I took him to the airport with me when we flew to Perth and you told me they might have to cut him open to check he wasn't hiding anything?"

"Well, he might have been full of drugs if we'd been travelling between countries."

"You never added that bit. I was worried the whole journey."

Julie went back to her search, she moved a box and behind it, sitting on top of some pasting tables she could see the old green and cream case of the reel to reel tape recorder. "I've found it. I just need to… Can you pass me a duster, please? They're under the kitchen sink." Julie went to the other side of the hatch to where the tape recorder was sitting. Next to it were three large brown envelopes containing the reels. "Jackpot," she said to herself.

"Pardon?" Her mum was at the bottom of the steps holding the duster.

"The tapes are all here too. I didn't think finding them was going to be that easy." Julie took the duster and cleaned the lid of the tape recorder. "Can I pass them down to you?"

"I'm ready." Sylvia said.

First of all Julie passed the brown envelopes. Then she lowered the tape player down.

"I'd forgotten how heavy this old thing is," said her mother taking the weight and lowering it down. "To think you can get ones now that fit in your pocket that can hold more than this. I'm surprised that the tapes look in such good shape after all this time. Your loft must be ideal storage conditions."

Julie appeared at the hatch. "Can you hold the ladder for me to climb down?"

"Don't forget the light." Sylvia called up as Julie put her foot out of the hatch. She pulled the foot back again and went across to the light switch. She turned the torch on and went back to the step ladder and climbed down. "Now then about that drink. I need it to strip the dust from my throat. It makes you wonder where it all comes from."

Her mother handed her a mug.

***

Noosa. Tuesday 18th September

"That's got Susie off to school. How are you doing, Mum?" Julie joined Sylvia at the table where the reel to reel player was sitting idly. Its cover was leaning against the leg of the table.

"It's so long since I've done this." Sylvia was threading the end of a tape through the sets of rollers and onto the empty reel the other side. "Can you remember which button does what?"

"I think we need to plug it in and try a few," said Julie picking up the plug and looking round for a spare socket. "Hang on, I'll find an extension lead."

"I've no idea what dates these tapes were last used, or even if they were last recorded in England or here."

Julie plugged the machine in, "Well, we seem to have an 'on' light, so that's a start. Which button shall we try?"

"Not this one," said Sylvia pointing to one that was larger than the others and coloured red. "I'm almost certain that's the record button and whilst I've not plugged the microphone in, it will still wipe the tape."

"If it works."

"Oh ye of little faith. Of course it'll work," said Sylvia. "We built things to last in the old days, not like the modern throw away rubbish. I think it was this button." Sylvia pressed the one on the end which turned out to be rewind. The tape slid effortlessly back onto the main reel with its end flapping as it continued to go round.

"Well, that moved the reels," Julie burst out laughing.

"All right, if you think you can do any better. I'll just

rethread the tape through and we'll try again. Just remember that that one is the rewind button."

"I'll get a sticky note to label it," Julie said, trying to keep a straight face.

On the second attempt, the tape player started to move in the right direction, but the muffled sound made the words being said impossible to hear.

"Which was the volume switch?" Sylvia looked around the outside of the case and found a wheel marked 'volume'.

She turned it one way and the noise disappeared and then the other and a slow strung out voice could be heard "Heeelllooo, juusssst teeessstttiiinnnggg"

"Mum, I think it's on the wrong speed."

"Oh thank goodness for that. I was trying to think who on earth spoke like that." This time they both laughed. Sylvia pressed the off button whilst she looked for the switch to adjust the speed of the tape.

She started it again and this time the voice was clear. "It's Dad," said Sylvia. "I haven't heard his voice in..." her voice faltered. "Do you have some tissues, darling?"

Julie went to her bedroom and came back with a box of tissues. "This is going to be hard." She put her arm around her mum.

"Yes it is, but nice too. I've missed hearing those voices all these years. You still think you can hear how they sounded in your head but to hear the real voice again is very special. Who'd have thought we had something so precious and just forgot it was there. I don't suppose Susie has even heard her great grandfather's voice as far as she'll remember. She was three when he died."

"She still remembers her great gran though."

"Yes, she'd have been nine by the time Mum died.

Shall we listen to them?"

"We know this one is before '96 as Granddad started it, but then I suppose we knew it must be, as we weren't using this machine by then. It must be quite a bit earlier."

"Oh yes, this goes right back to when I first moved out here. It wasn't long before communications were modernised and we were able to telephone."

They sat side by side listening to the tape, Sylvia holding Julie's hand as they did so and dabbing her eyes with the tissue that was scrunched up in her other hand. For the next half hour they shared tears and laughter as they listened to everything from Granddad singing to Grandma updating the family news and saying how much she missed her daughter. "Did you hear that? It's 1977. Mum just said 'your sixth birthday', that was February '77."

"We're close then, but that was before Patricia or Lisa were born."

"Well, this is after your birthday. It must be too early for Maureen to have known she was pregnant. Hang on, what are the dates we're looking for again?" Sylvia stopped the tape and got some paper.

"I was enjoying listening to that so much I'd almost forgotten why we're doing it." Julie found a pen.

"Right," said Sylvia. "Your birthday was February '77." She drew a time line on the piece of paper. "Patricia was born in December that year, so Maureen must have been expecting her since about the March. She'd have known in the April."

"We need the time closer to when Patricia died, which was the following spring, 1978."

"I'm not sure, but it sounds as though this was recorded at least a few weeks after your birthday. They'd just received your thank you note. I suspect I may have written as much of it as you did, but they always loved to get a note from you. Let's listen to the end of the tape."

There were no further clues to place the timing. When they finished they rewound the tape and put it back in its holder. "Can you face another one?" Julie asked. "The tapes are numbered, well lettered anyway. That one was 'B'. We've still got 'A', 'C' and 'D'."

"We used them in rotation so we knew their order. When we got to 'D' we went back to 'A'. It means that the other three could all be later than this one or 'A' might not have been reused and could be before this. There were a few months between each tape. We often did them around birthdays. Let's listen to 'C'."

The second tape turned out to have been sent from Australia to England around Sylvia's birthday that year. They listened to Julie's first attempts at playing the recorder and laughed as she sang 'Baa baa black sheep.'

"That was fun, but it didn't tell us much. I think we should play it to Susie later."

"What, and have her laugh at my singing?" They both laughed.

***

Noosa. Tuesday Evening 18ᵗʰ September

It was already 7.30pm by the time Julie came in. Susie was sitting cross legged on the floor talking to her grandmother.

"Hello, I'm home. It looks like you two are having fun."

"Baa baa black sheep, have you any wool?" sang Susie mimicking the voice of a small child.

"Hmm. Your gran's been playing you the tape then." Julie put her bag on the table and walked towards the kitchen.

"Dinner's all ready, darling," said Sylvia getting up from her chair. "I found some odds and ends in the fridge."

"You can stay more often," said Julie getting the bottle of wine. "Susie, you could learn quite a lot from your gran. Do you want a glass of wine, Mum?"

"Yes, please." Sylvia brought the plates out to the table and they sat down to eat.

"I don't suppose you've found out anything new have you?" Julie asked as she put butter on a slice of bread.

"No. I went through the diaries I'd found. I noted the more immediate stuff. I was never one to put the deeper thoughts down on paper, I think I was always worried that you'd read them. Although back then you would have coloured them in." They all laughed.

"I hate to say it, Susie, but when I was young I wasn't so very different from you. They say girls get more like their mothers as they get older. Maybe they're always alike if you compare them at the same ages."

"That is so not cool," said Susie. "Don't even begin to suggest I'm going to be like you. Besides you aren't much like Gran. For a start Gran's nice to me."

"O.K. fair point. I don't suppose you listened to the other tapes did you?"

"No. We've been waiting for you. Well, I've been waiting for you. I think Susie was asking if it was all right if she did her homework."

"Yeah right! Can I go over to Steph's house, Mum? There's a project we're working on together."

"No, love, not tonight."

"But, Mum. Tell her, Gran."

"I'm not getting involved. Count me out." Sylvia

picked up her glass and moved her chair back to allow the other two to argue between themselves.

"But nothing, Susie. I'm already part way through a glass of wine. I'm not driving to pick you up later. You'll have to do it another night."

"Can Steph come here and stay over?"

"Why does she need to stay? It's not fair with your Gran here too."

"Her Mum won't come and pick her up later either. Oh, please."

"What do you think, Mum?"

Sylvia smiled. "This is where I can be the fairy godmother or the wicked witch." She flashed a benevolent smile at her granddaughter. "How about if Steph stays tonight then you cook dinner for all three of us tomorrow? I'll help you."

Susie threw her arms around her Gran's neck. "Thanks, Gran, you're a treasure. Can I go and ring her now?"

"Go on," said Julie. "You're going soft in your old age, Mum." They both laughed.

They cleared the plates away and put the tape recorder back on the table. "It's 'D' next isn't it?" said Julie.

Her mum passed the tape marked 'D' across and Julie put it onto the machine. "How did you thread it through? It's years since I've done this." Sylvia helped to thread the tape through to the other reel and then started the machine.

"It's Mum," said Sylvia grinning when she heard the first voice on the tape. "It's a tape done in England. That's a start. What was the next big event in the year after July?" The tape continued rolling in the background as they listened for clues. "That's it. Mum's just said thank you for the birthday present. Her birthday was September so it would be sometime after that, October time. That makes it just before Patricia was born."

Towards the end of the tape, the voice said "and now for the adult news."

Sylvia stopped the tape. "That was always the point that we turned off until there was time to listen without you children present. If there is anything, it'll be in this section." She pressed start again.

"Aunty Maureen's baby is due on the 15th of January, so she's got another six weeks to go…" They both gasped. "…She's been having problems. She's in hospital now, so she's in the best of hands."

Sylvia stopped the tape again. "Well, that's one piece of information."

"Let's hear the rest of the tape, in case there's any more."

Sylvia restarted it and they listened intently to the end of the reel. No more was said about the baby.

"Well, we know for certain that tape 'D' was the beginning of December. That means that 'A' was either an earlier one or would have been the next key event, maybe Christmas or maybe a bit after that." Sylvia pressed the rewind button. "I don't suppose it's going to be after Patricia had died but it might tell us something." She put the tape back into its case and passed it to Julie who in turn passed her tape 'A'. "Here goes," she said threading the tape through and pressing the play button.

Sylvia and Julie both sat and held their breath, anticipating something to give them a clue whether this was the tape that could answer everything. There was crackling and the sound of furniture being moved. The volume came through much louder than the other tapes with background piano music and then Julie's voice boomed out. "This is a practical demonstration of the development of technology presented for my final college assessment on…"

Sylvia stopped the tape. "You recorded over it," she almost whispered. "This was the one that might have had the answers and you recorded over it."

"But…" stammered Julie, "I could never have known. I…. You knew I was going to use it. Oh, Mum, I'm so sorry. I'm so very, very, sorry. What am I going to tell Lisa?"

"The truth," said her mother then they fell into a stony silence.

CHAPTER 14

Billingbrook. Tuesday night 18th September

"Hello, yes it's Lisa Forster here." She nodded to Pete and mouthed. "It's her."

"Thank you, yes it was very sad losing Mum so young."

"It has been three years since Dad died, yes."

"No, I'm fine. It must be…"

"As long as that." She scribbled a note on the pad to Pete. 'She sounds lonely. I could be here all night.'

Pete scribbled back. 'Shall I go and leave you to it?'

She was horrified and wrote, 'Don't you dare!'

'I was just joking,' came Pete's swift response.

"Oh, I'm sorry to hear that. That can't be easy."

'I don't know how to ask her.' Lisa scribbled as she continued to make sympathetic noises into the phone.

'Just do it – as they say,' Pete wrote back.

Lisa took a deep breath. "Yes, no, I understand… The thing is Mrs Farmer … Dorothy, I wondered if you could help me? I've been researching my family tree and wondered whether Mum had ever talked about her family and when we all moved to Billingbrook?"

Lisa scribbled on the pad. 'Mum started working at the college – early 80s. Started part-time.'

"Anything at all." Lisa rolled her eyes.

"So, they already had me when they moved here."

As Dorothy continued to speak, Lisa wrote 'Triford Maternity Unit. Never really knew Dad.'

"Yes, I know about Mum's sister's family." Lisa hesitated, trying to find the right phrasing for her next question. "Did Mum ever talk about adoption?" She wrote the word 'NO' in big letters on the pad and drew a big circle.

***

Billingbrook. Thursday evening 20th September

"How soon do you think we'll get replies?" Lisa dropped her keys onto the table in the lounge and wrapped her arms around Pete. "Do you think we should go back to my place to see if there's anything there?"

Pete led her to the settee and sat her down next to him. He stroked her hair as he said. "It's too soon. I understand how desperate you are to know what's happening, but we posted the letters yesterday. We ordered the death certificate the day before, but the site said it would take seven days for them to send anything."

"I can't take much more." The tears welled in her eyes. "I don't think I'm strong enough to deal with this."

"Lisa, you are strong enough," he took her hand in his. "We can do this together, one step at a time. We've put the advert in the Stockport paper to appear on Saturday. We're going to Triford next Tuesday after work. We're doing everything we can."

She nestled her head into Pete's shoulder and began to cry with heaving sobs that overcame her whole body. Pete rocked her backwards and forwards. "Shhh shhh. Everything's going to be fine. You'll see. We'll get to the bottom of it all." He held her to him. "I promise I'll take care of you."

Little by little the warmth that flowed from Pete made

her relax. "Can we go back to my house tonight?" she said through gulping sobs.

"Of course, we can."

"I just want to check if anything's arrived there, just in case."

"Do you want me to drive?"

"I'm O.K. It would be better if we take both cars, then we can go straight to work in the morning."

"Don't you want your friends to know about me?" He pulled back a little way and grinned, but she could see the genuine concern that lay beneath it.

"No, silly. I've already told Trudy about you anyway. I just meant it would be easier as we go at different times. I don't mind the whole world knowing about you and I mean that."

She looked into his eyes and smiled. He wiped away a stray tear with his finger and then kissed her. He kissed her nose, then he kissed each cheek and then held her face as he kissed her lips. "I love you, Lisa Forster."

"And I love you, Pete Laundon... Right then," she said in a more business-like manner. "Shall we go?"

She drove back thinking about how things seemed to have settled into a comfortable pattern with Pete. For a moment she found herself thinking that maybe he was prince charming, bringing the slipper that would be her perfect fit. Then she laughed out loud admonishing herself for being no better than a teenager and reminding herself that 'the one true love' should be reserved for fiction and this was real life, where you had to be glad if you met anyone's true love, let alone the one meant for you. She looked in the rear view mirror and saw Pete driving behind. A little shiver ran through her.

She unlocked the house and picked the post up from

the mat before going through.

"Anything interesting?" Pete asked coming up behind her.

"A bank statement and the electricity bill, nothing else. I know, you've already pointed out it's too soon. It was just that…"

He put his finger to her lips, "I know, you just hoped."

She nodded. "Now we're here do you want a drink?" She went through to the kitchen and looked round for a bottle of wine. "I thought I'd got a bottle of white somewhere, but I can only find red."

"That's fine."

She poured two glasses and passed one to Pete.

"Let's try to look at this positively. Why don't we work out what we're hoping to achieve next week and book some accommodation?"

"I wondered whether we have any family down there we could stay with."

"Aren't they all in Australia?"

"Australia," gasped Lisa. "We haven't checked for email." She almost ran as she went through to the other room, her wine sloshing over the top of her glass and onto the floor.

Pete fetched some damp kitchen roll to clear the wine up before following her. "It's stained." He shouted to her rubbing at the wine on the carpet.

"Salt," she shouted back.

"What do you mean 'salt'?"

"Rub salt into it and it'll come out. I'll do it in a minute while the computer warms up."

Pete went back to the kitchen in search of salt. Lisa came through to join him, but was so much on edge that she couldn't even remember what they were looking for.

"Salt," said Pete as she turned her third circle.

"Oh yes." She opened the cupboard by the cooker and took out the salt, thrust it in Pete's direction and hurried back to the computer.

Lisa was still pacing up and down mumbling "come on, come on" under her breath when Pete joined her.

"It's all right now," he said.

"What is?"

"A record by Free. No, the wine."

"Right," she said, not listening.

Once the computer was ready she opened her email. She moved the cursor around the screen with the impatience of a child wanting seconds at tea, as the mail downloaded. When the email from Julie Faulkner dropped into her mail box she pounced on it. "It's here."

"Lisa," said Pete in a measured tone. "It's headed 'I'm Sorry'. Don't get your hopes up."

Lisa read Julie's abject apology for using a tape for her college project. "How could she? She's so stupid." Her fiery temper was getting the better of her.

"She didn't know it was going to be important."

"Oh that's it, you stick up for her. She's wiped the chance I had to find out who I am."

"Lisa, calm down. You don't know it was the right tape anyway. You can't blame Julie. She hasn't done anything wrong."

"Wrong, wrong, of course she's done something wrong. She was the one who told me I was adopted."

"You can't blame Julie for any of this. She's trying to help. It isn't her fault you don't know who you are."

"Oh you're a good one to talk, Pete Laundon. What do you know about any of it? You don't know what it is to lose your identity. You've probably never been hurt before."

Pete flinched but said nothing.

"Why don't you just go home? I want to be on my own. Just go away." Lisa sank into a heap on the floor sobbing. Pete gave her a minute and then sat next to her, wrapping her in his arms but remaining silent.

After a few minutes a little voice, through the blubbering said "'m sor…ry. I lub you Pete."

"And I love you, Drippy Nose."

She looked up at him and laughed. "I didn't mean the things I said. It's just…"

"I know."

He held her for another few minutes and then said "Why don't we try to make a plan for next week."

She nodded then wiped her eyes and nose on a tissue from her pocket. "I just hoped they'd find something out. I can't believe that Julie recorded over the tape."

"We are going to find out the truth. I don't know how, but we are." Pete got up from the floor and went back into the lounge in search of a pen. He was still looking when Lisa came through carrying a pen and some plain paper from the office. "They were in there."

"I suppose that's obvious." Pete sat on the settee and rested the paper on a copy of 'Red'. "Do you learn anything from this stuff?" he asked, pointing at the magazine cover.

"No, but I keep hoping."

He laughed. "I'm not missing anything then. Right, next week." He jotted some notes on the paper.

***

Billingbrook. Saturday 22nd September

The post fell on the mat with a thud. It was already eleven and Lisa was just contemplating the day when she heard it. She shot out of bed and grabbed her dressing gown from the hanger on the side of the wardrobe.

"What's the rush?" said Pete, rubbing his eyes. He rolled over and sat up, but Lisa was already through the door and on her way down the stairs. She came back two minutes later clutching a batch of letters.

"Phone bill," she said throwing the first one onto the duvet. "Junk mail," she threw the next one onto the pile. "Junk mail addressed to Miss L Forrester," another one landed on the pile. Then she held up an envelope marked 'Froggatt Boothby and Jarvis'.

"It's from the solicitors."

"I wonder which one's written to us, Mr Froggatt, Mr Boothby or Mr Jarvis?"

"It might be a Mrs or a Ms."

"Fair point. Are you going to open it or do I have to go on guessing?"

She threw the envelope to Pete. "You do it."

He slit the envelope with a pencil from the side and pulled out the letter. "Dear Miss Forster, I am sorry to hear about the loss of your parents," Pete paused. "They did know, didn't they? They dealt with the wills."

"Just read it will you. They're being polite. Oh, give it here." She took the letter and read out. "I would be delighted to see you in our offices at a time of your convenience. Please telephone my secretary, Jennifer Thomas to arrange a time."

"That's great."

"Oh, hang on. Then it says 'We understand copies of all relevant papers were passed to you at the time of your mother's death, however we will be more than happy to check our records.' That's it. I presume they must have the originals."

"More importantly was it signed by Mr Boothby or Mrs?"

"Pete!"

"Ok, I'll be serious. It might be good, it might not. It depends if they find anything. We could go in on Wednesday."

"Yes. For reference it's signed by Marcia Goddard."

"Maybe she doubles as Mrs Boothby, or Mr for that matter."

Lisa was already opening the next envelope. "It's from the Child Benefit Agency." She read the letter to herself. "Grrr."

"What's it say?"

"It's bloody ridiculous. Before they tell me whether I am who I think I am, I've got to prove my identity to them. How can I give them my birth certificate when I don't know who I am? It isn't as though we didn't explain in the letter." She threw the letter down on the bed. "What do I do? Do I produce the birth certificate for Patricia and then say, but I'm not that person?"

Pete picked up the letter, "Due to the requirements of the Data Protection Act... I don't suppose they ever imagined this sort of situation when they wrote the Data Protection Act. It isn't shaped to cover this type of event. I think we should ring on Monday and try to explain. There's no point ringing today."

"Will you do it, Pete? I'll just get cross."

"Well, I will but it's even less likely that they'll talk to me. Perhaps we'd be better to go in person. We can take the birth certificate and anything else you've got, with us."

"That's our lot, unless you want a credit card with MBNA in the name of the previous occupant of the house.

You'd think by now they wouldn't still be on mailing lists." She sat on the edge of the bed. "So what do you fancy doing today?"

Pete turned the corner of the duvet back. "You could get back in."

She leant across and pecked him on the forehead. "I could, but to be honest I'm not in the mood. I feel as though I should be doing something."

"Other than feeding Toffee, I've got nothing planned. We could drive over to Stockport to buy a copy of the paper, but then we won't be in when the phone rings."

"If it rings. I wonder where the nearest newsagent is for the Stockport paper?"

***

Billingbrook. Sunday 23rd September

Saturday had been a bit of a disappointment. They had driven to the outskirts of Stockport in the afternoon and bought the *Stockport Express*. Lisa opened it before even getting back into the car and found the announcements page. "Mr and Mrs Jones formerly neighbours of Hugh and Maureen Forster in Billingbrook. Please get in touch with Lisa on Billingbrook 314672." It was set in a black box with enough white space surrounding the advert to make it easy to see.

"What do you think?" she asked Pete.

"I'll buy it. Oh sorry wrong type of ad. Yes it looks fine. I just hope that they see it. Is there anything particular about them that you can remember?"

"Nothing. They were just nice, ordinary people."

"Well, that sets them apart from quite a few. Did they have any pets?"

She shook her head and sighed. "I can't remember. Let's go home." She climbed into the driver's seat of her

Fiesta. "I need to book this in for a service."

"We could take it to the Anglican Church tomorrow."

"Pete!"

"Sorry. It's not playing up is it? We can take mine to Triford next week. I'd like to do that for you."

"No, it's just its annual check-up. I'm happy to drive next week, besides isn't yours a bit past long journeys?"

"There's nothing wrong with my Mini."

Lisa realised she'd touched a raw nerve. What was it with men? Why did they insist on taking over when it came to things like driving? She was just as capable and liked driving. Besides, Pete's car was ancient. She took a deep breath before saying, "No, there's nothing wrong with your car. I wasn't saying there was. I was just saying that I'm quite happy to drive and there's nothing wrong with my car either."

"Please," said Pete. "I insist."

She hadn't got the strength for the whole equality debate right now. If things were ever going to work between them, Pete was going to have to understand sooner or later that there was a difference between taking care of someone and taking over. She was anxious as to whether Pete's car was reliable, but knew if she asked he would take it as a personal slight. "Ok, you can drive to Triford."

Pete beamed as though he had just been given a new toy. "Great. I'll work out which will be the best route so that you don't have to worry about map reading."

She bit her lip and sighed. 'Men!' she thought to herself. 'Bloody men!'

There had been no phone call on Saturday and Lisa felt that placing the advert had been a waste of time. Now it was Sunday and she had no idea what to do with herself.

"I just feel frustrated that we can't get on with any of the finding out. Why is everywhere closed on a Sunday?"

"They don't call it the 'day of rest' for nothing. I blame God personally. He set a precedent by resting on the seventh day and everyone else followed suit."

"I don't even know if I believe in God. It was never something we talked about."

Pete sat up in bed. "Well it's the right day if you want to find out. I'm sure we could find a church service that hasn't started yet, although you may want to miss out mentioning that we aren't married, but spent the night together."

She picked up a pillow and hit Pete with it. "Will you for once take something seriously?"

"Sorry. I seem to be saying that a lot recently. I suppose I don't know what else to say. I can't come up with all the answers for you on whether God exists and why you can't ring Social Services on a Sunday. I'm only human."

She relaxed and snuggled up to him. "It's me that should be sorry. I'm so on edge. To be honest right now whether God exists isn't the first thing on my mind. I'm on the more basic level of 'who am I?' The whole God thing is a bit further down the line. I need to do something to take my mind off things. What about…"

The phone rang and she bolted out of bed to the dressing table where the handset was recharging in the cradle. "Hello"

"Hello, is that Lisa Forster?"

"Yes, who is this please?"

"It's Phyllis Jones who used to live next door to you in Billingbrook. We were just coming out of church this morning when Mary who does the flowers said 'You aren't the Jones's from Billingbrook in the advert are you?' Well, I said to her 'What advert?' and she said..."

Lisa looked imploringly at Pete as Phyllis continued to move towards the point. "It's great to hear from you," she said with forced enthusiasm as soon as she could get a word in edgeways.

"Well, Brian, and I would love to see you and wondered if you'd like to come over for tea later today?"

Lisa racked her brain for an excuse, but knew that her desperation for information meant grasping this opportunity with both hands. Maybe somewhere in all the talking there would be some useful information. "We'd love to come."

"Oh, that's nice dear. Is five all right? I was saying to Brian the other day that I often think of those days back in..."

"Yes that will be fine. What address is it?" Lisa took down the details of where to go and then tried several times to end the call before Phyllis said goodbye.

"What do you mean 'we'?" Pete was laughing. "I don't need to have tea with a garrulous old woman."

"Oh, I think you do." Lisa said flopping down onto the bed. "I'm going to need your help to get out of there alive. It wasn't until she started talking that I remembered what she was like."

"Well, let's hope if she talks so much that we'll learn something."

"I hope so."

CHAPTER 15

Stockport, Cheshire. Sunday evening 23rd September

The Sunday drive to Stockport was no less nerve-racking than collecting the paper the day before.

"Are you expecting them to have two heads or eat people for Sunday tea?" Pete asked as they parked the car.

"Oh, that's good, coming from the bloke who wanted to be left behind."

"Well, they weren't my neighbours and you didn't give them an outstanding write up."

"I'm just nervous. Every time we come to another dead end the pressure on the next step increases. I'm even starting to ask myself whether any of it matters. Wouldn't it be easier if I could decide who I want to be and get on with it? The problem is it isn't that easy. I still feel driven to find out who I am." They'd walked along the road to number fifty-three and were standing on the step.

"Are you going to ring the bell or shall I?" Pete asked.

"What? Oh yes." She pressed the bell and heard a classic 'ding dong' sound in the hall beyond. The door had glazed panels and she watched a distorted human shape moving towards them. She guessed it was Phyllis Jones by the bright blobs of colour top and bottom. She imagined Brian being more conservative.

The door opened and Phyllis came into focus, the cerise top and purple skirt would not have suited Brian. It was enough to make her break into a genuine smile as she introduced Pete and got over the whole 'My, haven't you grown' conversation that was inevitable given how many years it was since they'd met.

"Come through, my dears," Phyllis ushered them into the sitting room. "Brian's just in the garden I'll call him."

Lisa sank into an armchair near the door and Pete sat in another by the fireplace. She was aware of a sensation of time having stood still as she looked around the room. It wasn't old fashioned. It had been newly furnished some time ago, but hadn't been updated. At a guess Lisa thought it was an early 80's style, complete with a television in its wooden surround. Lisa smiled at the sight of a 'state-of-the-art' Dual turntable with a Des O'Connor LP leaning against it.

Brian came through from the kitchen, "Hello, Lisa, dear and you must be Pete. Pleased to meet you." He shook them both warmly by the hand. "Phyllis was wondering the other day what had happened to you and here you are."

Phyllis bustled in with a tray of sandwiches and cakes. She put them on the table with the food she had already laid out. "Do tuck in. I'll just bring the tea in."

When Phyllis returned she was talking before she'd even come through the door. "I was so sorry to hear about your mum. It must have been very hard for you. I'm sure your young man will have been a great help." She beamed at Pete. Lisa thought it was too much effort to set the record straight and explain that Pete hadn't been around then.

Without the need for any prompting Phyllis launched into a lengthy update on how they had got on since they moved to Stockport with Lisa drifting in and out of concentration and wondering how to broach the subject of her possible adoption. She became aware of Phyllis saying, "Here's me talking so much my tea's gone cold."

Lisa saw her opportunity and turned to address Brian. "The thing is, one or two pieces of information about my parents have come up. I wondered if you could shed any light on them. For example, do you know how old I was when we moved to Billingbrook?"

"Now that's a hard one," said Brian. "I think if I remember rightly."

"You'd have been about 6 or 7 months or so. I know you weren't yet one because it was your first birthday just before that Christmas and I'm sure it was the beginning of the summer when you all moved in."

From that, Lisa knew without asking that they had no idea that she wasn't the original baby. Her heart sank, what possible use could there be in talking further. There was nothing else for her to learn from them. She wondered how they could bow out gracefully without causing offence, or whether she was going to have to suffer hours of Phyllis prattling. She became aware of Brian talking.

"I don't suppose you can ask much of your mum and dad's families can you, what with all the problems."

Lisa's brain raced. *Problems; what problems?* Her heart pounded. If she asked outright there was a risk they'd clam up, realising she didn't know. *What could she say to draw out some more information? She needed to appear that this wasn't news to her.* She looked away from Pete who was looking at her quizzically and cleared her throat. "No, it was always difficult. In fact I don't know where they are now."

"No, it was a rum deal that time your Dad's brother

turned up."

Brother, an uncle of mine. What uncle? "How old would I have been then?" She crossed her fingers that Pete wouldn't try to be helpful by joining in the conversation.

Phyllis put her cup down. "I remember your poor dear mother afterwards. She was quite shaken. She said they never expected to hear anything more from Laurence. He was after money, I think. Your dad was furious. I think you'd have been about seven at the time. Do you remember you stayed the night at our house?"

Lisa felt on safer ground. "Yes I do remember staying with you. It was fun. You let me stay up late and we had a pretend party with music and all sorts."

Phyllis laughed. "Oh yes, that's right. I had to do something to cover the sound of the shouting. Isn't it funny when you look back?"

"I don't know what happened to Uncle Laurence," said Lisa feeling strange saying the name for the first time.

"We never saw him again after that. Your dad said he didn't expect to hear from him again."

The conversation changed and they found themselves being shown the Jones's family photo album and having a tour of their immaculate suburban garden before being able to escape.

"Thank you," Lisa said. "You've been very kind."

"Think nothing of it dear. Do come again sometime or maybe you'll be ringing to invite us to a wedding." Phyllis beamed at Pete in a meaningful fashion.

"Now, now Phyllis, let the poor dears get off," said Brian mouthing an apology to Pete.

They waved goodbye and walked along the road to the car.

"You didn't tell me you've got an uncle Laurence."

Pete sounded confused.

"I didn't know I'd got an Uncle Laurence. If we're being accurate, I probably still don't have an Uncle Laurence and if I did, we wouldn't know where he was. I can't believe that in all those years Dad never mentioned he had a brother. Why would he not say anything? What was there to hide? I used to think I knew my Mum and Dad, now I'm not so sure."

"So, we went there to find out who you are and came away wanting to know who Laurence Forster is as well. At least, we've got a name for him."

"I don't think the important question is 'who is he?' it's 'why did no one speak about him?' I wonder if Sylvia would know," Lisa said as she drove back to Billingbrook.

"Don't you think she'd have mentioned it if she did?" Pete had the map on his knee but the road signs were clear.

"She may not have realised it was relevant. I'll send her another email later. I wish I could contact her direct, without going through Julie."

"I know. Just hang on to the thought that there may not have been anything on the tape anyway."

***

Billingbrook. Wednesday 26th September

It had been a restless night. Lisa had been lying there thinking about the appointments they had over the next few days. She couldn't help but worry about what she was going to do next if none of this provided anything useful. She was still none the wiser as to who Laurence Forster was and whether he was still alive. She'd looked on the listings of births, marriages and deaths but she wasn't even sure that his first name was Laurence or whether that was the correct spelling. She had no idea when he was born or for that matter any certainty over where he was born. She had found some Laurence Forsters but he could be any one of them and besides which, finding the quarter he was born in wasn't going to make him any easier to find now. She lay thinking about their first meeting with the lawyers, it was unlikely they would know anything that hadn't come up when they sorted out her mum's will, but she still hoped there may be a chance.

She managed a couple of hours sleep. It was still too early for the alarm to go off, but there was little likelihood of her dozing off. She lay with her eyes open looking through the morning gloom in a hazy unfocussed way, listening to the rhythmic breathing of Pete by her side. The curtains were thicker than the ones at her house, she could see little more than shadows, though she was sure it must be light outside by now. There was a snort and an exhalation from the sleeping Pete as he rolled over towards the wall, pulling the covers with him. It felt quite cool for September and she was about to pull the covers back when everything seemed to happen at once. A large furry object that turned out to be Toffee, jumped onto her bare midriff; then shot off again as the alarm burst into life. Pete threw an arm out in search of the snooze button.

Lisa sat up startled. "This is it then."

"What?" Pete responded.

"Well, it's the day we might find something out."

Pete rolled onto his back, "Don't get your hopes up." He stroked her arm. "Just see it as another step along the way."

That was all very well for him to say. He knew he was Pete Laundon. Lisa considered the fact that even Pete didn't understand what this was like for her. Without another word, she dragged her tired body out of bed and headed for the shower.

***

They were walking up the steps into the offices of Froggatt Boothby and Jarvis. "You O.K.?" Pete asked her.

"Do I look O.K.?" The tension was getting to her but she wasn't prepared to admit it, not to Pete and hardly even to herself. Pete didn't reply but held the door open for her to go through.

It was Pete who took the initiative when they got into the reception area.

"Miss Forster, Miss Goddard will see you now. Please follow me." The receptionist led them along the corridor to a suite of meeting rooms with glass sides and narrow Venetian blinds that could shield the occupants from prying eyes. They were led into meeting room three; a small windowless room with a circular table and four chairs. Marcia Goddard hadn't arrived, but there were pots of tea and coffee and china cups laid out on the table.

Lisa turned to Pete. "Shall I tell her the whole story?"

"It can't do any harm. It might at least help to get her to understand why we're asking such odd questions."

"I know. It's just…"

At that point, Marcia Goddard breezed into the room and greeted them. Shaking hands first with Lisa and then with Pete.

"How can I help you, Miss Forster?"

"Please, call me Lisa." She paused and looked at Pete. "I don't know where to start. It's a difficult story to believe." Then she explained the whole story, while Marcia Goddard sat nodding in all the appropriate places.

"I see. Well, that isn't quite what I expected and I don't know if we would have anything to help. Unfortunately, due to client confidentiality I wouldn't be able to disclose to you if we had anything in connection with any other matters than the will that you are directly involved in."

"I suppose that's what I expected," said Lisa, brushing away a tear. Pete put his hand over hers and she drew it away.

"I can explain some of the adoption process to you if that will help? Just give me a minute." Marcia picked up the phone and rang an internal extension. "Joyce, can you spare five minutes in meeting room three? I've got a client here who needs to understand what the adoption process would have been in ..." she broke off, "What year was it, Lisa?"

"1977 or 1978," she said blowing her nose on a tissue.

"1977 or 1978," Marcia repeated.

Whilst they waited, Marcia Goddard poured them all drinks, including one for Joyce. As she finished a tall lady with half glasses entered the room. Lisa guessed that she would be in her mid-fifties by the tight grey curls and the benevolent smile.

"Joyce is our specialist in family and matrimonial law," said Marcia once the introductions were out of the way. "She's been with the firm a little longer than I have."

Joyce threw her head back and laughed. "Marcia is being very kind. I've been here a terribly long time. Now, how can I help?"

Once the situation had been explained, with Joyce nodding and clarifying the facts they did have. She sat back. "It just goes to show that however long you've been in this game, there's always something new to learn." She reached across for a pad of paper and a pen and began to make notes as she spoke. "There were three types of adoption. The main route, as now, was through the local authority. I won't go through all the regulations. Children within local authority care who are eligible for adoption can be placed in suitable homes. Secondly, there were, and for that matter still are, other agencies through whom adoption can take place. These are known as voluntary adoption agencies."

Lisa started scrabbling about in her bag for a pen and some paper.

"Don't worry," said Joyce, "I'm writing the key things on here for you to take away with you. Lastly there were in the past, although they became much less common, private arrangements for adoption. These covered a very small number of cases. The time you're talking about, adoption from abroad was not as common as it is today and the number of babies born to single mothers, who were then placed for adoption, had already declined. It wasn't quite the taboo it had been historically. What all of these arrangements had in common was that they needed an adoption order through the courts. Which court it would be would depend on which area the adoption took place. Do you have any idea where that was?"

Lisa shook her head. "It might have been here, but I think it was more likely to have been Triford."

"We could get one of the trainees to go through all the records, but it might be like looking for a needle in a haystack. There would be a charge for our time, but I can't say how much it would be." Marcia said. "You might be better to talk to the authorities in Triford first, to see if they can help."

"Thank you. We've got a meeting with them on Friday," Lisa said. "Perhaps we can come back to you after that if we need you to do some work."

"Yes, of course."

"Have I forgotten anything, Pete?"

"No, I don't think so," said Pete, speaking for the first time.

They thanked Marcia and Joyce and putting the piece of paper that Joyce had given her in her bag, Lisa led the way out of the building.

The bank was an imposing building with stone colonnades and marble flooring. They were shown into a partitioned room that had once been part of the main banking hall. A young man in an ill-fitting brown suit joined them.

"I'm Mr Pritchard, how can I help you?"

"My parents had accounts with you before they died and I need to know whether you held any documents for them."

"We'd have sent you any relevant documents when you closed the accounts."

"What? Even if they were in a safety deposit box?" Lisa raised her eyebrows.

"Oh, you didn't mention a safety deposit box. No, they're dealt with separately. What was the number of their box?"

"I don't know if they had one. That was what I was trying to ask you."

"Oh, right. I see. Let me have a look on the computer."

He tapped at the keys for a couple of minutes and then looked up.

"Sorry, could you excuse me for a moment. I'm afraid they've obviously changed the password."

As Mr Pritchard left the room, Lisa looked across at Pete and shook her head.

Once he'd logged in, Mr Pritchard said, "What name is it?"

"Forster," said Lisa in a flat tone.

"And their main account number?"

She pushed the bank statement in his direction.

"No, I'm afraid there's nothing here. I can't help you."

"And you wouldn't hold any information anywhere else?" Lisa was clutching at straws.

"None, I'm afraid."

As they walked away, Lisa was thoroughly fed up. "I never did think much of banks. Today just confirms it."

"Don't be too hard on him. It's not the most usual situation."

"The bloke was stupid."

"He wasn't very bright, I will grant you that. But he did try to help. "

"I'm going home. I'll see you later." And with that Lisa walked off in the direction of her car leaving Pete standing on the pavement. *Bloody men*, she thought as she brushed past people in the town centre. *Someone must have known what was going on.* She kicked a can that was in the way and watched it bounce against the legs of the person in front. They barely reacted and for a moment she wished she'd kicked it harder. By the time she got back to the car park, she was starting to calm down and she sat in the driver's seat with her head in her hands feeling empty.

She jumped when she heard the tap on the window and as Pete pressed his nose against the glass to pull a funny face, she couldn't help but smile. She turned the ignition on and lowered the window. "You just don't take no for an answer, do you?"

"I'll take that as a sorry then shall I?"

"Get in. You're safe. I've calmed down."

Pete pulled a mock cowardly expression and pulled away from the car. "Sure?"

"Just get in, before I change my mind."

"Do you want to go home or shall we get some lunch?"

"Well, we aren't at the Benefits office until later so we've got quite a while."

"Ok, let's go to the Art Gallery and have lunch there. There's a café upstairs."

Lisa closed the window and got out. "Are you sure you're up to this. I'm not the best of company."

"Is that a challenge?"

***

The Art Gallery was busy with lunchtime traffic but it was still quieter than the Market Square itself. "Can we look round first and then eat? I'm not that hungry right now." Lisa said, stopping to read the board telling them what exhibitions were coming up.

"That's O.K. by me. I used to come here on a Sunday afternoon when I was on my own," said Pete, making his way through to the lower gallery.

"I've never been in before. It's not that I don't like art, it's just that you take the things on your doorstep for granted. You take a lot of things for granted when you come to think of it." She stopped to look at an exhibition of local scenes by different artists. "I don't think much of that picture of the Market Square. I'm surprised it's up."

"You could describe it as a modern impressionist, although to be frank it doesn't even give much of an impression of being the market. It's more 'swirls of colour on washed out background,' but I don't suppose that sounds as good as 'Market Square on a busy day'." They both laughed as they moved on down to the gallery.

"You never talk much about the time before 'us'" she said turning to Pete.

"I will one day," Pete replied turning away. "Just not yet."

Lisa stopped to look at a painting of a face in full scream. It was a woman, holding her head between her hands, with her head thrown back. It was a colourful derivative of the famous picture by Edvard Munch. "I can relate to this one right now. It seems to describe how I feel on the inside, but I just can't let it out."

"That's a scary thought. I would say 'let it all out', but to be honest if that's what's inside I'm not sure that's such a good idea. Could you just let a little bit of it out?"

"I don't think you can control that sort of feeling once it's started. It's a sort of 'all or nothing' type of scream."

"Right," said Pete. "Perhaps best leave it at nothing then."

***

"I don't think the Art Gallery is going to be remembered for its culinary skills," said Pete as they began to walk to the Benefits Office. "It's a good job you weren't hungry. What do we need to ask them here?"

"We need to know what you have to fill in to get child benefit."

"Right. Have you got some sort of ID on you?"

"I've got my passport and my birth certificate. Or at least I've got somebody's documents."

"It might be best here if you don't mention that they aren't yours. Somehow I get the feeling that you'd be better off letting them think they are."

"Yes, I know."

They stopped outside a multi-storey building that looked as though it had been put up in the 1960's without any thought to design.

"I guess they were on a tight budget," said Pete, frowning as he looked at it. "Was that plastic cladding ever in fashion?"

"I doubt it." As she looked at the queuing system with everyone taking a number, Lisa was grateful to see a separate reception for people who had an appointment. Once checked in, they were directed to the interview room at the end of the waiting area.

"It's a bit different to Froggatt, Whatsit and Whod'yamaflip," said Pete as they both looked round at the sparse furnishings and unwelcoming decoration. "They've even forgotten the tea and coffee."

"Pete, I'm sorry I'm just not in the mood for jokes."

A plump lady in a dress that hung at an awkward angle came into the room clutching a file.

"I'm Mrs Connors; your case has been assigned to me. How can I help you?"

There was not the least impression of help given out by Mrs Connors as far as Lisa could see, leaving her with no idea of where to start. "Well, I think I need to know when I was registered for Child Benefit and in what name?" She looked at Pete.

"Lisa has reason to believe that she may have been adopted and wondered whether any of the information that you hold would provide some answers." Lisa appreciated the warmth of Pete's hand as he put it over hers, whilst the stony faced Mrs Connors looked on.

"I can't see that our records will tell you anything. For a start," she said, sounding disdainful. "I am presuming that you are talking about a case some time ago."

Lisa nodded.

"Our computer system was installed a few years ago and I don't think we keep all the records before that." She snapped her file closed, as though she was signalling the end of the meeting.

The tears started to form in the corners of Lisa's eyes

and she sniffed to try to stop them. Pete looked at her and then in as charming a manner as Lisa had ever seen from him, he looked into the face of the case worker. "The thing is, Mrs Connors, or may I call you Violet?" he said as Lisa saw him glancing at Mrs Connors' name badge. "I know you must get a lot of very difficult and very awkward people, who seem to be wasting your precious time, in what must be an extremely difficult job..." Violet Connors looked Pete in the eye for the first time, "It's just that my girlfriend has discovered that she isn't her parents' natural child and she doesn't know who she is. Can you imagine what that feels like?"

It was clear to Lisa, from the look on Violet's face, that she was thinking about it and Pete was winning. To Lisa's surprise and delight, Violet's whole demeanour changed.

Mrs Connors nodded and gave a reassuring smile. "I've adopted a little girl myself. Yes, I can imagine." She laid the file down on the table, opened it and clicked her biro to the on position. "Now why don't you tell me everything you do know?"

The tears were trickling down Lisa's cheeks as she began the story and Violet made notes on the paper in front of her.

When she got to the end, Violet shook her head. "Well, in all my years in this job, I can honestly say I've never come across anything like this before. I'll see what I can find out and then I'll let you know. I can't make any promises. It's been twelve years since the file was closed, I don't know what I'm going to find going back that far."

"We'll appreciate anything you can do to help. Really we will." Pete gripped Violet's hand and shook it vigorously. "You're one in a million, Violet," he said, giving her a peck on the cheek. Violet blushed a deep red and gathered her things together as Lisa and Pete headed for the door.

CHAPTER 16

Wednesday evening 26ᵗʰ September

"We're all going…"

"Pete, will you just cut the singing and concentrate on driving?"

"Oh, go on with you. You know you want to join in." Pete grinned at her.

"I'm sorry. I'm just so wound up. Everything we've done has led nowhere."

"My best friend Violet might come up with something."

"Your best friend Violet needs to trace a record that's thirty years old. I know I'm hoping that she strikes gold, but I know what I'd find if I were looking for that with the library's systems," Lisa said.

"A very big fine for an overdue book. Can't you lighten up just a little bit and enjoy the fact we're going away together for the first time?"

Lisa looked out of the window of the Mini at the passing countryside. The truth was that she was still fed up that Pete had insisted on driving. She did need his help, she wasn't about to dispute that, but she didn't need him taking over. This was her past they were delving into and she wanted to be in control. In some ways, the journey was the thing she could have been in control of. She wasn't in control of the process itself. That all seemed to be something that was happening to her, rather than something she could direct. Pete had even insisted on booking the hotel "as a surprise" and wouldn't tell her where it was. She had wanted to stay right in the middle of Triford so she was conveniently placed for the meetings the following day, but all Pete had said when she asked where he was booking was, "Wait and see." She didn't want to wait and see. At the moment there were enough unknowns, without him adding any more.

"Sun arise…"

"Pete!"

"O.K., O.K. If I can't sing, at least talk to me."

"What about?"

"Oh, I don't know; anything. Tell me about when you were a child."

Lisa paused, thinking. "There was a park we used to go to, with deer and an old ruined house. Mum would make up a picnic and we'd sit down by the stream. Dad would help me fly my kite or I'd take my bike and cycle up and down while Mum and Dad had a gentle stroll. Sometimes, I'd just sit and read my book, leaning against the massive trunk of an oak tree, whilst Mum and Dad sat and talked."

They fell into silence for a while.

Even then, Pete failed to contain his exuberance and before long burst into a rendition of 'I am the one and only'.

"Pete, don't be so bloody insensitive."

"What? Oh sorry. Lisa, I am so sorry. I just didn't think. I love that song. I wasn't thinking about what the words might mean to you. I'll be quiet now. Please will you forgive me?"

"Just drive."

It was eight in the evening by the time Pete turned off the road and up the gravel drive of a country house hotel.

"Pete, it's gorgeous but aren't we still miles from Triford?"

"Well, yes, but I thought I'd like to spoil you a bit and it's a long time since I stayed in a hotel, so I thought I'd make it a nice one. It's ten miles to Triford from here. It won't take us more than half an hour."

She looked over the imposing stone building with its fountain in the middle of where the drive swung round in front of the house. They pulled up outside and a commissionaire came over to open her door. "Welcome to Triford Grange, Madam."

"Thank you," she said giggling. It felt as though the problems she was facing were a million miles away and she let herself think that maybe Pete had done the right thing booking them into such a beautiful place.

"This way, Mrs Laundon, Mr Laundon."

"But…" then she stopped herself and smiled. "Thank you."

She enjoyed the sound of her heels on the marble floor as she tiptoed through the hall toward the reception desk. She smiled at how feminine the surroundings made her feel. She wanted to throw her head back and drink in the quiet magnificence of the wood panelling and the oak staircase. As the porter took her bags, letting her walk unencumbered past the paintings of the house's former owners, in her own mind she was the current rich and famous lady of the manor.

***

Triford. Thursday 27th September

Triford Registrar's office was a red brick building. The gardens had short cropped grass and evenly spaced plants bringing a broad spectrum of colour. "I suppose that's where they do the photos after weddings," Lisa said, as she got out of the car. "I'm not sure I even know where Mum and Dad got married. You don't suppose it was here, do you?"

"You could always ask."

"I think I'll find out if there's any possibility that they are my mum and dad first."

Pete held the door open for her and they went in. She could feel her heart pounding as she approached the counter. She waited for the woman to look up from what she was doing.

"Can I help you?"

"Yes, at least I hope so. I telephoned to see if you could help me sort out whether this birth certificate is mine or not. I spoke to a lady called…"

"Alice, yes it was me you spoke to."

"Oh good," said Lisa, relaxing at the thought of not having to explain things all over again to another person.

"Do you have the birth certificate with you? And I need the details of the death that you'd like me to look up."

Lisa passed Alice the birth certificate and the reference to the death record for Patricia Lisa Forster. "Can you check if there were any other Patricia Lisa Forster's born at around that time in Triford?"

"I'll have a look for you, but the death record of a baby of that age will show the names of the parents, so unless the parents of two babies had the same names and called their children exactly the same thing, I think you can rule out coincidence."

Lisa nodded, "I was just… yes, I know. I suppose I'm clutching at straws." She turned to Pete. "Even though I'm certain I already know the answer to this, I don't know if I can face it."

He gripped her hand. "I know."

They waited a few minutes before Alice said "I'll just send this to the printer for you; then I can show you what we've got." She walked over to the printer at the other end of the counter, picked up the document and then came back to Lisa. "I'm afraid it's a definite match. Look. Here are the details of the person registering the death, in this case the father, Hugh Forster and the details of the parents and age of the child."

"What did she die of?"

"It looks as though it was one of those unexplained infant deaths, or cot deaths. I can't tell you anything more than that, I'm afraid."

Lisa stared at the paper in front of her.

"I know this is a long shot," said Pete. "But can you think of any other ways we could find out who Lisa is?"

"I've never come across anything like this before. I don't know what to suggest. Aren't there any relatives you could ask?"

Lisa shook her head. "Thanks, anyway."

"Look," said Alice. "Why don't you give me a contact number and I'll ask around amongst my colleagues to see if anyone else has any ideas? One of them might have come across something like this before, but I haven't."

"Thank you," said Lisa, then she and Pete went back to the car.

"Where now?" said Pete.

She took a deep breath, "Good question. I don't know." She thought for a moment, "Oh you mean where are we going next? I was thinking of the bigger picture. LloydsTSB on High Street." She looked at the map.

"That's the one we turned off to come down London Road. We might be as well to leave the car here and walk. Do you think they'd mind?"

Pete looked round at the empty car park, "Not if it stays as quiet as this." He relocked the car and came round and put his arm through Lisa's. "I do love you, you know. To me you are you and that's all there is to it. If you get what I mean."

"Yes, I think so. That's sweet of you. I wish everything else felt as simple as that."

The meetings with both LloydsTSB and the Natwest Bank in Triford were no more use to them than the bank in Billingbrook had been. The story was as difficult to explain, but despite all the details of both Hugh and Maureen, there was no evidence that there had ever been a safety deposit box in either or both of their names.

In one bank they were passed from person to person, until they found themselves back at the first person they'd seen, whilst in the other Lisa felt overwhelmed by the stuffy formality that seemed to be linked to the words 'safety deposit'. It was as though the whole concept belonged to a different age and class of society and she felt as out of place as she could ever remember feeling.

"Thank God that's over," she said as they came down the steps back onto High Street.

Pete grinned, "I was starting to think they were going to file us along with someone's family heirlooms. What does that leave us for today?"

"The hospital. The cemetery. Oh, I don't know. I can't face any more of the explanations and the sympathy, the incredulous looks and everyone saying they've never come across anything like this before. I don't want to be the source of so much novelty for people."

"What would you ask at the hospital?"

"I can't see what we could gain. I could ask them about other babies born around the same time, but there's no reason to presume I was born at the same time or even at the same hospital. There's no particular information that the hospital could give us that would prove a link."

"Unless there were twins."

"Wouldn't Julie have known about that though?"

"Yes, I suppose so. You're right, there's nothing that the hospital can help us with, unless we get some more information first. They aren't going to admit to us that there was some confusion and babies got switched."

"No. Let's call it a day. I wonder if I'm too late to get a massage at the hotel?"

"I could always give you one," Pete answered a broad smile breaking across his face.

Lisa smiled. "We'll see. Maybe. I'm not in the mood right now, but perhaps we could go to the spa and then see how we feel later."

***

Triford – Friday 28th September

It had been a lazy start to the day. The meeting with the adoption agency was not until the afternoon and even allowing for the time it would take to get into Triford and find parking, Lisa and Pete had decided to spend the morning in and around the hotel and have lunch before they left.

"Ready?" said Lisa, picking up her bag.

"But it's two-thirty. We don't need to go just yet."

"Pete, I don't want to be late for the Adoption Agency. It's important. If I'm going to find out anything useful, this is going to be it."

"O.K., I just need to go back to the room for the car

keys."

"Oh, please will you hurry up."

"Hey, calm down will you. We've still got an hour before the meeting."

"Oh, just get on with it, Pete."

Whilst Pete went off to get the keys, Lisa waited in reception. She paced up and down the corridor wondering what could be taking him so long. "We're going to be late," she said as he came towards her.

"What?" he said, but she was already half way out of the door on the way to the car.

He remained silent for a while as they got into the car and he began to drive. They were about half way from the hotel to Triford when there was a cloud of smoke from the engine of the Mini and the engine died, leaving them rolling to a stop at the side of the road.

"Pete, what's wrong? This can't be happening. It's three o'clock. Will it start again?"

"After that? I doubt it. I think I'm going to have to call the breakdown people."

"Pete, we can't break down. Not now. You've got to do something. I need to be in Triford."

"Now calm down, Lisa, I'm doing what I can. I didn't know this was going to happen. It's not deliberate."

"Don't tell me to calm down. You wanted to bring the bloody car. I wanted to drive my car, but oh no, you had to insist on driving. I don't know why I ever listened to you in the first place. It isn't as though I couldn't have done all this on my own. Men, they take over everything and look where it gets us. When we need you, you just let us down. We're better off without you." And with that she got out of the car, slammed the door and walked off in the direction of Triford.

"Lisa, we can sort this out. I'll call the breakdown people and tell them it's urgent. Maybe they can send a taxi for you. They might get here in time. Lisa come back."

Lisa marched off down the road searching for her mobile phone in her bag. There might still be time to call a taxi and get to Triford for the meeting. *Damn, no bloody signal. Why did they have to break down in the middle of nowhere?* She realised she'd left the map in the car and had no idea where the nearest village was. She prayed there'd be somewhere along the road where she could make a phone call. She looked at her watch, it was three-ten. Time was running out. Why hadn't she put on flat shoes? She normally wore flat shoes. O.K., so these ones had a low heel, but she couldn't run in them. It was years since she'd done anything as energetic as running, she didn't fancy the prospect of starting now. She looked round for signs of houses, but saw fields on one side and woods on the other. Maybe she could flag down a passing car, but she'd heard too many bad stories and the last thing she wanted was for the day to get any worse. She walked for another fifteen minutes before she saw the start of a village ahead. She wondered whether Pete was having any luck with the car, but pushed all thoughts of him away. As far as she was concerned he was history.

It was already three-thirty when she reached the first house. She wondered what to do. She could ring the Adoption Agency and ask if they could see her later and then call a taxi, or she could see how long it was going to take to get a taxi first. The first pub she came to was closed. She wondered whether such things as phone boxes still existed in places like this. She eventually found one and fished around in her purse for some money to pay for the call. Just as she picked up the receiver she realised it didn't take coins. It needed a phonecard and she didn't have one. There must be a shop somewhere. The village looked large enough to support one. This was the South of England though and there were lots of commuter villages full of people who did their shopping in the towns, then drove home, or ordered it over the internet.

She stepped out of the phone box and looked about. On the far corner of the village green, she could see a triangular ice cream flag fluttering in the breeze above the window of what she presumed was a shop. She went over and found a small newsagents who were able to supply her with a phone card and allowed her to look up the numbers she needed in their phone book.

By the time she got back to the phone box, it was three forty-five. She rang the taxi firm and they said they could get a car to her in fifteen minutes, at that rate she could make it to Triford for four-fifteen. She rang the Adoption Agency.

"I'm afraid Mrs Linford, who you were due to see, finishes at four on a Friday."

"Can't someone else see me? I've come all the way from Lancashire. I'm trying to find out who I am." Lisa felt the hot tears stinging her cheeks.

"Just hold the line a moment."

Lisa waited, hoping that her credit would last.

"Hello. If you can be here by four-fifteen then Mrs Pickering will see you. She will be here until four-thirty, otherwise I'm very sorry but there's nothing we can do."

"O.K., I'll try to be there by four-fifteen. Thank you."

Lisa left the call box and sat on a seat on the village green to wait for the taxi. She watched the ducks waddling around the banks of the pond greedily scrapping for food when a mum brought a small child to feed them. The child was clutching the end of a bag of bread. She watched the comings and goings from the newsagents and every so often looked at her watch. It hadn't occurred to her to check her mobile phone for a signal. When it hadn't worked, she had become so focussed on finding a payphone. She got quite a shock when it started to ring. She looked at the number calling and saw that it was Pete. She decided to let the answerphone take it and then listen to her message. She checked her watch, it was already four-ten and there was still no sign of the taxi. She rang them from her mobile and was told they would be with her any minute. She then called up her message.

"Lisa, it's me, Pete. I just wanted to make sure you were O.K. I'm still waiting for the breakdown vehicle. I'll see you back at the hotel later. I love you."

She snapped the phone closed. Did he think she had any intention of going back to the hotel? She had a few clothes and her wash bag there. He could take those back. Once she got to Triford, she would go to the Adoption Agency and then get the train back to Billingbrook. She looked at her watch again it was four-fifteen, she may as well get the taxi to take her straight to the station. It was going to be too late to find anyone at the Adoption Agency now.

CHAPTER 17

Billingbrook. Friday evening 28ᵗʰ September

It was late on Friday night by the time Lisa got home. She was tired after the journey and the house felt empty. She picked up the post, made a drink and took them both to bed. As she opened the first letter, the trauma of the week was compounded by receiving a copy of the death certificate that she and Pete had ordered over the internet. She already knew the content, but it was a stark reminder of the lack of progress she was making.

She turned out the light and lay in the darkness, thinking about what mattered. She knew it wasn't Pete's fault that the car had picked today to break down, but right now she didn't need to be let down by anybody else. If she was going to do this, she was going to do it on her own.

Lisa moped around the house for most of Saturday and Sunday, ignoring the messages Pete left on both her mobile and house answerphone, despite how much she was missing him. She hadn't realised what a big part of her life he had become. She wondered whether he stayed on at the hotel or if he came back to Billingbrook. He didn't even know where Lisa was, but she wasn't about to tell him.

She knew she needed to talk to the Adoption Agency, but there was nothing she could do until Monday, so she spent her time searching on the internet for any information about Triford or Billingbrook thirty years ago. Somewhere there had to be a clue as to what had happened.

***

Billingbrook. Monday 1st October

Lisa headed into work early on Monday, determined not to let anyone see how she was feeling, but her false jollity was obvious to all who knew her well.

"I've got grave news," she said beaming at Trudy. "I've buried my relationship with cemetery Pete."

She could tell that Trudy wasn't fooled. "We're going for lunch and no arguing. Meet me in the foyer at 12.30."

Lisa was grateful that Trudy knew better than to come over all sympathetic in public. Right now if anyone were to say 'Poor Lisa' or 'Are you all right?' she knew she would dissolve into a total mess. She went to see Derek in person this time, to ask for another day's holiday.

"I know it's inconvenient and I wouldn't ask if it weren't important, but is there any possibility that I could have this Friday off please? I did only take three days last week and…"

"Yes, that's fine."

She hadn't expected such an easy time. She was preparing herself for a more lengthy reasoning of the situation. "Right, yes thanks. Well, that's all then. I'll do the form." She shook her head as she walked away. What on earth had come over Derek? Maybe this was going to be her week. She felt brighter until the phone rang on the counter. "Billingbrook Library Lending Department, can I help you?"

"Lisa, it's me, Pete."

She froze.

"Are you there?"

"Yes," she said. "I'm here, but I'm working right now. This isn't a good time."

"I know. It's just that I had to know you were all right and I wanted to say I'm sorry. It was a lousy thing to happen and it was all my fault for taking over. Everything you said was right and, well, I was just hoping you might forgive me."

"I can't talk right now. Thank you for calling. Bye." And with that she hung up. She missed him desperately, but she just couldn't deal with him right now. She fought to pull herself together and struggled through the morning.

"Come on then, tell me everything that's happened." Trudy said as they made their way to Pizza Hut.

"Before I do, what's going on with Derek? He was nice this morning."

"He probably had sex at the weekend," said Trudy giggling. "Now tell me about you."

"I suppose you want the long version. I still don't know who I am. I've fallen out with Pete and I've got an Uncle Laurence."

"And that's the long version?"

They opted for the buffet again so that they could talk uninterrupted.

"No, I suppose not. O.K., where shall I start?"

"Pete."

Lisa told Trudy the saga of the car.

"He must have been mortified. Did he manage to fix it? It's his pride and joy."

"Whose side are you on? I don't know. I didn't stick around long enough to find out. It was all feeling a bit claustrophobic and seemed like he was taking over. I just needed some space."

"And what about now you've got some?"

"I'm missing him."

"Lisa! You've got to talk to him."

"I know, but not right now. We were on our way to Triford Adoption Agency. We never made it. They're the last, obvious, place that might know who I am. I want to see them on my own before I start involving Pete again."

"I think I see. What about Uncle Laurence?"

"Your guess is as good as mine. It was a neighbour of my parents who told me about him. Apparently he's Dad's brother, but I've never heard of him. Apart from his name and the fact that he had an argument with my parents when I was about seven, I don't know anything about him."

Trudy was quiet for a moment and then said, "You don't think you might be Uncle Laurence's daughter do you? I know it's a long shot, but he might have come to take you back or something?"

Lisa put her knife and fork down and stared at Trudy. "I hadn't thought... you don't think? But why wouldn't I have heard of him? It's possible, but it doesn't make any sense. Who was my mum in that case?"

"I don't know. It's just the other bit of jigsaw you've got to work with. I was trying to see if it fitted any of the holes."

"I don't think I feel hungry any more. I don't know what to think."

"Sorry. I was just trying to make suggestions."

"It's O.K. You're right. I don't know why I hadn't thought about it. I wonder if I can find his birth details and anything more about him. Maybe if I could find him he might know all the answers."

"Maybe."

"Do you mind if I go back to work. I don't want any more to eat and I want to see if I can find any information on Uncle Laurence on the library computers."

"I've had enough anyway. I'll come with you. Perhaps I can help." They paid for their meal and headed back to the library.

The computers were not in use, so they found two terminals side by side and logged in. "What are we looking for then?" asked Trudy.

"Can you see if you can find a birth record for Laurence Forster in Triford and I'll go onto Genes Reunited to see if I can find any matches there."

They tapped away at the keyboards for a few minutes.

"Bingo," said Trudy.

"What have you got?"

"Laurence Forster, born Triford, Jun quarter 1938."

"That makes him three years older than Dad. He'd have been 39 when I was born. You'd think he'd have sorted his life out, been married and able to look after children of his own by then."

"Unless his wife died."

"Have a look for a marriage record. I presume it would be before that, if your theory's right, so between 1954 and 1978."

"Hang on. . . I'm not sure if everything is complete on here but there's nothing coming up."

"Damn. Nothing here either. That's it. I'm going to see if I can make another appointment with the Adoption Agency for Friday. Thanks for trying."

"No problem. Let me know if you find anything and please speak to cemetery Pete."

"O.K."

***

Triford. Friday 5th October

It was a slow week. Nothing felt quite the same without Pete. Even though she spent time doing all the same things, researching on the internet, emailing Julie to ask about Uncle Laurence, trying to work out what to do next, none of it felt the same. When Lisa travelled down to Triford by train the previous evening, all she could think about was how much she missed Pete's annoying singing. In the short time they'd been together he had become essential in a way she'd never experienced before. It was as though without him all the flavouring had been taken out of life. She could still chomp her way through the activities of the day, but none of them had any taste. For the last three weeks, she thought what mattered was finding out who she was, now she realised that there was something else that mattered; it was Pete.

As she prepared to go to the Adoption Agency from her functional hotel room in the centre of Triford, she thought ruefully of the hotel they stayed in the previous week and how special it made her feel. She looked at her mobile phone, her appointment was in an hour. She knew it was going to take ten minutes to walk to the Adoption Agency as she'd passed it on the way from the station the previous evening. She picked up her mobile phone to ring Pete. She hadn't spoken to him since he rang the library on Monday, but it felt like the right time to call.

The phone went straight to message service. Lisa took a deep breath. "Pete, it's me, Lisa. I just wanted to say I miss you." She hung up and looked at the phone thinking of all the things she should have said, like "I'm sorry too," and "I'd like to see you," and "Don't ever let's fall out again."

This time she arrived at the Adoption Agency in plenty of time for her meeting. She turned her phone to silent as she went into the building and approached the reception desk.

"Please take a seat, Mrs Forster."

"It's Miss, oh never mind, sorry. Yes, thank you." She went over to the waiting area and sat in a chair which gave her a view of the corridor. She picked up a magazine, but couldn't concentrate as she tried to watch everything that was going on, wondering whether Hugh and Maureen sat in this same place all those years ago. Some of the posters looked as though they might have been up since then, judging by the tatty curled edges.

Despite the fact that she was watching, she still jumped when the receptionist called her to go through. "Miss Forster, it's the third door on the left."

"Right. Thanks." She took a deep breath, straightened her jacket and went down the corridor.

"I'm Mrs Linford, how can I help?"

She poured the whole story out to Mrs Linford. She told her about everything from the bet with Pete to the car breaking down the previous week, while Mrs Linford sat and listened.

"You're having a hard time," Mrs Linford said. "I hope we can help. We keep records of all the children we place into adoption, but we're not the only people who deal with adoptions in this area. There are a number of private organisations and years ago it was not uncommon for adoptions to be arranged privately. We also have records of all those who have applied for adoption through us, but who were turned down."

"Why are people turned down?"

"There can be a number of reasons. It may be that they

can't provide a stable home; it may be that in some way we are concerned that the child would not be safe with them. We do carry out extensive checks before we place a child."

"If I were adopted through your agency, would you be able to tell me who my real parents were."

"Well, as long as we have a record of who they are, that is something you now have a right to know. However, it's quite common that we only know the name of the mother," she hesitated. "And in those instances where a baby is abandoned and the mother doesn't come forward, then we don't know the identity of either parent, although it's not unheard of for the mother to come forward years later in an attempt to trace the child."

"How long will it take you to find out if you have any information to help me?"

"That's hard to say. We've transferred many of our records onto computer, but there are still some that we have to resort to the paper files. They're the ones for whom adoption was refused. It also depends on how much information you can provide us with."

"I have the names and dates of birth of the people who would be the ones adopting."

"Do you have their address at the time of the adoption?"

"It might be this one." She handed over a sheet of paper.

"Not to worry, we should be able to do it from the dates of birth. It's just to ensure that we get the right people. It's important if they have a common name. Right, let me take down the details and then I'll get someone to bring you a coffee whilst I see what I can find."

As Lisa waited she read the words on the posters

several times and stared at some of the flaking paintwork. In reality, it was about half an hour, but it felt considerably longer. Her mind raced through all the possibilities that Mrs Linford might come back with and she wondered how she would react to them. She was just thinking about the possibility of finding out that she was abandoned and how she would deal with that when Mrs Linford returned.

Lisa got up as she came in, "Have you found anything?"

"Well, I have, but I don't think it's what you were hoping for."

"What is it?" Lisa's excitement was hard to contain.

"Miss Forster, I'm sorry but this agency turned down the application for adoption by your parents."

Lisa fell back into her chair. "So I'm not adopted?"

"I can't say that. I can say that you weren't adopted through us. As I explained earlier, we haven't transferred the reasons for refusal to the computer system; they're still in our archive files, which aren't held here on site. It's possible you were adopted through a different agency or privately, but I can tell you that you were not adopted through Triford Adoption Agency."

"Right. Would the reason they were turned down provide me with anything more useful?"

"Probably not."

"Right." Lisa didn't know what else to say. She needed a definite answer one way or another and it appeared that she was never going to get one.

"If we can help you in any other way, then please do let us know."

"Yes, thank you." She started getting her things together. "Could you let me have a list of the other adoption agencies in the area?"

"Yes, of course we can. You may be better to go through the court records for Triford for that time though. They would include the private adoptions as well."

"Thank you, yes, I'll do that."

Once again she felt downhearted. She couldn't believe that finding out who she was could be so difficult. She wished Pete were here to give her a hug. For the first time that week she regretted deciding to do this part on her own.

The train journey home served to reinforce how lonely she was feeling. It seemed a lot longer than three weeks since the bet with Pete. The uncertainty over her identity felt as though it had gone on forever.

When she got back to Billingbrook it was raining and she arrived at the bus stop to watch the bus she needed pulling away. It was ten minutes until the next one, but Lisa couldn't face waiting in the rain. She went to the other side of the station and found a taxi to take her home. She arrived to find Pete sitting on her doorstep, dripping wet, holding a bottle of wine in one hand and a large bunch of roses in the other.

"I thought you might need these," he said presenting them to her.

Despite her tiredness, Lisa threw her arms around him. "I'm so pleased to see you."

"I wondered whether you'd come at all. I've been ringing your mobile since you left the message for me this morning."

"I turned it off when I went to the Adoption Agency. Where's the car?"

"Still being fixed. I had no idea that's where you were. How did it go?"

"Let's go in and open this wine. I think I need a drink."

CHAPTER 18

Triford. May 1978

We stopped the adoption process when I found out I was pregnant. There didn't seem any point in continuing if I could have a child of my own. I was all for stopping it completely. It was Hugh, being level-headed, who suggested we put it on hold for a while.

I had got to the point of ceasing to believe that we would ever have a child of our own and then we found that I had conceived that tiny beautiful baby. Before Patricia, we thought it was one of those things, either there was something wrong with one of us or we were incompatible. Adoption seemed to be the best solution; our only solution. I saw a piece in the local paper, asking for potential adopters to come forward. I laid the paper out in front of Hugh.

"What do you think?"

"I don't know," he said. "Would it feel the same? It would never be our child."

"Does it have to be our child to feel the same?" I asked. "There isn't any reason that the child should feel any different. She'd see you as her daddy and me as her mummy."

"Oh, so it's a girl now is it," said Hugh in a resigned voice, but smiling at me at the same time.

"O.K., or a he. It's just..."

"I know, love. I know."

"There's a woman at St Mary's who's adopted three children, a brother and sister and then another little boy. She's always brought them up knowing they're adopted. She and her husband have always explained to the children that they are extra special, because they were chosen."

"There's no harm in asking for some information, love. We can at least do that."

I hugged Hugh and planted a massive kiss on his cheek. "I'll get onto it right away."

I rang the number that was given in the paper, but it was too late, so there was no reply. I rang again the following day. When I got through, the lady from the Adoption Agency was lovely and started talking to me about how the process worked and what we had to do. She said she would include the application forms and all the necessary paperwork as part of their information pack. She said they would have to carry out a number of checks if we decided to apply and that would include visiting us in our own home and police checks into our background. I said she could carry out all the checks she wanted and agreed that it was vital that the right sorts of people should be tasked with such an important job.

To be honest, I think I'd made my mind up before I even received the paperwork. I just needed Hugh to reach the same conclusion.

From then on, I don't think I stopped talking about it. I wasn't one to talk non-stop, but I was excited. Even though no decision had been made, between me and Hugh, never mind with the adoption people, I felt that the end of being childless was in sight.

It took a week for the pack of papers to arrive. They

were on the mat when Hugh came downstairs for breakfast. I was in the kitchen and hadn't heard the postman arrive. The envelope was addressed to 'Mr and Mrs H Forster' so as he munched his Corn Flakes, Hugh opened the package. He didn't tell me what he was reading. He'd read the letter and turned it over and opened the brochure that came with it. When I looked over his shoulder, he was looking at two collages. One was of lots of wide-eyed children, in individual shots, all looking straight at the camera. Their smiling faces carried a sadness that went beyond the photograph itself. The second collage was of the same children in family photographs. In some, they were the only child, whilst in others they had brothers and sisters as well as parents. We both looked at it silently.

"We'll fill the application in this evening," Hugh said.

I couldn't answer for the tears. I wrapped my arms around him so tightly and nestled my face into his neck. "Thank you," I eventually managed to say.

We did fill the forms in and sent them off. We'd had our home visit and several further discussions with the Adoption Agency and were within days of their final decision when I found I was pregnant with Patricia. It was then that we put the whole application on hold. I think it was those collages that stopped Hugh wanting to stop the process altogether. He was such a good man. He wasn't going through the adoption for me, or even just because we wanted a child of our own. He was doing it because there were all those children that needed families and it was such a good thing to do.

I didn't know when we lost Patricia that he had got in touch with the Adoption Agency within three weeks. I was in no state to think rationally and Hugh was desperate for a way to help me. He thought that if we could at least get onto the list of people waiting for a suitable adoption, it might give me the strength to carry on.

The first I knew of it was the letter. It was May 10th. I shall never forget that date. It wasn't Hugh that picked the post up that day, it was me. The postman had come early and the mail was already on the mat when I came down. If it hadn't happened that way round, I might never have known that Hugh had been in touch with the Agency. The chances were that he wouldn't have shown me the letter.

It was addressed in the same way the other one had been, but as I wasn't expecting anything from the Agency, it didn't occur to me that it would be from them. I opened it as I went through to the kitchen. I stood in the dining room reading it, having put the other post on the table.

"Hugh!" I wailed. "Hugh."

He came running downstairs, still in his pyjama bottoms, shaving foam daubed across one cheek. "Whatever is it, love?"

"Hugh!" I wailed again. Clutching the letter and reaching for a chair.

Hugh helped me sit down and took the letter from my clenched hand.

'Dear Mr and Mrs Forster,

We regret to inform you that following the extensive checks and references that the agency is obliged to carry out, we are unable to assign you a place on the waiting list for adoption.

If you would like to discuss this matter further then please arrange an appointment with …'

"It's got to be a mistake." Hugh shook his head. He turned the paper over in case there was anything we'd missed. "How can any of their checks not have been all right?" He was talking to himself more than anyone. I was sitting rocking backwards and forwards crying as though Patricia had died all over again.

"I'll ring them from work, just as soon as they open. I'm sure this is something we can clear up. We'll go to see them. This has to be a mistake. We told them everything. We've got no secrets. Come on, Maureen, it'll be all right, you just wait and see." He wrapped his arms around me, trying to keep the shaving foam from going all over my hair.

I followed him back upstairs when he went to finish shaving. I curled up on the bed crying. I just wanted to die and be with Patricia. I was still lying there when the phone rang at 11.00. I dragged myself to the extension on the side in our bedroom. "Hello, Triford 6973."

"Maureen, love, it's me."

I wasn't used to Hugh ringing during the day. He wasn't the sort to make personal calls from work and to be honest I wasn't with it. "Me?"

"Maureen, it's me, Hugh. I've rung the Adoption Agency, they can see us this afternoon. I'll come home for lunch and take the afternoon off."

"Right," I said, but didn't register what he was saying.

I lay back on the bed and fell asleep. I woke with a start when Hugh came in. "What time is it? What are you doing here?"

Hugh sat on the edge of the bed and stroked my cheek. He quietly and patiently explained all over again that we were going for a meeting and then went to make me a cup of tea while I had a wash to wake myself up a bit.

"Mr Forster, Mrs Forster, Mrs Anderson will see you now, please come this way."

We were led down a dimly lit corridor, brightened by

the posters of smiling families displayed on the walls. After passing a number of closed doors, we came to an office with Mrs Anderson's name plate on the door. Our escort knocked then opened the door and showed us into a functional office where Mrs Anderson was seated behind a large desk. We had met her two or three times before and she had always been very sympathetic and encouraging to our application. Today it was a different case and we were met with a high degree of formality as she indicated that we should sit in the chairs in front of her desk.

I could tell Hugh was nervous as he sat on the edge of his chair. "Mrs Anderson, thank you for agreeing to see us so soon. We had a letter from you this morning, as you will know and there seems to be some mistake." Hugh fumbled in his pocket for the letter.

"Mr Forster, I have a copy of the letter here on the file," she said looking at the open folder on the desk. "And I'm afraid there is no mistake. I have here copies of the checks that were done."

"But I don't understand. Which of the checks is the problem?" Hugh readjusted his position in the chair, while I sat clutching my bag on my knee.

"It's the police check, Mr Forster."

"Police check! But we haven't done anything. How can anything come up on the police check?"

"Mr Forster, as we explained to you there are certain offences which preclude a person from adopting a child. This applies to anyone who is living at the address that the child will be resident."

"But there's only us and we haven't done anything." Hugh was starting to sound as much angry as confused.

"Mr Forster, what you did not tell us," said Mrs

Anderson, "was that there is also a Mr Laurence Forster living at your address and I'm afraid..."

"Laurence? What's Laurence got to do with anything? He doesn't live with us. I haven't seen him for twenty years."

"As I was saying, Mr Forster, there is a Mr Laurence Forster showing on the police records as resident with you and his previous activities disqualify you and Mrs Forster from being able to adopt."

"This is preposterous. Laurence doesn't live with us. There's a mistake. The report must be wrong. You can't just stop us adopting because of a brother I haven't seen for twenty years. You need to do the checks again..."

"Mr Forster..."

"I know my rights. You can't just start accusing me of associating with someone when I don't even know where he is. He could be dead for all I know. You're wrong I tell you. You've got it wrong."

"Mr Forster," Mrs Anderson said. "There is no point arguing with me. Our decision is final. You may consider reapplying if there is a change in your circumstances, but I must say that this is the sort of thing that the Agency takes very seriously."

Hugh dropped back into his chair, "What has Laurence done that's the problem?"

"I'm sorry, Mr Forster, but I am not at liberty to provide any more details on the matter." Mrs Anderson snapped the folder closed and stood up. "I think you know your way out."

I was dazed and confused. I knew that Hugh had a brother who was the black sheep of the family, but as far as Hugh had mentioned he was involved in petty theft. Hugh had last seen him just before he was sent to prison for an eighteen month stretch in about 1959 when Hugh was eighteen. He went away to college and never heard from Laurence again.

We were in reception on our way out when I broke my silence. "Did you know about this?" It was a question, but it was an accusation. I didn't think that something like this could happen without someone knowing about it.

"Maureen, I had no idea. I can't see how he can be registered at our address. He doesn't even know where we live."

"Well, he obviously does."

"I don't even know what he's supposed to have done. Theft isn't enough to stop an adoption. Reading some of the backgrounds of the kids waiting to be adopted, that ought to make them feel right at home."

"Hugh!"

"Well, honestly. How dare she say we aren't good enough to adopt a child because of some brother that I have no control over whatsoever and whose whereabouts I haven't known for years?"

"But she has said."

"We'll move. We'll go a long way from Triford. We'll go somewhere he can't find us, away from all the horror of the last few months, away from the past."

"But Hugh, I don't want to leave Triford I was born here."

"Maureen," he said, turning to look at me. "Maureen, let's go somewhere and start again, away from both our families, away from all the bad memories and the pain. Let's find somewhere that we can apply for adoption again and no one will tell us that we can't. Let's buy our own house. We've got enough for a deposit. We can take out a mortgage for the rest. I can't bear being weighed down by everything that's happened. I want a family too." He slumped down on a low wall at the edge of the car park and started to cry.

"Not here, Hugh. Let's go home." It was the first time he'd broken down since Patricia died. I didn't know what to do.

"Think about it, Maureen. What is there here for us?"

"How would you pay the mortgage without a job?"

"I'll get a job somewhere new. You could go back to teaching. We could have a fresh start."

"But Patricia's here."

"Maureen, we need a new start. We can visit her. Think of all the bad memories that are here."

"Where would we go?"

"I don't know. A long way away. Anywhere I can find a job. Somewhere where nobody knows us and we can start again."

"We could get a map out and stick a pin in it."

Hugh went quiet.

"What are you thinking?"

"It might be nothing, love."

"What?"

"It's one of our suppliers. I was on the phone to them the other day, to their Finance Director and he jokingly said they needed an accountant. Except, he wasn't joking. I laughed at the time but I could always ring him."

"Where are they?"

"I'm not sure. Somewhere up north."

"Do I have to tell you now?"

"Take as long as you like, love. There's nothing to stop me ringing him tomorrow to see if he was serious."

"Ok. I'll think about it."

CHAPTER 19

Billingbrook. Saturday 6th October

They were awoken by ringing. "What time is it?"

"I've no idea. Where's the phone?" Deep in sleepy confusion, Lisa found it under a newspaper on the side where it always lived. "Hello."

"Hello, Lisa. It's your cousin Sylvia in Australia."

"Sylvia?"

"Julie's mum."

"Oh sorry, yes of course. Wow, how great to hear from you. What time is it there?" She mouthed to Pete that it was Australia calling and he sat up in bed.

"It's 7.15 in the evening, on another beautiful day."

"Have you found something out? Is there some news?"

"No sorry, love, I should have realised that would be what you'd assume and maybe emailed you first."

"Right," Lisa felt deflated. "I thought you might have found something about Uncle Laurence."

"No, dear. I don't think I'd ever heard of your Uncle Laurence and it was your Mum's side of the family that Julie was researching. It's just that I haven't been able to stop thinking about how this must all feel for you and I want to do something to help. For a long time, I've been looking for an excuse to visit England. I feel too far away over here, so I'm coming over."

"Wow. I mean when?"

"I hope it's O.K. I've already booked my flight. I looked at the map and it seemed Manchester would be the best place to fly to."

Lisa felt a burst of excitement. "Yes, that's much nearer than flying to London." She mouthed to Pete that Sylvia was coming to England.

He mouthed back "What about Julie?"

"Is it just you coming?" Lisa asked before Sylvia was able to go on with the explanation.

"Yes at the moment it's just me. Susie has school so Julie's tied here, apart from which she can't leave the business for long. She's trying to arrange some cover so that she can come when Susie's on holiday, if I'm still over there by then."

"When are you coming?"

"I shall arrive at 8.00 on Tuesday morning."

"Tuesday! What this Tuesday?"

"Oh dear, is there a problem? Once I get an idea into my head."

"No, it's fine. It's just such a surprise. I'll be at work but..."

Pete waved his arms to attract her attention.

"Hang on a minute."

"I could take Tuesday off. I've got the holiday I carried forward that I need to use up," said Pete who was now looking almost as excited as she felt.

"Pete can pick you up. You can stay in my spare room, if that's O.K.?"

"That would be lovely, darling. I'd better get on and sort myself out. I'm going to bring the tape that was recorded over with me. A friend of mine suggested we might be able to go to an expert who can help us find whether any of the original message can be salvaged. We may as well do that there, there isn't time before I come and it would be good to know as soon as possible. I'll get Julie to send you an email with the details of the flight. See you on Tuesday."

"Yes, see you then. Have a good flight." Lisa put the phone down and stayed sitting where she was. "Wow. She's not even my real cousin and she's prepared to fly all this way to help me."

"We could do with a fresh pair of eyes to look at this. Someone must know something, but I'm blowed if I know what we ought to be doing next."

"Me neither. Maybe we should do something else for the weekend and leave all this until Sylvia arrives. If we go through it all with her, then maybe we'll have some new ideas. I just feel as though we're going round in circles."

"So what do you want to do?"

"Get ready for Sylvia arriving for a start. I need to make up the spare room and do some shopping. I could do with cleaning this place too. I'm not used to having visitors."

"Except me."

"You don't count as a visitor. You belong here," and she scrambled back into bed to be close to him.

***

Manchester Airport. Tuesday Morning 9th October

It was a damp drizzly, autumn morning when Pete headed for the airport. It was still dark when he left and developed into the sort of day that was never going to become completely light. The Arrivals Hall was warm and cosy in comparison and the bustle of travellers coming to and fro had a vibrance that was in stark contrast to the day.

Pete stood and watched the emotional reunions and business-like meetings that were taking place all around him. He was holding a sign that read 'Sylvia (Julie's Mum & Lisa's sort of cousin)' and had secured himself a spot in full view of the opening doors, right up by the barrier.

A lady pushing a trolley full of luggage came towards him. "Are you Pete?"

"Yes, that's me. Are you Lisa's cousin?"

"Yes," she said giving him a big hug. "I thought I was never going to get here. That's an awfully long time to be stuck on a plane."

"Sorry, I didn't know your surname. I forgot to ask Lisa before I left and I realised when I got here that I had no idea who I was looking for and that I needed a sign."

"I'm quite used to being known as 'Julie's Mum', although it usually went with her being in trouble for something. A parent would appear at our house and start the conversation with, 'Are you Julie's Mum?' I'd always know it was bad news." They both laughed.

Pete took the trolley and led the way towards the car park. "I expect you're tired aren't you?"

"Not too bad. I had some sleep on the flight, although now my body thinks it's night time again. I might just have a short nap when we get home, to keep me going."

"Well, welcome back to Blighty."

"I always planned a trip back sometime. I just didn't expect these to be the circumstances. Where have you got up to? Have you found anything out yet?"

"Nothing new. I think Lisa was hoping to go through it all when she gets home later, as long as you're not too tired."

"I'm sure I'll be fine. Why don't you tell me some more about you and about Billingbrook?"

"Well, I'm Pete and Billingbrook is where we live. That's about it."

"Nonsense! Now give me the unexpurgated version."

***

Billingbrook. Tuesday night 9th October

Lisa came through the door to the smell of dinner cooking and the sight of a table laid for three with candles lit and wine poured out ready. "I could get used to this. Am I pleased to see you?" Lisa gave a broad smile as she addressed the woman who was hurriedly getting off the settee to greet her.

"And you must be Lisa. I am so pleased to be here." She enveloped Lisa in a huge hug as an aproned Pete came out of the kitchen with a wooden spatula in his right hand.

When she had escaped from Sylvia's greeting she gave Pete a hug and a kiss, steering well clear of the cooking utensil. Pete handed her a glass of wine.

"We ought to fall out more often, if this is what happens," she said kissing Pete again.

"Don't push your luck," he said grinning.

"How was your flight?" She sat herself down on the settee next to Sylvia whilst Pete went back into the kitchen to finish preparing dinner.

Dinner was out of the way by the time anyone mentioned the investigation.

"I might see something that you two have missed. Why don't you go through everything and I'll chip in with questions as you go along?"

"I'll make some notes of any ideas that come up," said Pete getting up to fetch paper. He hesitated, "If that's O.K. with you Lisa?"

"It's O.K. Pete. I'm not going to bite your head off for

taking over." She went and gave him a hug, "But thanks for asking." Then she turned to Sylvia, "We had a bit of a disagreement about the way things were going, but we've sorted it out now."

"I'm not surprised. This whole process must be very stressful. I'm used to Jules shouting at me, so if you do need to let off steam, I'm not about to take it personally."

"Thanks, Sylvia." Lisa leant over and gave her a hug. "Shall we sit somewhere more comfortable? Are you sure you're not too tired tonight?"

"I'm fine. Besides I was rather hoping we might find some loose ends that I could start helping with tomorrow."

"O.K." said Lisa beginning, "we know that I'm not Patricia Lisa Forster. She died and we have her death certificate so we know she was the same child. We know that I grew up in Billingbrook from when I was quite small, but we don't know if I was born here. We know I wasn't adopted from the Triford Adoption Agency, although we do know that Maureen and Hugh did apply to them to adopt a baby, but were turned down."

"Really? That's news to me." Sylvia shook her head.

"The other thing we've found out is that Hugh had a brother Laurence who nobody seems to know about. He turned up when I was about seven and had some big argument with my parents."

"Have you managed to find out where he is now?"

"No."

"So that's something we could follow up."

"The Adoption Agency said it would be worth checking the court records, as they cover all adoptions. I don't know how we go about that."

"I suppose that's something I could have a go at,"

Sylvia offered.

"It makes it harder," said Pete "that we don't know which court the adoption took place in. It might have been Triford or it might have been Billingbrook."

"Could it have been anywhere else?" said Sylvia looking thoughtful.

"What do you mean?" asked Lisa.

"Well, is it down to where the parents live or where the child comes from that determines the court it's in?"

"Oh, I see what you mean. If it's the child then it could have been through any court anywhere."

"Not quite any court," said Pete. "It would at least have to be the Family Court rather than say the Criminal Court."

"I think we assumed that," said Lisa, smiling.

"Have you thought about using the newspaper?" Sylvia asked.

"We put an ad in the Stockport paper to find Mum and Dad's neighbours. Other than that I don't know what we could do."

"You could always get them to run a story about what you're doing and ask anyone with information on you or Laurence Forster to come forward."

"Maybe this is how you'll become famous," said Pete, laughing.

"I don't think that was quite what I had in mind when I said that. I suppose we could. I'm not sure I want my life plastered across the newspaper."

"No, I can see that. It's something to think about." Sylvia patted Lisa's hand.

"I could take tomorrow afternoon off to help if you need me."

"I'm sure I'll be fine, thanks. I can get Lisa to call you if

I get stuck."

Lisa got up and went to the door with Pete.

"Someone somewhere knows who you are. I'm sure of it. We're going to find the answer." He hugged her. "I think Sylvia's as determined as we are. Goodnight, beautiful." He touched her cheek with his finger and then gave her a long, lingering kiss.

"Do you have to go? Couldn't you stay?"

"I've been out all day. I do need to get back to feed Toffee. I'll come over after work tomorrow, or maybe we could all go out."

"I'll ring you to let you know what we're doing." Lisa stood leaning against the doorway, watching him go to his car. As he turned before he got in she blew him a kiss, before closing the door and going back to Sylvia.

"Can I get you some more wine?"

"That would be wonderful," said Sylvia, stretching out her legs. "He's all right. He quite suits you."

"You sound like my mum... well, like Maureen anyway. It's funny I know you're Sylvia but... well, you're not actually my cousin are you?"

"Well, I'm not a blood relative, but you're as much a cousin now as you were before. To me, anyway. Are cousins anything more than people with labels? Do they feel any connection? Other than a shared history they often don't even know about."

"Oh, I don't know. I've thought so much about things like that in the last few weeks. I keep going in circles. They say you choose your friends but you can't choose your family, but in some ways I feel as though I'm having to choose both. It's either that or have no family."

"I don't know all the things that happened in our family over the years. I sure had enough of my own fallings out. Your Aunty Elizabeth never approved of Barry, my ex-husband. That's why we got married the day after my eighteenth birthday. None of the family came. We didn't even tell them until we'd done it. I'm not in touch with any of Barry's family now; they were relatives for as long as I was married to him. Of course, they are still related to Julie, though she doesn't hear much from them, but they aren't related to me anymore. I know I only found out you existed a few weeks ago, but I like the idea that I have a cousin, even if you aren't."

"In a funny way, I could do with Mum being around right now. I know that if she were here then I could get all the answers I need, but I mean in the sense that even as an adult there are times you just need your mum, someone to take care of you and listen to you."

"If Maureen was anything like her sister, you'd be lucky if she would just listen."

"It's difficult to admit right now, I feel a lot of anger and confusion, but in reality she was a good mum. She did used to listen and never judged me. She and Dad always encouraged me to fulfil my dreams. I miss them. All of this has made it feel as though I've lost them all over again."

"I know you hardly know me, but I feel a responsibility to try to fill the gap for you. You can tell me to butt out if you want to, but I'd like to offer the support you need. I know you've got Pete, but…"

"That's different. Pete's great, but it isn't like talking to your mum."

Sylvia got up and went to get something from her bag. When she came back she was carrying a CD. "I thought you might like to listen to this. You don't have to do it now if you don't want to. It's one of the tapes I told you about. I got it copied for you. There's just a short bit where Maureen is on the tape. She must have called when they were doing it. There's not a lot, but I just thought you might like to hear her voice."

"Oh, Sylvia, is it Mum? I don't know if I can face listening to it or not."

"It's up to you. I'll leave it here for you to decide. Even if they did adopt you, they most certainly loved you. They were good people, Lisa. If they didn't tell you, they must have had a good reason."

"I know. I've been thinking about that. It may not have been quite the childhood I thought it was, but it was still happy. I always felt that I was loved, there was never any doubt about that and I always loved them. I keep telling myself that nothing needs to change, but I can't just leave it."

"Well, tomorrow I'll see if I can do anything useful to help."

"Thanks, Sylvia. I think I need some sleep. I'm going to leave listening to the CD until another time. I don't think I can face it now."

"Good night, dear. I'd better get myself off to bed too. My body clock is starting to wake up again; all this wine should help."

Lisa lay in the darkness thinking about what was happening to her. Was this what trust was all about? Should she put her trust in Hugh and Maureen and know that their reasons would have been good ones? Perhaps it was best that she didn't find Uncle Laurence. Perhaps she should just accept that she was Lisa Forster and get on with her life. She rolled over and tangled her foot in the duvet, which was now at right angles to where it started.

She sat up and turned on the bedside light. Sleep just

wasn't happening. She could have counted all the flocks on the Welsh hillsides, let alone the sheep around Billingbrook. She slipped her feet into her sheepskin slippers and picked up her dressing gown.

She went downstairs trying not to wake Sylvia, then went into the lounge and closed the door. The CD was still sitting on the side where Sylvia had left it. She put it into the player and turned the volume to a low setting. Most of the speaking was by her Aunty Elizabeth and Uncle Andrew. There was a bit with Granny Richardson, but none of them were people she had known. She listened to the inflections in Aunty Elizabeth's voice and smiled as they reminded her of her mum and then, there she was, Maureen. Lisa gasped and replayed that section of the CD. As she heard her mum sending greetings to all those in Australia she felt the tears fill and overflow her eyes. Maureen didn't say much, but it was the voice she missed hearing every day of her life. She longed for her mum to be there in the room with her, talking to her in person rather than from the hifi.

Lisa was engrossed in her grief. She sat on the floor replaying the half minute of the CD over and over, whilst the tears streamed down her face. When Sylvia knelt down beside her she jumped, but then welcomed the arms that wrapped around her and held her tight while she sobbed for the loss of a mother and of the certainty and security that had always gone with being her parents' child.

CHAPTER 20

Billingbrook. Wednesday 10th October

It was a struggle for Lisa to get up for work that morning. She was tired and still more than a little emotional from the night before. She was surprised to find Sylvia already up and in the kitchen.

"I thought you might appreciate your breakfast being ready. How did you sleep in the end?"

"Not too badly," said Lisa although she was conscious from her quick look in the mirror that the black bags under her eyes told a different story. "I'm sorry that I've got to go to work. We might have achieved more together."

"I'll be fine. It'll be quite an adventure as long as I can find the places I'm looking for."

"You can always look them up on the computer. If you're in town, you could use the ones in the library. There's usually at least one of them free," Lisa poured some cereal into a bowl. "We could go somewhere for lunch. Maybe I could show you a bit of Billingbrook?"

"That would be great." Sylvia hesitated. "At some point, I would like to go up to the cemetery, but perhaps we'll do that another day."

Lisa nodded.

A-Z in hand and armed with the tape that Julie had recorded over, Sylvia headed for the security firm who offered forensic disclosure. The internet site said it was possible from disc, but said nothing about whether the same might be true of tape.

"I'm sorry," said the assistant who greeted her. "We can enhance an audio recording, but once you've taped over it, there's little we can do. Now if it had been a disc…"

"As you can see, it's not a disc. Thank you." Sylvia turned and left.

Once outside, she looked at the A-Z. It wasn't clear which courts were located in Billingbrook itself, but Sylvia went in search of the building marked on the map.

It was an imposing structure, although modern, with a wide flight of steps leading up to the main entrance. Before she even reached the reception desk, she was confronted with a sign which said 'Security' and she had to put her bag through the machine whilst she went through a separate metal detector.

Once inside, there were various signs pointing to the Probate Office, the Magistrates Court and the cafeteria. Sylvia approached the reception desk where there were already a couple of people waiting. One was neatly dressed in a suit, shined shoes and carrying a smart leather briefcase, whilst the other was tattooed, sporting extensive body piercings, wearing torn jeans and a tatty t-shirt. They were not together.

When Sylvia's turn came she started to explain the situation. "I need to know where I can look at the records of the Family Court from thirty years ago. I may need more than the Billingbrook records. Can you help me, please?"

The man at the desk was brusque in reply, "We don't have public facilities here, Madam."

"Can you point me in the right direction, please?"

"You might try the Family Court."

"I'm sorry, I thought that might be here too. Can you tell me where I can find it?"

The man's pager went off and he immediately checked the message. Without so much as a word to Sylvia he moved away from his position to the phone at the side of the desk. He then walked away from reception leaving Sylvia waiting.

"Well, really!" Sylvia muttered as she was left alone.

It was a few minutes later when a lady arrived and rather more cheerfully said, "How can I help you?"

Sylvia began her explanation again. This time she included a bit more information on what she was trying to do.

"Just wait here a moment, I'll see if I can find one of our clerks to help you. We don't have all the paper records here, but we do have computer access to all the case information."

"Thank you so much," said Sylvia, "I'll certainly wait." She stepped to the side of the counter and looked around.

She had only been there about five minutes when a fresh faced young man came down the corridor towards her. He looked at the lady behind the desk, who indicated to Sylvia.

Once again she told Lisa's story, whilst she was talking the man directed her down the corridor and into his office.

"What date range do you need to check between?"

Sylvia hesitated, "I don't think we need to look before about January 1977 or after around 1980. Can you search on as wide a date range as that?"

"So Jan 1977 to Dec 1980?"

"Yes, that should more than cover it."

"And what name am I looking under?"

"Forster, Hugh and Maureen Forster."

The man started to input information and then asked Sylvia one or two more questions before sending a search to the database. "I'm sorry there's nothing here. There's an adoption by Joseph and Penny Forster in London and there's another one in Leeds, but there is nothing at all for Hugh and Maureen Forster between those dates."

"Would all adoptions be on there?"

"All that were done through the courts."

"Right." Sylvia sat for a moment and then said, "Well, thank you for your time. It was very kind of you to help."

"I'm sorry I haven't found anything for you."

"Yes, so am I. The whole thing is making no sense. Somebody must know what happened." She got up and with her head down, walked away from the court.

She emerged into the daylight. There were still two hours until she was due to meet Lisa. The cemetery was quite close. She set off in that direction.

It took her a while to find the grave of Maureen Forster. "So there you are, Aunty Maureen. A fine mess you seem to have left behind. What's going on? How am I supposed to be able to help Lisa? You seemed such a normal aunt, so level-headed." She stood looking at the grave. "There must be somebody somewhere who knows what happened. Is it something to do with this Laurence, Uncle Hugh's brother? I can start to see why people go to psychics or whatever they're called. I could do with you telling us something. How could you keep something like this so secret?" She shook her head and went to look for Uncle Hugh's grave. After she'd found it, she spent some time wandering round the graveyard reading all the inscriptions. Then with time to spare she headed off in search of the library.

Lisa was working in the Reference department that day and had no idea that Sylvia had already arrived. She went to the foyer in time to meet her for lunch and was surprised to see her come from the door to the Lending Library rather than in from the road. "You should have told me."

"That's O.K., I wanted some time to think."

"That sounds ominous. Have you had a good morning?"

"I don't know. That's what I wanted to think about. I wanted to work out what it all meant."

As they talked, Lisa led the way out of the library and towards a small Italian Restaurant on the corner of the next side road. "Billingbrook isn't blessed with many good eating places." They went in to Frascati's where Lisa had already rung ahead and booked a table. It was in the window giving them a good view of all the passing people on the main road. "This one's new. I haven't tried it before but some of the others came here from work last week and said it was good."

After they sat down, Lisa said, "Have you reached any conclusions?"

"What about?" Sylvia was already looking at the menu.

"About what your morning means. Tell me everything."

"Let's order some food first and maybe some wine and then I'll tell you what I've done."

"I don't normally drink at lunchtime."

"It's up to you, but I think you might be glad of a glass of wine."

"That bad is it?" Lisa looked serious. "Do you know who I am?"

"No. I'm no closer to that."

Lisa let out a heavy sigh, "O.K. we'll order first."

She chose the spaghetti bolognese and Sylvia chose the cannelloni. They also ordered half a carafe of the house white wine, which was brought to their table almost immediately and placed on the blue and white checked table cloth.

Sylvia poured them each a glass and began her account. "I took that tape into a little place here that I thought may be able to recover the previous recording, but as it turns out, they can't."

"Right. I shouldn't say this to you, but how could Julie be so careless?"

"I said something like that to her as well. I suppose at the time we had no idea it would be significant. It's as much my fault as hers."

"I'm getting used to disappointment."

"That's a good job."

"Oh, no, why?"

Sylvia took a deep breath. "I've been to the Court."

"And?" said Lisa grabbing Sylvia's hands.

"I'm sorry, love. They couldn't find any record of an adoption."

"You mean in Billingbrook?"

"No, I mean anywhere."

"Nothing?" Lisa felt as though she had been kicked. "Nothing at all?" she could feel her eyes filling with tears and wiped them with her serviette.

"Nothing. I searched for the whole of the time from Jan 1977 to Dec 1980. It couldn't be outside that date range, could it?"

Lisa thought for a moment. "I didn't ask Triford Adoption Agency what date they turned the application down. I presume any actual adoption must have been after that. As for a latest date, I don't know. In the photo album, there's a family holiday picture of me as a toddler with Mum and Dad at Lulworth Cove in June 1980. At least, I presume it was me. I suppose it's possible that the whole thing was faked later, but even then they would have needed a photo of them with a small child at about the right time. I don't know what to believe any more."

"We still don't know if there might have been some private arrangement that didn't go through the court," said Sylvia passing Lisa a tissue. "And we still don't know who Uncle Laurence is. Have you thought any more about going to the newspaper?"

"I've thought of little else," said Lisa wiping her eyes. "I don't know. I'm still hoping something will turn up. What are you going to do this afternoon?"

"I don't know. I'm feeling quite tired. I think the jet-lag has caught up with me a bit. I might just go back to your house, if that's O.K."

"Yes, of course it is." Lisa looked at her watch. "I haven't got time to take you now, but the bus goes from just over there." She pointed out of the window to a row of stops opposite.

***

Billingbrook. Wednesday evening 10th October

"You've got to go to the paper." They were going through the events of the day. Pete had listened to Sylvia recounting the details of her trip to the court. "It's the only thing we've got left. That and Uncle Laurence." He put down the letter that Lisa had received that day from Violet Connors at the Child Benefit Agency. "This is all very odd. They aren't saying that their records don't go back that far. What they're saying is that they do have records, but there was no Child Benefit being paid."

"Mum and Dad never claimed any Child Benefit for me. Why wouldn't they do that?"

"When you start to look at that and the fact that there's no record of the adoption, it makes it look as though for whatever reason, none of this went through official channels. I even started to understand why people might go to a psychic today. I didn't mention that I called into the cemetery. I guess I was looking for inspiration. I'm sorry. I should have told you earlier."

"That's O.K. Just because I can't face the cemetery, doesn't mean you have to stay away. I don't feel as though any of this belongs to me. Whoever me is! What would we say if we went to the paper?"

"Would someone like to be my parents?"

"Pete!"

"Sorry."

"I think you'd have to tell them the whole story," said Sylvia. "I suppose they would guide you on what to say."

"I don't want it to be sensationalised."

"That's always the problem," said Pete, being serious for a minute. "The papers always look for some angle to make it interesting to readers. The stories when Dad was killed in the car crash gave no thought to the family."

"Oh, Pete! I'm sorry. I had no idea." Lisa put her arms around him. She looked at him, feeling real concern. For a moment, her troubles seemed insignificant.

"It's not your fault." He looked away. "I've never told you before. Anyway," said Pete getting up and walking round the room, "let's keep this focussed on you."

Sylvia nodded at Lisa and then said, "I think the

papers will find this is interesting enough without looking for an angle. It's up to you Lisa, but I don't know what else we could do. They may have information on Laurence Forster as well."

"We could ask," said Lisa who was starting to weaken. "I can't leave things as they are and I can't see what else I can do."

"When are you free to go?" asked Sylvia, "I could always go in tomorrow and ask if there's someone who could talk to us after you finish work."

***

Billingbrook. Thursday 11th October

Sylvia had no difficulty in getting the newspaper interested in the story. She spoke to the news desk who said they would be more than happy to run a piece in the next available edition. She arranged to go back to the offices as soon as Lisa finished work so that they could run through the facts.

"There's one other thing," said Sylvia as she was about to leave. "Do you have any way to check your records for the last thirty to forty years, to see if there are any stories about a Laurence Forster, born about 1938?"

"Yes, sure. All our archives are now on computer. I'll have someone take a look and see if I can get something by the time you come in later."

Lisa was fidgeting with her bag as she and Sylvia headed for the newspaper. She had passed the offices of the Billingbrook Mercury often enough, but with the exception of placing the death notices for her parents, she had no cause to go in. It was one of the smaller daily papers, but still did well in Billingbrook itself. The printing of the paper had long since moved to a bigger press away from the town, but all the other activities concerning editorial, advertising and newspaper sales continued to take place at the original location in the centre of town.

It was past six when Sylvia and Lisa arrived and the main doors of the building were closed to the public. They went to the manned security entrance and rang the bell, as Sylvia had been instructed to do earlier. They were expected and it wasn't many minutes before the reporter was showing them through to a meeting room on the editorial floor of the building.

"I'm Andrew Sutherland," he said, shaking Lisa by the hand.

"Lisa Forster," she said. "Well at least I am as far as I know." She laughed nervously and the others joined in.

"O.K." said Andrew, "Sylvia has outlined the story. Why don't you run through things and tell me a little bit about yourself and your parents and we'll take it from there?"

"What sort of stuff do you want to know?"

"Oh things like, where you went to school, where your parents worked, where you lived, anything that might jog people's memories."

Lisa did her best to comply and every so often Andrew would ask a question, "What hobbies did your parents have?"

"Dad used to paint, watercolours mainly and he liked his gardening. Mum liked crosswords and reading. Nothing very exciting."

The reporter took notes for about half an hour and then said, "I think that gives us enough to be going on with. By the time I get chance to do a little research myself and write this up, I think it will be Saturday before it appears. Is there a number I can call you on, if I have any other questions?"

Lisa gave him her mobile number. "I don't suppose you found anything about Uncle Laurence did you?"

"No, sorry. There's no mention of his name in our archives at all. I took the liberty of searching for your parents' names too. I found a piece on your mum retiring from the college."

"I think I've already got a copy of that amongst Mum's papers."

"This may generate some calls from the public. We often do very well on this type of story."

"Thanks."

Lisa and Sylvia headed towards Pete's house, where he was cooking dinner for them all.

"You know," said Sylvia as they drove away from the newspaper. "We might be doing this in the wrong place."

"What do you mean?"

"Well, maybe it should be the Triford paper we go to. They're more likely to have something on Laurence Forster. We don't know he ever had anything to do with Billingbrook."

"We know he visited my parents when I was seven."

"Yes, but we don't know that he ever lived here."

Lisa thought for a moment. "So what you're saying is that we ought to go to Triford and see if the paper there will do some research."

"We could ring them first, maybe when the story comes out here in Billingbrook."

"I'd quite like to go back down there, as long as Pete can come too. I'd like to have more positive memories of going there with Pete than I have at the moment. I wonder if I can get any time off next week. At least with the story going into the paper, I may as well explain to my boss what this is all about. He might be a bit better about me taking time off then."

***

Billingbrook. Saturday 13ᵗʰ October

The story came out on Saturday.

"I can't read it. Tell me what it says." Lisa handed the paper to Pete.

"'Local Girl in Identity Search' is the headline. It's not a bad photo."

"They came and took that at work yesterday. I was glad I'd already told Derek what was going on. I'm already getting an idea of the sort of responses I'll get. 'Oh, poor you', 'Oh, how dreadful'. I just wanted to bury myself under a stack of books."

"At least it means they're on your side. I shouldn't imagine there's a person out there who wouldn't help you if they could." Sylvia was settling in well as a mother hen figure, making them cups of tea and coffee and taking care of both Lisa and Pete. Lisa was enjoying having a surrogate parent and as she'd said to Sylvia earlier, she had as much of a right to mother her as anyone else seemed to have.

"Go on, Pete, read it out."

"Local girl Lisa Forster (30)."

"Why do they always do that? I might have wanted to keep my age secret."

"Well, in this case, I can see a good reason. It's part of the information people might need in order to help you." Sylvia put the tea down on the side and went to carry on making lunch.

"…talked exclusively to the Mercury about her recent discovery that her birth certificate is for a baby who died nearly thirty years ago," Pete continued.

214

"They have made it sound sensational then." Lisa groaned.

"I suppose they had to, to some extent, to make it interesting," Sylvia said.

"Why don't you read it for yourself?" said Pete passing Lisa the paper. "At least the contact email and phone number they gave are for the journalist and not for you. We aren't at risk of hearing from loads of cranks."

"I don't mind cranks as long as they've got some information," said Lisa taking the paper from him.

She read the piece through. It was on page three of the paper in quite a prominent spot. Not quite front page but near enough. She wondered what her work colleagues would have to say on Monday. It had been bad enough yesterday, when one or two of them knew. She wished she could have taken the whole of the following week off, but it was hard when they were so stretched and besides she had a limited amount of holiday to play with. Friday would have to do. This time they would be going to Triford in her car, but she had conceded to staying in the nice hotel away from the town again.

CHAPTER 21

Triford. Friday 19th October

"Welcome to the last chance saloon," said Pete as they drove into Triford.

"Oh, Pete!" both Lisa and Sylvia said at the same time and then giggled. It was hard for Lisa to believe that she and Sylvia were not related, given how well they were getting on. She wondered whether Julie was as much like Sylvia as she was.

"Well let's face it, girls," Pete said, winking at Sylvia, "we have now officially tried everything else."

It was amazing that despite the constant setbacks they were all in such good spirits.

"We haven't even had any crank calls."

"That's because they called the newspaper," Lisa replied.

"It was a shame we didn't get anything from the tape, but then I suppose it was a long shot. I don't know why it didn't occur to me then, just how precious it was to be able to hear the voices of past generations, quite apart from the information it might have contained."

"Don't blame yourself, Sylvia. No one was to know just how vital that information might be. Besides, given there doesn't seem to be any trail as to what happened, I can't believe Mum would have given all the answers on that tape."

"No, I suppose not, love. I just wonder whether it would have helped."

The Triford Gazette was much smaller than the Billingbrook Mercury. It was a weekly rather than a daily paper and its offices felt as though they were stuck at least thirty years ago. Lisa had already spoken to them by phone to make sure they were interested and had sent them a copy of the story from the Billingbrook paper.

They were ushered through from reception into a small meeting room, where a wiry gentleman with a wizened expression soon joined them. "Hello," he said, his voice in complete contrast to his face. "I'm Henry Snelgrove, the Deputy Editor."

As soon as the introductions were out of the way Mr Snelgrove turned to Lisa, "Can I just start by saying how dreadfully sorry I am for the difficulties you're facing. I've been thinking about it a great deal since you called and I would just like to assure you that the paper will do anything we can to help."

"That's very kind of you, thank you. If you can find anything out for me, I'll be extremely grateful."

Henry Snelgrove went over much the same material that they went through with the Billingbrook newspaper, but then asked what they knew about the family from the time they lived in Triford.

"Not a lot," said Lisa. "Sylvia might be able to tell you more about the rest of the family, but we don't know a lot about Hugh and Maureen. I suppose we do know that they were turned down by Triford Adoption Agency and we know that their real daughter, Patricia, died here when she was just a few months old. I've got their old address."

"My parents were still living here in those days," Sylvia added, "Elizabeth and Andrew Summers.

Although my grandfather John Richardson had died just before that, in 1976, my grandmother Margaret Richardson, lived here until she died in 1982." They gave Mr Snelgrove as much detailed information of names, dates and places as they could and he noted it all down.

"There is one other thing," said Lisa. "We wondered whether you might have any information on file about Hugh Forster's brother? We've come across the name Laurence Forster in trying to put this all together, but he was never mentioned while I was growing up. We wondered whether the newspaper might have anything on him. He was born here in Triford in 1938, but that's as much as we know about him, apart from that he had an argument with my parents when I was about seven."

Henry Snelgrove scratched his head. "I might be able to do a quick search on Laurence Forster while you're here, if you don't mind waiting. I'd also like to get our photographer to take a picture to go with the story if you don't mind."

Lisa looked at the others, who both nodded. "That's fine."

"Right," said Henry Snelgrove. "I'll get one of the team to have a quick look into this and then get someone to take you along to our photographer. I'll come back here as soon as I can. Can I get someone to bring you some coffee?"

It was about forty minutes later when Henry Snelgrove came back to them, clutching several pieces of paper that had been printed out. He ran his finger round his collar and coughed.

"Well, I've found some things on Laurence Forster. I've printed one or two of them off to give you the general idea." He coughed again. "I'm not sure how to put this, but I don't think you're going to be overly happy."

He passed them the sheets of paper.

Lisa felt the colour drain from her face as she read the first one, 'Local Man on Indecent Exposure Charge'. She looked at the date of the story, it was from 1964. She moved it aside and read the next one 'Triford Stalker Jailed for Four Years.' The date for that one was 1979. She couldn't speak, she pushed them over to Pete and Sylvia and with a shaking hand picked up her cold coffee and took a gulp.

"So that's why no one talked about Uncle Laurence and you thought they just had an argument." said Pete. "Phew that's some history to hide from. Are you all right, Lisa?"

She nodded, but still said nothing.

"Mr Snelgrove," Pete said, appearing to choose his words carefully, "You will still run the story for us won't you?"

"Oh good heavens yes. This is all rather unfortunate, but your story is completely separate.

"And in the story you run about Lisa, you won't make any link to this, will you?"

Henry Snelgrove shook his head. "No," he said, "you have my word on that. We aren't the tabloid press here. We pride ourselves on our professionalism. I see no reason for Laurence Forster to ever get mentioned."

"But what do we do if we find Laurence Forster is mixed up in all this somewhere?" Lisa said in a shaky voice.

"Well, we cross that bridge when we come to it," said Henry Snelgrove. "It's possible of course. Would you still want to know if that was the outcome?"

Lisa nodded.

"Right then. The best I can do is to let you see a copy of the story before we go to print. That should at least put your mind at rest. We'll be able to email it to you on Monday. That gives enough time for any changes before we go to press on Tuesday night."

"Thank you," said Lisa as she started to think about what this might all mean. She'd claimed she might be descended from somebody rich and famous, but it had never occurred to her that they might be notorious.

As they walked away, Lisa's shoulders were stooped and her head down. Pete went to catch her up, but Sylvia put her hand on his arm. "Just give her a bit of space."

"But, won't she need a hug?"

"In her own good time. For now she needs to be alone to think."

Lisa walked past the car and onto the main road. "Where do you think she's going?" said Pete.

"Nowhere in particular. She just needs to take it in."

"So what do we do?"

"We stay here until she comes back, or phones us."

"I feel so helpless," said Pete. "Who'd have thought that the bet we had in the pub would lead to this? It's all my fault."

"It's not your fault at all. Whenever Lisa had chosen to trace her family tree it would all have come out one way or another. You might have influenced the timing, but you couldn't have caused the events."

"She must be feeling dreadful. Do you think she's thinking she might be Uncle Laurence's child and Hugh and Maureen brought her up?" Pete leant against the side of the car.

"I don't know what she's thinking. I don't know what to think myself. All those years and our family never knew about Laurence. At least if they did, no one ever told me."

"Do you think they were the only crimes he committed?"

"I doubt it. The sentence he got for stalking was quite a long one. Either the judge was hard or there was more to it than meets the eye."

"It's no wonder Hugh and Maureen didn't want to see him when he turned up in Billingbrook. You don't think he'd come to take Lisa back, do you?"

Sylvia shook her head, "I think you're jumping ahead a bit now. The worst bit is that we may need to find him to get answers."

"The worst bit," said Pete grinning for the first time, "is that the car keys are in Lisa's bag and we don't know how long she's going to be."

"Pete, you are incorrigible."

"Thank you."

"I didn't mean it as a compliment." They both laughed. "Oh dear," said Sylvia. "It doesn't feel right to be enjoying ourselves."

"No, I know. But we can't just stay sombre all our lives."

Pete's phone beeped with a text message and he delved into his pocket to find it. He was all fingers and thumbs trying to press the right buttons. He sighed, "It's O2 telling me how to check the balance on my contract."

It was another half an hour before first Sylvia's and then Pete's mobiles beeped with a message to say that Lisa was in Starbucks, with a request that they join her.

"Thank goodness," said Pete. "I was starting to think she'd gone home."

Lisa was sitting staring into her mug of coffee at a table

as far from the public gaze as she could find. She stood up as they arrived and Pete put his arms round her.

"I just feel numb," she said. "I'm sorry that I walked off and left you. I wasn't thinking straight. I'm still not."

She pulled away from Pete and sat down again. "Shall I get us all a coffee?" Pete said.

"I'm O.K. with this one thanks," said Lisa, nursing the cup that was now almost cold.

Sylvia sat with Lisa while Pete joined the queue.

"Do you want to do anything else while we're in Triford?" Sylvia asked, putting her hand over Lisa's.

Lisa nodded. "I'd like to go to the crematorium to visit my namesake." Then she smiled and looked at Sylvia. "And I'd like to see where you grew up."

"I was kind of hoping you might. I wasn't going to say anything otherwise. It's a long time since I've been back there. I suppose it's changed. It's more than thirty years since we emigrated."

"Have you never been back?"

Sylvia looked down. "I came back briefly when each of my parents died, but they were flying visits with very little sight-seeing. Mum came out to Oz to see us a couple of times."

"I'm honoured, that you've come back for me."

"I'm honoured to be here with you," Sylvia replied, smiling at Lisa.

***

It didn't take long to find the crematorium but the book of remembrance sat in a locked case displaying October 19th.

"This is it then," said Lisa, biting her lip.

"Are you all right?" asked Pete.

She shrugged. "I don't know." She slumped down on a

bench in the garden of remembrance and began to sob. "Somewhere, here, are the ashes of a baby that should have been me."

"No," said Sylvia. "Somewhere here are the ashes of a baby, but you should always have been the person you are. Do you believe in fate? You were always meant to live. It wasn't your time."

Pete moved away to another bench and sat with his head in his hands.

Sylvia put her arms across Lisa's shoulders. "Are you O.K.?"

Lisa nodded, but said nothing. Then she looked up and saw Pete and went over to the bench he was on. "I'm O.K." she said, trying to reassure him. He looked up, the tears running down his face. "Pete?"

"I can't tell you right now. The time's not right." He wiped his eyes with his sleeve and forced a grin. "I will tell you, one day." He put his arms round her and they clung to each other. "One day," he said again.

***

Triford. Wednesday 24th October

"This is Triford Radio bringing you the latest news and views from around the region. We've got an interesting story from today's paper about a girl who's trying to trace her family tree. What makes this story unusual is that she found out that the birth certificate she thought was hers was in fact for a baby that died here in Triford thirty years ago. I've never come across anything like this before, Briony, have you?"

"No, Carl. Lisa Forster, grew up believing that Hugh and Maureen Forster who used to live in Triford, before they moved 'up North' to Lancashire, were her parents. She's now trying to find out if anyone knows anything about her background. So, listeners, if you think you can help why not call our usual

number and we'll pass the information on for you. Maybe we can try to get Lisa on the radio to talk about her search."

***

Billingbrook. Thursday 25th October

It was strange coming home to an empty house. Lisa had got used to Sylvia being around and the sounds and smells of dinner being prepared as she came in, but whilst they waited for any news there had been little she could do, so Sylvia had taken herself off to the nearest big city, Manchester, for the day, to do some shopping and have a look.

The phone was ringing as Lisa came through the door, but it stopped before she could answer it. To her surprise, the message light was flashing that there were five messages. She couldn't remember ever having more than two before and that was when she went away. Her heart was racing as she fumbled to put her bag down and find a pen and paper.

Damn those digital answering machines, she thought as she struggled to hear everything that was being said on the message.

"This is a message for Lisa Forster from Henry Snelgrove at the Triford Gazette. Perhaps you could call me? I'll be here until 6.00." She looked at her watch, it was 5.50, she paused the messages and rang Henry Snelgrove from her mobile.

"Ah, yes, Lisa, thank you for ringing back. We've had a number of calls to the paper since we ran the story yesterday, but there's been one that I thought you might find useful. I have it here somewhere..." There was the sound of rustling paper. "Yes, it's from former neighbours of your parents. They say that they are certain that Hugh and Maureen didn't have a baby when they left Triford."

"Didn't have one?" said Lisa confused.

"Yes, that's right, I've got their details here if you want to give them a call." Lisa jotted them down on the pad and thanked Mr Snelgrove.

"We'll let you know if we get anything else."

Lisa sat back and thought about what he'd just said. If Hugh and Maureen didn't have a baby when they left Triford, and Phyllis and Brian Jones were convinced that they did have a baby when they arrived in Billingbrook, someone must be wrong. Either that or it was the same time they had taken her from Uncle Laurence so that nobody knew the background. She shivered as a chill ran through her. She wished more than anything that she had never started this process, but now that she had it would have to run its course. It looked as though she was going to have to find Laurence Forster.

She pressed the play button on the answerphone and held her breath. The next message began to play. It was a woman's voice that Lisa didn't recognise. "Hello, this is Stella Walton at the Daily Mail. I heard your story on Triford Radio and I want to run a piece in tomorrow's paper. Call any time on …" Lisa sat in disbelief and replayed the message. How had this woman got her number? But then she supposed she was a journalist and it went with the job. The National Press. Lisa played the message for a third time and noted the number down. She wasn't sure whether or not she would return Stella's call. She wanted to talk to Pete and Sylvia first.

The next message started, "Hello, this is Briony Thornton at Triford Radio. We read out the piece from the paper on our show yesterday and were wondering whether we could interview you on air to give our listeners an update on the story? Please call me on…"

Lisa added the number to the pad feeling stunned as the next message began to play.

"Hi, this is Stella Walton again, trying to get hold of Lisa Forster. Please ring me as soon as possible."

Nothing if not persistent. Expecting it to be Stella again, Lisa waited for the final message.

"Lisa, it's me Pete. I've rung the wrong number. I meant to ring your mobile. Speak to you later. Oh, and I love you."

Lisa laughed and pressed the save button.

She was about to get up from the chair when the phone rang again. She hesitated before answering it. She wanted to talk to the others before talking to another journalist. She let the answer machine do its job.

"Lisa, it's Sylvia. I'm just…"

Lisa picked up the phone.

"Oh, you're there."

"Yes, I'll explain later."

"Is there any chance you can pick me up from the station in ten minutes? I seem to have rather a lot of shopping bags."

"I'm on my way." Lisa was glad of the distraction.

Pete was already waiting on the doorstep when she got back. "It would be easier to give you a key." Lisa laughed. "You practically live here anyway."

"Yes, but then Toffee would need a key too," said Pete.

"Don't push your luck. I haven't invited you to move in just yet."

They went in and settled down to a Chinese takeaway and Lisa began telling them about the messages.

"It all seems to hinge on Uncle Laurence. I can't help but think that if we find him then we'll find the answers."

"So what are you waiting for?" Pete asked.

"I don't know whether I want to find Uncle Laurence."

"The *Daily Mail* will probably run the story whether you talk to this Stella woman or not. Wouldn't it be better to put things as you want them? I mean," said Sylvia, "if they can find your phone number, just think what else they could find."

"I guess you're right. It's just," before Lisa had finished, the phone rang again.

"Why don't you answer it?" Sylvia said.

"Hello," Lisa said picking up the handset.

"Yes, I'm Lisa Forster."

"Oh right, you're the one who left the messages." She then ran through the story with Stella, missing out anything about Uncle Laurence.

"They're putting it in tomorrow's paper," she said as she sat back down at the table. She could no longer face the chicken chow mein in front of her and pushed the plate away.

"Is that going spare?" said Pete replacing his own empty plate with Lisa's.

The other two stared at him. "What?"

"Men!" said Sylvia, shaking her head.

CHAPTER 22

Billingbrook. Friday 26ᵗʰ October

"What's it like now you're famous?" Trudy called to Lisa as she walked up the steps into work.

"What?"

"Haven't you seen the paper?" Trudy held out the *Daily Mail* in Lisa's direction.

Lisa could read the headline from where she was. Above a photograph of her was the caption 'Thirty year identity mystery.' "Oh no, where did they get that picture?"

"I've no idea, you look about 18."

"I am, or at least I was in that photo. It was in the Billingbrook Mercury when I won a prize for English at school. I wonder why they didn't use the one the Mercury took for their story?"

"Maybe they thought people would respond better to the picture of a younger you. You'll have to wait to find out if anyone comes forward. Maybe someone will notice a family resemblance or something."

As she went about her work that day, Lisa was conscious on several occasions of people staring at her and being the subject of whispered conversations. It was like that when the story ran in the Mercury, so she knew it would die down again in a day or two. It never ceased to amaze her how quickly people could forget. Normally, that caused a problem with people searching for half-remembered books, or worse, ones they thought they remembered and then got the author and title wrong, but on this occasion it was a reassuring thought.

The afternoon was quiet in the library. Lisa took the opportunity of finding a computer to do some research. What could she find about Uncle Laurence and more to the point, where was he. He seemed to be the key to finding the truth.

There was nothing available under general internet searches. She started to search for prison information, but without knowing whether he was in prison and if so which one, it was impossible to make any progress.

She thought that it would be ironic if he'd changed his name. Given the sorts of crimes he'd been involved in, that seemed quite likely. She sighed. It was probable that Uncle Laurence was on the sex offenders register, so she began to search for that before hitting another brick wall. She could find records for America available to the public but not for this country. She could talk to the police, but that would have to wait.

***

Southingham, Gloucestershire. Friday 26th October

Matt Kirby was sitting with his feet up on the desk eating a sandwich and reading the *Daily Mail*. It was rare for him to get a lunch break and be in the office at the same time. Usually, he went from one appointment for a photograph straight to the next and called back into the *Express*'s offices to download images and pick up an up to date list of the day's jobs. He was often sent new assignments by phone, but he liked to come back in, now and again, to make sure he wasn't missing anything.

He wasn't ambitious. He loved what he did and had

been with the *Southingham Express* man and boy, surviving every change in technology and working practice that successive editors had thrown his way. It wasn't that he hadn't been offered the position of Picture Editor; he had, but he preferred the comparative freedom of life on the open road and settled for the title of Senior Photographer.

"Got a job over Cheltenham way. You could fit it in and still get back for the Southingham Brass Band later," Charlie called to him from the other side of the office.

"Can't Bob go? I've been out all morning, I was just enjoying a bit of a snooze."

"Go on, you lazy good-for-nothing." Charlie came over and prodded him with a ruler. "Bob's out at an accident on the dual carriageway. Head on collision."

"Some people get all the luck. I just get a lousy band to photograph." Matt kicked away from the desk with his feet, using the chair's casters to propel himself towards the bin.

"You might like this one. It's a tip-off that our dodgy councillor is visiting his lady friend. If you can get there in time you might catch them on the doorstep. The caller said he's generally there for a couple of hours."

"You're the boss," said Matt, picking up his camera bag and slinging it over his shoulder. He picked up the paper from the desk, "At least, I'll have something to read while I'm waiting." He waved the *Daily Mail* at Charlie.

"Yeah and don't miss the picture because you're engrossed in the Sudoku!" They both laughed.

Matt sat outside the house, far enough away not to be conspicuous, but close enough to notice any sign of movement. He got his camera set up ready and then placed it on the passenger seat while he went back to the paper. He'd got as far as the headline 'Thirty year identity mystery' when the door of the house opened. He grabbed the camera and took a series of photographs as the councillor backed out with his hood up, kissed a negligee clad figure goodbye and hurried off down the road on foot. Matt followed at a reasonable distance in the car, but lost him down a footpath that led away from the housing. He hoped that with some enhancement back at base the photographs might provide something worthwhile, but from experience, he doubted it.

He parked the car and finished reading the story. He was in no hurry to photograph the brass band. He didn't want to be early. He read another couple of pages of the paper and then set off. He couldn't stop thinking about what it must be like to find you had no idea who you are. Thirty years was a long time for a secret like that to be hidden. In fact, it was as long as he'd worked at the *Southingham Express*. He'd started as a trainee journalist way back in the summer of 1977, when he finished university. He switched to photographer a couple of years later. How must the girl feel? Matt scratched his head. It was an impossible thought.

He couldn't get the story out of his head as he drove back. He felt as though there was something he ought to be remembering, but he didn't know what it was. Something from when he first started. He searched through every crevice of memory he could find the key to, but just couldn't place it. He tried to put it out of his mind and think about other ways of catching the councillor up to no good, but try as he might he couldn't stop thinking about Lisa's story.

Back in the office after photographing the band, Matt had finished trying, unsuccessfully, to enhance the pictures of the councillor, when a thought crossed his mind. He tried to push it out again and looked at the jobs schedule to see if there was anywhere else he was supposed to be. There was nothing else listed for the day so he picked up his stuff to go home. But the thought he'd had was nagging away at him. He needed to follow it up, see if it had legs.

The light was still on in the editor's office. Matt had always got on well with this editor, throughout his now five years of tenure. Matt knew he was well thought of and his previous year's detective work had been generously recognised.

He knocked at Dan McIntyre's door.

"Come."

Dan was a sharp and very astute businessman. Despite his surname he'd been born and bred in Wales and his tone alternated between the soft lilt of the valleys and hellfire and damnation, depending on his mood.

"Hey, Matt, how's it going?"

"Yeah, great. Trying to track down our dodgy councillor for you, but still not having any luck. Dan, I've come to ask a favour."

"Shoot."

"There's a story in the *Daily Mail* today, about a woman who's trying to find out who she is and I've got a hunch."

"What? One of your long lost love children?" Dan laughed heartily.

"No, I think there might be a Southingham connection."

Dan sat up a little straighter. "Go on."

"It's a hunch at the moment. I don't want to say anymore until I've looked into it. What I'm asking for is a bit of time to do that?"

"Matt, you know we don't work on hunches. We work on facts, real stories. I haven't got the resource to let you go gallivanting after hunches. This isn't another spot-the-difference between the photographs. You're a bloody photographer, not an investigative journalist. Admittedly, you're a damn good photographer, but I can't go sending you off on a wild goose chase at the drop of a hat, just because you managed to solve a murder investigation last year. Look, this is the best I can do, you tell me about your hunch and I'll put one of our best people on it. Even then I'm stretching my resources to the limit."

"No deal. If this comes off, it's my story." Matt left the editor's office, pulling the door closed behind him. He wasn't asking for much, just a bit of time to look into it. He went back to his own department and looked at the holiday chart on the wall. It wasn't a question of whether he'd got spare holiday, he'd always got spare holiday. He never took any and that was apart from all the extra shifts he worked at weekends. He needed to see whether there was anyone else off from his department. He ran his finger along the line. This week was half-term, but next week the schools were back and Jo would be in. Now all he had to do was get Charlie to approve his time off and get his jobs rescheduled onto the others.

It was already late and there was no chance of seeing Charlie tonight, so Matt headed home.

"Hi honey, I'm home." He shouted as he went into his haven from the world, near enough to the centre of Southingham for convenience, but close enough to the edge to escape. He'd shouted the same thing every day for the last eleven years, since Caroline left him, taking their daughter with her and every day he hoped to hear her voice reply.

He poured himself a small whisky, conscious that at any moment he might head out again on the trail of the latest crime or other horror in Southingham. He tuned his radio into the emergency services broadcasts and went through to the kitchen. He was always the one to do the cooking, even when Caroline had been at home, so whilst the working hours and the whisky drinking might have increased, at least he wasn't living on takeaways.

It was after dinner before he allowed himself a second whisky and began to make notes of the facts he had so far. He got out a map and looked at where Billingbrook and Triford were. There was no reason to suppose that either place had a connection with Southingham, so why did he have such a strong feeling? Was it just because he was remembering one of the first stories he'd worked on and the timescale was a coincidence?

He tapped the pencil on his pad as he wondered how he could prove or disprove a link without raising anyone's hopes. He was too painfully aware of what it felt like to be separated from a child, but even then he still got to see Rachel occasionally. It was much easier now she was old enough to be independent of her mother. She seemed more understanding of his work as she was training for a career herself. He liked to think that his work over the last couple of years might have had some influence over her choosing a career in law, although in truth she'd already chosen to study the subject at university before Matt became wrapped up in the murder investigation.

He wondered whether it was worth ringing Rachel to discuss his hunch, but decided that his starting point was the *Southingham Express's* archives. He needed to find the story from thirty years ago and see whether there had been any follow up to say that the mystery had already been resolved.

***

Southingham. Saturday 27th October

"Hey, Charlie, what's cooking?"

"You're not on duty today, Matt. Couldn't you keep away again?"

"That's just it, Charlie. After today I do want to keep away. I want to keep away for a week or two."

"What are you talking about?"

Matt pushed the holiday request in the direction of his boss, who had just taken a mouthful of coffee. Charlie spluttered the coffee over the desk and began mopping it with his shirt sleeve. "You, Matt Kirby, asking for holiday! You're not serious?"

"Sure am."

"But I don't remember the last time you took time off. What's up?"

"Just something I want to do."

"It's pretty hard for me to say no, when you're owed more days than there are to the end of the year. But could you not have given me just a little more notice?" Charlie shook his head and signed the form with a flourish. "You'll be the death of me, Matt Kirby, or at least of my career. So are you going to tell me what all this is about?"

Matt shook his head. "Maybe later, Charlie, but then again, maybe not."

He went to his own desk, leaving his boss to finish clearing up the coffee and work out how to reschedule the week's work.

Matt tapped away at his computer, searching for stories that ran thirty years ago. He knew it must have been in his first year at the Express, so he entered a date range of August 1977 to August 1978 and searched. Bingo! Stephen and Felicity Newman. He printed the story and then began to search for any follow up stories over the intervening years. He found very little. There had been an interview done about two years later, but by then the couple had separated. Matt printed out the follow up and added it to his pile.

He searched for the names of Stephen and Felicity Newman in the electoral register and found nothing. It was quite possible that they had moved away or changed their names. He searched on the address that they had lived at thirty years previously, but the house had been knocked down to make way for flats. He sat back and wondered where to go next. It was no good approaching Lisa if he couldn't find the parents and still no good if he found them and they didn't want to know.

He did an open internet search on the names and revealed thousands of hits, but no obvious clue to link any of them to Southingham. He needed someone to bounce ideas off and wondered whether he could get hold of his daughter. He could drive up to Birmingham to see her if she were free. He rang her mobile and got the message service, "Rachel, it's Dad. I wondered if I could buy you a pizza? Ring me."

He packed the print outs into his bag and headed out to the car. As he did so his mobile rang, "Hey, Dad, what's up?"

"Hi, sweetheart. Nothing's up. I just wanted to see my little girl."

"And the real reason?"

"You read me like a book. I need to pick your brain. Are you free later?"

"I could be. What time?"

"I'll be there by four."

"O.K. Do you know where I'm living now?"

"Is it that place I came to last time?"

"No, Dad. That was last year. We're in a house in Edgbaston now." She gave him the address.

"I'm on my way."

***

Birmingham. Saturday 27th October

It was great to see Rachel. She was 5' 9" tall, slim, with symmetrical features and an hourglass figure and even without her intelligence, Matt would have been proud to call her his daughter. She reminded him of all that was best about her mother.

"Whatever happened to student slums?" he asked as he arrived at the house.

"They're so last year." Rachel hugged her dad.

"At least, it's your loan that's paying for it," said Matt as they got into his car. "How's your mum?"

"Is that what this is all about?"

"No," he said. "It's just that I still miss her."

"You want the truth? She misses you too, but she can't deal with the hours you work."

"I know." He felt sad. He knew it was in his own hands to change, but he just couldn't stop himself. He guessed when all was said and done, however much he loved Caroline, he loved his work more. He couldn't blame her for not being able to deal with that.

"So, what is this about?"

"Can't a father want to see his daughter?"

"Yes, he can, but you're not a normal father."

"And you're not a normal daughter." He smiled. They were very alike, which at least meant that Rachel could understand his more extreme tendencies. "Right," he said. "I need to trace a couple who lived in Southingham thirty years ago. I know they split up and I know they must have moved house. What I don't know is where they are now. I've got a strong feeling that the woman won't be far from Southingham, I don't know about the father."

"So why do you need to find them?"

"I don't want to tell you that part at the moment. I might be wrong."

"Dad, is this something dodgy?"

"No, it's a story. It's a good story, but it's just a hunch. More especially I want it to be my story."

"But you can trust me."

"I know that. It's just… well, let me do a bit more work on it first. I want an idea of how I can find the couple."

Rachel thought for a minute. "I suppose you've already searched on the woman's maiden name. It's too obvious to miss."

"Right. Erm…"

"You haven't have you?"

"Er, honestly? No."

"It's a woman thing. It's a way of reasserting your identity if you break up. It's like Mum."

"What do you mean 'like Mum'?"

"Oh, you didn't know? Mum goes under her maiden name now."

Matt felt as though he'd been punched. "And you?"

"I'm still Kirby, Dad. I've always been a Kirby and I plan to stay that way."

"Right." He sat for a while, then said, "So you think I should search for the woman under her maiden name."

"Yes. At least I'd start there. I'll think about what else I'd do and let you know."

As he drove back to Southingham later that day he couldn't help but reflect on the fact that his beloved Caroline had moved on. He shook his head and wondered whether Felicity Newman had moved on too and wouldn't want to re-open old wounds.

***

Billingbrook. Saturday 27th October

"We've got to find Laurence Forster. It's the loose end we've got left." Lisa was enjoying a boiled egg with carefully cut bread soldiers.

"And you say there's nothing on the internet?" said Sylvia as she poured some coffee.

"Nothing I could find. I suppose I could have tried other search engines. We could have a quick look after breakfast."

As they were finishing the phone rang.

"It's Henry Snelgrove," said Lisa cupping her hand over the receiver. Pete and Sylvia sat watching her.

Lisa started waving her arms and mouthing "pen". Sylvia passed one to her and she started scribbling on the pad.

"So sentencing was this week?"

"Did it say where he was taken to?"

"Thank you so much for letting me know."

She whistled as she put the phone down. "You aren't going to believe this, but we've found Uncle Lawrence. That request for a visiting permit that I found on the internet might come in useful after all."

"I hesitate to ask," said Pete, running his finger round his collar. "But do you know what he's done this time?"

"Same sort of thing," said Lisa, shaking her head. "Oh, God, I do hope that I'm not his daughter. To be honest, I think I'd rather not know if I am. After all this, can you imagine the shame of it? They say you love your parents whoever and whatever they are, but this is a circumstance I just can't imagine."

Pete went over to her and took her hands. "I'll still love you whoever you are."

"Really?"

"Nothing he has done affects who you are, unless you want it to. You'll still be my Lisa."

"Thank you. I needed to hear that."

CHAPTER 23

Triford. Late May 1978

God knows, Hugh and I needed that weekend away. The emotion was as raw as it ever had been and there wasn't a day that went by when I didn't spend hours in tears. Almost anything could set me off; the sight of a toy, a photograph, another child, even the colour pink was enough to do it. I was desperate to hold my child. Coming away from Triford felt as though we were leaving her behind, but if we were going to make a new life in Billingbrook then we would have to make the break at some point.

Back in Triford, people would pat my hand and say things like "God willing, you'll soon have another." I wanted to scream back at them "I can't have anymore and who is this God anyway?" Instead, I held it all in until there was no one else around and then I cried. I railed at a God I didn't believe in, a God who'd let me down and whose purpose for me seemed too cruelly twisted for the 'bountiful, caring God' that other people spoke of.

Hugh was always there for me, always supporting me. He was hurting too, but in his pain he could be the rock for me to depend on. He knew how I felt. In his own way, he was desperate too; desperate that we couldn't have another child, desperate that we'd lost the one we had and desperate that he felt it was his fault that we couldn't adopt. In my more rational moments, I thought we were even. My family had killed Patricia and his family prevented us having any more. In my less rational moments, I'm ashamed to say I took my loss out on him. In those times it was 'my' loss rather than 'our' loss. I was the one that could never be a mother.

Although we'd already found the perfect house in Billingbrook and Hugh had a job lined up, there were still another four weeks until we were due to move. It was Hugh's idea to go away for the weekend and we'd found a little guest house in a valley in South Wales so that we could 'get away from it all'. The truth is we couldn't get away from the things that mattered. I'd still spent hours at a time crying. I'd still wanted to scream at the world for how unfair it all was.

We left the guest house on Tuesday morning and decided to go home via Southingham, to do some shopping before the rest of the drive back.

"Will a couple of hours parking be enough?" Hugh asked as he sorted through his pocket for change. "These new machines are so much harder than having a human being to pay," he grumbled. "We could have an early lunch and set off after that."

"O.K." I said, taking my old-fashioned wicker shopping basket out of the boot of the car.

We found a space on the first level of the car park. We didn't bother with the lift and walked down the stairs into the shopping centre below.

The first thing I saw was Mothercare. I just stood looking through the window, with my back to the passing shoppers so that they couldn't see the tears coursing down my cheeks.

"We don't have to stop at all," Hugh said as he put his

arm round me. "We could go straight back to the car."

"No," I said, as I rummaged through my handbag for a tissue to dab my eyes. "I've got to deal with it. Things like this are going to happen all the time."

"I know, love," he said, full of genuine understanding.

"Right," I said, pulling myself together. "What bits of shopping do we need?"

"Why don't we go and get something to eat first and then find a supermarket? I know it's a bit early for lunch, but I think we both need a cuppa."

I nodded and allowed Hugh to find our way through the row of shops to a board showing all the facilities throughout the centre. It wasn't a large place, but there were a couple of cafés on the upper floor, so we made our way there. I didn't look at any of the other shops we passed. I just focused on following Hugh. We found a quiet table in the corner, away from prying eyes.

"What are we going to do, love?" He said, putting his hands over mine.

"I don't know." I fought back more tears. I couldn't go on like this. I was falling apart.

"We've got the move coming up. A fresh start in Billingbrook, but is that going to be enough?"

I shook my head and watched the tears splash on the polished surface of the table. I was grateful that we were out of view of the other customers. "I can't live without children. I can't go on, Hugh."

My life meant nothing without Patricia. I wasn't afraid to die. Killing myself had woven through my thoughts regularly since Patricia died. It was the way to be with her. I would stare at her photograph, feeling her in my arms, imagining day by day the way my baby was growing. I imagined what she weighed; how much hair she had; heard the noises she would make. Did she need new clothes? I'd even bought some of those clothes, ready for her to grow into. I couldn't bear the thought of going on without her.

We'd ordered omelettes, but I wasn't hungry. It's hard to find comfort and flavour in food when you'd rather be dead. At least, my breast milk had dried up now and I didn't have to face the ignominy of producing food for a non-existent baby.

We sat in silence as Hugh ate and I moved the food about my plate.

"We'd better get a move on if we're going to get the shopping done and not overrun our time," he said looking at the clock in the café, which said twelve-fifty.

I nodded and put my knife and fork down. "The toilets are on this floor. I'll go and freshen up a bit, before going anywhere else."

"O.K." he said, "I'll pay the bill; then come along to meet you."

I picked up my handbag and the shopping basket and went along to the toilets.

I wondered why the ventilation was always so inadequate in shopping centre toilets, as I opened the door and was greeted by the stale smell of disinfectant. The wash basins were behind the door and the cubicles were opposite them. There wasn't a lot of space in there and I was glad I didn't have lots of shopping bags as I squeezed into the empty right hand cubicle. I heard someone come in soon after me with a pram. I could hear her, struggling to get it through the door and putting it next to the basins. Then the woman was offering reassurances through the cubicle door to the child, as she went to the toilet. I flushed my toilet and came out and there she was, the most beautiful baby, loosely wrapped in a tiny pink outfit, lying unattended in a pram outside the cubicle.

I had moments to think. I went to the basin to wash my hands. Everything I did must appear normal. I looked in the mirror to check that I didn't look too dishevelled from crying.

I could hear from the noises coming from the cubicle that the mother was going to be indisposed for a little while yet and despite the reassuring voice, she must have been regretting whatever it was she'd eaten.

My heart pounded. My mouth went dry. In that split second, I knew exactly what I was going to do. I started the hand dryer. It emitted a loud whirring sound as the rush of warm air filled the already stuffy room. The noise drowned out all other sound. The tiny sleeping mass was so easy to lift. She didn't stir at all as I picked her up and laid her at the bottom of my empty shopping bag, tucked under her little pink blanket. I restarted the dryer to keep the sound going. Then I put the basket over my arm, straightened up and walked confidently out of the door and back towards the café. Hugh was coming towards me as I approached.

"We're not going to the supermarket. We're going home. Let's go back to the car."

"O.K., love," he said.

We headed for the door at the end of the level that went directly into the car park at the other end from our car. Pushing open the blue swing doors and escaping from the possible gaze of any other shoppers or security was a huge relief. Hugh walked innocently and ignorantly by my side. There was a rustle from my bag as the baby shifted position.

"What was that noise?" Hugh asked looking round.

"Just the wind blowing the litter." I replied pointing to the empty crisp and cigarette packets dancing with some old dried leaves in the corner of the car park. I continued my purposeful walk towards the car.

"You would think they'd take more pride in the place. It doesn't look as though it's been up long."

I have never been so glad that we owned such a mundane and inconspicuous car as I was that day. I put my bag in the footwell between my feet and we set off. It was about five minutes since I'd left the Ladies but by now, someone would have raised the alarm. I was banking on the obvious lack of personnel around the centre meaning it would take the mother a bit of time to get any kind of search organised.

I was willing the baby to stay quiet until we were well away from Southingham. Hugh was going to find out sooner or later, but I wanted enough time to convince him to continue with the plan and not be able to make a snap decision to turn back. I thanked the God I didn't believe in for the soothing effect that cars have on babies, as she continued to sleep. I stole the occasional glance down in her direction, my heart missing a beat every time I looked at that tiny hand clutching the edge of the pink blanket.

We were some distance outside Southingham when I turned to Hugh. "Now I want you to pull over so that I can talk to you, but as soon as I have, we need to start driving again."

"Maureen, what's going on?"

My voice was level. "Don't argue with me. Just pull over as I've asked. I want you to stay calm and listen to me."

"Maureen, you sound as though you're hijacking me." He pulled over without further complaint.

My bag moved between my feet. It wouldn't be long until she woke up and needed feeding. Hugh turned to look at me. "What is it?" He was starting to sound irritated.

"I've done something. I'm sure you won't approve, but I've done it for both of us and I'm not about to undo it." I kept my voice as level as I could, trying to hide my excitement. "It took us so long to get Patricia and then we lost her. We can't have any more of our own and thanks to your brother we can't adopt." I'd thought about what to say. I needed to make sure that Hugh felt as responsible for this as possible. Now was not the time to find him taking the moral high ground and making us go back.

Hugh glanced across at me and then looked away. "Maureen, what are you trying to tell me?"

At that moment a wail erupted from the basket.

"Maureen," he said. The shock was written across his face. "I'm going to drive to the next services. We can make a phone call from there. We can put this right, Maureen. You're ill. They'll understand."

"I'm not ill, Hugh. I know what I've done and if you love me then I want you to be part of this with me. If not, then I'll do it on my own. I'll disappear and you'll never hear from me again."

"Maureen, you can't do that. You'll never get away with it. There'll be people looking."

"Where are they going to look, Hugh?"

"Oh, I don't know. Someone probably saw you. What about the waitress?"

"Hugh, the waitress didn't pay any attention to us. It was more effort than she wanted just to serve us. She was more interested in her finger nails." I stopped. "How did you pay? Cash or cheque?"

"Cash."

I breathed a sigh of relief. "There you are then. No one saw me in the toilets. No one saw me leave with a baby and a couple in a beige Ford Escort is a common sight."

I could tell Hugh was nervous, but I was relying on his placid nature to maintain the calm exterior.

"What about when we get home?"

"We're moving in four weeks. I'll stay at home during that time. Just tell people I'm ill. Tell them I've had a breakdown or something."

"Some would say you have."

"Hugh, this can work. We never told people that we'd been refused adoption. We were too ashamed. In time, when we've moved, we can say she's adopted." I could see him starting to waver as I lifted her out of the basket and rocked her in my arms.

"How old is she?" He glanced across and a smile broke across his lips as he saw me cradling the tiny, fragile bundle.

"I don't know. She looks a bit older than Patricia was before we lost her, maybe five months or so."

"Look, love, I know you want to keep her, but what about her parents? What are they going to be feeling? Besides how are we going to register her for healthcare and school and the like?"

"I don't want to think about her parents. We're her parents now. Our baby died, what about us? As for the rest of it…" I went quiet as I tried to think how things worked. There had to be a way. Once we moved to Billingbrook, how would anyone know? We hadn't seen my family since Patricia died. I couldn't stop seeing them as responsible. Oh, I'd heard all the arguments about how these things just happen and how it was nothing they'd done wrong, but how come it happened on the one night she stayed with them and not on all the nights she was with us? We hadn't seen Hugh's family since the adoption request was declined. We couldn't face them and Hugh knew there was a risk of my saying something I shouldn't. I sat thinking.

"If we call her Lisa we can use Patricia Lisa's birth certificate to register her for things in Billingbrook. Surely, no one will contact anyone in Triford to check? We'll be ok, you'll see."

"Maureen, I don't think I can go through with this."

"Oh, Hugh, please say you can. Otherwise, I'm doing it on my own. You don't want people to know why we can't adopt do you? If I'm in trouble with the police for this, then after your brother's record, they are going to look pretty closely at you, too."

"Are you threatening me, Maureen? Because if you are..." His voice trailed off and I sat wondering what to say next. I knew he was right. I knew there was a huge risk involved, but I also knew that some things were worth taking a risk for and this was one of them.

"I'm not threatening you, Hugh. I'm just telling it as it is. All I want is for us to be a family. All three of us." I bounced Lisa on my knee and she began to gurgle with pleasure. "All three of us," I said again and smiled, the most contented smile I'd felt since we'd lost Patricia. "A family."

CHAPTER 24

Southingham. Sunday 28th October 2007

Matt was asleep in the chair when his mobile rang. The empty bottle of Talisker from the night before was on the table beside him.

"Hello," he said in a distant voice.

"Dad?"

"Yes, who's this?"

"How many people call you Dad?"

"Oh, sorry, Rach, I wasn't with it."

"Dad, have you been drinking again?"

He looked at the empty bottle, "Only a dram."

"Dad! You promised."

"I know it's just…"

"It's what I told you yesterday about Mum, isn't it?"

He was quiet.

"Dad?"

"Yes. Yes it is."

"You've got to move on. It's been a long time. Mum hasn't got anyone else, if that makes you feel better."

"A little. Did you just ring to check up on me?"

"No. I've been thinking. Your woman could have remarried."

"Yes, I was thinking about that. I'm going into work later to see if I can unearth anything."

"Make sure you're sober before you drive. I love you,

Dad."

"You too, Rach."

He looked at the time. It was already past noon. He put some coffee on to brew and went to get cleaned up.

There was one other hardy soul in the *Express's* offices when he went in. Matt didn't bother to speak as he passed on his way to the Editorial Department. Once there, he spread the stories he'd already printed out on the table in front of him and began looking for clues. He realised there must have been other news reports from when the baby was abducted, Sophie her name was. He looked at the picture of Stephen and Felicity holding their newborn baby girl. He logged into the computer and began to search in the archive. He read all the other follow up stories that happened around the time of the abduction.

He dismissed the stories about the improved security in the shopping centre after the event and concentrated on those that covered the family themselves. There were theories put forward by the local police, including one linking it to a similar case in London, two months previously. He began to search for stories about the London abduction. He realised it was possible that Lisa was the child abducted in London, rather than the one taken from Southingham.

He found an article reporting that the body of the London baby had been found on waste ground three months later and took a deep breath. He hoped the same fate had not befallen Sophie. Then a thought struck him, if he was right, was this just a family reunion he was trying to bring about, or a criminal investigation? He wondered how Lisa had ended up where she was, if she turned out to be Sophie. Could the person who brought her up have been the one who took her from the shopping centre or was there someone else involved? He went back to the report on Lisa and read that the person who brought her up had since died. Of course she must have done, otherwise Lisa would have been asking her. He pondered whether it was best to leave things as they were, but hell, there'd be no story if he did. He might be accused of having a caring streak, but the story always won. Occasionally ethics tried to creep in the way of a good story and even then it was more about how he got it, rather than whether he got it at all.

Matt went back to his original search for the parents. He needed to find the marriage record of the Newmans to find out what Felicity had been called before she was married. It never ceased to amaze him how easy it was to get hold of maiden names, given that they were used for security questions. He wondered whether anyone had set up a 'favourite colours' site on the internet, for people to publicly log their preferences to make it even easier for criminals.

It took him ten minutes to find the marriage of Felicity Aldwich to Stephen Newman. He jotted down the information on his pad, then went back to searching for information and stories on Felicity Aldwich. There was no telephone book entry, but the electoral roll provided a hit. He noted down the address and planned to take a trip out to see Ms Aldwich later.

He thought about how he could prove the link between the two and whether there was any way to do it without raising hopes that might later be dashed. He wondered if it would be possible to do a follow up story on how Felicity Aldwich had coped with the years of not knowing what had happened to her daughter and whether there was any way of picking up some DNA evidence that could be tested at the same time. The mother's DNA would be similar to her daughter's. He thought that the first part would be easier than the second. It was too late to turn up on a Sunday evening and he suspected that a Sunday visit might raise too many questions anyway. His best bet was to wait until Monday. In the meantime, he could make contact with Lisa Forster with a view to meeting up and running a story on her.

***

Billingbrook. Sunday 28th October

It had been a quiet weekend in Billingbrook, after the events of the last few weeks. Pete and Lisa took the opportunity to show Sylvia the sights, though as Pete had pointed out, that was not something which would occupy the whole weekend. They went out onto the hills behind the Town and Lisa talked to Sylvia about her childhood. "Do you remember our dog, Spotty? I don't suppose you met him. He was quite a character… I'm starting to believe there must have been a good reason for Mum and Dad's silence."

"Every family has its secrets, love, and it seems that ours might have had one or two more than most, but they were a good lot - with the possible exception of Uncle Laurence."

"I can understand why no one ever talked about him. I'd rather forget about him myself." Lisa was walking arm in arm with Sylvia with Pete walking a little ahead of them. He was quieter than usual. When they caught up with him Lisa was concerned, "Are you all right?"

"Yes, I'm fine. Look, you and Sylvia are enjoying a bit of time together, do you mind if I disappear off for a while? There's something I'd like to do."

"I'm sorry, I wasn't meaning to leave you out."

"No, I said I'm fine."

Lisa was taken aback, Pete didn't usually snap at her. "We'll include you more."

"It's not that. Look, there's just something I need to do. Maybe I'll come over tonight." Then without so much as kissing her, he turned and walked back down to Billingbrook.

"What was all that about?"

"Sylvia, I don't know. There are some days that I think I don't know very much about Pete at all."

"That's men for you."

Lisa and Sylvia continued their walk, but it didn't feel quite the same to Lisa now and after a short while they headed for home. As they approached the cemetery, there was a man coming out with his head stooped. They were some way off but Sylvia said "Isn't that Pete?"

Lisa turned to look, but he'd already gone and she saw nothing but the chilling sight of the iron railings guarding the dead. She shivered and they carried on.

Sylvia and Lisa had been back for a while and were sitting relaxing with a glass of wine. There had been no word from Pete. The phone rang and Lisa sprang to answer it. "Hello."

"Hello, is that Lisa Forster?"

Lisa sat down with the phone, "Yes, who is this?"

"My name's Matt Kirby, I'm a reporter with the *Southingham Express*."

"Oh, right. Look to be honest, I've had enough of journalists and newspapers and radio stations. I just want to…"

"Yes, I can understand that, but I'd like to help."

"What can you do that the others haven't?"

"I can't promise you anything. I just think I can. Is it

possible to meet you and perhaps do an interview? In exchange I'll see whether I can do some background research and unearth anything for you."

"Look, I don't know who you are. I don't live anywhere near Southingham. I've already done as many interviews as I want to give and I've got nowhere. Why should I talk to you?"

"O.K. what about if I paid you?"

Lisa took a deep breath. "What? Why would anyone want to pay me for this?"

"At least meet me and let's talk. I can come up there on Tuesday. There's something I need to do down here first. What do you say? I'll buy you lunch and if you don't want to talk to me after that, well, fine."

Lisa could feel curiosity weakening her resolve. "O.K., meet me outside Billingbrook Library at twelve-thirty, bring some ID with you. I'd like to know you're not a crank."

"Oh, trust me there are plenty of cranks work as journalists, but I'll bring the ID anyway."

"A reporter with a sense of humour," Lisa said to Sylvia as she put the phone down. "Let's see what he's got to say on Tuesday."

***

Southingham. Monday 29th October

Matt Kirby rang the bell of Felicity Aldwich's house and waited. He rang it a second time and heard heavy steps approaching. The door was opened to reveal a thickset man with a shock of grey hair. He looked to Matt to be in his fifties, but looked to have the fitness of a younger man.

"Yes?" the man said.

"I'm looking for Felicity Aldwich."

"Why?"

Matt was beginning to feel uncomfortable and he suspected that revealing that he was a journalist wasn't going to help matters. He thought quickly, "I'm a friend of the family."

"She's not here." The man closed the door before Matt had chance to say anything else.

Matt rang the bell again, but this time the man didn't bother coming back to the door and Matt was left standing on the doorstep. He went back to his car and waited to see if anyone came out or arrived back at the house. He'd been sitting there for about half an hour when the man from the house strode out to where Matt was sitting. Matt wound his window down and smiled, "Does this mean you're ready to talk to me?" He knew he was pushing his luck but had no idea what else to say.

"No, it means you can go away. I don't know who you are, but you aren't going to talk to her. Is that clear?"

"I'll talk to her as long as she's happy to talk to me. Who are you, her minder?"

"Just clear off. If I see you here again, I'll make sure you can't come back."

Matt held his hands up. "O.K. I get the message."

He started the engine as the man walked back over to the house. Matt didn't like being threatened. It made him more determined to find Felicity Aldwich. He headed back to the *Express's* offices to do some more research.

It wasn't long before Matt had checked the electoral role again to make sure that the thug wasn't listed at Felicity's address. He took it as good news that he wasn't, although wondered whether he ought to be eligible to vote anyway. He then started to search the internet to see if he could find anything about Felicity Aldwich that might give him a clue to where else he could find her. It didn't take him long to find an article in a medical journal, written by Felicity, that gave details of the pharmaceutical company where she was research manager. He wondered whether the thug was a personal friend or whether he was protection from campaigners against testing on animals. At least, that might explain his describing Matt as 'You people'. He would have to approach carefully so as not to raise an alarm. He thought it might be best to telephone first, so looked up the number for the company.

He hesitated but decided that his media credentials were more likely to get him put through, "It's Matt Kirby from the *Southingham Express*."

"One moment please."

He felt his sweating hand stick to the phone handset as he was put through and the line rang once more before being answered. He was buoyed up ready to make his pitch.

"Hello, Felicity Aldwich's secretary. Can I help you?"

Matt felt deflated, "Yes I'd like to speak to Felicity Aldwich please, it's Matt Kirby here from the *Southingham Express*."

"Can I ask what it's in connection with?"

"I'd like to do an interview with Felicity Aldwich for a profile in the newspaper." It wasn't a lie, but it wasn't the whole truth either.

"Felicity is away from the office at the moment. She isn't due back in until Thursday. I'll pass your message to her then."

Matt was frustrated by the possible delay. He'd given himself these two weeks to get to the bottom of the case. Thursday seemed a long way off. "Is it possible to get a message to her before that? Does she have a mobile I can call her on?"

"I'm afraid we don't give out direct information on our staff. I'll pass your message on."

"Wait, can I give you a number that she can call me, night or day, any time is fine?" Matt gave her his mobile number before she had time to decline.

"I'll pass it on. Goodbye."

The line went dead and Matt sat back in his chair to think.

"I thought you were on holiday?" Charlie came over to his desk.

"Yeah," said Matt. "What are you doing on my beach?"

"What are you up to, Matt?"

"Charlie, can you do me a favour?"

"What's new?"

"I need to put a letter through a door, but I don't think I can go back to the house."

"Matt, have you got woman troubles and the husband's found out?"

"No, Charlie, trust me, it's nothing like that."

"I can do it on my way home, but will you tell me what it's all about?"

"Later, Charlie, later."

Matt set to writing a note to Felicity. He reasoned that if she was out of town, the minder would have gone with her. His logic might be flawed, but it had to be worth a shot.

***

Billingbrook. Tuesday 30th October

Matt arrived in plenty of time for his meeting with Lisa. He wanted to have an opportunity to look round and get a feel for the place before they met. He wondered how different it was to Southingham. Would her upbringing have been the same, even though the location was different? His first impression was that it was more solidly built on the industrial heritage of the eighteenth and nineteenth centuries than on the cultural foundation laid down by the Romans. He had no idea whether this still affected today's way of life, although there were fewer grand houses than he was used to seeing.

For all that, it was clear from the grand Town Hall and surrounding square, that Billingbrook had once been wealthy and now showed hints of its faded glory, rather than the flourish of youth. The market was lively enough and Matt started to get the impression of a warmer friendlier place, where the people were less isolated and where they, rather than money, made the world go round.

"Are you lost, love?" asked a woman with curly grey hair as Matt walked backwards a few paces, looking at the scene before him.

"What? Oh no, thank you. Well, you couldn't point me in the direction of the library could you?"

The grey haired woman was happy to help. Matt thought it a refreshing change from the people of Southingham travelling in their cushioned silos.

It was a fine day and Matt sat on the library steps as he waited for Lisa, continuing to observe the passing traffic and thinking about how he might describe it in his story.

"Have you been waiting long?" asked a tall slim figure coming down the steps behind him just before half past twelve.

"How did you know it was me?" asked Matt, wrong footed as he took a proper look at Lisa. He'd seen her picture in the paper so already knew who it was that he was looking for. She was more attractive than the paper had shown her to be and her shoulder length brown hair shone in the daylight.

"Let's just say I've met one or two journalists over the last couple of weeks and you've got that look about you."

Matt thought he'd better check out what "that look" was and change it before it blew his cover on any stake outs.

"Right," he said, still trying to recover some control of the situation. "Where to?"

CHAPTER 25

Billingbrook. Tuesday 30th October

"So, Matt Kirby, this is just lunch and not an interview." Lisa smiled, she was in control of the situation and it felt good.

Matt held his hands up in surrender, "Not an interview."

"Why have you come all this way just to take me out for lunch? What's in it for you?"

Matt looked taken aback. "The papers never said you were quite so feisty."

"They didn't say a lot of things." She looked down at the menu, which was already beginning to have a familiar feel to it. They were in Frascati's. It was the same waiter as the other day and he was already treating her as though she were a cherished regular.

Matt gave her a quizzical look. "Are you trained at dealing with media or do you just learn fast?"

She laughed. "Is that your first question? What's this really about? If you're honest and I trust you, then I'll co-operate. If I don't think you're being straight with me, then I won't answer anything."

She'd spent a long time the previous evening trying to decide how to play this meeting and, feeling stronger from the time she and Sylvia enjoyed out on the hills, she felt ready for anything. Almost anything at least, she'd been disappointed when Pete hadn't shown up in the evening, but at least he sent a text to say he was sorry but just needed a bit of time to himself. She wondered whether it was him going into the cemetery, but they never pushed each other on things like that and she wasn't about to start now.

She focussed her attention back on Matt, who seemed to be weighing up her offer. "Well?" she asked, raising an eyebrow to reinforce the question.

"You're quite something, Lisa Forster! O.K., it's a deal." Matt sat quietly for a moment. They were interrupted by the waiter who had been lingering for a drop in the flow of conversation before approaching to take their order.

After the waiter had gone back to the kitchen to request the spaghetti and the Marguerita pizza, Matt began to speak. "I've got a hunch. I don't want to say too much now as I don't want to raise your hopes or send you off on a wild goose chase, but let's just say that I might have an idea about your past."

Lisa widened her eyes. She felt her composure slipping away. "What? How? Where? I mean... Oh, I don't know what I mean! Can you tell me some more than that?"

"Not at the moment and you have to understand it is just a hunch. I could be wrong."

She shook her head in disbelief. "Do you often have hunches?"

"Let's just say that I'm doing this in my own time and not the paper's and it's the first holiday I've taken in as long as I can remember. No, I don't often have hunches."

"What do you want from me? I mean, how are you going to prove your hunch and what happens then?"

"From you I need some information and maybe

something that can be tested for DNA. But you have to realise that to prove anything, it's not just you that I need cooperation from. You're already searching for your parents. You've dealt with finding they weren't the people you thought they were. You may still be dealing with it; I don't know what it must feel like. To prove anything I have to find your real parents and they have to be prepared to deal with this too. I might not find them. They might not talk to me. They might not want to do this. It's quite possible that they've already gone through enough and don't want to revisit the past."

As Matt talked, Lisa felt broken at the prospect that her real parents might not want to know her.

"I'm not saying they don't want to see you. I haven't spoken to them. I'm just saying it's one of the risks. Even if I'm right, I can't promise that I can prove it yet."

Lisa nodded. This wasn't what she'd been expecting. She no longer knew what to say or how to feel. It was as though she was sinking through the depths of a dark ocean, gasping for air that wasn't there.

"O.K. so let's just say that I believe you. Can I have some time to think about it?"

"For DNA, I need something physical. I could stay somewhere overnight and maybe see you again tomorrow."

"Or I could post something to you?"

Matt shook his head, "As I explained I've had to take holiday to do this. I'm pressed for time. I've got two weeks."

Lisa nodded. "I'll have an answer for you by seven this evening. I'll call you and if it's a yes then I'll come and meet you."

"That seems fair," said Matt. "Now are you going to

eat some of your lunch?"

Lisa smiled. "No, sorry I'm going to leave you to it. I need to make a phone call if I'm going to be able to give you an answer later. I need someone to talk this through with."

Matt got up as she left the table and then sat down and continued with his meal. By the time Lisa reached the door and looked back, he was already tucking into his spaghetti as though he hadn't eaten in days. She wondered if he would eat her pizza for afters.

Lisa walked along the road away from the busiest part of town and made her phone calls as she walked. She left a message for Pete, asking him to call her.

Then she rang her home number and as the answer machine picked up she said "Sylvia, it's me, Lisa. If you're there can you pick this up?"

There was a click and then she heard Sylvia speak on the other end, "Hello."

"Oh good, you're there."

"You sound out of breath."

"No, I'm fine. I've just been talking to that journalist. He thinks he can help me find my parents. I want to talk to you and Pete about it before I do anything. I'm going to suggest we meet at home at six this evening. I can't get Pete at the moment."

"I'll be here."

"Great, see you then." Lisa hadn't expected Sylvia wouldn't be there, but she felt agitated by the lunchtime conversation and she just needed to hear a friendly voice. It was Pete she needed to get hold of. She thought about ringing him again, but knew he'd get to her message in his own time.

The afternoon dragged for Lisa. When she heard

nothing from Pete by four, she started to wonder what had happened to him. There was still no word as she arrived home at a quarter to six, but her heart skipped a beat as she saw his car parked by the house.

As she opened the front door she could hear voices in the kitchen, "Hello."

There was a chorus of greeting and Pete came through to meet her.

"How did you know to be here if you didn't return my call?"

"Telepathy." Pete answered and laughed. "Sorry, I left my phone at home. I just came over straight from work to say sorry for the last couple of days and Sylvia told me you'd called a council of war, so here I am, your warrior in chief." He grinned.

"Pete, this is serious."

"I know. Come on then spill the beans."

Lisa kicked off her shoes, put her bags down and went through to the kitchen where Sylvia was already preparing dinner.

"I thought we could eat as we talked," she said. "Do you want a glass of wine?" She started pouring the wine before Lisa had chance to answer.

"No, thanks. I might have to go out again."

"Oh, right. Pete, there's a glass of wine here." She looked up to find Pete standing in the doorway. "Oh you're there." Sylvia passed him the glass.

Lisa updated them on the meeting.

"Well that's great isn't it?" said Sylvia.

"It might be. The people, my parents, don't know yet. He doesn't even know if they would want to know. It's just, well, I'm scared."

Pete moved across to where Lisa was sitting and put

his arm round her. "We've come this far, you can't give up now."

"No, I know you're right. I suppose I just needed to hear someone else say it."

"Lisa, if things don't work out, we'll still be here for you. We'll still be your family," said Sylvia.

"It's funny," she said. "Almost all my life I've had a family who aren't my real family. Now might be my one chance."

"You've got to try," said Pete, holding her. "You get one shot at life. You've got to try."

Lisa wondered what had made Pete so philosophical all of a sudden, but it wasn't the time to ask. She got up and fetched her mobile phone from her bag. She dialled Matt's number. As he answered she said, "It's Lisa. Let's do it. I'll see you in the Red Lion in half an hour."

When she'd finished she turned to Sylvia and Pete, "Will you come with me?"

"Try stopping us," said Pete and went to put on his coat.

They found Matt already sitting on a stool at the bar. He got up as Lisa approached. "What are you having?"

"Matt, I'd like you to meet my boyfriend, Pete Laundon and my cousin Sylvia Peterson."

"Pleased to meet you." Matt shook their hands. "Now, can I buy you all a drink?"

They got their drinks and settled at a table in the corner. "This is where it all started," said Pete.

"Shh," said Lisa. "Today isn't supposed to be about a story, it's about how Matt can prove whatever he thinks he can prove."

"Right," said Pete. "Scratch that, nothing started here." The others laughed.

Matt took out a notebook and wrote Lisa's name at the top of the page, scrawled the date and then said, "O.K. so what I need is anything that might be a distinguishing feature. I'll take some hair or something to test for DNA. To be honest I haven't yet found somewhere to do the test, so we may have to come to that when I know what they want. There's no point my sorting that out until we've got something to compare it to. Do you have any birth marks, anything that might be able to identify you from birth?"

"What are you going to do with anything you find out?" Pete asked.

"I just want to see if my theory is right. If it is, then Lisa will work with me on a story. If it isn't then you have my word that I won't do anything with it."

"The problem is," said Lisa. "That I can't think of anything that would be helpful."

"What about your blood group?" Sylvia asked. "That's one of the things you get from your parents."

"How funny," said Lisa. "I should have realised years ago that Hugh and Maureen weren't my parents and I just never thought."

"What do you mean?" asked Matt with his pencil poised.

"My blood group. Hang on." Lisa started to rummage through her bag. "I used to give blood. I haven't done it for a while. My blood group is 'B positive'. I'm sure they said that there was something like eight percent of the population in that group. Then when Mum and Dad were ill, before they died, I saw the charts in the hospital and neither of them were that group. It's just that I never connected it."

Matt was grinning. "I'm sure that's something I can use. It won't prove anything, but it would give me a good indication. Can you think of anything else or shall I get on my way back to Southingham?"

"I think that's all," said Lisa still feeling stunned that she'd missed something so obvious.

***

Southingham. Tuesday 30th October

Matt was disappointed that he hadn't heard anything from Felicity Aldwich, perhaps she was really out of town. He wondered whether it was worth another attempt to make contact with her or whether he should wait for Thursday, even then he was not convinced that his message would be passed on. He sat back in the armchair and looked at his pad. The things he'd written down were 'it all started in the Red Lion pub – need to find out how?' and 'B+', which he had circled heavily.

He turned to a new sheet of paper and scribbled 'blood group' in the middle. Then he drew lines from it to headings reading, 'parents', 'hospital', 'police records'. He underlined the last one and reached for the phone.

"Hello."

"Rob, it's Matt Kirby. What's going down?"

"Matt, long time no speak. How's the newspaper world?"

"Ticking along. What about crime?"

"So so. We haven't stopped all the criminals yet, but you've got to give us marks for trying. I'm guessing this isn't just a social call?"

"Am I that shallow? No, on second thoughts don't answer that. I was ringing to call in a favour."

"Uh oh. What you after? I struggle with getting speeding fines waived."

"No, nothing like that. I think I might be about to close one of your unsolveds, if you haven't already closed the file."

"O.K. I'll buy it. What are you looking at?"

"At the moment it's just a hunch. I don't want to lose control of this thing right now, there's a big story in it for me."

"And the criminal?"

"It won't hurt you to wait. If I'm right, then they're dead."

"Blimey, Matt, not another murder?"

"No. Have you read the story in the papers about the girl who's trying to find out who her parents are? She's about thirty and has just discovered that the people who brought her up aren't her parents."

"Yes, I saw something."

"Well, I want some information from an old abduction case. Just under thirty years ago Sophie Newman was taken from her mother here in Southingham. I've got a gut feeling that tells me it's the same person."

"Based on what?"

"Just call it journalistic instinct."

"So what do you want from me?"

"I want you to get hold of the file and find out what blood group the baby was. I don't want you to do anything else right now. I want to break it to the parents and get the story. After that, it's up to you. But if I'm right then there's no one to prosecute because the people involved in the abduction have died."

"I'll see what I can do. But if questions get asked, then I might have to hand it over."

"I know. Call me."

"O.K."

Matt hung up and smiled, he knew that Detective Inspector Rob Grant wouldn't let him down. He owed him one from last year and won his promotion based on the information that Matt had handed over to him. Matt was sure that he'd be happy to repay the favour.

Matt turned another page of the notebook and headed a page 'find the father'. Then he started to think about the story he would write when this all came together. 'When' this all came together, he thought, not 'if'.

Matt picked up the pile of stories he'd printed out about the abduction. If he were going to find the father he needed to build a profile of the man. He began to search through looking for specific details and as he found them made notes on the pad. 'Stephen Newman, born about 1950, married Felicity Aldwich 1975', none of that was new information. Then he spotted a background story telling him Stephen had an Economics degree from Birmingham University. He wrote it down on his pad and circled the word 'alumni'. Bingo. He was sure that Rachel would be able to make enquiries about a former student.

He picked up the phone and dialled.

"This is becoming a habit." She laughed.

"Watch out, I'll start remembering birthdays next."

"Only if they're part of a story."

"Ouch. Harsh."

"But true. Come on then Dad, what is it this time? You know I love talking to you, but I can see right through you."

"And out the other side, or so it seems. It's the girl's father."

"I thought you were finding the mother."

"I did but she's got a minder who doesn't seem to want me to see her. I'm looking for the father instead, Stephen Newman."

"And where do I come in? Am I the bait?"

"Are you having a bad day? Should I call back later?"

"Sorry, Dad, I had a row with Mum earlier. I'm O.K., it's not your fault."

Matt hesitated. He wanted to know what the argument was about, but knew better then to ask his daughter. "He went to your university."

"Wow."

"Yes, I know. This could be the break I need. I need to trace him and I wondered whether you could ask at the alumni office?"

"I can try. It won't be until tomorrow. What do you know?"

"He did Economics and was born in about 1950."

"So we're looking for someone graduating in about 1971?"

"Yes, I think so."

"I'll see what I can find out. Ring me tomorrow night."

"Thanks, Rach." He hung up and sat back in the armchair. What else could he do than wait?

***

Southingham. Wednesday 31st October

Matt didn't know what to do with himself when he awoke on Wednesday morning. He wasn't used to taking holiday and his immediate thought was to go into the office anyway. The least he could do was treat himself to breakfast first, so grabbing his bag he was just on his way out in search of Starbuck's when his phone rang.

"Hello."

"Is this Matt Kirby?"

"Who is this?" Matt couldn't place the gruff voice addressing him from the end of the phone.

"Stay away from Felicity Aldwich."

"But," Matt became angry, "who is this? What right

271

have you to tell me what to…"

"If you know what's good for you, you'll stay away from Felicity Aldwich."

"Now just you…" But he was talking into a dead phone. Matt put his bag down and looked for the last caller, but they had withheld the number. He wondered whether it had been the heavy from Felicity's house the other day, but whoever it was, it made him more determined to see her.

Matt found a table in a corner of Starbucks with two easy chairs. He pushed one of them away so that no one would join him. As his Americano steamed in front of him he took out his notebook and began to scribble questions and ideas.

'Who is the thug? What or who is FA being protected from? What is the best way to get to her?'

He sat back and realised he was beginning to write an altogether different story than the one he'd set out to investigate. He turned the page and tried to focus on the immediate problem. As he did so his phone rang.

It was Rob Grant. "I've got copies of some of the case file for you. Can I meet you in half an hour?"

"I'm in Starbucks. Is that any good?"

"I'll be there. Mine's a latte."

Matt grinned as he closed the phone. He got up and moved the other easy chair back into position and put his bag on it. Whilst he waited for DI Grant he began to put together a plan for waiting for Felicity Aldwich and following her to a convenient location so that he could talk to her.

He didn't go to the office after he met DI Grant. He headed home with the brown envelope containing the case notes. He set them out on the dining table and began to go through them one by one. He was looking for three things. He wanted a clue that could confirm Lisa's identity, anything, her blood group, a birth mark, anything that could rule Lisa in or out. In his own mind he was already certain that it was the same person so he was looking for two other things as well. He wanted a clue as to how he could find her father, but more importantly he wanted the story.

He poured a small glass of Talisker over some ice and settled down for a long afternoon. It was obvious that the initial investigation had been thorough and the inability to trace the baby was due to some other factor than ineptitude. There had been so little to go on. The shopping centre had no closed circuit television. No one saw the person who took the baby. The toilets were close to the car park, making it easy for someone to leave. How would you trace a baby in that situation? Matt scratched his chin with the end of the pencil and began to make his own case notes. They were more unanswered questions than observations.

By five o'clock, he was still in search of a vital clue. He couldn't believe that he hadn't come across her blood group in all the papers he'd looked at. He wondered whether Rach would consider it late enough to count as evening and decided to try her number anyway.

"Rach it's me, Dad. Have you got anything?"

"You're a lucky one, aren't you?"

"What do you mean?"

"He's registered. I've managed to get his work details. He's a management consultant with a small firm in London. Have you got a pen?"

"Have I got a pen? Have I ever not got a pen? Go on."

He wrote the office number on the top of his pad,

"Thanks, Rach. I owe you. Gotta go, I want to call before five thirty."

Before he even heard his daughter's response he'd hung up and was dialling the number of Able Benjamin Consultants. A well-educated voice answered, "This is the voicemail of Stephen Newman. I will be out of the office until Monday 5th November. I will be checking my messages or you can call my mobile…" Matt wrote down the number on the pad and hung up.

CHAPTER 26

Billingbrook. Wednesday 31st October

"Do you think he's found anything?" Lisa was opening a bottle of wine for dinner.

"You've got to give him time, love," said Sylvia, putting her hand on Lisa's arm. "It can't be easy trying to piece this jigsaw together."

"Do you think he knows anything? What do you think, Pete?"

"I don't know. He could just be looking for a story, but something tells me that's not the case. There was something about the light in his eyes as he was talking about it last night that tells me he really does have a hunch. Of course, a hunch can be wrong, but he seemed like a smart guy."

"Perhaps I should ring to ask what's happening."

"I'd give him a bit longer," said Pete. "Let's wait to see if we hear from him before the weekend."

"Do you think we should go to Southingham?"

"Oh, I don't know, love. We seem to have done quite a bit of running around already. It may be nothing to do with Southingham itself. We need to hear what he's got first." Sylvia started to put the vegetables onto the plates. "Don't get me wrong, I'd like to see more of the country while I'm here, but I want to see places for a reason, not just because I met a journalist from there."

"You're not thinking of going back just yet are you?" Lisa felt anxious. "I've rather got used to having you around."

"Well it's nice to know I'm not outstaying my welcome, but I'll have to go back to Australia eventually."

"I thought you might like to stay and cook for us permanently," said Pete, winking at her.

"Don't push your luck," said Sylvia handing him a plate with perfectly cooked roast rib of beef. "We couldn't afford to eat like this forever."

"No, I suppose not, unless Lisa does turn out to be rich and famous. Then…"

"Pete! Honestly you just don't give up." Lisa shook her head as she carried her plate through to the lounge.

***

Southingham. Wednesday evening 31st October

Matt dialled the number for Stephen Newman's mobile, even after all these years in the job he could feel his heart pounding. It was going to be a difficult conversation, that he did know. The phone rang with the long international ring tone that meant Stephen must be out of the country. Matt already thought he would rather break the news in a face to face meeting and this just confirmed his thinking.

"Stephen Newman," answered the precise voice.

"Mr Newman, this is Matt Kirby from the Southingham Express. I wonder if it would be possible to meet you to discuss an important story that I'm working on right now."

"Is this a hoax?"

"No, sir, you're very welcome to check with my editor if you have any concerns. I can give you his number."

"Yes, I'll do that. Can you tell me what the story is

276

about?" He sounded guarded.

Matt weighed up how much he should say. He couldn't afford to be rebuffed, but he didn't want to give too much away. "There's some new information that has come to light which may relate to the disappearance of your daughter thirty years ago."

There was silence on the other end of the phone.

"Mr Newman, are you still there?"

The voice that replied was no longer so clipped and professional. "Can you tell me some more? Why haven't I heard from the police?" Stephen sounded defeated.

"This isn't in the hands of the police, Mr Newman, although DI Grant knows that I'm working on something. It's some work I've put together myself. Is it possible to meet you?"

"I'm in Paris right now, but I'll be flying back on Friday, although the flight isn't booked yet. I could meet you Friday night as long as I'm back in time?" He paused, "Have you spoken to Felicity yet?"

"Friday night's fine, but no, I haven't managed to get hold of your ex-wife."

"She's not my ex-wife. We never divorced. Strictly speaking she's still my wife, though I haven't seen her for a long while. Anyway, if you give me your number and your editor's I'll call you on Friday when I know what time I'll be arriving. I can sort out with you then where we'll meet."

Matt gave him the information and hung up. He was quite pleased with how the call had gone, but disappointed with more of a wait.

***

Southingham. Friday 2nd November

Matt was already sitting in the corner of the Joie de

Vivre wine bar, when a tall suited figure entered, looking out of place by his nervousness. He was the sort of figure that Matt imagined would stride in, looking in control of any situation, but not tonight. Matt got down from his stool and went across.

"Mr Newman?"

"How did you know?"

"Let's just say it's my job. I've already got a bottle of St Emillion and two glasses, I hope that's agreeable?"

"Yes, that will be delightful."

"I was sitting here so that I'd see you coming in. Perhaps we should move to somewhere more comfortable."

The wine bar was busy. The crowd looked as though they had come straight from the office. The girls looked as though they had taken time to change, judging by their short black skirts and high heels. Matt wondered if any of them went to work dressed like that and for a moment thought he might be working in the wrong office. They found a table right at the back of the wine bar that was just being vacated by a young couple who were too busy, lost in each other's worlds to reply when Matt asked them if the table was free.

He put the bottle and the two glasses on the table and sat down. Stephen followed hastily behind.

"So what's this all about?" Stephen accepted the glass of wine that Matt poured and swirled it round the glass, sniffing the freed aroma.

"I need to be honest with you. I'm working on a hunch. It's a strong hunch, but it's a hunch none-the-less. I don't want to lead you to think that I have anything conclusive at the moment. What I've got may come to nothing, but if you work with me, well ..." He left the sentence hanging.

"Look, Mr Kirby."

"Please, call me Matt."

"O.K., Matt, this isn't easy for me. There have been crank calls and letters over the years and a number of false starts. If there's going to be anything on this, I think it's better you speak to me and don't trouble my wife. She may not be able to take it."

"I haven't managed to get past her minder yet."

"Hmm. The heavy squad still on the prowl? I've taken a lot of hurt over the years and survived. I can take one more dose if that's what it's going to be. I may have a great career, but that's all there is. I lost everything that mattered because of this. What have you got?"

Matt thought he may as well plough in rather than build up the story. He got the impression that Stephen Newman would want the blunt facts. "I think your daughter's alive."

There was silence from Stephen. He opened his mouth to speak, but closed it again. He nodded.

"There's been a story, you may have seen it," Matt pushed a copy of the story about Lisa across the table. "It's about a girl of thirty who's trying to find out who she is."

"How can she not know?" Stephen shook his head. He didn't pick up the cutting but looked intently at Matt.

"The people who brought her up are both dead. She has a birth certificate, but she's found it belongs to a baby that died thirty years ago. It isn't her certificate. I know it's a long shot, but the story about your daughter took place when I was just a cub reporter. It stayed with me all these years and there's something about this story that made me sit up. You can dismiss me as a crank if you want to, but I think it's worth you getting a DNA test done."

"Why are you doing this? What's in it for you?" Stephen's hand was shaking on the table.

"Mr Newman, I'm a journalist. I spend my life pursuing a story. I've met this girl. She's already ruled out that she was adopted. At the moment she has no idea who you are. I wanted to talk to you first. All I ask is the chance to break the news if it's true."

Stephen Newman nodded.

"I don't think this is a wild goose chase. I've met her twice and I'd say there's a resemblance to you, around the eyes and the cheekbones. The one thing I've got to go on at the moment is her blood group. Do you know what blood group your daughter was?"

Stephen shook his head, "Her mother might know. What do I need to do?"

"Well there's a DNA test that you can do, both you and Lisa Forster. It would tell us if you aren't her father for certain and would give a near one hundred percent answer if you are. I'm sure Lisa would be willing to take the test if you are?"

"What about her mother?"

"It can be done with her mother or without. It doesn't need both of you."

"I still love her you know."

"It's natural you should love your daughter, Mr Newman."

"Please call me Stephen. I don't mean my daughter. I mean her mother. I still love Felicity. She always blamed herself, but I didn't. In the end, she couldn't look at me, because I reminded her of Sophie. She hated me because I wasn't Sophie. It meant I started to hate Sophie. I wished she'd never been born. I lost everything because of her.

Everything."

Matt was torn between thinking what fantastic material this was for a story, beginning to wonder whether there was a whole book in there and realising he needed to say something to Stephen to comfort him. He shifted in his chair and ran his finger round his collar.

"None of this was Sophie's fault. She was just a tiny baby. She wouldn't have chosen this to happen. If I'm right and it is Lisa Forster, then you've got a lovely daughter, Stephen and, even without my story, I think it's worth your while having the test to find out."

Stephen shakily lifted his glass and took a large sip of wine. He nodded as he put it back down on the table. Then he looked straight into Matt's eyes. "How long will it take?"

Matt forced himself not to show the smile he was feeling. He knew that he'd got his man and that the next stage in the process would happen. "We need to send for the testing kit. The website says it will take four working days from when they receive the samples back."

"And the sample from this Lisa?"

"I'll sort that out, if you'd like me too."

Stephen nodded. "I have to go back to Paris on Monday. I won't be back again until Friday evening next week. Can we do the test then?"

"I should be able to get everything by then. I can get Lisa's sample ready to send with yours on the Saturday."

"How do I know that I can trust you?"

"Stephen, I've got a daughter myself, I can only begin to imagine what this must be like for you. If it would help you could ask DI Grant his thoughts on whether I can be trusted. He'll vouch for me. There's nothing to stop you going ahead with this without me. It's up to you. You've got my number." Matt stood up to go.

"Wait," Stephen grabbed his arm. "Don't go. I'm sorry, yes I do trust you. I'm just terrified. I've spent thirty years hoping that my daughter had come to no harm and yet deep down believing that she had been murdered and we'd never know what happened. Thirty years wondering if there was something else I could have done, something I should still be doing. I've had to force myself to carry on. I drowned myself in my work, because then I didn't have to think about it. I didn't have to feel any more guilt, any more hurt. Matt, I'm terrified."

It was Matt's turn to nod. "Don't put all your hopes on this. It may still come to nothing, but you wouldn't thank me if you didn't at least try."

***

Billingbrook. Saturday 3rd November

It was eleven o'clock when the phone rang. Lisa had been up for a while and was cooking brunch for the three of them. She was just in the middle of breaking the eggs into a pan when she heard the ringing.

"Can someone get it?" she shouted from the kitchen. Another ring and then the phone stopped. She wasn't sure if the answerphone had taken the call or whether Pete or Sylvia had picked it up. She carried on cracking the egg shells, when Pete came through with the handset.

"It's Matt Kirby, can you take it?"

Lisa thrust the egg into Pete's hand and grabbed the phone. "Matt, hello, is there some news?"

"Hi, well maybe. I'd like you to take a DNA test. If you'd be prepared to, then we'd know in a matter of days whether my hunch is right or not."

"Can't you tell me some more than that?"

"No, not yet. If it comes to nothing then I'm sorry, but

if it works out then you'll know the whole story."

"O.K., but when?"

"It'll be sometime this week. I've got to send for the testing kit first. I could come up there on Thursday."

"Right, what time?"

"How about lunch time?"

"What do I have to do? Isn't it a blood test?"

"I don't know. There are no needles. I think it's a swab that takes cells from your mouth."

"Right. Same place then? Shall we say one o'clock? I should be able to make sure I get that time for lunch."

"See you Thursday."

Lisa went back through to the kitchen where Pete had got everything under control and was ready to serve the food. "Whatever would I do without you?"

"Well, firstly you would overcook the eggs on a regular basis, secondly…"

Lisa hit him with the oven glove. "It was a rhetorical question, Pete."

"Shame, I'd got quite a list to give you. What did Matt want?"

Just then Sylvia came into the lounge. "I slept like a log, was that the phone that woke me?"

"I thought you were already up, breakfast's ready." Lisa replied putting the plates on the table. "It was Matt Kirby. He wants me to do a DNA test. He won't say why, so I still don't know where this is leading. He sounded positive though so I can't help but feel excited. The strange thing is that I don't quite know what I'm excited about. You don't think he could find my parents do you?"

"I don't know, love. It's a long shot. It would be good if he could, but after all these years it's got to be a fairly small chance." Sylvia sat at the table.

Pete went over to Lisa and hugged her. "Anything's worth a try. When will it be?"

"He's coming up Thursday."

"Do you want me to be there?" Pete asked, pushing her chin up with the back of his hand so that he could look into her face. "No," he said, "it isn't a question, unless you object, I'd like to be there to support you. If you don't mind?"

Lisa shook her head. "How about all three of us go?"

"I'd like that," said Sylvia. "It does rather feel as though we're all in this together."

"Yes," said Lisa. "It does."

***

Billingbrook. Thursday 8th November

It had been an odd week for Matt. He was determined to take his week's holiday, even though there wasn't a great deal he could do with the time. He'd sent for the DNA testing kit on Saturday and it arrived on Tuesday. He felt frustrated that he could do nothing with it immediately. He had thought of going into the office on Monday but contented himself with working at home, researching the company that Felicity Aldwich worked for and trying to get a better picture of why she needed a minder.

He remembered why he didn't take holiday. It gave him too much time to dwell on the things that had gone wrong in his own life and invariably led to increased levels of drinking. He couldn't help thinking that if he took too many holidays he might have to switch to a cheaper drink than malt whisky.

By Thursday, he was more than ready for the drive to Billingbrook and set off early to give time to get a feel for the place and put together some background for his story.

He'd started to scribble some notes on the contrasts in the life that Lisa had growing up in Billingbrook, compared to the life she might have had in Southingham. It was hard to put his finger on the difference in the essence of the places. He could feel there was one, but he could only find words like 'pretension' and 'snobbery' when considering Southingham, without being able to put his finger on what they meant. He was sitting in the Market Square of Billingbrook, when a shopper stopped to say 'hello'. Having passed the time of day, Matt realised that wouldn't have happened in Southingham. The word 'egalitarian' came to mind to describe Billingbrook. Somehow, here everyone was equal, whereas in Southingham there were beautifully dressed people in their expensive clothes and their four wheel drive vehicles, who set themselves apart from the stolid local working class. Maybe the proportions of the classes, in this classless society, were different in Billingbrook than in Southingham, but whatever it was, Billingbrook felt more down to earth and as though everyone was welcome, even Matt.

He began to wonder if Lisa would have gone to a private school rather than the local comprehensive and what difference that might have made to the person she became. He'd met her a couple of times, but he liked her the way she was.

He patted his pocket with the DNA testing kit tucked away and headed for the restaurant.

Pete was already sitting at the table when Matt went in. He got up to greet Matt as he approached.

"You're early."

"Yes, I've got to get back by half past, but I didn't want to miss the excitement."

"You care a lot about Lisa don't you?" He said it more as a statement than a question.

Pete nodded. "Is it that obvious?"

"Just help her to understand there are no guarantees in all this. I hope I'm right, but I might not be."

Just then Sylvia and Lisa came into the restaurant to join them. "What are you two scheming about?" Lisa asked as she held her hand out to shake Matt's.

"I was just divulging all our intimate secrets," said Pete getting up to give her a hug and a kiss. They laughed and sat down at the table.

"O.K., what do I have to do?" Asked Lisa, launching straight in. "I can't face food until we get this out of the way."

Matt took the testing kit from his pocket, "The instructions are all there."

"I'll do it in the ladies if that's O.K.?" She got up, but sat down again. "Who's providing the other sample?"

"I thought you might ask me that," said Matt grinning. "But even expecting the question I'm not sure what to give as the answer. I don't think I should answer it at this stage."

Lisa looked disappointed. "O.K., I guess I'll have to wait."

"I'll come with you, love," said Sylvia following Lisa towards the toilets.

"They never go in ones," said Pete smiling.

"I suppose this is an exceptional time," said Matt.

"You're all right for a bitter twisted journalist."

"That's a back handed compliment if ever I heard one." Matt was laughing.

"I'm sorry, it's just you're not what I expected."

"I've been through the mill enough in my own life to

have some compassion for others in difficult situations."

"It's good to see. I suppose it helps if people trust you, but I don't get the impression it's an act."

"That I will take as a compliment."

"Good heavens they're coming back already." Pete stood up and went towards Lisa and Sylvia. "Was it O.K.?" He sounded worried.

"Yes, it was fine. There's nothing to it. It's amazing that such a minor process can give anyone enough information to work out anything about me."

Pete kissed her. "I love you, you know."

"What was that for? I'm not used to these sudden bursts of affection."

"Well, I think it was sweet," said Sylvia as they got back to Matt. "Now, I'm famished."

Matt felt in high spirits as he drove back to Southingham that afternoon. The story seemed to be coming together and he was looking forward to the outcome. As he was driving down the M5 his mobile rang through the built in system in his car. "Hello, Matt Kirby."

"Mr Kirby this is Felicity Aldwich, you left a message for me."

Matt drew a deep breath and straightened the car from the odd path he had taken. "Thank you for calling back, I didn't think you'd got my message, with the threat from the heavy at your house and everything."

"You've been to my house?" Felicity Aldwich sounded shocked and flustered. "Mr Kirby, what is this in connection with? If it's to do with my work, you had no right going to my house."

This wasn't going to be an easy conversation. Matt pulled into the service station he was approaching as he continued. "This is not connected with your work, Ms

Aldwich, please give me the opportunity to explain." He was already on the wrong foot and he needed to win her trust. "I had a meeting with your…" he hesitated over the right term to use and settled on "former husband and he suggested that I should talk to you too." This wasn't true, but he hoped it would get her interested.

"You've spoken to Stephen? What is this in connection with?"

"I think this would be easier in person, Ms Aldwich. Would it be possible for me to meet you?"

There was a pause. He hoped it meant she was looking at a diary or at least considering the proposal. "I can see you at six."

Matt looked at the time, it was already three forty. It should take another hour and a half to get home. "Where will I meet you?"

"There's a bistro on Sands Lane, L'Escargot, you can meet me there."

Before he had chance to reply she'd gone. Matt shook his head, beginning to form an impression of a woman who was very used to having her own way. He'd warmed to Stephen but something told him this was going to be an altogether different matter.

CHAPTER 27

Southingham. Thursday evening 8th November

Matt was five minutes early arriving at L'Escargot. He always liked to watch the person he was meeting come into a room and appraise their manner. He was looking round for a suitable table when he was surprised to hear a very precise voice greet him with "Mr Matthew Kirby, I presume."

He turned to find Felicity Aldwich already seated at a table to the left of the bar. His eyes were drawn to her long slender legs, which were crossed beneath the chair. He brought his gaze up to the perfect lines of the impeccably tailored burgundy suit and for the first time in ages felt inadequately dressed in his jeans and open neck shirt. He reached out a hand to shake hers, almost expecting her to decline or to examine the cleanliness of his nails before accepting. "Have you been here long?"

"Long enough to watch you coming in."

The sharpness of her reply told Matt that this was not a woman to be messed with. Despite his years of interviewing a wide range of people, Matt felt his mouth go dry and his brain begin to feel ridiculously addled.

He was looking for the right words but Felicity got there first and in a bored tone said, "Mr Kirby, what is this all about?"

He was tempted to be as blunt in reply and knock the

wind out of her sails, but he felt he needed to tread carefully, for Lisa's sake if for no other. "Ms Aldwich, I am undertaking an investigation following up on your daughter."

"How many times do I have to tell you people to leave me alone?" She stood up and picked her bag off the chair. "I've been hounded by so many for your 'how is she bearing up?' stories and your 'Ten years on' stories. I've got a life to live. Good night, Mr Kirby." She almost spat his name out as she went to walk away.

Matt couldn't risk her walking out on him, not now he'd got this far. "Ms Aldwich, please." He put his hand as gently as he could on her arm to restrain her. "This is different. I think I might have found her. I'm having DNA testing done."

Felicity dropped back into the chair. She looked much older and fragile. "Is she, I mean is…"

"The person I am testing is alive, Ms Aldwich. I'm having her DNA compared to your husband's."

"No! I mean. You haven't got the samples yet have you? Is there still time?"

"I'm seeing him tomorrow. I've got the sample from the girl and now I need your husband's DNA to compare it with."

"Don't use Stephen's. Use mine. You can do it now." It came across as an order and Matt was struck by the sternness with which it came out.

"I can't do that. I don't have the kit on me." He was lying, but he wanted to see how she would react.

"Then go home and get it. I'll wait here. Damn, I'll come with you if I need to. It would be better to use my DNA; I could be her mother for God's sake."

Matt decided that he could use the kit in the car for

Felicity and still have time to drive to collect another sampling kit tomorrow before seeing Stephen. He tried to remember where the testing laboratory was based and seemed to recollect it being Kent, but he was sure there would be a nearer lab he could get a kit from. "I need to get it from the car. Give me five minutes." He went out into the damp evening and hoped that Felicity Aldwich would still be there when he got back. There was something about her anxiety that told him she would be.

When he returned, Felicity was pouring wine from a bottle on the table into both glasses.

"I took the liberty of ordering while you were gone."

"Yes, that's fine," said Matt, surprised by her cool calm manner. She had recomposed herself and was behaving as though this were any business meeting. "I'm sorry it took me a week to contact you. I didn't come back to the office when they were expecting me and by the time I did get back, your note was amongst quite a large pile of things on my desk."

"What about the note I left at your house?" Matt asked, making the most of the defrosted atmosphere.

"I didn't get that." She took a sip of wine. "My bodyguard is sometimes a little over-protective."

"Bodyguard? Has the follow up on this been as bad as that?" Matt wanted to know if there were others chasing the story.

"Good heavens no. Most of the story relating to Sophie went away years ago. There has been the odd prying hack on the key anniversaries or when other children go missing; the whole 'how will the parents come to terms with it in the future?' thing. And before you ask, you don't come to terms with it. You blame yourself. You hate yourself. You hate your husband. You hate the world and yes, I'll admit there are times you hate the child, but you never come to terms with it. It eats away at you, leaving you angry and bitter and at times even a little bit crazy. You wonder what they look like now; what they might be doing. Sometimes you have to tell yourself they're dead just to make yourself move on, move house, whatever it is you need to do and sometimes you have to tell yourself that they must still be alive, that as their mother you'd know if they weren't and if they weren't still alive…" She took a large mouthful of wine before finishing the sentence, "there'd be no reason for you to live either."

"And the minder?" said Matt trying to prompt the flow to continue.

Felicity threw back her head with a touch of controlled madness and laughed. "He's because of the death threats. Ironic isn't it? I've thought of killing myself, but I'm provided with protection to stop someone else doing it for me."

"Why the death threats?" Matt wished he could get his notebook out and write all this down, but it wasn't the time.

"The little fluffy wuffy animals," Felicity said in a sarcastic voice. "We're a pharmaceutical company. We test our products on animals. We follow all the appropriate guidelines, but that isn't good enough for some people. They say they are against cruelty and then threaten us with death. Doesn't balance, does it?"

"No, I suppose not."

"It's not that I don't understand in some ways. God, I prefer animals to people, but it hardly makes sense if you look at the whole picture. There are days when I wish they'd just get on and do it. The ones when I think Sophie is dead. It's probably better that I don't know the truth of what happened to her, my nightmares are bad enough. Then people like you come along and bring everything back. Maybe I'm better not knowing." She got up. "Keep your DNA test, whoever she is she's nothing to do with me. Let Stephen do it; that will prove it for you." She made to leave.

"But that won't prove it, will it?" Matt stood up.

She swirled round to face him, anger flared in her eyes, "What do you mean by that?"

"I think there's something else. I think there's something you've never told Stephen. I also think you do want to know if she's your daughter." He knew he was treading on dangerous ground, but he had to get her to take the DNA test. It was another of his hunches, but he had to go with it, otherwise he could see his story slipping away. If he was right then the story had just got a whole lot bigger.

"Please," he said, "will you take the test? For Sophie's sake."

"You're a bastard, Matt Kirby! I wish I'd never phoned you."

"But you did phone me and the fact that you're here tells me that you still need to know." He reached into his pocket and took out the testing kit. "Why don't you do it now?"

"What here?"

"You could go to the Ladies."

"I'll take it home to do it. I'll return it to you tomorrow at one o'clock."

"I can't do that. I'll be out of town." He was still holding the kit. He didn't want her to leave with it. He was worried that someone would talk her out if it. "Why don't we go somewhere more private now? We could go back to my place."

There was still anger in her face, but it was fading to defiance. She appeared to think for a moment then conceded and in doing so adopted a resigned expression.

"Shall we take my car? I'll bring you back for yours afterwards." He took some money out of his wallet and signalled to the waiter, then followed Felicity towards the door.

As the cool night air hit them, Felicity seemed to calm down. "What's involved in doing the test?" She asked, while they were still in the doorway.

"It's just a swab that you wipe around the inside of your cheek."

"Could I do it in the car?"

"I don't see why not. I can't remember what it said about washing your hands first, but you could always go back inside to do that before we leave."

Felicity's face clouded. "I've hated using public toilets since the day that Sophie was taken. I just think to myself, if only I hadn't gone to the toilet."

"You only need to wash your hands," said Matt. "You don't need to go into the cubicle."

"I'll be two minutes. Will you hold this please?" She handed him her coat and went back inside.

***

Southingham. Friday 9th November

Matt spent Friday morning ringing to find the nearest laboratory that would provide him with a DNA sampling kit. They weren't set up for those who didn't want them to do the testing and having already paid the fee to the laboratory in Kent, he was in no hurry to pay for the whole process again. Eventually he rang DI Grant who smoothed the way for him. He had already explained to the original lab that there would be an extra kit to test and for a small additional fee, they had agreed. *Let's just wait for the results of that, Ms Felicity Aldwich.* Matt began planning the next few days.

Once again he was early for his meeting with Stephen Newman and as he poured himself a glass of wine he wondered how much he should tell Stephen about the meeting with Felicity. It was possible it would be better not to mention it at all, but Matt wanted to see what reaction he got. He'd warmed to Stephen and decided he was a genuine enough chap. He didn't feel that Stephen was the one with the secrets, but unless he had misread the situation with Felicity, he was sure there were a lot of things she wasn't telling him.

"Sorry I'm late," said Stephen removing his dripping raincoat. "Damn, weather. I couldn't get a parking space anywhere close to here. It was dry in Paris. If it hadn't been for our meeting I wouldn't have minded staying there for the weekend." He went back towards the door to hang his wet coat on the stand and propped his umbrella in the corner.

"I took the liberty of getting a bottle," said Matt pushing a filled glass of Chablis towards Stephen when he returned.

"Jolly good. It doesn't matter how often I drink French wines, I never tire of them. Not like these New World ones that are always the same." He swirled the glass before taking a long slow breath through his nose to savour the aroma. "There is so much depth in the smell and flavour of a good French wine. Don't you think?"

"Stephen," said Matt, when he could get a word in. "There's no need to be nervous. The test isn't difficult."

Stephen's shoulders dropped, "Yes, I suppose I am a

touch anxious. I don't think it's the test itself. It's the result I'm worried about. I haven't been able to think of anything else all week, just the prospect of getting my little girl back. Oh, I know she won't be so little now but she'll always be my little Sophie. I've never stopped believing that this day might come." He looked at Matt's face. "You know, when she went missing, what I needed was Felicity to put her arms around me and tell me everything would be all right. But I was expected to be the strong one. When I needed love, she pushed me away. Said I didn't know what she was going through, as though it was only happening to her. It was almost a relief when she asked me to leave, I was hurting so much and there was no one to take care of me. Setting myself up in a functional bachelor pad meant I could switch off more easily, almost pretend it never happened. Don't get me wrong. I still thought about my little Sophie every single day, but I immersed myself in work and pushed Felicity out of my mind. There were times that it almost felt as though it was supposed to be just Sophie and me. I'd go to the park some weekends to feed the ducks, all the time thinking this is what I would have been doing with Sophie. She'd have to have been a tomboy. I used to buy her presents," his voice wavered. "I bought her a toy hovercraft one time. We took it to sail on the river. I'm not sure sail's the right word for a hovercraft. I'd stand there explaining to her how it all worked, even though she wasn't there to listen. I hope very much that the girl you've found is Sophie. We've got so much catching up to do." Stephen took his handkerchief from his pocket and dabbed his eyes. "We'd better do this test. I'm sorry."

"There's no need to be sorry," said Matt thinking about the times he'd missed of his own daughter's growing up.

"I hope it's Sophie too. I don't think I even care about the story anymore." He took the envelope out of his pocket and passed it to Stephen. "I'll send all three samples tomorrow."

"Three?"

"I saw your ex-wife yesterday."

"Oh," Stephen sounded disappointed. "You don't need my sample then?"

"Oh yes, please. It's best to have all three. Then there can be no uncertainty at all."

"Right. Yes, of course. I'll just..." He took the kit out and read the instructions. "I'll wash my hands first. I'll..." He didn't' finish his sentence. A sadness had come over him since Matt had mentioned seeing Felicity. Matt nodded and Stephen headed off towards the cloakroom.

Matt was topping up his glass when Stephen returned.

"How was Felicity?"

Matt smiled, "She seemed well. She wasn't what I expected."

"No? Why not?"

"She seemed harder than I'd imagined."

Stephen laughed with false jollity. "She's still covering up the real person with a tough exterior then. She's much more sensitive underneath, though it can take a lot of digging to get through." He sipped his wine. "What happens now?"

"I send these off for analysis and we wait a few days for the results. I think we'll hear by about the end of next week."

"Right." He swirled his glass, looking deep into the wine as though somewhere in there lay the answers. He put the wine down. "I think I should go. I don't think I want to spend my evening looking into the bottom of a glass of alcohol. There's a new art gallery opening tonight. I've been invited. You can come if you're interested. It would at least take my mind off things."

Matt shook his head. "No, but thanks all the same. I've got some thinking to do." As Stephen left, Matt looked to the bottom of his own glass of wine and wondered if it held the answers to his question. What was he going to tell Stephen if his suspicion turned out to be true?

***

Billingbrook. Saturday 10th November

"Is that you, Lisa?" Pete shouted down the stairs as he heard the front door bang closed.

"No, Pete. Sorry, it's me." Sylvia put the shopping bag down on the side in the kitchen and came back to the lounge where Pete joined her.

"I don't know where she is?"

"She'll come back, love, when she's ready. She may have just needed a bit of time to think. This can't be easy."

"No, I know that. It's just that she went out so early. I was awake at eight and her side of the bed was already cold. I need to go home to feed the cat. Will you call me if she comes back?"

"The way you two are, you'd be better to move the cat here." Sylvia laughed. "Are you sure you don't want a cuppa before you go?"

"No, I'd rather go now and come straight back. She might be back by then."

"Pete, there's nothing you can do. Lisa's worrying, she's bound to. She might be about to find out who her parents are. That's a big thing for anyone."

"Yes, I know. It's just I want to be there to take care of her. I want to do the hurting for her. I want..."

"Pete, you've got to stop this. You can't do those

things. Lisa has to go through this for herself. Our role is to be here to support her. Come here." Sylvia gave Pete a big hug. "Now go on with you." She went into the kitchen to put the kettle on.

***

It was cold walking out on the hills. Lisa had taken a thick coat but she'd been out here for ages. The damp had wheedled its way in through all the layers of material and was beginning to chill her to the bone. Her brain was frozen from the emotional turmoil, she had come out here to find space to think, but now it was just plain frozen. What she fancied was the idea of sitting in front of a log fire with a mug of hot chocolate. She made her way back to the car park. She knew the others would be worrying about her, but she didn't feel as though she could cope with playing cosy happy families right now. She drove out of the lane to the main road and instead of turning left to Billingbrook, she turned right in search of a village pub. She didn't need to look at the clock to know it was lunchtime, her stomach had been chiming noon for the last hour and she would be very glad to force it to be quiet.

As she drove along, Lisa tried to decide what mattered to her. Trust and loyalty were high up on the list and so was honesty. She thought about the people around her. Her family right now was Sylvia and Pete. It was true that they weren't blood relatives or even legal ones, but they were her family none-the-less. She smiled as she thought of Pete's gentle snoring as she crept out of bed earlier. He'd snuffled like a truffle pig as she'd got out of bed and she'd stood in the darkness for a few minutes to make sure he didn't wake up. She thought about how worried her little truffle pig must be by now and despite the thunderous noises from her stomach, she turned the car round in the next gateway and began to drive back to Billingbrook.

As the front door closed, she heard Sylvia call, "Is that you already, Pete? There's no sign of Lisa but we did get a call from Matt..." Sylvia stopped when she saw Lisa in front of her. "Oh you poor dear. You look ice cold. Let me get you a cup of something."

"Wait, Sylvia," said Lisa, the tears welling in the corners of her eyes. "Can I have a hug?"

Sylvia wrapped Lisa in her arms. "Of course you can. You know the longer I stay, the more it feels as though I've got two daughters."

"That's a nice thought," said Lisa smiling as she stepped away again. "Now what's this about a phone call from Matt?"

"He just rang to say he sent all the tests off to the laboratory for checking. He wanted you to know they'd gone."

"Did he say any more about what he was matching my sample to?"

"No, darling. He didn't give me any idea."

"Right. Where's Pete?"

Pete had noiselessly entered the room and was standing behind her. "Pete's here," he said.

Lisa twirled round startled by his voice. "How long have you been there?"

"I've just come in."

"How come you can get through that front door without anyone hearing? It always sticks for me."

"You got out without me hearing this morning."

Lisa nodded, "Yes, I suppose I did." She went up to him and wrapped her arms around his neck. "Pete

Laundon, I just want to tell you that I love you."

"Now what's brought on that sudden rush of emotion?" He grinned and added, "I'm not complaining because I love you too."

"Oh my! Young love. Perhaps it should be my turn to go out." Sylvia headed back towards the kitchen.

"No, don't go. Let's all go out for lunch, somewhere with a log fire."

"I like the sound of that," said Pete. "I could murder a pint."

"Do truffle pigs drink pints?"

"What are you talking about? Come on you two, you can tell me on the way."

CHAPTER 28

Southingham. Monday 12ᵗʰ November

Matt went to work early that morning. It felt strange not having been there for two weeks and he wondered just how much would be waiting for him on his arrival. It was even stranger to pick his camera bag up after a fortnight of investigation. He hadn't stopped to think how good it all felt until now. It was odd though, it all started as just a story. He'd followed his nose thinking this was going to be 'the big one' and now he was within sight of the finishing post, he was plagued with a conscience that made him wonder how much of the story he would tell.

"Hey it's the part-timer," said Charlie, coming in not long after Matt. "How was the holiday?"

"You know, sun, sea, sand, sex - the finest that Southingham could offer."

"Last time I looked it didn't offer any of those."

"It still doesn't. Actually, Charlie, I might need another couple of days off later this week or early next."

"Give a bloke the taste of the good life and he gets a liking for it! Shouldn't be a problem. You're not going to make holiday a regular thing are you? We might have to reconsider our opinions of you."

"I did wonder about asking Rach if her old dad could take her away somewhere in the holidays."

"A bit late to start with the family holidays, isn't it?"

"Perhaps, but maybe it's not too late." He'd been thinking a lot about Rach over the last few days after what Stephen Newman had said. Matt had known where his daughter was, but still hadn't made the most of her.

He'd been at his desk for half an hour when he was called in to see the editor.

"Morning, Matt. What've you got for us?"

"Morning, Dan. I've just got back from holiday."

"Holiday you took to track a story down. When are we going to run it?"

Matt couldn't help feeling this was a little unjust, being pressurised for a result on a story that Dan McIntyre wouldn't even give him the time to pursue.

"I'm not there yet."

"When will you be? I need to keep the front page ready I presume?"

Matt realised that Dan was angling for details and decided to play the game. "I won't be filling it this week, so you'll need to get the reporters to do some work."

"Next week?"

"Dan, I can't give you a specific day. Yes, you'll want to run it on the front page when it breaks, probably for several days, but no I'm not telling you what I've got right now."

"Good man. If you'd given in and told me everything I wouldn't have believed it worth it. There's something else Matt, depending on how this goes, I've got a slot for a senior reporter, if you want a break from photographing the local amateur dramatic group putting on Cinderella, for the third year in succession, then it's yours."

Matt felt his heart leap. This was what he wanted, he knew that, but he wanted it on his terms. "We'll see," he said. "I'll talk to you about it when I bring you the story."

"You're a cool customer," Dan smiled. "We'll talk next week."

***

Southingham. Friday 16th November

Although he was kept busy at work, Matt's week had gone about as slowly as an old steam train on a branch line. It ran out of steam yesterday and he had resolved to wait one more day before ringing the lab for the results.

"I'm sorry I can't give the results over the phone, but if you can give me your reference number I'll check whether they've been sent out yet."

Matt read the number from the original order form and as he waited he pictured the woman the other end looking at the details on her computer screen.

"That sample didn't arrive with us until Wednesday."

"Damn the postal system."

"I'm sorry, what was that?"

"Oh, nothing." Of course, Matt thought, he'd used the return label provided, but there had been three tests rather than just two, it had probably taken it into another postage category. Why couldn't the Post Office cut you some slack when you needed it. Although, they could have decided not to deliver it at all, so at least that didn't happen. "When will they be ready?"

"They're being processed today. It looks as though the results should be with you by Monday or Tuesday next week."

"Thanks, but are you sure there's no way you can provide the answer by phone?" He wished he'd got DI Grant involved in the process, at least then they could have been rushed through.

"I'm sorry, sir, it's against company policy."

"Yeah, I know. Thanks, anyway."

He hung up and thought he'd better let Lisa know of the delay. He left a message on her mobile and did likewise for both Stephen and Felicity. If it was going to be Monday or Tuesday that the results arrived, he was going to need a few days off to see all the parties in person. He toyed with taking the whole week off, but once he'd broken the news, what part did he have in it, except to write the story? He thought about Rach and the family he was missing.

He filled out a holiday request form and then made one more phone call before getting on with the day's workload. Once again he went through to a mobile answering service. "Rach, it's me, Dad, I wondered if I could take you out for Sunday lunch and before you ask, this time I don't need advice, I'd just like to see you. Oh and I'm cutting down on the drinking too. Call me."

***

Billingbrook. Monday 19th November

It had felt crazy to have to drive back down the motorway to Southingham from Birmingham the previous evening after seeing Rach, but Matt had to go home to collect the results before setting off again. Now he was driving to Billingbrook. He hadn't spoken to Lisa yet to tell her of his arrival, he didn't want all the questions to start on the telephone. He knew he wanted to deal with this face to face, as much so that he could see her reactions to the story as any sense of doing things right. He hadn't telephoned Stephen or Felicity either, but they would have to be called as he couldn't be in two places at once.

His fingers had been tingling as he opened that envelope this morning. Was it going to prove that Felicity had been keeping a secret for thirty years? He had

305

scanned through the letter summarising the results. The sample between Felicity Aldwich and Lisa Forster was positive. Felicity was the mother. He had continued to search for the second result. His breath caught as he found it. Bingo! The result between Lisa Forster and Stephen Newman was negative. He was not the real father. Matt's suspicions had proved right. If he hadn't had that sample from Felicity he would have concluded that he'd got the wrong person, instead of which he'd got the right person, but more story than he'd bargained for. Now the question was, how much of that story should he tell?

He had taken his overnight bag with a few days clothing so that he was prepared to travel with Lisa to any meetings that took place, as long as she was prepared for him to be there. He reasoned that he had a right to be there, after all, without him she still wouldn't know what had happened. He reminded himself that at the moment she didn't know and wondered how you broke the news to someone that they had been abducted.

The one phone call he had made that morning was to DI Grant to tell him the case was solved and that by the end of the week, before Matt went to press, he would provide him with all the details.

Matt toyed with the idea of turning up at Lisa's house without notice and then wondered about going to find her at the library, neither approach appealed. He stopped at a service station and rang Pete.

"Pete, it's Matt Kirby. I need to talk to Lisa this evening. I've got the results of the tests. Do you think I'm best to come to the house or should we meet up somewhere else?"

"How do you think she's going to react?"

"It's complicated. I don't know."

"Come to the house at seven. I'll forewarn her."

"Right. See you later."

Matt phoned the Red Lion to book a room. It was the only place he had a number for. Then he continued driving to Billingbrook and went straight to the pub. He killed time for the next couple of hours. There was no point arriving at Lisa's house early, but sitting in the bar drinking coke was killing him. He'd promised Rach that he would cut down on the drinking and he meant it.

It was exactly seven when he rang the bell of Lisa's house. It was Pete who answered.

"She's waiting in the lounge. She knows you're coming." Pete took Matt's coat and hung it up as Matt went through.

"Well," said Lisa pouncing on Matt before he had chance to say hello.

Sylvia got up, "I'll put the kettle on and leave you to it, shall I?"

"Oh no. Please stay. I feel this is about all of us now," Lisa said. She looked at Pete for support.

"If you don't mind my saying so," Matt interrupted. "I think you might want to talk about this on your own first."

Lisa laughed. "What can you possibly have to tell me that I can't share with Pete and Sylvia?" Then she stood still. "Is there something really bad to tell me?" She felt shocked before she even knew why. "It's not Uncle Laurence is it? No, I'm sure this is going to be fine."

Matt raised an eyebrow. "If you're sure. Shall we sit at the table? I've got some newspaper cuttings to show you."

Pete moved the remaining pots from dinner so that the table was clear. He left the wine glasses where they were, together with the rest of the bottle. "Can I get you one?"

He asked Matt.

"No, thank you. I'm fine." Lisa watched Matt put his bag on the table and sit facing her. "Let me start by telling you that I do know who your parents are."

"Are," said Lisa, "You mean they're still alive? Where are they? Can I meet them? They don't want to see me do they? That's what all this is about. It's all so long ago that they wish you'd never found me." She got up from the table and started pacing the room. "I'm never going to know. All this has come to nothing." She could feel the pitch of her own voice rising, but had no control over it. "Have I got any brothers and sisters? Don't any of them want to meet me?"

"Lisa come and sit down," said Pete taking her arm. "Let Matt tell us everything before you start to reach conclusions.

Lisa turned on him. "Do you already know all this? Has he told you?" She pulled her arm away from him. "You know, don't you? I'm the last to find out."

"No, Lisa, I don't know anything. I just knew Matt was coming here. Please will you give him a chance to explain it to us?"

She sat with one leg under her on the dining chair ready to spring up at a moment's notice. She nodded. "Go on."

"I think it's best if I show you," said Matt taking a pile of newspaper cuttings from his bag. He pushed the first one across to Lisa. It was headed "Baby girl abducted from shopping centre."

Lisa gasped. "That's not me is it? How can it be? I must have been found and returned, otherwise Mum and Dad wouldn't have brought me... They weren't my mum and dad..." She felt a wave of horror. "Are you saying? You mean?" She took a deep breath. "Is this why there's no adoption record? They wouldn't do that. They were good people. You're wrong. You're wrong." By now she was angry, angry with Matt, angry with everyone. "How dare you suggest..." the tears were streaming down her face and then unable to find further words she bolted from the room.

Sylvia sat with her head hung, tears dripping down her cheeks. It was Pete who broke the silence. "Can you explain it to us as simply as possible? I think we're going to have difficulty taking this in."

Matt had been expecting this at some point and had tried to rehearse the facts in his head, ready for this moment. In his mind he had envisaged explaining it to Lisa, but he was content to run through it for Pete and Sylvia first. "You've got to understand that there are some facts I don't know. There are some things we may never know, but I will tell you what I can. In 1978, I was a cub reporter with the *Southingham Express*. This was a major story not long after I started. Things like this don't happen in Southingham every day. A baby called Sophie Newman, who was then about four months old, was taken from her pram in the ladies toilets in the Broadway Shopping Centre. She was never found. There was a big police search. It was on national television and radio and in the newspapers. The progress of the investigation was reported for months, but there were no sightings of the baby anywhere. There was no proof of who took the baby, there still isn't. It's unlikely that there would be a criminal prosecution now, even if Hugh or Maureen Forster were still alive, but the DNA tests of Sophie Newman's mother and Lisa Forster show that Lisa is that baby."

Sylvia looked up at Matt. "So you believe that it was

my aunt who took her?"

"I don't know what to believe, but yes, it looks that way," said Matt hating to break the news to her.

"Can I get this straight?" Pete asked. "Hugh and Maureen lost their own baby in April of that year and then, in May, Maureen abducted Lisa."

"Yes," said Matt. "That's what it amounts to."

"Oh, those poor people." As Pete spoke, Lisa came back into the room and stood noiselessly by the door. "They must have gone through so much, losing their own child, not being able to adopt. I can understand what drove them to it."

"How dare you? How dare you defend what they did? They were criminals. They were kind to me, but they were still criminals. How could they take me from my real parents? What about them? What must they have felt in all this?"

"I was only saying I can understand what drove them to it. I didn't say it was right," said Pete.

"Right! Of course it wasn't right. I was abducted."

"But think what they'd been through. Their baby had died."

"And you think that gives them an excuse? Get out of my house," said Lisa in calm anger. "I don't want to see you again. Get out."

Sylvia looked up. "Had I better go too? Oh Lisa, I am so sorry. I had no idea. I'm so ashamed."

"You didn't do it. I can't blame you, Sylvia. Besides, I think I need you right now." She turned back to where Pete was lingering in the doorway. "Just get out. I don't want to see you."

Pete said nothing further as he went out through the front door.

310

Lisa turned to Matt, she bit her lip as she asked. "Do my real parents want to see me?"

Matt nodded. "Yes, how much of what I told Sylvia and Pete did you hear?"

"All of it. I was on the stairs. It's where I always go. Can you tell me about them? Where do they live? Do I have any brothers and sisters?"

"I don't know where to start in telling you about this," said Matt, feeling out of his depth. "I feel as though it shouldn't be me telling you all this, but I guess someone has to. Felicity and Stephen Newman are no longer together. They were the parents of the missing child," he picked his words as carefully as he could. "They both want to see you. I haven't told them the news yet, I thought it fairer to see you first."

Lisa nodded and looked helplessly at Sylvia.

"Are there any brothers or sisters?" Sylvia asked, taking Lisa's hand as she did so.

"No," said Matt, shifting in his seat. "I think the search and the police investigation rather took their toll. Felicity never forgave herself and their relationship never recovered."

"Where do they live now?" Sylvia looked at Lisa and then asked, "What do they do?"

"Stephen is a management consultant and Felicity works in the pharmaceutical industry. They both live in Southingham, but travel a fair amount with their work."

"I can't take all this in," said Lisa shaking her head. "For the last couple of months, I have been desperate to know the truth and now that I do, I want you to tell me it's different somehow. Nothing is real anymore. I thought I had a happy childhood, but it was just a myth. They were criminals," she almost spat it out. "I can't even bring myself to say their names. Do you think it would be possible for me to read all of this and then talk to you again tomorrow?" She turned to Matt.

"I'm staying at the Red Lion, why don't you call me when you're ready?"

Lisa nodded but said nothing.

"I'll leave this envelope with you," said Matt, pushing his cuttings file towards her. "I'll see myself out." Then he left Sylvia and Lisa at the table, picked up his coat from the hall and headed out of the front door.

He went in through the bar of the Red Lion and ordered a drink. As he stood at the bar he had a good look and then nodded to himself. He took his whisky over to the table in the corner.

"I thought I might find you here. Do you mind if I join you?"

Pete looked up. "Be my guest, although I'm not much company at the moment. How was she when you left?"

"Confused, as you'd expect. What is it that you aren't telling her?"

"Me?" Pete looked shocked.

"Yes," said Matt. "You. And don't give me the act. I need someone I can trust in all of this too. You tell me your secret and I'll tell you mine."

"How did you know?" Asked Pete, swirling his beer round in his glass.

"Your reaction. Most people don't see the point of view of the abductor. Most people would start by saying 'How dreadful for her real parents'. You didn't, your first thought was for Hugh and Maureen. I'm guessing it struck a chord with you."

Pete continued to look into his beer. "You're quite incredible. I suppose that's what's makes you good at your job."

"If it was all about the job, I wouldn't have a dilemma myself now, but let's start with yours. I'm not sure how, but you've been there, haven't you? You've felt that level of desperation."

Pete looked up with tears in the corners of his eyes. "I don't suppose crying over my pint is a very manly thing to do in a bar, unless it's over a football result." He laughed an empty laugh and sniffed hard. "You won't use any of this in your story will you?"

"Not without your permission, no."

"I haven't told Lisa any of this. I haven't talked to anyone about it. In ten years, I haven't talked to any living person about it. It's strange though, it was because of this that Lisa and I met." He sniffed again, then drew a large white handkerchief out of his jeans pocket and blew his nose loudly. "I was married once. It doesn't matter when and it doesn't matter who to. We had a daughter, Annie. She was the most beautiful little girl. She was everything I'd always dreamed of about having a family of my own. She was perfect. Then when she was ten months old, she caught meningitis. Everything happened so fast. One minute she was fine and then the next minute we were rushing her to hospital with a raging temperature and…" He dabbed his eyes and blew his nose again. "She didn't make it. My world ended right there in Billingbrook hospital. Janice and I couldn't console each other. We were lost in our own worlds of grief. We divorced the following year. I didn't think I would ever love anyone again. It was my wedding anniversary when I went to the cemetery to talk to Mum and bumped into Lisa. In that moment, I felt hope as I hadn't felt it for so very long and now look." Pete went back to twirling his pint around his glass. "I've blown it. . . I haven't had much chance to talk to Mum recently, though I did go a couple of weeks ago, the anniversary of Annie's death. Lisa doesn't know."

They sat for a while considering their own glasses of drink. Matt's whisky was still almost at its original level. He pushed the glass away across the table. "I promised Rach. Can I get you anything else from the bar? I'm getting a coke."

Pete nodded. "I'll have another pint please." He put on a forced smile and swigged the end of the first pint so that Matt could take the glass.

When Matt sat back down Pete looked more composed. "You said you had a secret too?"

Matt swirled his beer round the glass. "I met both Stephen and Felicity Newman, although Felicity is now known as Aldwich. I took DNA tests from both of them. Felicity only wanted me to test her, but I'd already met up with Stephen and agreed I would test him. It set me wondering why Felicity didn't want Stephen tested." He took an envelope from his pocket and passed it to Pete. "Go on, read it. It's the test results."

Pete studied the document, "So you're telling me that Stephen isn't Lisa's father. Then who is? Does he know this?"

"That's my dilemma. He doesn't know, although Felicity does. Felicity doesn't know I used both tests. Stephen has grieved for a daughter. He's dreamed of a daughter and now he's found his daughter and Lisa has found her father, unless I tell them the truth. I'm a journalist goddammit. Telling the truth is what I'm supposed to do." He downed the glass of whisky that was still sitting on the table. "Sorry Rach," he muttered.

"What a pair," said Pete, already half way down his

pint.

"Yes," said Matt. "What a pair. There are some truths that are better off being known and there are some truths that are better being kept secret. I think we've got one of each."

Pete looked into Matt's face and nodded.

"Are you going to break it to her or am I?" Matt asked Pete.

"I think it might be better coming from you."

It was Matt's turn to nod, "I'll do it tomorrow."

CHAPTER 29

Billingbrook. Tuesday 20ᵗʰ November

Matt's mobile rang and stirred him from the depths of sleep. It was quite late by the time he and Pete had parted company and he slept fitfully thinking about his meeting with Lisa that day. He reached across to the table for his phone, knocking his watch onto the floor in the process.

"I waited until there was at least some chance of you being awake before I called."

"It's O.K." He rubbed his eyes with his free hand and fumbled for the switch on the cable of the bedside light.

"When's my birthday?"

"That wasn't the first question I was expecting."

"Sorry, it's been bothering me and I forgot to ask you yesterday."

"I'll have to check. January sometime I think."

"Right. How soon can I meet my parents?"

"Now that was the question I was expecting. I don't know. I'll have to call them."

"I need to book some time off work. I think if I explain what's happened, I should be able to get the rest of this week. I'll have to go in today to sort a few things out first."

"Let me make a few calls and come back to you."

Matt looked around the room. It was dominated by the bed, but there was a small table and chair squashed in the corner. It was better then he'd expected from a pub. He went through to the en suite bathroom and turned the shower on.

By the time he emerged from the steamy room he'd missed two more calls on his mobile. He rang his message service and found one from Pete asking him to call and another sounding equally anxious from Stephen Newman. He dialled Pete's number first.

"I just wanted to make sure you were happy to tell her," said Pete.

"Happy isn't the word I'd use, but I'll be all right. I need to start drafting the story as well. I'll let you see it before it goes to print. I'd like to make sure you're ok with it, as well as Lisa."

"I don't suppose she much cares whether I'm happy about things. I appreciate the offer. Do you want to meet up later for a drink?"

"I expect we'll be travelling to a meeting with her parents."

"Oh, yes, right. Well ring me when you know anything."

When Pete had gone, Matt dialled Stephen's number. It was answered on the first ring.

"Stephen Newman."

"It's Matt Kirby returning your call."

"Matt, thank you. Is there any news?"

Matt took a deep breath, "Yes. Yes, it's Sophie." He could hear the other man break down and waited for Stephen to compose himself.

"Are you still there?"

"Yes, I'm here," said Matt.

"Does Felicity know yet?"

"No, I haven't called her yet."

"Right. When can I see Sophie? I'm in Paris now, but I can come back. I could get the train to Waterloo, no, wait a minute, it's St Pancras now. I could get the train to St Pancras and meet her there. Will you bring her? How soon? I could come now."

"Yes, I'll bring her. Sophie or rather Lisa needs to get some time off work first. Shall I ring you when I know when she can come?"

"Yes. I'll keep my phone on."

May as well complete the set. He looked for Felicity Newman's number. It rang through to an answer message.

"Hello, this is Matt Kirby. Please can you ring me as soon as possible?" He didn't think leaving a message to say that he'd found her missing daughter was appropriate. When he'd finished he had one final call he wanted to make. It was seven-thirty and he knew that she'd be asleep, but he just wanted to hear her voice.

"Hello," the sleepy voice came through the receiver.

"Rach, it's me. I just wanted to tell you that I've found her and…"

"What? You mean you were right? Wow, Dad, that's amazing. I forgive you for waking me."

"Thanks, I wanted to tell you that I love you as well."

"Bloody hell, this story has got to you, hasn't it?"

"It's taught me a thing or two, yes."

She laughed. "What is it they say about old dogs? I love you too, Dad."

He smiled, they were the best words in the world to him and he knew for certain how much of the truth he would tell Lisa when he saw her.

***

Train to London. Tuesday evening 20th November

"Do you think I'll recognise him?" Lisa asked.

"I doubt it. He'll recognise me and know it's you." Matt put his camera bag on the overhead rack. "You won't mind if I take a picture for the album will you? And maybe the odd one for the story." He grinned.

"It was always part of the deal. To be honest, it's a small price to pay for what you've done."

Matt was looking at her quizzically. "I talked to Pete yesterday."

"I don't want to hear it," she said, giving him a sharp look.

"There's something he hasn't told you that you might want to know. It could help you make sense of his reaction."

"I said I'm not interested. Case closed." She made a show of going back to her book.

"You're your mother's daughter all right."

She shot another look at him. "What's that supposed to mean."

He smiled at her. "She's a determined lady."

"She's had a tough time."

They fell into silence for a while before Lisa picked up the conversation. "It was funny finding I've never celebrated my birthday on the right day, not even my first birthday. I need to do something to make this year's special."

Matt was typing away on his laptop. She was watching him while he thought. Eventually he looked up.

"What should I call myself?"

"That's a good question. What do you want to be known as?"

"I don't know. I've been named after a dead baby for nearly thirty years, somehow being called Lisa Forster just

319

doesn't feel right anymore. It's hard to change though. For a start, how would I let everyone know?"

"I could use it for one of my headlines."

Lisa laughed. "What? 'Just call me Sophie'. Don't you want something a bit snappier than that?"

"It won't be me that comes up with the headline anyway. The sub-editors do that."

"Where will the story run?"

"Just about everywhere I should think. It'll start in Southingham on Saturday and then I've done a piece for the *Sunday Times*. After that, it will be a free for all. I hope we can arrange for you to see your mother before I have to finalise my copy. The message she left said she'd ring again later."

***

St Pancras. Tuesday evening 20th November

As the train pulled into Euston, Lisa felt her mouth going dry and her heartbeat racing. "What if he doesn't come?"

"Don't worry," said Matt smiling. "He'll be there."

"How do you know?"

"I'm a father, trust me, I know." He pulled his camera bag down off the rack then led Lisa off the train and along the platform towards the station concourse. "It's about a mile to St Pancras, do you want a cab?"

"No, thank you. I'd rather walk. Unless you'd rather get one? You're the one with the heavy bag. I've got this little case." Despite the fact that she had no idea how long she'd be away for, she had still managed to keep her packing to the minimum. She followed Matt out onto the Euston Road. It was hard to walk alongside him as they weaved between the oncoming passers-by. "What time's his train getting in?" she called above the noise.

"We've got plenty of time. He's not due to arrive for half an hour. I might take some pictures of the station if you don't mind?"

"I'll be fine, as long as you don't go too far away. I can't believe how frightened I feel. What if he doesn't like me?"

Despite the flow of people Matt stopped. "Lisa, this is the moment he's longed for, for almost thirty years. He adores you. You may have grown up differently to the little girl he imagined, but a day won't have gone by that he hasn't thought of you."

Lisa felt the tears coming to her eyes. She pushed her way forward into the crowd. "I guess I hadn't thought about it like that. It's all so new to me. I can't imagine this person who has spent all that time longing to see me, desperate to know whether I'm still alive. And all the time I thought I was having a happy, normal childhood." If not knowing who she was had been hard to comprehend, the truth was proving even harder.

The red brick of St Pancras loomed ahead of them.

"This is it then," she said, taking a deep breath. "Where do we go?"

"We need to find the Champagne Bar," said Matt readjusting the bag on his shoulder.

They passed through the gleaming lower level of the station with its glass fronted boutiques and the check in points for the Eurostar and arrived at the escalators that were signposted as the way to the Champagne bar. As they came out at the top into the expanse of powder blue metalwork standing out against the Victorian red brickwork Lisa felt speechless. She stood at the top of the escalator and looked at the unfolding scene.

She was right by the Champagne Bar, but she decided

to have a look round first. Matt came and stood by her, lifting one of his cameras out of his bag as he did so.

"What do you think?" he asked as he raised it to take a photograph.

"It's... well I don't think I can find the words," Lisa replied as she walked towards the end, gazing up at the clock with its bright gleaming gold numerals. She stopped at the end of the walkway in front of the statue of a couple saying farewell.

"It's perfect," she stammered as the tears began to roll down her cheeks. She looked back at the clock; the time was showing as 8.20. "Had we better go to the bar?"

Matt took his camera away from his eye. "Yes I suppose we had."

There was something comforting about the dull humming of the idling engines as they were shown towards one of the intimate tables with old fashioned train table-lamps. Lisa looked anxiously about, wondering which direction her father would come from. A waiter came to their table, "Can we wait to order until he gets here?" Lisa said to Matt.

She didn't see the man who was following the waiter until the waiter moved aside and a tall man fiddling with his cufflink said, "In which case we'll have a bottle of your finest Champagne."

"Mr Newman. Dad!" said Lisa feeling almost nauseous with shock.

"Sophie," he said reaching out his arms to greet her. "My Sophie," then as he took his daughter in his arms she felt the shakes of his heaving sobs against her.

It was a few minutes before they separated. Matt sat waiting, his camera away in its bag allowing them their private moment. Stephen turned and took Matt by the hand and shook it vigorously.

"Thank you. Thank you. I can't begin to tell you what this means to me."

"You don't need to," said Matt. "I'm a father. I know."

Stephen sat next to Matt, opposite Lisa, holding her hand and just looking at her.

"I've got so many questions, but I don't know where to start."

"Nor do I," she said, trying to take in every detail of the man sitting in front of her. Although it was grey, he still had a full head of hair, which with his clear blue eyes and tailored suit, made him look distinguished.

"Have you spoken to your mother yet?"

"No, we're waiting for a call."

"She's probably finding this all as hard to take in as I am."

Lisa nodded. "And me."

"Tell me all about yourself. Tell me what I've missed. Were they kind to you? Did they treat you well?"

"Can we start with you first? I want to know all about my family and what life would have been like."

"There doesn't seem much to tell. I had a beautiful baby daughter who was everything in the world to me and I lost her. Since then my life's been empty - until now."

"Tonight is going to be too short. When do you have to go back?"

"I've got a train back later this evening, but I can come back to Southingham on Thursday. We could have the whole weekend together."

Lisa nodded. "I'd like that. I just don't know where to start right now."

As they drank the champagne, the conversation

became easier. Matt left them to it for a while and then came back before Stephen had to leave. They walked with him down to the check in area then watched as he went through. Even after he was out of sight, Lisa continued to watch.

"Come on," said Matt, taking her arm. "There's no point standing here all night."

Lisa looked at him, "We haven't got a hotel."

Matt grinned at her. "I had that thought while you were drinking champagne. I've got us into a little hotel not far from here."

As they walked, Lisa said, "He's not what I expected."

"How so?"

"I don't know. He seems nice. Part of me wanted not to like him, so that I couldn't feel I might have missed something. It's hard to explain. I keep alternating between feeling angry with Mum and Dad, Hugh and Maureen and trying to cling to the good times we had. Finding out that Stephen Newman is so nice, has made it harder not just to think of Hugh and Maureen as criminals. I thought they loved me. Was none of it real?"

"Strange as it might seem right now, it doesn't mean that Hugh and Maureen didn't love you."

She fell into silence as they continued to walk. She felt torn between a past she might have had and the one that although real, seemed to be slipping away.

***

Train to Southingham. Wednesday 21st November

The train had barely left Paddington when Matt's phone rang.

"Yes, Matt Kirby here. Damn, it's always the same getting out of London." He put the phone down and turned to Lisa, "Signal's gone. I'm not sure, but I think it was your mother."

Lisa gasped. "Should I talk to her?"

"She'll need to ring back first, there was no number given," said Matt as they went through another tunnel.

"Right. I'm not sure what to say. It's just."

Before she had time to finish Matt's phone rang again, "Hello."

"I've got Felicity Aldwich for you."

The line went quiet. Matt took the phone away from his ear to see if it had dropped the call again and then heard a distant voice coming from the earpiece, "Hello, hello, is there anyone there?"

He answered as quickly as he could, "Yes, sorry, we're on a train out of London."

"We?"

"Yes, I'm with Lisa, would you like to speak to her?"

"Lisa? Lisa who?"

"Sorry, Sophie. I was forgetting that I haven't spoken to you yet. Oh dear, I'm getting this all wrong. The test was positive. I'm with your daughter."

There was silence at the other end of the phone.

"Hello, are you still there?" Matt looked at the phone to check he still had a connection and returned it to his ear.

A husky voice said, "I'm still here. Can you just say that last bit again in case I didn't hear it right?"

"You did hear it right," for the first time Matt could hear none of the harshness in her manner. "I'm with your daughter. The tests were positive."

There was another pause. Then a more controlled voice asked, "Did you only test me?"

Matt knew what she was referring to. She needed to know whether he realised that Stephen wasn't the real father. He thought for a moment of the story and then looked at Lisa's eager face. "Yes," he said. "Just you."

"May I talk to her?"

Matt smiled with relief, "Yes she's right here. Hang on a moment." He passed the phone across to Lisa. "It's for you."

Her hand was trembling as she took the phone from him. She raised it to her ear and mouthed to Matt. "I don't know what to say." He raised an eyebrow in return.

***

"Mum?" Lisa said.

"Sophie, is that you?"

"I guess so, although I know myself as Lisa. Where are you? When can I meet you? Oh, there's so much I want to know." Lisa could feel the tears flowing and wished she was having this conversation somewhere more private.

"I'm in Switzerland at a meeting. I'll be back Friday. Maybe I could meet you then."

Lisa could hear diary pages turning.

"Yes, I'm free on Saturday."

It felt strange to be treated as an appointment by her mother. She hadn't expected such a business-like response. Her mother came back on the line and it was as though the reality had sunk in.

"My Sophie! Alive! After all this time. I'd given up hope and yet I did nothing but hope. All these years I've blamed myself. I thought that someone had killed my baby." Her voice faltered.

"Mum, are you all right?"

There was a cough and a clearing of the throat. "I'll be fine. I'm free Saturday. We'll arrange to meet then. I have to go now. I'll call you."

Lisa turned to see Matt returning clutching some

buffet-car bags. She hadn't even noticed he'd gone.

"Bacon sandwich?" Matt said as he passed a bag to her.

"Thank you," she said turning to him. "Not for this, although thank you for this as well, but, thank you."

"It's been a pleasure. When will you meet her?"

"Saturday. She's away until then." Lisa bit her lip. "She's busy."

He nodded, "Now that things are working out, will you give me five minutes to tell you about Pete? As a favour to me."

She looked away. "I suppose when you put it like that, I can't say no."

"Good. When I've finished, what you do with it is up to you."

"All I can see is Pete always taking the other side."

"O.K., but you need to look beyond that to what's made him feel that way." Matt took a deep breath. "Pete had a daughter."

"What! You're kidding, right?"

"No. Pete was a dad, but his daughter died."

Lisa put her hands over her mouth and shook her head in disbelief.

"No! But he's never said anything. How can he keep something like that secret from me?"

"Because it's too painful. He's never talked to anyone until he told me the other night."

"How long ago? Was he married? Who was the mother?"

"It was about ten years ago. Yes he was married, to someone called Janice. Their daughter was about eighteen months old when she died and their relationship couldn't take it. I think Pete should tell you the rest, if you'll talk to him."

"The cemetery. Is that what that's about?"

Matt nodded.

"So he could see how Hugh and Maureen felt."

Matt nodded again.

"Why didn't he just tell me?" Lisa sat and looked out of the train window, watching the green fields and hedgerows give way to stone built villages and back to fields. Why hadn't he told her? She might have understood how this had made him feel then, instead of which... She bit her lip, wondering where he was right now and whether she should call him. Not just yet. She needed some more time to think first. She also wanted to find out if her suspicions about her own body were right first. Until now, she'd thought he might be pleased if it turned out that she was pregnant, but now she wasn't so sure. Why was everything happening at once?

***

Southingham. Thursday 22nd November

"I have to go into the office for a couple of hours," said Matt putting a cup of coffee down on the side for Lisa. "I've put the spare key on the table in the kitchen, feel free to come and go as you please."

"Dad's picking me up tonight when he gets back. It does feel funny saying that, to call someone who was a complete stranger until a couple of days ago 'Dad'. It's very good of you to let me stay here. I'm not sure I fancy wandering round Southingham on my own. Although I need to find a chemist."

"I should be back by eleven. Perhaps I can show you the town then, unless you'd rather wait to go with your mum or dad. As for staying here, well, stay as long as you want. The room is set out ready and waiting for Rach to stay, it's just that she never has. You've made me think about her a lot."

"Thanks," said Lisa snuggling back into the duvet. "I might just lie here for a while and think about things."

As soon as Matt arrived at the Express's offices he went in search of Dan McIntyre. The editor's office door was open as always.

"Matt, about time too. I was just organising the search party." He winked at the deputy editor Sian Richards, who was sitting opposite him.

She got up, "Don't take any notice of him," she grinned at Matt, "the old codger's trying to wind everyone up this morning."

"Less of the old," fired back Dan. "And I'll wind up who I like until someone's calmed me down with some coffee."

"Don't go, Sian," said Matt. "I think you might both want to hear this."

"Let me just get my coffee and I'll be right back. I'll bring one for the old codger too," she turned and raised an eyebrow at Dan.

"Ah, you'd miss me if I wasn't here," Dan called after her. "Come in, Matt, sit down and tell me what you've got."

"How about front page for today and the next few days?" said Matt barely able to contain his excitement.

"Confirmed?"

"Yes."

"Well I'll be." Dan shook his head, then getting up from the black leather chair he went to the doorway and bellowed across the newsroom, "Sian, Rob, Charlie, here, now!"

The buzz coming from the newsroom raised a notch.

Dan returned to his chair, which gave on its hydraulics under his weight. He faced the long editorial table in front of him. Within seconds his key team were assembled and Matt was ready to tell Lisa's story to them all.

When he'd finished Dan took control. "So we're ready to go?"

"As soon as I've updated DI Grant with all the details."

"And when will that be?"

"He's coming in at ten."

Dan nodded, "The thing we won't carry is the 'reunion' photo from Saturday, which is going to the Sunday Times."

Matt nodded.

"Seems fair as you had to use your holiday to do the work. O.K. guys, get to it. Sian, I'd like you to stay. I've called another meeting with production and newspaper sales to change everything we said earlier. They should be here any minute. This could be the best sales day we've had in ages."

Matt couldn't help thinking that Dan looked like the fox that got into the hen house. He wondered how soon other media would pick up the story and whether Lisa's reunion with her father would be quite so private later. For a moment, he wondered at the advisability of her staying at his house, but decided it was unlikely to be the first place they'd look for her. Once he'd seen DI Grant, he'd ring to forewarn her that she may be famous sooner than she thought.

Lisa was still in bed when Matt rang her mobile. He was expecting to leave a message when it rang several times before being answered, but then a sleepy voice said "Hello,"

"Lisa, it's me Matt. I thought I'd better warn you that

the story is running in the Express today."

"What? The *Daily Express*?"

Matt laughed, "No, the *Southingham Express*. What time do you think it is? No, never mind. Anyway, don't answer the phone or door to anyone unless you know who it is."

"Why not?"

Matt realised that she hadn't understood the scale of the media scrum that would follow the story. He wondered whether she was ready for it and whether the whole thing was fair to her at all. It was too late in his career to start developing too much of a conscience. "Once the story is out, other media will pick up on it." He paused hoping some of this was going to sink in before he had to say it. "There will be a national as well as a local media circus for a short while."

"So, I've got the famous, but without the rich?"

"That about sums it up, although I'm sure you could sell your story to get the rich. You might want to ring your mum and dad and warn them too."

"Oh great, hello, Mum, I'm the daughter you haven't met for thirty years and by the way I've brought a hundred of the paparazzi with me. Can they come in?"

"Look," said Matt, worrying for a moment that his story might slip away from him. "You don't have to talk to any of them. You don't have to let any of them in and I'm hoping that my place is the last location they'll look for you."

"You've got me in hiding now then." It was Lisa's turn to laugh.

Matt felt relieved that she was taking the prospect so well. "I'll be back in half an hour."

***

Lisa felt very lonely when Matt had gone. She needed

someone to talk to. She couldn't ring Pete, though at that moment she missed him desperately, but she still didn't feel ready. She hadn't even met her mum yet and had no idea what she would be like and she didn't feel that she knew her dad well enough. She rang her own home number, after all she had better warn Sylvia that the media may be in touch. The phone was answered almost immediately and Lisa didn't know what to say.

"Hello, Sylvia."

"Who is this?"

"It's me Lisa, I… well."

"Oh my darling, I'm so glad to hear from you. I've been worried about how everything was going and I didn't like to call. I didn't know if you'd want to hear from me."

"Sylvia, I don't want you to think about that. You didn't know. It was nothing to do with you. I'm confused about so many things, but I do know that having found you I don't want to lose you again."

"That is so good to hear. How is everything?"

"I've met my dad. He seems great. If I'd never had a dad and had been asked what I would like my dad to be like, well, I think it's him. Does that make sense?"

"Yes. Yes, I think it does. And your mum?"

"I've spoken to her, but I won't meet her until Saturday. I don't know what she's like yet. Before I forget, the story is running in the paper today, you might start getting phone calls from other newspapers and things. Just unplug the phone, except when you want to use it. Oh and Sylvia."

"Yes?"

"Have you heard from Pete?"

"Why don't you talk to him, Lisa?"

"No. I don't want to talk to him. I just wanted to know if he was O.K."

"He's as you would expect him to be. He's lost the woman he loves."

There was no reply from Lisa.

"Are you still there?"

She replied, "Yes, I'm still here. I'll talk to you in a few days."

Then she sat on the bed hugging her legs and thinking about what Matt told her about Pete.

CHAPTER 30

Southingham. Saturday 24th November

Things were quiet on Thursday and Lisa had been able to spend time with her father without interruption. By Friday, the story had gone from local news to breaking national news and as Lisa and her father tried to take in the sights of Southingham they had been stopped by well-wishers on more than one occasion. Lisa was still staying at Matt's house, it had, as they hoped, afforded a little privacy and after her father had dropped her off on Friday evening and returned to his own apartment, he rang her mobile to say there were photographers outside.

It was now Saturday morning and Lisa was due to meet her mother at eleven. The original plan had been for her dad to pick her up from Matt's and drive her to her mum's house. It was going to be a chance for all three to meet and Matt to take the 'reunion photo' for his piece for the *Sunday Times*. Given the media scrum that was developing they had adopted 'Plan B' and long after Lisa returned from seeing her father, Rachel had arrived and slipped in through the back of her Dad's house. The plan for the morning was carefully choreographed. The meeting place was to be a country hotel in the Malvern Hills, where a private room had been booked in Rachel's name.

At ten past ten they were ready to leave.

"Good luck," said Rach, holding out her hand to Lisa. "Maybe I'll see you again when this has all died down."

Lisa smiled. It was funny seeing Rachel dressed as Lisa Forster in some of her spare clothes, while she was wearing some of Rachel's. They were a little tight, but not too bad. She couldn't help thinking that Rachel looked better in her clothes than she did, but there wasn't time to dwell on that. She put on the hat and dark glasses and stuck her thumb up to the others as she looked outside the back door.

That was the cue for Matt to lead Rachel out of the front door, underneath her coat so that all the reporters would think he was escorting Lisa. Their route was to the train station, where Matt would see Rachel onto the train back to Birmingham before driving out to their agreed location.

Matt's garage was at the end of the garden, giving Lisa a different exit route. It was Charlie, the Picture Editor who was waiting there to drive Lisa out of Southingham to a point where, if all went according to plan she would meet her dad for the final part of the drive. Her mother, to avoid the media had gone straight to the hotel the night before instead of returning home. The biggest question that they had difficulty planning for was how Stephen ensured that he wasn't followed. He assured them he had a plan, but wouldn't reveal to any of them what it was.

Charlie pulled into the lay-by where they were due to meet Stephen. It was set back from the road and as they drove in Lisa felt anxious waiting to see whether her father was alone. There was no sign of him. The only other person in the lay-by was a leather-clad, helmeted biker standing next to a flame red Ducati bike.

"I guess he's not here yet," said Lisa biting her finger.

"Oh, I think he is," said Charlie, grinning. "Look."

The biker gestured towards them and approached the car.

"He can't be serious. He can't expect me to go on that thing." Lisa began to get out of the car, still unconvinced that the figure in front of her could be her father.

He took his helmet off as he got nearer. "If they even thought to follow me on this, they were never going to catch me." He grinned as he hugged his daughter. "I've got another helmet, shall we go?"

"But I've never been on a bike." Lisa could feel her legs wobbly with fear.

"Don't worry. I'll look after you. You're my little girl," and he touched her cheek with his gloved hand.

Lisa laughed. "I would never have imagined that my dad rode a motorbike."

"I didn't think the journalists would imagine it either. I thought I'd be safe going out of the underground car park on this. I don't think they paid me any attention at all. I don't ride it very often these days, but when I do, well even an old-timer like me feels young again."

Lisa waved to Charlie as she climbed onto the bike behind her dad. She didn't see whether Charlie waved back, she was too busy holding on as they set off out of the lay-by. The good thing, as far as she was concerned, was that this took her mind off how nervous she was about meeting her mother. The journey to the hotel flew by and it wasn't long before they were turning onto the gravel drive.

"Ready?" said Stephen as he pulled off his helmet.

"Wrr yrrr hhhh mm," came the reply as Lisa gestured that she couldn't get the helmet off.

Stephen put his helmet on the bike's handle and then

tugged at Lisa's. As it came off she stepped backwards and nearly fell over.

"I shouldn't think that's done a lot for my hair," she said. "I suppose you're going to tell me that Mum is one of these people with not a hair out of place."

"Well, actually..." said Stephen. "Look, there's bound to be a mirror inside. You can get straight before we find the room."

"That's probably a good idea. I do wish Pete were here."

"Pete?" said her father as they walked into the hotel lobby.

"Yes, I've not told you about him yet. He's my..." she paused to think. "Ex-boyfriend I suppose."

"Oh, I'm sorry. His choice, I presume?" said her father, holding the door open for her.

"Not at all," Lisa looked up, surprised by her father's assumption. "No, it was my choice."

"It's no good asking me," he said shaking his head. "I can't pretend to understand these things."

"What happened between you and Mum?"

"Honestly?"

"Yes, honestly."

"My marriage to your mother was over years ago. In fact, I don't know if she ever loved me."

"I'm sorry."

"Yes, so am I. Despite the problems, I still carry a flame for her. That's not the thing to tell you when we're all about to meet up. It's just, I guess I'm nervous too."

Lisa hugged him. "I think it helps me to know that. Wait here. I'll just make myself presentable." They were outside the wood panelled doors of the downstairs cloakrooms and Lisa went in search of a mirror.

When she came out her father looked at her appraisingly. "You look great. It's hard to believe that this is how my daughter has turned out. Shall we go?"

He stood so that she could link her arm through his. To Lisa it felt like solidarity in the face of a shared fear and she wondered whether he saw it the same way.

They made their way to the Gloucester Suite which was on the first floor. Lisa knocked tentatively at the door.

"It's open." The voice sounded distracted.

Lisa tried the handle and finding it locked, knocked again.

A woman came to the door, flung it open without looking and as she walked away said "You can put it on the side. I did say it was open. I'm in the middle of…"

"Felicity!"

The woman swung round, "Stephen! I thought… Oh never mind what I thought. Sophie!"

Felicity came back to them in the doorway and held out her hands to take Lisa's in a theatrical fashion. "What must you think of me? What a greeting. I thought it was room service. I've just rung for some coffee. I thought reception was going to call me when you arrived."

"We didn't tell them we had," said Stephen winking at his daughter. "We preferred the element of surprise."

"Well, you certainly managed that," Felicity replied in a testy voice. As though what was happening sank in, Felicity deflated in front of them. "Oh, what must you think of me. I sound as though I'm still addressing people at work. The truth is I don't know what to say. I don't know what to do."

"You could give me a hug," ventured Lisa.

"I could do with one too if we're being honest," said her Dad moving from foot to foot.

They moved into the room and Felicity wrapped her arms around her daughter. "I never thought I'd see this day. I'd given up hope. I'd told myself you were dead. It was the only way I could carry on. But then it was my fault. All my fault. I should never have left you outside the toilet, but there was nothing else I could do. Then when I came out you'd gone. I couldn't believe it at first. I kept looking in your pram, presuming you were under the covers, but I'd checked them. I kept checking them and you weren't there." Felicity had let go of Lisa and fallen back onto the settee with her head in her hands. "I can see it now as though it's happening again. I ran out of the toilets leaving your pram in there. I shouted for help. I looked along the corridor, but there was no one around. Then I went back to get the pram, in case somehow I was wrong and you were there all along. It was all my fault."

Felicity was crying by this stage and Lisa and Stephen looked at each other. Lisa thought Stephen looked as though he had no more idea what to do than she had. She had expected a celebration, she hadn't thought it would bring all her mother's guilt flooding back. She sat on the settee next to her mother and put an arm around her shoulders. Stephen sat on a chair opposite and shrugged at Lisa.

Lisa felt she needed to say something by way of reassurance. "My life's been O.K., Mum. I had no idea about any of this until a couple of months ago. I grew up in what I thought was a happy family."

Felicity turned her tear-stained face towards Lisa. Lisa was half-expecting her to express her anger at Maureen and Hugh, but instead to her surprise she said, "She probably made a better mother than I would have been for you."

"Oh, Felicity stop it." Stephen got to his feet. "Don't say that."

"It's true, Stephen and you know it is. Look at how I treated you. I made your life hell and what had you done wrong? Nothing. You were just too perfect."

Stephen laughed. "I've been called a lot of things in my time, many of them by you, but I don't think anyone has ever told me I'm too perfect before. Why don't I go for a walk and give you two some time together? I think it will be a little while before Matt joins us."

"Thank you," said Felicity, smiling for the first time.

Lisa wasn't sure she was ready to be left alone with her distraught mother. She thought she'd prefer to be the one going for a walk, but as her father closed the door her mother looked at her properly and as she moved a strand of Lisa's hair away from her eyes, in a softer, kinder voice said, "Why don't you tell me about you?"

"He still loves you, you know."

Felicity laughed. "You've known him a couple of days and already you're trying to match make. I know he does, but it's too late for us. There's too much water under the bridge. Tell me about you."

Lisa found herself pouring out the whole story about how Pete had stuck up for Maureen and Hugh and even before she had gone as far as telling Felicity about Pete's own past, her mother said, "He's right."

"What?" said Lisa.

"He's right. I can understand what drove them to it. When I lost you, I found myself looking at other people's children and thinking 'why couldn't they be the one that was dead instead?' It's no different. I didn't do anything about it, but loss can make you do and think strange things. Oh, don't get me wrong. I was angry with whoever had taken you. I hated some nameless person and thought they must be evil, but that's not the same as not being able to understand how a perfectly normal person could get to that position. Of course, it's never the right thing to do, but look at you now. If I'd brought you up, your dad and I would still have separated. I would never have given you the balanced upbringing you've had. What would you have been like then?"

"I don't know. I've thought about that a lot. I just didn't know what I was comparing to. Pete lost a baby daughter too."

"Is it any wonder then that he could understand?" Felicity got up and walked over to the window. "If being with Pete will make you happy, you've got to fight for it." She turned towards Lisa and leant back on the window frame. "I threw away the best thing that ever happened to me." She indicated with her head towards the gardens where Lisa presumed her father was. "Don't get your life as wrong as I did. I was too young to appreciate a good man when he came my way and I sure as hell didn't appreciate my own child until I lost her. Don't be like me. If you are, you end up a wizened old crone who thinks of no one but herself."

Lisa didn't know what to say. She found herself wanting to tell her mother about how she'd met Pete and about Maureen and how hard it had all been for the last few years, but as she opened her mouth to speak there was a knock at the door and the moment was gone. This time it was room service, bringing the ordered coffee and Lisa wondered whether she would ever feel close to her mother, a woman who seemed to have developed a hard exterior to deal with her own feelings of inadequacy.

As Lisa poured the coffee, she started to think of all the

questions she wanted to ask. Did she have any family left alive? How long had the family lived in Southingham? What did her Mum's job entail? But as she looked at her mother staring out of the window, she realised now wasn't a time she was going to find the answers. She thought she might get further asking her father and as she sat back down on the settee, she wished he would come back soon. She felt that for now she'd had enough time alone with the woman she now called Mother. She wanted to reassure her mother that she wasn't 'a wizened old crone', but watching her standing there, Lisa couldn't help but wonder whether, from the way she'd been treated as a business appointment, the description might not suit her rather well. She thought of how close she'd felt to Maureen and more recently how well Sylvia had fitted the role of surrogate mother in her life and she wondered where this real mother fitted in to all of it.

As though she were reading her mind, her mother turned to face her. "You must think me very rude, standing here ignoring you. There must be so much you want to know," she laughed. "There's so much I want to know, it's just… I think it's shock. I don't think I can do all this right now. Every day of my life I have driven myself, almost as punishment for the guilt I felt. I thought you were dead. I thought it was all my fault. I've never eaten an Indian takeaway since." She laughed again, an unnatural laugh. "I had to blame someone, but there wasn't anyone to blame except me. What if I hadn't been ill from the takeaway? What If I hadn't been selfish enough to want some new clothes? What if I hadn't left you outside the cubicle? If if if. I couldn't let myself think about it. If I had, it would have killed me." Then that laugh again. "In some ways it did kill me, although there are some that would say I was dead emotionally long before that. I need some air." Then she rushed from the room, leaving Lisa alone to drink her coffee.

**

Lisa had been sitting thinking about her mother's reaction for about fifteen minutes when her mobile beeped with a text message. She had a quick look. It was from Pete's number 'Ring me when you can, Sylvia.' Lisa wondered why Sylvia was using Pete's mobile and wasn't sure whether it was a trick by Pete to get her to call, but that wasn't his style. He'd already left her a message saying that he hoped the meeting went well and that he loved her.

She tried her home number first, but it rang unanswered. Sylvia must still have it unplugged. Hesitantly she rang Pete's mobile. It was Sylvia who answered.

"Hello, Lisa?"

"What's wrong? Has something happened to Pete?"

"No, love, don't worry. It's nothing like that."

Lisa felt herself sigh in relief. "I'm so glad to hear your voice. I miss you."

"Really? And there was me thinking you'd be so wrapped up in getting to know your mum that you wouldn't want me interrupting."

"If only that were the truth. Oh Sylvia, why can't she be like you? Why can't she be like Maureen?" She began to feel the heat of tears streaming down her cheeks.

"Oh, Lisa, come on. It can't be that bad. I feel so helpless here. Do you want me to come down?"

"That would be great, but I think I might come back up there tonight. I think I need to talk to Pete too."

"We could both come down there. I could bring the

letter with me."

"Letter? What letter?" Lisa stopped thinking about her mother and wanted to know what Sylvia was talking about.

"I don't know. There was a piece in the paper here yesterday about what happened. We'd plugged the phone in for ten minutes. A man called, from the company that Hugh used to work for. When they moved premises they had to clear out the safe and they found a letter addressed to you from Hugh, to be opened in the event of his death. Until the newspaper article, they didn't know where to find you. The man had been meaning to track you down but hadn't got round to it. The story jogged his memory. We've already picked it up from the paper for you."

"Right," said Lisa. "I don't know what to say. Why would Hugh leave a letter there for me? I'm not in Southingham. I'm at a hotel in the middle of nowhere. Why don't I see if they've got any spare rooms and we could all stay here for the weekend? It's nearly lunchtime now. If you set off soon you could be here by mid-afternoon."

"That's the answer we were looking for. My bag's already in the car. I had a job to convince Pete that it would be O.K. for him to come, but he's almost finished packing. We're on our way."

Lisa hung up then used the room phone to ring down to reception to check availability. The receptionist confirmed the rooms and then asked Lisa if she was ready for Matt Kirby to come up. Lisa smiled, "Yes, please. Send him up."

When Matt arrived at the door, her father was with him and they both greeted Lisa with a hug.

"I saw your mother brooding in the grounds. Is

everything O.K.?" Stephen asked, still holding her hand in his.

"Maybe," she said. "I think it's going to take a while. I don't think I understand her."

Stephen laughed, "I'm afraid I can't help you much there."

"One thing I did decide while I was sitting here, I'd like to change my name. I'm not sure about the Sophie bit yet, I need to think some more about that, but I'd like to be known as Newman rather than Forster."

Stephen looked into her eyes and cupped her face in his hands. He opened his mouth to speak, but there were no words. Then he wrapped her in the biggest hug and as he pulled away she saw the tears in his eyes. When he spoke, all he could say was, "I don't think I've ever felt this happy."

CHAPTER 31

The Malvern Hills. Saturday afternoon 24th November

By the time Pete and Sylvia arrived it was late afternoon and Lisa was sitting with her father having tea from a beautifully laid out tray of cakes and sandwiches. They were still using the private sitting room that the hotel had made available to them, but Stephen had arranged for enough bedrooms for them all on the top floor of the hotel. He'd also told reception to expect his guests and it was an impeccably dressed valet who knocked at the door to announce their arrival.

Pete stood in the doorway as Lisa rushed across the room to greet him.

"I'm sorry," he said. "I didn't mean to…"

Lisa put her finger to his lips and then replaced it with her own lips. When they parted she said, "Let's start again."

He nodded, as Lisa led him by the hand into the body of the room.

Sylvia was waiting for them to finish, then she embraced Lisa and said, "This place is fantastic."

"It is," said Lisa. Then with a beaming grin she said, "Dad insisted that he's paying for everything." Then turning to her father she said, "I'd like you to meet Pete and Sylvia." She turned to Sylvia. "I've already explained everything to Dad. He doesn't bear any grudge towards you."

"On the contrary, I'm very grateful for the help you've given my daughter. I'm sorry for how difficult this must have been for you too."

"Thank you," said Sylvia, then turning to Lisa. "Is your mum still here?"

Lisa shook her head, "No, she's not quite as ready for this as Dad is. She went back to Southingham after we did the family reunion photograph. She may join us for lunch tomorrow. Matt's coming back to join us later, I hope that's O.K.?"

"It's more than O.K.," said Pete. "I think I owe him a pint."

"I think I owe him a bit more than that," Lisa laughed. "He's busy finishing his story for the *Sunday Times* at the moment. He took some lovely pictures of me with Mum and Dad out by the fountain." Lisa looked at Sylvia, biting her lip she said, "Do you have the letter."

Sylvia nodded and opened her bag. She handed to Lisa a white sealed envelope, which in ink was addressed 'Lisa Forster, to be opened following the death of Hugh Forster.'

Lisa looked at the others, her hands were shaking.

"Why don't you sit down and I'll pour you another cup of tea while you're reading it, love," Sylvia said, leading her to a comfortable chair.

Lisa took ages opening the envelope. She read the date at the top of the letter. "I wonder if he knew he was about to die when he wrote it?"

"We all know we're going to die," said Pete. "… Sorry, that wasn't the thing to say."

Lisa read the letter to herself before passing it to Pete.

Sept 2002

My very dearest Lisa,

I have never been one for many words, but I feel that I owe you an explanation and I doubt that Maureen will ever have the strength to do it. I need you to know that I am deeply sorry for what we did. If you blame anyone and hate anyone, please make it me. Forgive Maureen, she meant no harm. I should have stopped it; I know that. It was all my fault. I just couldn't do that to her.

If you are reading this, then I assume that I have died, although Maureen may still be alive. Please forgive her. She has always loved you and we have always done our best for you, the best any parents could have done.

I don't know how much you know of what happened and even now writing this on a piece of paper, I don't know where to start.

Lisa, the truth is, you aren't our daughter. There I've said it now. We had no right to you. We had no right to love you or to be loved by you. But we did love you. From the first time you started to cry as we drove back to Triford, I loved you as if you were my own, our own.

I set out to put the record straight for you, not to win your approval for the dreadful thing we did, so let me go back to the beginning.

Maureen and I knew we wanted a family of our own. I don't know how long I'd had those thoughts, but for Maureen it was part of her life. She couldn't imagine a world in which she wouldn't be a mother. We talked about it long before we married and started trying for a family almost immediately.

At first, it didn't matter to me that no children came along. I was still young and enjoying being married to my lovely girl, but the more I saw how much it was hurting

Maureen, the more it started to matter to me too. When we found out that she was pregnant with Patricia, it was the best news anyone could have given us.

When everything went wrong, the cruelty of the situation was beyond endurance. I thought I was going to lose my girl as well as Patricia. I didn't think she wanted to live anymore. I was so scared. I would have given her anything to make sure she could get through the pain, anything within my power.

When Maureen said she wanted to adopt, how could I refuse her? I couldn't see that it would feel the same, not then anyway. Having loved you, I now know it could. I didn't know that Laurence being registered at our address was going to mean we couldn't adopt. How could I tell her that I knew? He was my brother when all's said and done. He'd just asked me, when he came out of prison, if he could use our address while he got himself sorted, applied for benefits, that sort of thing. What was I supposed to do? I couldn't see that it could do any harm. Oh God, when I think of the harm it did.

At the end of the day it was all my fault. I don't know why Patricia died, but not being able to adopt was my fault. I took Maureen away for a few days to get her out of herself a bit. I never thought for a minute she'd do something like this. It was when we were on the way home. We'd stopped at Southingham for a bite of lunch. I didn't know she'd done it until we were in the car driving away from Southingham and there you were in her shopping bag, this beautiful baby girl. Oh, I wanted to be strong enough to take you back, but I looked at Maureen and for the first time in weeks she had a glimmer of life in her eyes. She had a reason for living and you were that reason. How could I deny my girl that, when it was my fault that she couldn't have it any other way?

It wasn't just for Maureen though. I loved you. Your perfect little fingers and toes, so beautiful. Your fine hair all wispy on your head. I am so deeply sorry for what we did. I know that it was wrong. There were so many stories in the paper about your disappearance, I was sure someone would find us. There were days when I wished they had found us and we could have made it all right. Then we moved to Billingbrook, a family with a young baby and no one questioned it. No one thought it was odd. The stories in the paper reduced and we brought you up as ours. How could we ever tell you the truth?

The last time I heard from Laurence he wanted money and I sent him away. You were quite small then. I didn't want him anywhere near my family.

I hope that your life has turned out well. I hope you are happy, despite what we did. I have enclosed a cutting from the paper that will help you to find your real parents. Goodbye my precious girl.

With all my love always,

Hugh Forster.

Lisa sat in silence as Pete read. When he finished he held out the letter to Lisa.

"May I?" asked Stephen, looking at his daughter.

Lisa nodded.

Stephen read in silence with Lisa watching him. He nodded occasionally and when he'd finished, he put down the letter and looked at his daughter and smiled, while at the same time raising his eyebrows and shaking his head.

"If I'd found him twenty years ago I don't know what I'd have done to him. Whatever it was, it wouldn't have been pretty. Now," he said, his eyes searching his daughter's face. "Here you are before me, safe, happy and having come to no harm. I don't feel anger anymore. I think relief is what I feel most. I'm glad they're not still alive. I don't think I could face the emotions a trial would bring." He passed the letter back to Lisa and put his head in his hands. "What an awful mess life can become."

Lisa went across and put her arm round her father, she couldn't find any words. She felt confused enough herself. Her father moved his arm and embraced his daughter and held her.

"Thank God I've got you now. Thank God," then Stephen began to shed heaving sobs, whilst Sylvia and Pete slipped out of the room to leave father and daughter to some privacy.

"I don't know what to think about any of it anymore. I never felt different. I never doubted Mum and Dad, Hugh and Maureen. They weren't the sort of people you would ever imagine doing something wrong." She laughed as she thought back. "Maureen had her moments, but Hugh was always the quiet reasonable one. They say it's the quiet ones you have to watch."

"Lisa Newman," said her father stroking a strand of hair away from her eyes. "Lisa. It's a nice name. We might have chosen it at the time if we'd thought of it. Sophie was your mother's grandmother's name. She wanted it to be a family thing. My grandmother's names were Florence and Elisabeth and your mother didn't like either of those. To be honest, I don't think they were good enough for her. I don't think she'd have liked anything I suggested. So what happens now?"

"I don't know. I need some time to think about things, to get to know you and Mum, to forgive Pete, to try to understand everything."

Stephen nodded.

"Do you think Mum will join us tomorrow?"

"I don't know. I hope so."

***

The Malvern Hills. Sunday 25th November

They all gathered round the *Sunday Times* over breakfast.

"It's not bad of you," Lisa said to her Dad.

"I don't think your mother will be quite so pleased." He laughed. "She looks as though she's pouting rather than smiling."

"I always hate photos of me. At least Matt has been good with the story. I don't think there's anything there we can complain about."

"He doesn't even give himself much credit for solving the mystery," said Pete. "We'd never have got there without him."

"No," said Lisa. "It's a shame he and Rachel couldn't join us for lunch. It does feel as though they should be part of the family too."

"Maybe next time," said her Dad. "Have you heard anything from your Mum this morning?"

"No," she said. "I wonder if she'll join us?"

"I wonder if the journalists are camped out on her doorstep," her father replied.

"I hadn't thought of that."

They spent a leisurely morning around the grounds of the hotel, enjoying an unusually bright day for November. There was no word from Felicity and no reporters seemed to have found them either.

It was later when they were sitting down to lunch at a quiet table in the corner of the dining room that Felicity breezed in.

"Darling, how are you?" she said greeting Lisa with theatrical kisses.

Lisa felt startled and looked across at her father for an idea as to whether this was normal. Stephen grimaced and shrugged.

"And you must be Pete." Her mother continued holding her hand out to the now standing Pete.

He caught Lisa's eye before spluttering, "Lovely to meet you," as his serviette fell to the floor from where he'd tucked it in his shirt.

"And who might you be?" said Felicity addressing Sylvia who was sitting at the far side of the table.

"I'm Sylvia, Lisa's cousin from Australia." Then Sylvia looked embarrassed. "Well, when I say cousin, what I mean is..."

"No," said Lisa, "cousin is fine."

Felicity looked surprised by the intervention, but continued unperturbed, "You mean, you were related to those people! Well I'm not sure how you've got the nerve to be here."

Stephen rose to his feet. "Felicity, you're out of order. Sylvia is here as my guest, she's been very kind to our daughter."

Felicity glared at him. "Well, Stephen, if Sophie says so."

"I'm not using the name Sophie. I'm keeping it as Lisa. Lisa Newman."

"Well how ridiculous! Even I don't call myself Newman now," her mother snorted. "Wouldn't you be better to change to Sophie and then take my surname of Aldwich?"

"I've never been Aldwich. I wasn't Aldwich when I was born and I haven't been Aldwich for the last thirty years. I've made my mind up that I will be Lisa Newman." Lisa felt the tears brimming on her eyelids. "Excuse me." She walked away from the table and out of the dining room.

She was in the ladies toilets when Sylvia found her. "The boys looked helpless, so I hope you don't mind that it's me who came."

Lisa threw her arms around Sylvia. "I have never…" she gulped back the tears, "…been so humiliated…" she gulped again, "…in my life."

"No," said Sylvia in a steely voice, "I can believe that."

"First she treats me like a business appointment and now this. How dare she tell me what to do? And why does she have to be so unkind to my father? It's impossible to think she's my mother."

"I suspect it's going to take a little bit of time. It may just be her way of dealing with the confusion and the pain. People react differently."

Lisa dabbed her eyes with the tissue. "I know. I suppose we'd better go back in. Do I look ok?"

"You look perfect," said Sylvia smiling at her. "Any parent would be proud to have you as their daughter. You know that reminds me, if you'll still put up with me by then, Julie and Susie want to come over to join us for Christmas."

Lisa's face brightened. "Really? Yes of course I'll put up with you." She laughed. "When will they come?"

As they walked across the hall to the dining room, Sylvia replied, "As soon as Susie breaks up from school in a couple of weeks."

"That's fantastic. I can't wait to tell Pete."

By the time Lisa entered the dining room she had a beaming smile on her face. "You'll never guess what…"

she said as she approached, before noticing that her mother wasn't there. "What happened to Mum?"

"She rather flounced out again in much the same manner as she arrived," said Stephen looking non-plussed. "I never will understand women."

"Oh," said Lisa feeling a little as though her balloon had been burst.

"I'm sorry, there was no stopping her. Now what were you about to tell us?"

"Oh yes, Sylvia's daughter and granddaughter are coming for Christmas."

"That's brilliant," said Pete getting up to hug first Lisa and then Sylvia. "When did you find out? Why didn't you tell me?"

"I heard a couple of days ago," said Sylvia. "I just wanted to tell Lisa first."

"I suppose that's fair," said Pete.

"I was wondering," said Stephen looking at Sylvia. "Whether you might like to stay down here for a few days and let me show you the sights of Southingham."

Lisa could see Sylvia blush and waited to see how she would respond.

"Oh well, that's kind, but if Lisa needs me..."

"Oh, I'll be fine for a few days if you'd like to," Lisa chipped in. "I'd stay down here with you, but I'm going to have a great deal of catching up to do when I get back to work." She held her breath waiting for Sylvia's response. She couldn't help but think how nice it was to see two people who were so special to her getting on so well.

Sylvia looked down. "Well if it wouldn't be too much trouble, I'm sure I'd like that very much." She looked up at Lisa, who nodded her approval.

Stephen had ordered a bottle of champagne to be

brought to the table while the girls were absent. He tapped his glass. "I'd like to propose a toast," then raising his glass, "To happy families, old and new."

"I'll drink to that," said Pete raising his glass and looking at each of them in turn. "Happy families."

"There was one other thing," said Pete twisting his napkin in his hands. He looked at Lisa, then getting down on one knee. "I wondered whether you might like to be Lisa Laundon?"

Lisa looked into Pete's eyes and in a measured tone she said "No…"

Before she could continue Pete had staggered to his feet, "I'm sorry. Oh God, what must you think? I just…"

Lisa took him firmly by the arm, "Stop, Pete. Now get back down on your knee and let me finish." She smiled and put her hand to his face.

Without question, but looking embarrassed he went back down onto his knee. This time he looked uncomfortable and awkward.

Lisa got down on her knees in front of him and took his face in her hands, forcing him to look at her.

"If you're asking 'will I marry you?' The answer to that is yes. It would be an honour and a privilege to marry you. It's just that, if you don't mind, I'd like to keep the name Newman, I've had enough of trying to work out who I am for one lifetime."

By now Pete had tears in his eyes and he put his arms around Lisa and kissed her.

They could have stayed on their knees for the whole lunchtime had they not been interrupted by the hotel manager, who having witnessed the scene brought over another bottle of champagne, "With the compliments of the hotel." He said before retiring.

"I think we need another toast," said Stephen as Lisa and Pete got up from the floor. "To my daughter and my future son-in-law."

CHAPTER 32

The drive back to Billingbrook. Sunday 25th November

"Christmas is going to be so different to the one I imagined a couple of months ago," said Lisa as they drove away from the hotel.

"If you think I'm dressing up as Santa Claus then think again."

"Oh, Pete, don't be a spoilsport," she said in a teasing voice. "Red wouldn't suit you anyway."

They laughed together.

"Where are we going to live?" Pete looked across at her as he drove.

"Your house is great, but you get fewer footballs kicked at the car near mine. We could sell them both and move to something a bit bigger. We might need the space." She looked across at him to see if he would pick up on what she'd said.

"No," said Pete. "I meant do you want to live in or near Billingbrook at all."

"As opposed to what?" asked Lisa, forgetting that he hadn't picked up on the point about space.

"Well, I just wondered whether, after everything, you might want to consider a move to somewhere else, like Southingham."

"Wow, I hadn't thought of that. I want to spend time

getting to know my family, but what about you? What about your job and your roots?"

"I've felt ready to change for a while. I could live out all my days in Billingbrook, but I've got ghosts there as well as you. As for my job, I don't know. There's nothing to stop me looking for something else. They do have engineers in Southingham."

"Pete, there's something I need to tell you."

"Uh, oh, now what?"

"Look it's quite important it's just that I haven't had any chance to talk to you about it. You might want to stop the car before I do."

"Don't tell me you've abducted a baby as well?"

"Now isn't the time for jokes, Pete, this is important."

He pulled into a lay-by, "O.K., I'm listening."

She took hold of his hand, "I don't know how to tell you this. I haven't said anything to anyone yet. I'm, no, I mean we're, expecting a baby." Her eyes searched his face for a reaction as he sat motionless for a moment. He took his hand away from Lisa's. She didn't know what to say next.

In a measured tone Pete asked, "Is that why you said yes to marrying me?"

Lisa laughed with relief. "Oh Pete, thank God that's what you're worrying about. I said yes because I love you. I said yes because I couldn't bear my life without you. If I'd wanted to make you marry me for the baby, I would have told you as soon as I saw you."

He nodded as though that made sense to him.

"Pete, I know about the things that have gone wrong for you in the past. I can't pretend they aren't there or make them go away, but I can tell you that I want to spend the rest of my life with you. I want to grow old with you and yes of course I would love to bring our family up with you, but marrying you isn't about the family we may have, it's about the love we already have."

Pete was still looking serious. "Do you know whether it's a girl or a boy?"

She shook her head. "It's too early yet. I only found out last week. I haven't even had chance to see a doctor yet. I don't know how long it's been. I just thought I was late because of all the stress."

"Lisa, I'm frightened."

Lisa nodded. "Yes, I thought about that. I don't know what I can say, except that I love you."

Pete took her hand. "I think right now, I am probably the happiest and most frightened man on the planet."

"How far have we driven?" She asked.

"About twenty miles. Why?"

"Do you think Dad and Sylvia will have left the hotel yet?"

"Perhaps, although they did look quite settled in front of the log fire," said Pete.

"Can we go back to tell them the news?"

Pete looked at her and for a moment Lisa didn't know what he was going to say. Then he broke into a smile, "For you, anything."

He started the engine and turned out of the lay-by back the way they had come.

"If you're going to be Newman and I'm going to be Laundon, then what will the baby be called," he asked, sounding hesitant.

"Oh, I don't know," said Lisa pretending not to understand the question. "How about Tom, Dick or Harry if it's a boy."

"You've spent too long with me. You're even pinching

my lines. No, seriously."

"I don't know. We could double barrel it. How about Newman-Laundon or Laundon-Newman?"

"It's a bit of a mouthful." Then he grinned. "I suppose we could all be Newman."

Lisa was stunned, "Really? Or are you just joking again?"

"I think I'm being serious. You're changing your name after all these years, why shouldn't I? There's none of my family to object and it would be nice to all have the same name."

"I suppose it is easier to have the same name. It would get very confusing at school otherwise," said Lisa.

"You're a bit old for school."

"Pete!"

"O.K, O.K."

"You know, it would be nice to bring up a family of our own, with other relatives nearby," she said.

"Have you got a three sided coin?"

"Why three sides?"

"Well, by my reckoning that gives us a choice of Southingham, Sydney or Noosa," said Pete.

"I'm not sure I'm ready to emigrate," she said.

"How about Southingham then?"

"If you're sure?" Lisa smiled to herself at the thought of starting a new life, but as she did so she thought of the parallel with Hugh and Maureen and their move to Billingbrook. More than anything at that moment she wanted to move away and where better to go than where she belonged.

"There is one other important question," said Pete, breaking into her reverie.

"What's that?"

"When are we going to get married?"

"Actually there are two. Where are we going to get married?"

"Isn't that supposed to be the girl's parent's home town?"

"Southingham," she said.

"And when? Christmas is probably too soon."

"Oh Pete, that's four weeks away."

"So what about your birthday. Your real one."

"That's still only six weeks away, but it would be lovely."

"Well, you could ask Sylvia to help you."

"Aren't I supposed to ask Mum?"

"Well, you could, but something's telling me that you may see things quite differently to your mother and it may not be the best way to build a relationship with her. Besides, if we're moving, you could resign from the library tomorrow and finish at Christmas. That would give you some time to do a bit of the organising too. If you wanted to."

"Damn, I'd forgotten the library. What are they going to say? I can't just go back and resign... Can I?" Why not, she thought? It was true she'd loved the job, but one way or another she was leaving, why not resign tomorrow?

"It's got to be your decision. You dumped me last time I tried to take over. I'm not taking that risk again."

Lisa smiled, grateful that he'd learnt his lesson.

"I didn't think I was going to have the chance of my father walking me down the aisle."

"Yes," said Pete. "That's going to be quite a moment." He paused, "Do you think Matt Kirby would agree to be my best man?"

"What a wonderful idea. If they're still going to be here

by then, do you think that Julie's daughter Susie would be my bridesmaid?"

"You're getting the hang of this extended family idea. I think that would be great," Pete said as he turned the car through the gateway of the hotel drive.

"I can't help thinking about the irony. The people who brought me up loved each other enough to cover for a crime and my real parents may not have loved each other at all. Yet in their own ways, they all loved me. Some might say I've been very lucky."

"And you?"

"I don't know what I think. It's going to take a long time to come to terms with it all."

***

Billingbrook Cemetery. Sunday 2nd December

Lisa gripped Pete's hand, as they walked along the rows of graves. They had paused to acknowledge Pete's Mum's grave and laid some carnations on it as Pete told her all their news, but the main purpose of their visit was for Lisa to speak to Maureen.

She felt butterflies bursting from their chrysalises as she approached the grave. She wasn't sure if her nerves were because of the confrontation she was about to face, or the fact that she was speaking to a dead person with someone witnessing her doing it. She hadn't brought flowers and that felt very strange, but for the first time her visit wasn't about sentimentality.

"I've come to say goodbye. I can't say I forgive you, I don't know the answer to that yet, but in time I'll come to accept, if not to understand what you did. You did take good care of me and for that I shall always be grateful. Pete and I have decided to move to Southingham. We want to bring up our child close to his or her real family.

Maybe one day I'll bring them back here to see you, I don't know.

I did have a happy childhood. I know that's still real, but the memory has become distorted. Maybe one day I shall be able to accept what happened without judgement. Maybe one day my memories can be restored to their rightful place, where I can look on them in my old age with pride.

Goodbye, Maureen, goodbye, Hugh, rest in peace. You did me no harm."

As Pete guided her away, the sun came from behind a cloud, casting a long winter's shadow across the gravestones.

"Pete, what does a groundhog look like?"

"I'm not sure. Why?"

"I'd like to go to the toy shop and see if we can buy one for the baby. I know it's the start of December, but it's the end of winter."

Pete took her hand and together they went out through the gate to the other side of the cemetery's iron railings; the side where the living belong.

ABOUT THE AUTHOR

Rosemary J Kind writes because she has to. You could take almost anything away from her except her pen and paper. Failing to stop after the book that everyone has in them, she has gone on to publish books in both non-fiction and fiction, the latter including novels, humour, short stories and poetry. She also regularly produces magazine articles in a number of areas and writes regularly for the dog press.

As a child she was desolate when at the age of 10 her then teacher would not believe that her poem based on 'Stig of the Dump' was her own work and she stopped writing poetry for several years as a result. She was persuaded to continue by the invitation to earn a little extra pocket money by 'assisting' others produce the required poems for English homework!

Always one to spot an opportunity, she started school newspapers and went on to begin providing paid copy to

---

her local newspaper at the age of 16.

For twenty years she followed a traditional business career, before seeing the error of her ways and leaving it all behind to pursue her writing full-time.

She spends her life discussing her plots with the characters in her head and her faithful dogs, who always put the opposing arguments when there are choices to be made.

Always willing to take on challenges that sensible people regard as impossible, she set up the short story download site Alfie Dog Fiction in 2012 and has built it to being one of the largest in the world, representing over 400 authors and carrying over 1700 short stories. Her hobby is developing the Entlebucher Mountain Dog in the UK and when she brought her beloved Alfie back from Belgium he was only the tenth in the country.

She started writing Alfie's Diary as an internet blog the day Alfie arrived to live with her, intending to continue for a year or two. Nine years later it goes from strength to strength and was named as one of the top ten dog blogs in the UK in 2015.

She is currently working on a novel which is a departure from her work to date, being set both a hundred and fifty years ago and in a foreign country. It is involving a huge amount of research, which she is enjoying almost as much as the writing. If she can tear herself away from the research, she hopes to complete it early in 2016.

For more details about the author please visit her website at www.rjkind.co.uk For more details about her dog then you're better visiting www.alfiedog.me.uk.

Alfie Dog Fiction

Taking your imagination for a walk

For hundreds of short stories, collections
and novels visit our website at
www.alfiedog.com

Join us on Facebook
http://www.facebook.com/AlfieDogLimited